# THE LADY OF CASTELL MARCH

# THE LADY OF CASTELL MARCH

## BY OWEN RHOSCOMYL
AUTHOR OF "THE JEWEL OF YNYS GALON," "FOR THE
WHITE ROSE OF ARNO," ETC.

NEW YORK
DOUBLEDAY, PAGE & CO.
1902

# THE EPISTLE TO THE READER.

It is just possible that the reader unfamiliar with Welsh History may feel somewhat bewildered at coming upon such a state of society as is implied in the pages following. Unfortunately there is as yet no good history of Wales to which to refer him. But, to give some idea of it, let him take all that he has read about the Highlands under the clan system, about the Scottish Borders in the old days of the Raiders, and about the Ireland of the Pale. To these add something which outdid them all as fostering turbulence ; namely, the Welsh "lordships Marcher" which for centuries wielded the chief influence over the English crown on the one hand and the fortunes of Ireland on the other ; making always for the profit of the strong hand. Shake all these together into inextricable confusion and the result will give some idea of the Wales of Tudor times. Out of this cockpit, however, the old trickle of students to Oxford and the Continental seats of learning not only continued but swelled to a recognised stream, an appreciable percentage of which ran the whole course to its natural finish in the Italian Universities, before returning to settle down in England as part of that swarm of Doctors of Divinity, Law or Medicine, familiar to the Welsh reader of Tudor history. But, this apart, the one really national profession was that of arms. For centuries the Welsh had served as mercenaries beyond their own borders. In Elizabeth's day they added the sea to their swordland, and though James I. in his ignoble truckling to Spain used all severity to put down their sea roving, yet it was not till the Cromwellian wars had finished draining the country of its fighting population that the old order really ended. It is true that it is often assumed that Bishop Rowland Lee ended Welsh lawlessness in the fifteen-thirties; but those who know most of Welsh history and have the clearest grasp of the essential continuity of the inner forces which guided Welsh evolution, can smile the broadest at the assumption. Pages of incidents could be here enumerated to show the mistakenness of any such view, were it of any benefit to prove the matter. But the reader may very well wait till the promised history of Wales appears, and then pick out the points for himself—meanwhile here is the story.

O. R.

# CONTENTS.

| CHAPTER | | PAGE |
|---|---|---|
| I. | The Veiled Man.......................... | 1 |
| II. | The Man That had a Quarrel with Brynglas. | 11 |
| III. | The Valley of Vortigern................... | 21 |
| IV. | "The Lady of the Mound"................. | 33 |
| V. | The Night Hag of Castell Vortigern........ | 43 |
| VI. | The Veiled Woman of Nevin Fair.......... | 55 |
| VII. | Tracking the Prey...................... | 70 |
| VIII. | The Seizing of the Lady of Castell March... | 80 |
| IX. | The Face Behind the Veil................. | 87 |
| X. | The Mocking Mask of Fate................ | 91 |
| XI. | The Elfin Child........ ................. | 97 |
| XII. | The Escape from Castell Vortigern ........ | 103 |
| XIII. | Love's Labour more than Lost............. | 119 |
| XIV. | The Oath She Swore to Brynglas........... | 130 |
| XV. | "Madre Mia"............................ | 142 |
| XVI. | The Witch that Walked in Darkness........ | 154 |
| XVII. | Grim Respite............................. | 161 |
| XVIII. | Keeping her Oath to Brynglas............. | 168 |
| XIX. | Renunciation ............................ | 181 |
| XX. | Cast Off................................. | 190 |
| XXI. | The Captain Captured........ ............ | 201 |
| XXII. | The Utter Death of Hope................. | 213 |

| CHAPTER | | PAGE |
|---|---|---|
| XXIII. | Darker and Darker | 224 |
| XXIV. | Cry of Doom to Nant Vortigern | 234 |
| XXV. | The Prisoner fror Oversea. | 242 |
| XXVI. | Returning Reason | 249 |
| XXVII. | The Lord of Castell March | 258 |
| XXVIII. | Trapped | 269 |
| XXIX. | The Elfin Boy's Revenge | 276 |
| XXX. | Foulk of the Feet | 285 |
| XXXI. | The Deed of the Disinherited | 294 |
| XXXII. | The Last of Foulk of the Feet | 305 |
| XXXIII. | The Coming Again of the Hag | 311 |
| XXXIV. | The Last of Castell Vortigern | 319 |
| XXXV. | Conclusion | 329 |

# THE LADY OF
## CASTELL MARCH.

### CHAPTER I.

THE shadow of that black East gate of Carnarvon seemed to thrill me with a strange sort of foreboding as I rode through it. It is true that the feeling was not altogether that chill which bodes disaster, yet assuredly it was not that wine i' the blood which makes a man catch a quick breath and turn his face suddenly to look all ways, because he is subtly aware that down some pleasant path strange happiness is coming. I do confess that at any time my mind would have misgiven me upon entering a walled town; especially a town whose castle was so great and strong as the Castle of Carnarvon. But this case was worse, as the common saying of the country showed—"The Gentlemen of Conwy: the Merchants of Beaumaris, and *the Lawyers of Carnarvon.*" The lawyers; and yet I, of all men in the world, was riding right into their hold, though I had only come to the place at all by the way as I fled from killing a judge, the chief amongst lawyers.

The porter, too, was as long of his red beard and

1

as crafty of his visage as any false thief that ever rode down by night out of Mawddy, to strip and pill a valley by the full light of next day.  The aspect of him sent my glance up to the teeth of the portcullis hanging above me, ready to drop, and they seemed as black and grim as he was red and hairy.  One sweep of his hand and those teeth would rush down : I should be trapped !—and he seemed one who would find pleasure in it.

With that thought I glanced again at the portcullis above me and half checked my horse to turn and ride away.  But in the same flash I remembered how the idlers in the meal-market behind me had stared as I passed.  In front the porter eyed me with a sudden suspicion, and, before my horse had time to fully answer the check of the rein, I felt that to draw back now was also to draw the hue and cry after me.

There was nothing for it but to go on.  Accordingly I made my pull at the rein into a sharp jerk, that the porter might think me merely a bad horseman who petulantly jerked his horse's mouth to make him mend his pace.  Neither did I look at the porter again, but pushed through, scarce waiting for him to pull back the bars before my horse was brushing shoulders with him in passing.  He gave me a growl and a curse, but I answered him nothing ; continuing as if I had not heard him.  Once inside, I saw a fair old inn at the top of the High Street, over against the Exchequer at my elbow, and so drew rein at its door.  Unluckily for me, this was neither a court nor a fair day, and so not only was the town empty of strangers—which made me more conspicuous—but I found the common room of the inn as empty as the streets.

At least it seemed so at first glance, and not till
1 had almost reached a seat at the window table
was I aware of any mistake. Then I made out the
figure of a man, sitting at the end of the long table
which fitted into the shadows of the corner of the
room. More yet, I saw at the same time that this
one man was as potent of possibilities as two or three
ordinary men. He did not wear green clothes like a
merchant, nor white linen coat and frieze hood like
the men of the country, neither the gown of a lawyer
in this town of lawyers. His chief garment seemed
to be a dark cloak of rich stuff wrapped about him
completely, though yet in a manner carelessly also.

But it was not his dress that struck me so much
as the wrappings of his face. Under the gold-trimmed
hat his head was bound round, Spanish fashion,
with a ruby-colored kerchief of silk, tied over his
left ear, and covering his forehead so low that it over-
hung his eyes. And this was only a part, for below
the eyes, shrouding all down to the upper lip, was
a broad bandage of fine white linen, but having a
great bloodstain dried black on the right side. Only
a narrow crevice was left for vision between this
bandage and the kerchief above, so that his deepset
eyes seemed to be lurking in two caverns. His nose
was high and bold under the bandage, and of his
beard that on the upper lip was a ruddy brown,
while that on his chin was black, heavily streaked
with grey. And of a truth it came upon me,
strangely enough, that it was more of a veil than a
bandage which hid his face so completely.

He did not move his head or seem to take any
notice of me, yet I felt sure that from behind that
bandage he had already looked me over, as the porter

on a castle gate measures through his loophole the
newcomer without.

I, being the newcomer, yet felt no resentment at
his discourtesy in that he neither bowed nor excused
himself. I was indeed somewhat relieved at his
aloofness, since it would enable me the better to keep
my own counsel and company. I confess I should
have liked to have found him sitting over the fragments of a meal of some sort, however good or however plain ; for then I could have called the serving
man and with a gesture towards the dishes have said,
"Bring me something to eat also." The serving
man would have thought it well enough on my part
and have treated me as being of proper degree ; not
as that serving man had done at the Bala, who, noting my rustic manners by comparison with those of
the judge upon whom he had just waited, treated me
with an insolence which nearly provoked me to drawing upon him, and thereby losing the great object I
then had in view, namely, that of killing the afore-
said judge.

Few men however, servitors or other, would have
cared to cock an elbow in the presence of this man's
empty dishes even. Therefore, as I say, I was disappointed at finding him with no more than a tall
pitcher and a cup before him, for now I did not
like to order a meal by dishes, wherein I might betray
myself for a stranger, and so cause too narrow a scrutiny of myself, as well as lest the server should treat
me with disrespect, which, if I resented it, would
draw dangerous attention to me, while, if I took it
meekly, it would cause the bandaged stranger to hold
me in contempt. Thus I ordered a can of March
beer instead of the meal I needed, and I could feel it

biting and burning all the way down as I drank it;
for the proverb is true that says, " Carnarvon ale, the
farther off the better." So hungry was I that I felt
the first draught of the ale mounting to my head as
well as exploring my stomach.

While I sat and drank, however, there came in a
man at sight of whom I thought I should now hear
food ordered, for he appeared to be a person of some
estate and was followed by three fellows of his people.
It would seem that this seat in the window was the
seat of honour, for the newcomer kept his way towards it, while his three men took seats on the bench
half way along the room.

When he sat down he seemed not to expect any
greeting from us, and I began to think that perhaps
this seeming discourtesy was but a custom of this
lawyer-town. But my speculations soon shifted to
whether he were going to order food or not—the
biting ale had made me more hungry still.

Evidently he was well known at this inn, for the
innkeeper himself followed at his elbow to take his
pleasure. "Yes, sir, and how is all at Brynglas?"

At that word, " Brynglas," the stranger started.
It was the least motion in the world; not a half-inch
turn of the head, but still enough to be significant.
It was the movement of a man who comes suddenly
and unaware upon one whom he had not expected to
meet, though he well knew of him. Yet my hunger
was more concerned just then with what viands the
newcomer would order than with wonder why the
other should start at his name. Therefore I felt all
the disappointment of it when he ordered only some
ale for his men and a cup of Gascon wine for himself; such wine as is commonest in Carnarvon.

Here, however, the stranger interposed, rising and speaking to the innkeeper while bowing to the newcomer. " Good host, why do you not recommend this Bilbao wine more to your guests ? Sir ! "—turning to the newcomer—" pardon me ; but if you will take it as kindly as it is offered, then I think this wine, with a quantum of which they have just furnished me, is as good a drink as ever crossed the Bay of Biscay. Let me pour for you ; here, host ! a cup and another bottle "—and with the word he lifted his pitcher and cocked the lid back ready to pour, taking the other's consent without waiting for yea or nay ; indeed quite in the best tavern manner though so belated.

The newcomer rose and bowed awkwardly in return —a man of good enough stature, loosely built ; his long sharp nose keeping kin with his long thin fingers and his long and narrow feet. Light, empty eyes— the first thing that you came to in him and the last you would leave—beard thin and scanty like his hair and eyebrows, and all of the same colour of unbleached flax, framing a heavy jowl in which the mouth was merely a wide, straight slit, midway between nose and chin. His dress was finer than his manners and would have been courtly on a courtly man, but a rustic garb would have sat with most ease on him.

To see him so much set by here, and yet a man who impressed me so meanly, gave me courage, however, and as soon as the innkeeper returned with the cup I spoke up without misgiving. " Bring me a meal of whatever you have ready."

With a brisk " Yea, sir," the innkeeper went to serve me, which in the ordinary way should have been the end of it. But the newcomer, being a boor who could not sit gracefully under the courtesy from the veiled stranger, now turned and addressed himself sharply to me, by way of putting himself at ease. "You are not an Arvon man," asserted he accusingly.

In my new scorn of him I had almost forgotten my great need of secrecy, and before I was aware I had begun : "No! I am from——" Then I remembered and broke off.

"From where ?" he went on sharply.

"From where no man would think of meddling with what does not concern him, or prying into the affairs of a stranger," retorted I, the fumes of the ale helping my natural heat to rise. In truth the strong drink had already made me light-headed, for all I had taken so little of it, which was only to be expected, seeing that I was famished and exhausted with hunger and fatigue, having eaten nothing since dawn of yesterday.

But here the stranger broke in : "Tush ! let us not quarrel. You are from Powys, sir, your speech betrays you. Well, Powys or Arvon, what of it ? I'll warrant this wine will taste as good to the one as the other. Here, pardon me "—and with the word he emptied my ale out of the window and poured me wine in the place of it—" tell me now if that be not as good a vintage as a man could expect to find without going to Spain to drink it ?"

This was not the end of all his speech. He saw that the boor was opening to answer my sting, and so he turned and continued to him, "Tush, sir, what does it matter ? One likes a lad of spirit ! what would you have ? Drink, man. Come, we will drink on it—and presently we shall be hearing the news from Powys."

He thrust the cup into the hand of Brynglas while he clinked his own with mine, and at that we drank, though perhaps with not too much spirit. Even then the boor had not sense enough to avail himself of this help to peace. It was only to have kept his mouth shut for a minute or two ; yet no,—" I always want to know who it is I sit at table with," persisted he.

" Unless he furnishes you with better wine than you ever buy for yourself," answered I, mad at his nagging foolishness, and so not realising the full extent of my answer.

For before he could reply the stranger took up the thrust, saying somewhat sharply, " Sir, now you hit me. I am ready with my name if it is wanted."

" Then why do you keep the stone of your signet ring turned inward on your thumb ?"—I had lost sense as well as courtesy over this mangy Brynglas.

Nevertheless I had pricked the stranger and he showed it as he answered, a little confusedly : " Did you never see the stone of a man's ring work itself round before ? "

" Aye, if his hand were lean and shrunken ; but yours is full and strong, so that the ring fits too tightly to turn of itself. But what of that ? If you do not wish to babble your name in the ear of every ill-conditioned rustic, why, whose business is that but your own ? And so with me ; am I to tell this fellow my name simply because he demands it ? "

I thought this last very well put, as having shifted my refusal from its real reason, the fear of betraying myself, to what was a very good tavern reason,

namely, that I stood upon my dignity and allowed
no liberties from louts. Pleasure at the neatness
of the thing swelled in me and helped the drink to
puff me up. In my new and comfortable courage I
even joined, too, when the stranger broke into a
ready laugh as I ended. "Nay, nay." said he, "I
sailed the seas for thirty years, but I come home to
find you all just as ready as ever to carve each other
for the first 'good morrow.'

"But I'll have none of it, for this one day at least.
Look you, you are both my friends and you are both
to drink with me—it is a black insult to the maids
who trod the vine in Spain that you should quarrel
at the same table with such a wine. It is thirty
years since I first sailed to find the city of gold that
dreams beside the source of Ooronoka. But I am
come home to-day, and on this first day you shall
neither of you quarrel, except with me. Drink now
and pledge me ; both of you."

My heart smote me as he spoke. Thirty years on
the coasts of the Spanish Main ! I was but four-
and-twenty : he had been an old rover, then, before
I was born. He might well have many happy reasons
for turning his signet. I were no better than this
Brynglas to stand at quibbles with him at such a
moment. And the city of gold on Ooronoka, too !
What tales I had heard of the Ooronoka, and what
dreams I had dreamed of wearing a blade there myself ! Perhaps now, through this veiled man, I
might come to sail there myself ; that would be
better far than Ireland for me. In Ireland was nothing but fighting for some chief or baron who was not
a drop of kin to me. On the Spanish Main were
wedges of gold and stacks of treasure ; and I should

be fighting for mine own share of it, just as the captain fought for his, though in different degree. One offered mere refuge, the other opulence. Aye, if I could only strike up a friendship with this old rover ; do him some signal service or other here at home, then he might perchance take me as one of his company when next he sailed. I could but try. I clinked my can with his cup. " Aye, forgive me, sir ; we will drink lovingly to you."

Then, that I might leave nothing undone, I turned to Brynglas, saying, " I pray you give me your grip ! " and without waiting for him to move I seized his ungracious hand and shook it warmly, the while I clinked my can on his ; though his surly chaps were still close and dumb, for he had not the grace to speak a single fair word. He himself was not near thirty, and yet he would yield nothing to this old rover's home-coming after so long at sea.

As for me I drank that pledge royally and as deep as if it had been in small beer. I was not used to such good wine—or to any great drinking of even the common wines in fact—and this liquid sunlight did not bite to warn me as it went down. The ale had already set my brain buzzing, and here was a health of the goodliest on the top of that. I did not dream then of all that was to come of that wine. If I had—well, if I had, what then ? I believe I should have gone just as deep. Believe ! nay ; it were mere folly now to say that I should not have gone even deeper.

# CHAPTER II.

In the same breath, while I put the can down, the wine mounted in me, and I felt new scorn of this Brynglas fellow; for I saw that he did but sip, as if it had been doctor's physic instead of the glow of the Spanish sun that brimmed in his cup.

"An insult to the maids that trod the press," had said the stranger. And he was right, for all the dark eyes that ever smouldered under a mantilla were in that wine. And yet this boor wiped his thin slit of a mouth with the back of his hand as if it had been a draught of whey from his own lean table. Compared with him I loved the bluff and ready stranger who sat and seemed to smile under his bandages.

Awkward still, Brynglas could not be easy. Instead of finding a word or two with which to bury his mistake in manly fashion, he turned his back on me and plunged straight at the stranger. "You say you have been thirty years on the Main. Now——"

"Aye, thirty years," broke in the other; "and I have been thirty minutes returned. I feel like a boy of fifteen again. Drink!"

But Brynglas only sipped and then returned straight

11

to the point. "So long on the Main!—you have seen some sharp work then, I'll be bound."

The stranger appeared to smile again as he tossed his cloak and sword upon the table and leaned forward to rest his elbows beside them. "Yea, things happen on the Main."

"And laws are not much set by there," pursued Brynglas.

"Except the laws we make ourselves. Those are stronger on deep water than any laws at home," answered the stranger.

"Aye," followed the other, "but they are only laws to ensure that each man gets his proper reward; those are right laws and should be kept. St. Beuno! after a man has run into danger he should get every penny of his pay. The man that would cheat him out of so much as a farthing of it should be hanged, I say." And with this generous speech he took a miserly sip of the wine.

But I did not believe in his fine words. He looked just the fellow who would not only cheat a man out of his eye-teeth but hang him afterwards to stop his reproaches. To keep my stomach from rising at such hypocrisy I took another drink, for I thought then he was but fawning upon the man who paid for the wine.

In the next breath however I saw that he was driving at something, for he continued. "And yet there is money to be made by the right sort of man here at home as well as yonder on the Main."

He paused and looked very straight at the stranger, but the other only replied carelessly: "Doubtless. A good sword can usually find use in any country."

"Aye, but special use. A special stroke, specially paid for," pursued this weasel of a Brynglas.

"Yea, special pay for special work—that is good custom all the world over," replied the other.

Brynglas plunged. "Now if you had a friend or two to back you. One or two good swords would be enough for what I mean. Even your own and another only might do, for yours is a long one and hath the look of having seen rare work."

The stranger seemed to catch fire at last. "Aye, rare work!" Seizing the scabbard he drew the blade a hand breadth out till we could see its double edge and broad channel. "Here is the sword that hath carried many a doubtful day!"

I thought of the Ooronoka; the wine suddenly surged into my temples and I felt scorn of fleeing to Ireland. My pot valiance would not seem to be unworthy of the stranger's company: I was a tall fellow too! Drawing my dagger I struck it upright into the table between them. "And here is the dagger that stabbed a judge on the bench, with the sheriff and all his javelin-men round him," cried I.

Straightway the weasel turned his face to me. "Oh!" he said, cold pleasure in every inch of the tone as he brought it out: "So that was why you would not tell me who you were. You murdered a judge in Powys and now you are fleeing to Ireland like any other redhand."

I stuck my face close to his in defiance of him. I knew that I had betrayed myself here in this town of lawyers; but a man from the Ooronoka would think nothing of a judge slain, and I would teach this weasel of Brynglas to be glad to keep his mouth shut. In my reckless contempt for him I brought out the whole tale, for he had pricked me in calling it murder.

"Murder! I did no murder. Murder is to hire

another man to do that which you dare not do yourself—as you were trying to do just now.   Yes, I am
from Powys.   My father went into the Bala, and there
a red-headed thief of Mawddy struck him.   Was he
to take that?   No! not if it had been in Dinas
Mawddy itself.   He wiped it clean with the steel,
but the judge was sitting in the town and within
three hours my father had been tried and hanged on
the Tomen.

" They brought me word over the mountains that
night, and next day as the court was rising I stabbed
the judge and escaped this way for Ireland.   And
how do you like it now that you know what I am?"

" Redhand!" he answered: " Redhand!   If I were
to cry out across the street to the porter there at the
gate you would be fast in the town.   Then you would
see whether it was murder or not to kill a judge."

" Should I?"—with the word I had his head back
on the table and had caught up the dagger.   " Would
I?   And what are you more than the judge that I
should not kill you too, or the porter more than a
sheriff that I should not escape?"

I had no intention of striking: all I wanted was to
teach him a lesson.   But his three men had sprung
towards me at once and I might have ended then
and there in my folly had not the stranger been so
cool and ready.   At a bound he seized my wrist with
one hand while with the other he put back the foremost of the men.

" Hold!" he said; not loud but in the tone that
is obeyed.   Then to me: " Put up your knife."

" Aye," answered I, readily enough; " for I
never intended to use it."

" That I saw plainly," replied he.   Then to Bryn-

glas : "You were just saying that you wanted a
good sword or two to back my own. I'faith we found
one sooner than we thought, and one that I will take
in place of any two I know of. Aye, that was a
lucky speech of yours in putting our friend here on
his mettle. Now this project of yours will have a
good chance of winning. Let us hear it then."

Talking thus he kept the other silent for the moment to give him time to take second thought before
he should speak. Yet, as his nature was, even the
second thoughts were still but folly. "Yes," said
he ; "he is just the man we want ; a redhand. So
I will keep his counsel if he does what is wanted
without question."

He was right. It struck me almost sober. I had
played the fool—or the wine had played the fool
with me—to the hilt. If I tried to flee now he had
but to call out of the window, as he said, and the
gates would be shut upon me. If I killed him here
to silence him, I should have his three retainers to
fight through and the porter would hear the uproar
and shut me in just the same. I was as fast as a
wolf in a trap—and as ready to turn and fight.

Thoughts were goads to me. I flung my grip out
to seize him and end all lessons for him in one, but
though I was quick the stranger was quicker to
seize my hand in an iron clutch. So close, too, did
he lean his face to mine that I seemed to feel the
gleam of his steely eyes out through the crevice of
the bandages as he said, in a tone that struck like a
blow, "No more ; put up !"

Then to the weasel, "Sir, we are wasting time.
We have not yet heard what your proposal is, and as
to the other point; this is a town of lawyers and I

think they would inquire more curiously into why you wanted to hire swords in Arvon than into why our friend left Powys. Go on therefore and unfold your proffer."

Slowly the weasel looked first at me and then at the other, till at last he answered cunningly—"Aye, but this is hardly the place to explain it in full. Come then to Brynglas with me and I will show you the whole plan. It is very simple—and as safe. It is only that I am so well known or I would do it myself. Will you come then ? There's my hand : will you come ? " He held out his long hand flat as he spoke.

The stranger stretched his palm and held it over that of the other. "Free to come and hear your offer and free to go if I do not like it : I and my friend here with me ? "

"Upon the relics, free," answered Brynglas. Then the other smacked his hand down, and so they struck faith between them.

I heaved a little quiet sigh of relief. I was saved for the moment, thanks to this stranger. Then another, a glad sigh, came on the top of that, as I recognized that I had also attained the height of my desire, and was become the comrade of the sea rover. If I did but act circumspectly and show myself bold and resolute, he would doubtless be ready enough to have me for a volunteer on his next voyage to the Main. Out of my extremity I had, instead, come to the very top of fortune. My heart rose at a bound so that I could have trolled a stave for sheer joy.

"Now," went on Brynglas ; " we had better not be seen to go out together. I'll ride out first then, and you shall follow presently after——"

"Nay," I put in : "it were best we went first and that you came after." I was thinking how. easy it would be for him to whisper a word to the porter as he went out, and so have the town gates closed after all to shut me in.

He came near to smiling as he looked at me again. " Well, that will do, too, if you like it better. I only wanted to arrange for a guide, since you must not ask your way to Brynglas. Go then," he went on, turning to the stranger, "and when you have passed out of the gate, and through the oatmeal-market outside, turn then to your right, down the Street of the Bowyers, and on over Pont y pridd. At the far end of the bridge, sitting in the shadow of the bank, you will see a little dark man with one eye. Here is my ring, show him that and tell him to guide you to the cromlech of Clynog and wait for me there."

The stranger rose, and as he stood out from the table to go I saw that he was more notable for breadth of shoulder than for height. His shoulders almost seemed to be built out from his body so that his arms had the freest of play, yet nothing uncomely, only seeming to speak of strength and activity. With his figure and that bloody bandage he looked in truth a man for the Ooronoka.

Without a word we mounted and rode out ; through the gate ; through the meal-market ; down the Street of the Bowyers ; abreast of the Street of the Arrow-makers, and then, at the head of the bank-bridge, my companion drew rein, motioning me to check also.

" What name shall I call you ?" he asked abruptly.

" Rowland," answered I, giving him my father's name for mine.

2

"Then remember it," said he. "And now yonder at the other end of the bridge is our guide. But before we go any further there is one thing I wish to teach you. You must quarrel no more with Brynglas."

"It is he who quarrels," replied I. "He used rank discourtesy to me from the first, as if he meant to provoke me."

"Aye, but that was because he was drunk," returned the stranger.

"Drunk!"

"Drunk!" repeated he bluntly. "Aye, you did not know the signs, for when he is most drunk then he is most sober to look at. I have not met more than one or two of his stamp, but always when they are in their cups then they are most awkward and stubborn. Do you think if he had been sober that he would ever have made such a proposal as he made to me, a stranger, in the presence of you, another stranger; and all at a chance meeting in a common inn?

"And there again, how well I worked, for if I had not also given you wine enough to get into your brain you would have seen it and so kept your temper. Thus you would never have confessed, and I should never have got you for a helper. But the mixture of the ale and wine kept you from thinking of anything except quarrelling with him for his discourtesy."

"But the wine did not make me drunk, but only warm; I was not at all overcome," protested I warmly.

"Not overcome at all," answered he: "you are one of those whom wine first makes merry and then sends to sleep. But there were many signs. For one you kept your hand on your knife haft whenever you broke out upon him : you did not do that when you went about to kill the judge."

"What did I do then ?" I asked, keen to hear what he could answer.

"You went about with a face as empty of meaning as a dish of skimmed milk. Your hands hung open and you looked anywhere but at the one you were there to strike. The last thing that you touched was the haft of your knife and the instant you did touch it you struck and were gone."

"How do you know that ?" demanded I, startled into fear. It was as if he had been at my elbow the whole time.

"Nay, never fear," said he ; "I do not believe in witchcraft. The thing is simple ; you stabbed the judge and yet escaped. It could only have been done in one way ; the way I have just described. It is because you did it so well that I have taken you to be my comrade in this affair which is before us. I want either the very top and flower of tall men with me in this, or I want none. That affair of the judge shows what you have in you ! 'Sdeath ! such a thing hath not been done before since the day when David 'apJenkin slew the Red Judge at Denbigh."

"This judge hanged my father," answered I.

"Tush, Rowland !" rejoined he ; "such a deed so well done needs no excuse. It can stand alone. Moreover—tell the truth—was not the danger itself half your reason for doing it ? You could have done it so much more safely anywhere else than in the court."

Inwardly I flinched, I felt that he had touched the truth in me there. But I would not show it. "He hanged my father from that court," repeated I. " I wished to avenge my father in the same place, openly for all Mawddy to see. But I promise you that when next I quarrel with Brynglas I will be as sure as I was in that court."

"That is just the thing you must not do," replied he upon the instant. "You are to keep your tongue and to keep your hand. You are not to quarrel with him no matter what he says."

"Why ?"

Firm and inflexible came his reply. "All in good time. You will know well enough before we have done with him."

Then I spoke out boldly. "Sir; to-day you and Brynglas both knew me at once as being from Powys. Now by your speech you are a man of the same country as he, and yet you are both supposed to be strangers to each other. Who then are you ?"

His shrouded face, with its featureless impassiveness, struck a chill through me as he leaned a little towards me while he answered. "Who am I ? I am the man that hath a quarrel with Brynglas !"

# CHAPTER III.

## THE VALLEY OF VORTIGERN.

ALREADY as he spoke the stranger had lifted his rein, and now he put his horse into motion before I could think of any word wherewith to answer that boding avowal. My own horse followed without pressure from me, for as we went along the packed bank and over the sod-covered timbers of the culverts, I was striving to piece out this strange puzzle of which I myself was now a part.

Until the innkeeper pronounced the word " Brynglas," the newcomer was no more to the stranger than I had been a little while before. At that one word, however, all had changed. All that had been slack and indifferent in him then sprang to quick and secret purpose, as keen and as flexible as the blade of his own sword.

And now he had decided (for I was certain that the thing was settled in his own mind) to undertake some dangerous adventure for the man; although he had just avowed himself to me as that man's deadly enemy. It could come to no good for Brynglas in any event : I would take oath on that on any relic. One way or another this stranger was going to avenge his quarrel with him ; of that I was full sure.

And what could that quarrel be ? This thirty-years-a-rover and that home-stayer who was not thirty years old—strangers—what could they have between them ?    Above all, what did I, riding here in the quarrel ?    I who had been desirous only of getting safely away to Ireland till the death of the judge should have blown over ; a few years at most, since he had no kin in the country to carry the blood against me? for it was not enough now that by helping this sea rover I should come to make that long desired voyage to the Ooronoka.    I would cheerfully have gone through with any adventure, no matter how desperate, to purchase that.    But here was an adventure undertaken treacherously, in that it was to end with the death of the man for whom it was undertaken.

Neither was it enough excuse to say that, since the veiled man had me into *his* secret, namely, that he cherished a hidden quarrel with Brynglas, he would in no case allow me to draw back, but force me to go through with him to the last stride. Doubtless he was better mounted than I, besides that my horse was tired ; while also he was perhaps a better fighter than I, so that I could not hope to threaten him into letting me go.    I could at least try flight or fight if that were all.

Nor yet could I tell myself that I was following this errand because Brynglas held *my* secret, for here outside the town I might try a dash to get away on my first road to Ireland : not to speak of the fact, which the Captain had before mentioned, that we held *his*—Brynglas'—secret ; since the lawyers would most certainly desire to know why he wanted to hire swords in their town.    We were all three level so far as secrets went.

What really did move me as much as anything was
that I could not stomach the thought of breaking
faith, even with Brynglas.   When he had had it in
his power to have me laid fast in the town for the
death of the judge, he had refrained from doing so
on the understanding that I would join in this adventure.   It did not matter that he did it for his own
profit and private ends ; I had permitted the stranger
to strike hands with him for me as well as for himself, and so was sworn.   I must go on now or be dis-
honoured.

Assuredly it was no desire of mine to help to compass the death of Brynglas in revenge for his insults
that caused me to continue.   I was never quarrel-
some, and if I did not end with a man at the moment
of bickering, then I never troubled about it afterwards—unless I happened to meet him again or to
hear that he went about boasting himself against me.
Then, of course, it could hardly be reckoned against
me if things happened.

But here I carried no grudge against this Brynglas,
for I held him but for a boor at best, who had only
meddled with me because, the wine being in, the wit
was out.   Boor as he was ; fool as he had shown himself to be ; suborner of murder as he stood confessed ;
yet it seemed cruel that he should set out to find a
tool for his own ends and straightway deliver himself
unwittingly into the hands of his own secret and
pitiless enemy.

I knew well that his chief reason for agreeing to
my joining in this errand was that, after using me to
accomplish his purpose, he believed he could then
knock me on the head in revenge for what I had done
in resenting his hobbinol insults to-day.   I was cer-

tain that when he became sober his anger against me,
instead of giving place to shame, would but be cherished and hidden deeper, to burn as surely and as
patiently as the fire in a charcoal-burner's pit.    It
was not alone that his nature was to be crafty and
murderous.   His three retainers had seen me stretch
him back over the table, my dagger at his throat, and
so he must either wipe out the insult by my death or
lose all he had.   He would be disgraced and undone
if he took it quietly, for his kin would put him down
from being chief and the next best man of it would
take his office.   He was thus bound to kill me, or at
least attempt it.   But yet I liked not this thing in
myself, that I should be knowingly riding art and
part with his secret foe.   It seemed so black a treachery, although again that foe was my one hope of
coming alive out of this affair into which I was
going.

   For it was deep in my mind that I should owe more
than a little to this stranger before I was done with
him.   And yet herein lay also another source of
danger too, for it fascinated me to think that, should
it the better serve his purpose against Brynglas, he
would not hesitate to sacrifice me, though then he
would apportion a goodly share of his vengeance to
me when he took it in the end.    Further, it irked
me to think that I should be no more than a waif
dragged into this quarrel to suit other men's plans.
I was but corn between the upper millstone of my
companion and the nether one of the fool behind us
in the town.   And perhaps it was my impatience at
filling such an ignoble part which left me more
nakedly open to the pricking of my conscience, telling me that I was already an accessory within the

nine degrees [1] to the coming death of Brynglas.
There was little pleasure in it all for me. I had
liever just then have been riding for Ireland, or at
best heading alone for some port whence sailed the
ships that harry the Spanish Main.

At the middle one of the three culverts my companion turned suddenly to me, saying—

" Of what dreamest thou ? "

" Of the Ooronoka," answered I, giving him my
last thought instead of my chiefest.

" Of El Dorado at its source or the Spanish swords
that guard its mouth—gold or fighting ; which is it
stirs thee most ? "

" Adventures that bring both," replied I, this time
with the whole truth.

He seemed satisfied and his high questioning came
down.  " Well, you shall have an adventure that may
bring both, and have it here at home too.  Then,
afterwards, you shall tell me whether El Dorado still
allures you.  Meanwhile prove yourself fit for that
by your conduct here in this.  See all and say little ;
and by my commands you shall learn how we expect to be obeyed on the Main.  For the present ;
silence."

This was because we were now come within ear-
shot of the end of the bridge, where presently we
found our guide.  He was lying close to the bank,
full length and seemingly asleep, but as soon as we
checked abreast of him he opened his one eye, and,
at the single word " Brynglas," sprang to his feet as
swiftly as a wild-cat.  A wild-cat for readiness he

[1] Old Welsh law marked out nine degrees within which
a man might be accessory to a murder.  Suitable punishment was laid down.

looked, too ; one-eyed, red-eyed, fierce-bearded ; lean
and lithe ; unkempt and ragged ; redhand in every line
of him, from his rusty black head to the spreading
toes of his naked feet. The sight of him gave me
comfort. This thing that we were to do for Brynglas
was plainly no matter of murder. Had it been that,
then this fellow had been enough of himself to have
done many murders.

The stranger showed him the signet ring for a sign.
"Thou art to guide us to the Cromlech of Clynog,
where we are to wait for Brynglas."

The answer the fellow made was to drop a pair of
hide shoes from under his arm and then to feel for
them with his toes and thrust his feet into them,
all without taking his eye from the stranger's shrouded
face for a single glance. In the same way he next
thrust his foot into the weeds amongst which he had
been lying, and with a flip of the toe jerked up one
end of a strung bow into his hand. The bow was
shorter than common, even for a short man like him,
and I eyed it as he unstrung it. As if he had seen
the question in my eye he spoke at last. "Aye, it is
a short bow, but he who would rather hit his mark
should shoot at short ranges." Then turning to the
road—"This way," ended he, striding out with a
short quick step that seemed in a hurry to be gone
from the town. "Short ranges !" Aye, a rank lier-
in-wait he was, by that speech alone.

Presently the last house was behind us and then,
a mile or so along the road, our guide stepped into
a little wood and brought out a pony, as unkempt
and wiry as himself, which he had tied there in
coming. If he had looked an ill carcase afoot, his
appearance now would assuredly have hanged all

three of us, had we two been seen at the tail of him anywhere within a dozen miles of Montgomery. No ; on the face of things it was no murder for which Brynglas required our help. My heart lightened.

At this point I took out and began to eat the piece of white manchet bread and the cheese which I had stuffed into my wallet at leaving the inn. This went to settle my stomach somewhat and, together with a deep draught of water from a rill that leaped down a rocky bank as we passed, served in a measure to abate the dizziness in my head, caused by the un-accustomed wine. Yet even so I have but a broadly tinted memory of that ride to the meeting place.

One by one we strung the miles out behind us and anon we came into a desolate and waste country, where low knolls and long swells covered with gorse and brambles stood out from the low swales between, that were dark with rushes or white with the cotton grass of the bogs. The water was brown with peat as it lay in the pools, or brawled through the boulders in lonesome streams that hurried along nakedly, or at best had no better clothing than a line of gloomy and dreary alders. And always the mountains of Snowdon walled us in on our bridle hands, and always the burnished sea stretched shining along on the other. Always the blue peaks of the Eivl in front of us beckoned us further forward into the peninsula of Lleyn. Also, all this time the guide kept silent, while my companion might have been a dead man in his shroud for all the word he ever spoke. It would seem that men grow but grim company by the banks of the Ooronoka.

At long length, however, we passed between the

famous great church of Celynog and the sea, and as
we drew rein at the gray old cromlech our guide
broke the stillness saying, " This is where you are to
wait for Brynglas."

Dismounting, we lay for nearly half an hour before
the guide spoke again.   Then " Yonder he comes,"
said he, and, looking back, we saw one rider coming,
attended by three others.

As they drew nearer I saw that the guide was
right, for the one rider was Brynglas.

Boorish as ever, he had no other salutation as he
drew rein than, " I was wondering if you had come
or if you had rued."

" Did we not strike hands upon it ? " demanded the
stranger, a little sternly.

" Aye ; but you might have rued for all that," answered the other.

" Well, before we go further," rejoined the stranger, " it will be better if I say at once that when I
give my hand on anything then I keep faith.   And
I expect a like faith from the man who strikes hands
with me."

" Aye, you may expect ; but do you always find
it kept ? " returned the weasel with a little sneer in
his face as he spoke.

That sneer faded as the answer came, so hard and
even was the voice.   " There is no man living who
can say that he ever broke faith with me.   One did
it and escaped—because he died."

Even Brynglas had sense enough to turn from
following that topic.   " What is your name ? " he
asked clumsily.

For a flash of time the other hesitated, but the
bandage prevented me from guessing whether it were

from confusion or only scorn of such ill manners. Then he said quietly, " Captain Meirion."

" Captain Meirion," repeated the other ; " I never heard that name before."

" Then you shall make up for lost time and learn it well in the future," returned the captain. " And now what is the thing you wish to propose ? "

" Oh, not here," said Brynglas hastily, though we might have been in Merlin's ship of glass for any peril of our being overheard. " Wait till we get home to Castell Brynglas. Yonder in the Eivl it is, on the other side of the peaks in front of us. There is no fear of mischance there : a fox cannot come near Brynglas without the leave of me ; and once there he cannot get out again till I show him the way.

" Aye, it is a goodly place for a man to be master of. Whenever a man makes a mistake in any part of Lleyn he always comes to visit me at Brynglas. And he stops there till I can get him his pardon, if his estate will stand the cost. And if it will not furnish enough to buy his pardon of the Council it will usually pay for his lodging with me royally for awhile. If not, there are ways of earning the shot money and I never inquire too closely as to where they spend the hours between dusk and dawn : in the daylight I know they must be within bowshot of Brynglas to be safe."

Either he had not yet had time to get sober or else he thought that we, as strangers, were so far from Carnarvon that we were committed wholly to his scheme. Otherwise he would surely not have revealed what kind of a den it was he asked us to enter. He must have thought us very thick skulled, or very foolhardy ; or else he deemed us now in his clutch and beyond the power of drawing back.   And yet he was but five, counting our guide, against our two ; while I would almost have backed my companion against any odds.

In the end I set him down as being still mazed with drink, for otherwise he would surely have grown suspicious of the readiness with which the captain answered, " Lead on then," while at the same time he mounted again.

Mounting also, and seeing the guide do the same, I rode close beside the captain now, while the guide fell back to the rear of all.   From here on Brynglas kept the way, along a track which climbed steeply to the left, inland, between the bald hills at our bridle elbows and the easternmost of the three peaks of the Eivl which barred our way to the south—for on the west the mountain stepped straight down into the sea at a single stride.

When at length we had topped the neck of the pass we headed south again, keeping forward under that eastern peak, which now I saw to be crowned by the vast walls and fortifications of a dinas, the hugest of all the dead cities of old time in the land. But for the present I knew neither its name or anything else about it ; nor durst I break the silence of this dumb ride by asking questions.   Past this peak and its empty city we went and then we turned to the right and mounted again till, gaining the top of a broad ridge, we suddenly saw a deep and narrow cleft open right under our horses' heads ; falling away from us towards the sea on the west.

So steep and narrow and winding was the cleft that my startled look could not reach the bottom of it ; but all the rim of it, where it met the grey nakedness of the upper mountain, was clothed with a broad belt of every kind of briar and thorn, growing so close and thick on the steep sides that not only no fox, but hardly a mouse could have crept through it.

Nor was this all, for wherever the sides of the valley were not natural precipices, there in old times great walls had been built, and then the upper sides filled in to the level of the mountain above, so that if one jumped down off these walls he would stick fast in the thorns below, and neither could he climb back again without help. And lest rocks should be rolled down upon the men in the valley, all the sides below the thorn belt were covered with a close growing wood of birch and oak. I saw all this in the first glance, and for a moment it seemed as though there could be no other way of entering it than by leaping our horses straight into the abyss, like thieves thrown from some rock of execution : some Careg y llam.

And in truth the head of this dingle is broader than the waist of it, being a sheer rock for the most part, but now Brynglas led us a little to the left, where, under a boss of ruddy rock, a rampart of loose stones was pierced by a gap just wide enough to let one man through at a time. As we halted here I could see a trail beyond, so narrow and so winding as it dropped down through the thorns that I thought the deer must surely have made it until Brynglas said—" This is the way in : this is the Valley of Vortigern " (Nant Gwrtheyrn).

At that name I turned my face to look to the right and left. On the topmost peak of the Eivl above us I saw the figure of a sentinel sitting beside the carn. I looked behind me and caught sight of our late guide disappearing to the south-east towards distant Pwllheli.  The Valley of Vortigern !  I had heard the dark tales of it.  The traitor king of old time fled hither for refuge from the fury of the subjects he had betrayed.  Into its deeps the lusty sun never shone, but only at his angry setting burned into the mouth of it from the sea.  These rocky peaks of the Eivl cherished no green thing upon their naked shoulders.  That dinas we had just passed was peopled only by ghosts and demons.  My heart sank and my knees were loose against the saddle.  Brynglas, I knew, meant to compass my death in the end ; and already he had dismounted and was leading the way down ; already the captain was following him ; already also the three men were waiting to follow me.  I was undone.

Heavily I got down and passed the reins over my horse's head to lead him.  All my safety went before me in the person of this man of the bandages, eerie and ghoulish in his unknown features and his mysterious quarrel with the man he followed.  It was a weird voyage on which I was engaged and I took a long last look at the sun and the warm rocks about me before I plunged after the two in front.

# CHAPTER IV.

## "THE LADY OF THE MOUND."

As I passed through the gateway, or gap rather, I saw by a quick glance to the right that three men kept a loose guard there ; one sitting on the rock as sentinel, a spear across his knees and a flag for signalling beside him, while the other two sat playing at chess. Nor did they interrupt their game by taking the slightest notice of us. Then, after that glance, I had only eyes for my footing on that steep trail, and all my attention was to see where to place my next stride in front of me, and to keep my horse from treading upon me from behind—though he was a colt bred in the Berwyn mountains and therefore used to steep pitches.

Thus we passed first through the tangle of the belt of tall thorns, higher than our heads, and next through the great oaks that went soaring up as straight as pines, reaching and struggling aloft for air and light as if they choked down here in the gloom of this cleft pit. And so at last we came to the bottom, dark and dolorous even on this summer day, and my dread rose twofold within me as the first flash of the eye showed all the head of the valley crowded with a cluster of wicker and plaster cabans. A redhand's town that ; refuge of every stark thief and murderer in Lleyn.

Women looked out of the crouching doors to see us ride ; children looked up from underfoot ; unkempt, long-daggered men paused as we passed ; and on our left, under the gloomy steep that shut out the sun, a mound green with coarse grass was left unresorted to, unplayed and unsat upon. " That is Vortigern's grave,"[1] said Brynglas curtly as we skirted it. A fit grave that was for the king who betrayed his country, and fit fate that even redhands should shun it and come no nearer to it than that path which wound by the foot of it.

Below the cabans a larger one was used as a drinking house. Here were men, some sitting over the ale and mead ; some wrestling, some leaping, some putting the stone ; playing with glaive and buckler, or shooting at a mark. Oaths, and jests, and scowls ; some bandages, and one fellow with his feet cut off, who went on hands and knees and yet, kneeling as he shot, drew a short heavy bow to his breast, loosing it with a double oath and treble blasphemy —and clapping fair in the clout with every shaft. "The best archer there," as his backers boasted in triumph.

A little further on through trees and then a building of shaped stone showed itself for a gwindy (wine house), though by every sign and mark it had been the church of some hermit saint in the old days. Here some men of a better sort sat careless over the wine, giving us an easy salute and no more as we passed, for they were listening laughingly to the tale which one of them was merrily telling. Even the

[1] Brynglas was wrong. Modern tradition points out the other grave, overhanging the sea, in the slack under Glan y mor or Brynglas itself, as being Vortigern's.

harper by the door let his wrest dangle idly in his fingers while he leaned forward to hear.

Then as we passed a clump of oaks we saw that the steep upon our left drew away to the south before turning again and striding in one sheer step down into the sea, twin cape with that which shut us in to the north. The long, green, level margin of the shore was on our left, but in front of us the breadth of the valley's mouth was all webbed and broken by a tangle of narrow and steep little ravines, slipping, grass-grown and brambled, down to the sea. The chief thing, however, was beyond them, where, on the north side of the valley, set on a high knoll that hung over the strand, the grey walls and towers of a strong, square castle showed broad and high against the shimmer of the sea and sky to the west, wherein the sun had begun to look down for a place to couch him. "Castell Brynglas," said our leader with a nod towards it. "It was Castell Vortigern in the old days, but my father renamed it when he rebuilt it."

A chill crept in my flesh at the word, for I remembered the story. Aye, it had been Vortigern's Castle till outraged Heaven sent down the lightning and destroyed it, a thousand years ago. And Vortigern's Castle it had lain, desolate and shunned by man, till this man's father with impious hands rebuilt its fire-marked stones into shape again, challenging Heaven once more with its black turrets.

But we were drawing near to it. A narrow ridge, just wide enough to carry a footpath, connected the castle knoll with the lower slope of the mountain behind it, and a massive bailey wall, which compassed the foot of the knoll, came up both sides of this ridge to a double towered gate that barred the way. Dismounting then at this gate, we gave our horses to the three men, while we passed through afoot, into the shadow of the two towers beyond, from between which frowned the door of the castle hall.

As we passed along the ridge I felt an eerie dread of the company we should find sitting in that hall, and much I feared it would be of no mortal men, but of the shades of Vortigern of Repulsive Lips and his court, doomed still to haunt it. But when we crossed the unportered threshold no company was to be seen.

No harper harped there, nor any other minstrel made music on pipe or crwth ; neither any officer kept order among the household men, for no household men were there. No servants waited upon any guests, for guests were none ; nor any one seeking boon of the lord of the place. There was no kind of man soever within save only a little elfin-faced lad crouching by the embers of the hearth. If I had dreaded that hall when I thought of finding it full, truly I thought it was more wist yet in its echoing gloom and emptiness. It was as if it had been the hall in some castle of the dead.

But the lord of it seemed to find nothing lacking as he strode up its length, till he came to the edge of the upper half. There the captain at his elbow stepped up with him on to the dais and I had put my foot to follow, when suddenly Byrnglas turned as if he would have bidden me remain below on the earthen floor of the lower half.

At the bare thought of so foul an insult, however, my blood roused like fire. Here in his own castle, with the sea in front and the redhands' town behind, I yet could not stomach so deadly a slight. My hands hung open and I kept all sign of heat under as well as I could ; but with one stride I was up on the dais so close to him that he had to take a half step back or I should have jostled him.

One glance at me and then he looked furtively at the captain. But, as ever, he could read nothing in that shrouded face. Only the resolute pose of the head, as the other looked at him, seemed to challenge his next act. With a muttered oath in his throat Brynglas turned and led the way to the seat.

Whether it were that some grace yet lingered in him, or whether he were hungry himself, he called now to the little lad for the board to be set. I looked then by this unprepared for meal to learn what state he kept, but when the maids, dressed all in green, had placed the board, they spread it with a fair linen cloth and laid out white bread, with butter, honey, cheese, and cold meats of flesh and fowl roast and sodden ; well enough, even if not so lavish as most gentlemen like to set before guests. Yet while the little lad poured the water over my hands to wash, I noticed that he looked hungry as well as elfish. Still, I marvelled that a child should dwell in this grim castle at all, and so turned my mind from him when he went back to the hearth.

I had had enough of wine that day and now therefore took only the mead horn to wash down my food. But I noticed that the captain drank freely, at the same time drawing the other by every smooth artifice to drink deep also. I was certain however that the wine would have no more effect upon himself than if it were poured into a steel casque, and I felt persuaded that he had an object in deepening the other's potations.

When the meal was done, the board taken away, and the hall emptied of its servants again, Brynglas looked at the captain and then glanced meaningly at me.

The veiled man answered him plainly in words, "Yea, it were best we settle it between our two selves." Then to me, "Rowland——" he began.

But I did not wait for the words. I saw what he wanted and I was full ready to let them draw the plot between themselves. I could trust the captain and I could not trust my own temper under the slights which I was sure the boor Brynglas would put upon me though I was here a guest in his own hall. And moreover I desired to be out of this gloomy castle to draw a breath of free air, even if that were only the air of the grim valley of Vortigern.

"I understand," said I. "Truth to tell I would rather leave the planning to you. Tell me after it is all settled. I am in no fever meanwhile. I will walk by the shore for a space."

"It is not worth while for you to go to the shore," put in Brynglas, with the usual half sneer under all. "The boats are fast by chain and lock. The only way out of this valley is the one you came in by and that is guarded as you saw."

"Aye, and perhaps you may yet wish there had been some other way out of it," answered I, as if in sour jest. "You may presently find that it was easier to pick me up than to shake me off. I have ridden all the way from Carnarvon at your desire— when I go back it shall be at my own, and neither shall I go as empty as I came." I thought it well to be bold with him.

The captain gave me the ghost of a nod of approval,

but I saw Brynglas open his mouth with a grin. Some veiled half-jesting threat was on his tongue I knew, and to be beforehand with him I turned brusquely on my heel and passed out without further word or any courtesy.

Outside, however, I paused. Before I went out of the gate in the bailey wall it were well that I should walk the round of the bailey itself and see what fashion of place this was ; for we might have need of every scrap of knowledge before we were done with Castell Vortigern and its lord.

As I turned to go the fresh sound of the sea was in my ears, and as I rounded the first corner to the right the shimmer of it was in my eyes. Till yesterday I had never seen the sea, nor had any fit conception of its mystery of power over men's hearts ; touching on this side, as it does, the edge of one's own homeland, and on the other those lands of gold and adventure that fill the longest nights with tales that never tire. Another stride, and as I kept my shoulder to the castle wall the sea was all before me, catching the first of its thousand splendours from the near setting sun.

From my present height I could see, over the top of the wall, the clear, light green wavelets curling upon the beach with gentle roar, and I sent a swift glance to see if perchance any mermaiden might be sitting there, combing her yellow tresses with the gleaming sea-shell comb. Yet, thought I, next moment, mermaids were little likely to come so near to such a valley as this.

Then I looked about for some way of getting nearer to the water still, for I had forgotten all need for examining the bailey. Just below my feet was a little

postern gate, and going down to it I found it standing ajar.

My eyes were eager for the sea as I passed out and so I
saw nothing but the flaming sun and the gorgeous
welter of his path below, while with long strides I went
down the stony beach till I stood upon the narrow strip
of sand whereon the foam splashed itself like spilt
jewels.   Much I marvelled if those wondrous lights
were not of wizard's magic.   Yea, for this shore was
haunted.   Here it was in old time that Vivien had cast
her spells on Merlin, and when all the rest of Vortigern's retinue had perished with their king and castle,
under the dolorous stroke of the lightning, she lured
him here from this beach into the Ship of Glass that
carried him away across the sea to her island of enchantment.   Well might that isle be enchanted which
must be sailed for over such a shining sea as this.
All things were possible here, for the glamour of this
unchristian place was creeping through my eyes into
my very bones.   Then, still with my eyes to the sun
and sea, I began to walk towards the great grey cliff
that cut off the beach to the south.

I had gone perhaps three score paces when something drew my eyes inland, over my other shoulder,
and no sooner had I looked than I stopped in my
stride, as suddenly as though a warder had challenged
me.   There, on the margin of the shore, swelled a
little green mound, no bigger about in compass than
a lady's bower, and draped all with the purple arras
of blossomed thyme, while on it sat a lady such as the
old Knights saw when they rode on quest from
Arthur's Court.

Young she was; a maid yet; clad in a robe of
flame-coloured silk like a maid of old-world story,

and her arms shone round and smooth and white as
a narwhale's tooth where she sat, with elbows on
knees, holding her face in her hands while she looked
full pensively out over the glittering sea.   About her
brow was a fillet of twisted silver, set in front with a
great round jewel which blazed and quivered blinding bright in the rays of the level sun.   Her heavy
tresses were aflame with the ruddy light as they
hung down by cheek and neck and shoulder, and all
the lustre of that radiant sea glowed in the softened
glory of her eyes that shamed the jewel above.   Fairer
maid did never meet the eye of mortal man, nor in
a fitter place.

I had come almost between her and the sun before
I was aware, and now as I paused she shifted her gaze
just long enough to see if I were a man or what, that
walked that way and disturbed her.   Then calm and
unmoved her eyes went back to the sea and the sun
and the bannered west, as if I existed no longer ;
while I went backward for a pace or two like one who
finds himself over his mark.

So dreamily and so steadfastly she looked before
her, that I could no more pass between her and the
sun than I could have passed betwixt her and the
harp of her minstrel had she been sitting in the hall.
And yet had I turned about and gone straight back,
then that had been uncourteous too.   Therefore I
made as if I had changed my notion and would now
go up to the foot of the mountain behind.   Crossing
the shingle then I reach the edge of the grass,
sauntering along and looking on the ground a spear
length in front of me as I went, yet always out of
the corner of my eye seeing her sitting there, like
the lady of some harper's tale.

She had not so much as turned a second glance
upon me, yet when I had passed inland it was as if I
could still feel the glow of her eyes as they burned
there in the sunset, and without a struggle I turned
southward again till I had reached the shore once
more a little way beyond her.  There I threw myself down on the grass that I might steal a furtive
look at her, but before I had well settled myself I
saw that she felt my neighbourhood and resented it.
Without deigning to look my way she rose.  Slowly
she folded a mantle of the grass-green silk about her,
and then, with a grace full stately in a maid, went
calmly back towards the castle, till she passed through
the little wicket in the wall and was gone.

Straightway I rose and followed.  As I passed the
little mound whereon she had been sitting I saw that
the trefoil grew thickly at the foot of it.  " She is
like Olwen," I said to myself aloud.  " Harpers tell
that, in Arthur's day, where Olwen walked three
white trefoils sprang up in her footsteps as she
passed.  Now do I know that Olwen was no dream
of bard but living woman, for this is she, surely.".

With quick strides I gained the wicket, but the
green slope was empty, no sign of her was there, and
all in a maze I turned to the sea again.

I looked at the giant cliffs that cut off the beach
at either end.  "There is no way of escape by the
sea," said Brynglas—I spoke the words to myself,
but with exultation.  I wished to feel that this lady
of the mound was as fast prisoned as myself in this
valley of Vortigern.

# CHAPTER V.

## THE NIGHT HAG OF CASTELL VORTIGERN.

TURNING, I walked along the margin of the land till I came again to the thyme-stained mound and stood regarding it. Westward the edge of the sun struck the sea and flashed it into flame from edge to edge. The sky above took colours that the inland never sees, while landward the gray mountain wall flushed into sudden glory. I had never seen the sun set over the sea before and this was a mystic sight to me.

The voices of the wavelets on the strand tinkled clearer : strange cold whispers came up over the gleaming waters, and a dread of witchcraft and of elfish glamour crept into my breast. This valley was enchanted said all the stories, and I began to fear that the maiden of its strand was some lady of spells to lure me to destruction, as Vivien had lured Merlin.

So did the weird time work in me that presently I began to doubt the captain himself and his enmity with Brynglas, and to fear that both were but emissaries of this Vivien to bring hither victims from the outer world. I recalled the silence of the ride hither ; the emptiness of the castle till the little elfin boy summoned attendants, and the fear grew in me.

43

Yet I felt no desire to escape : only to see again the enchantress who walked in green mantle as fairies do.

Was she of faerie [1] or was she Christian maid ? Here on the shore was no one save wild sea-birds to tell me ; but I remembered the gwindy and started towards it.   I could ask some one there.

Swinging along, I was presently striding at top speed, the fever in my blood so strong that only an impatient oath roused me in time to avoid a mischief. The archer without feet, whom I had seen shooting, was now sitting right in the line I was making, and a third stride from where I paused would have landed my foot in his lap.   His knees were bent before him, his shins along on the ground, so that he knelt and yet sat upright in a manner impossible to a man with feet.

I say the third stride, but the second would assuredly have been my farthest, for the fellow had straightway nocked an arrow to the string and begun to draw.

In my surprise I almost laughed.   "Nay," said I, "thou art mistaken.   I am no intruder.   I came here with Brynglas himself.   I saw thee shooting as we passed and I was glad to see thee win.   Here is a groat to add to thy winnings," and with the word I tossed him the coin.

As he caught the money I saw the scowl on his face blacken, till for a moment I thought he would have thrown the coin back at me.   Then his look changed and he lifted his head in a great laugh. "Fool !" said he ; " see thy groat ! watch it," and with that he flung it high up and out in front of him.

---

[1] Celtic fairies are of human stature.

I saw it rising slowly and then, just as it kept its level for a second or two before beginning to sink, the bow twanged beside me and the arrow struck the white silver and sent it spinning out of its flight, Often had I heard of that trick, when archers were drinking deep at the ale, but I had never believed it could be done by mortal bowman, and I took a new breath as I turned to look again at this fellow without feet. Was he part of the enchantment of this place ? would he presently turn into a brown leaf or a toadstool ?

"A groat," said he with a scornful voice : "a groat to the man that can do that. Who are you that I should not have put the shaft through you and taken your whole purse ? "

" Just what you see ; a man with a man's weapons," answered I, somewhat sternly.

" Oh ! "—he laughed again in scorn. " Oh ! a man and with weapons ! I tell thee this valley is full of men that are here because they were men and had weapons. This valley, nay, the Pit itself is so full of men that had weapons that they trap the arms and legs off half of them every time they shut the gates. That's where I lost my feet and so I've been let out for a few years more on earth, and here I am making the most of it."

His insolence angered me. " What good art thou here except to shoot at a mark and win other men's money ? " I answered, giving him his own scorn again.

" To shoot at a mark ! " repeated he, but with a grin of contempt. " There you confess yourself a stranger indeed. No other man in all Lleyn would ask that. I am good to shoot at a mark, but ask any man from Aberdaron to Carnarvon what mark I like best; ask him what he thinks of me, Foulk of the Feet."

" Of the Feet ? " repeated I.

" Aye; the feet I have not got. When once you hear the tale you'll never come babbling here again that I am only fit to shoot at a mark. There is no raid made out of this valley but Foulk of the Feet is in the front of it. Aye, if I can but reach the stirrup with one hand I'm into the saddle with the other, and then I'm as good a man as ever rode."

" Are you the chief then ? " asked I.

" Not by name. The drinkers yonder at the gwindy; they have the name of it. But not one of them all will plant his spear between the gwindy and the alehouse, as a call for men to a raid, till he has first made sure that I am willing to go. There are a hundred men and more in Nant Vortigern, but the best of them all is Foulk of the Feet, and in that no man dare give me the lie."

There was a grim quiet about this boast that kept my face sober and I thought well to change the point. Said I, " But how can this peninsula of Lleyn support a hundred outlaws ? "

" It cannot, but the sea can support all the men Lleyn would hold. Have we not ships and are there not coasts on every hand ? If we land in Pembroke and sweep half a commot clean, how are they to know that we are not pirates from Lundy ? And the ships that go to and fro; what tales can they tell of us after we catch them ? They never heard of Vortigern's Valley in the first place. No; no; the land for sport but the sea for spoil."

" But in time you will be known. All these losses

piled up on one another will rouse the whole land against you."

"Piled up; we do not pile them up; Brynglas sees to that.  He is too red a fox for letting us run up the score too high.  That is his part of it; to keep in touch with the governors; Chancellors, Chamberlains, Constables, or what not at Carnarvon, and note what the effect is on them.  If a whisper spreads he soothes it with gold pieces.  If some man begins to open his mouth too wide and nothing else will do, then that man's heirs presently divide his estate between them, for a hand's breath of steel or a shaft that comes suddenly out of the moonlight will quiet a man when all else fails.

"No, we may growl at having to lie quiet sometimes till we get hungry enough, but we know he's right; he loves the red gold too well to make a mistake.  A week ago we had a rousing haul at sea, and two nights ago some of us had a merry ride inland.  Now therefore we must lie quiet for a month or more till the stir settles—not so much as a hen's nest must be robbed till then."

Here was news for me.  This thing for which Brynglas had said he wanted one or two good swords that thought little of the law—what could it be?  He had been to Carnarvon to-day, to see if last week's piracy had made any stir there—but why had he brought us back?  True, he had said that the thing to be done was one he would have done himself if he were not so well known.  If he spoke truth at all it must be something well out of the usual run of piracy, raids, and murder.

Then like a knife it struck me that perhaps this captain with the bandaged face had been a sufferer

by that piracy, and coming to Carnarvon had fallen
a victim to a cunning plot of Brynglas to lure him
out here, that he might be murdered quietly where
no word of his death would ever reach the outer
world. And I had merely been included because
I had quarrelled with Brynglas over the wine and
could as easily be done to death as not.

This then was why we had been caused to leave
the town so clandestinely. And the reason we had
not been slain by the way hither was that our bodies
might in that case have been found and added to the
account of the known crimes of these men of the
Eivl. Oh fool, fool, that the captain had been to let
his quarrel blind him to the trap ! and double fool
I who had in pure emptyheadedness joined him.
Wine ! if I could but once win out of this danger,
then I would stick to mead and ale as long as I
lived !

This, too, was the meaning of the captain's quarrel
with Brynglas. Doubtless he had recognised him as
the head of the pirates who had wrought him such
harm. That was where he got the bloody bandage
upon which he relied for disguise. He was a man of
this country by his speech, and so probably knew what
Foulk of the Feet thought would never be discovered,
namely, where the pirates came from. But if he
knew that, then why had he ventured to come thus,
with only one companion, right into the outlaw's
valley ? Had he some ship coming to attack it, and
was he come here that he might show a light to
guide them in their attack to-night ? I looked to
seaward, but there was not a fleck of boat or sail on
all the greying expanse.

I do confess my throat began to feel full of frozen

lead. It was all very well to have slain a judge on
the bench with only a dozen or two of tired javelin
men and officers about him. To stab and be gone
or slain was one thing ; to find oneself in a place like
this, lured thither by a plot for one's own destruction,
was quite another. Moreover in that affair I had
been following out a plan of my own making, so that I
saw every stage of it ahead of me clearly to the end ;
while here I had ridden blindly in at another man's
bidding, seeing only the Ooronoka ahead of me, and
nothing of the way between. This captain was a
bold man and bitter in his quarrel, but Brynglas
was deep and crafty, and so had trapped him. We
were undone. Perhaps even now, while this man
held me here in talk, the captain was being done to
death in the castle behind me. Even so he might be
more fortunate than I. He had a proper cause of
quarrel with these pirates, and so his death would be
no more than a thrust and done with ; while my
quarrel, having had no such heavy provocation as
his, might land me in a much more horrible death,
to satisfy the hatred of Brynglas. My muscles seemed
to stiffen as I stood, and I had to check my tongue at
first till I could bring my voice more full and steady.

I wished to make some fit excuse for returning, that
I might at least try to warn the captain of his danger,
" I left them at the wine," said I, " while I came out
thinking to drink a cup at the gwindy with the
gentlemen there. But if there be no stir afoot, I
will wait till my friend comes with me later to-night.
Till then, therefore——" and I made as courteous a
sweep to this footless thief in parting as if he had
been lord of the widest cantrev in the land.

He did not return it by word or motion, and in my
4

dread I could not tell if it were suspicion or mere
disdain which looked so darkly out of his eyes.   All
the way as I went I tried to go carelessly, yet fear
tugged at my heart, for at every step I was listening
for the twang of his bow behind me, sending an
arrow into my back.   But the porterless gate in the
outer wall still stood open, beckoning me, and when
at last I reached it, whole and sound, I could have
leaped through it at a single bound for joy,
though the castle still hid the captain's fate from
me.

And as if this relief were but a beginning of good,
there, just inside, I met the captain himself, cloaked
and hatted and coming out to seek me.   "Are you
ready?" said he: "we start at once."

"Start," cried I joyfully.   "Whither?"

"You shall see in time," returned he.

"I care not where if it be only out of this valley,"
said I.

"What do you fear in this valley?" asked he
openly.

"Treachery," answered I.

There was no one near to overhear him, nevertheless
he whispered as he said, "Not yet at least.   All goes
so well that if I had planned it I could not have
bettered it."

"Thank God," replied I quickly.   "But I was in
great dread for you when I heard just now that they
had pirated your ship a week ago.   I feared that
they had recognised you again and had drawn a draft
to end you.   I was coming to warn you."

He did not trouble to unravel my words, but answered like a man to whom it is nothing.   "I do
not know what tale you have heard, but a week ago

I was off the coast of France and I have never lost a
ship to pirates yet. That is not my quarrel with
Brynglas."

With that he led the way out and along a path going down to the beach, where the boats lay fast by
chain and padlock. Here men were already leading
our horses aboard one of the broad shallops under the
stern of which the incoming tide was beginning to
lap while other men loosed the mooring chain from
the ring in the rock that held it.

" Do we go by sea then ? " asked I.

" Partly," said he.

Presently we too stepped aboard and the rowers
after us, four on each side down in the waist, though
for the moment they leaned idly about as they waited
for the tide to float us. By this time the colours of the
sunset were gone, save for the line of primrose afterglow far down on the livid sweep of the farthest sea.
The grey bulk of the Eivl deepened and darkened on
shore against the rising silver of the coming moon,
and still we sat, with our cloaks drawn about us,
waiting the lifting tide. I was thinking that if we
were but once safely out of that valley, I should need
to know well why I moved if ever I returned to it
again ; charm the captain never so rarely.

Then round and full and queenly white the soft
moon stood above the high peaks, and the flood of
her glamour washed every line and turret of the castle,
till it stood out of the shadows that had wrapped it
like a castle summoned by a wizard's wand. All the
weird dread which sunset and the fairy maiden had
bred in me came over me again like a rush of waters,
and then, like the ninth wave for volume, all the
swelling power of love swept me in. For in the sheen

of the moon's light I caught sight again of the lady of the strand.

She stood on the slope of the castle hill at the spot where I had halted when first I saw the sea after leaving the hall. She did not move. Her mantle of the green silk hung motionless, and a shawl of darkling crimson was wrapped about her face and shoulders, covering her heavy hair from sight. Then, as she turned her head, the gleam of the moon caught the jewel on her forehead and the light of it shone like another star.

Hungrily I gazed until at length a great sigh from my own breast startled me out of dreaming. " Do we go far ? Shall we be long gone ? " asked I of the captain, before I was aware.

" All in good time. You shall see," answered he.

At that, like an echo love gifted me with a ready lie. " Because," said I, " there is something I have left in the castle bailey, and I think it were well that I hastened back now and brought it——" And before he could remonstrate, or suggest sending a rower, I was ashore and speeding for that wicket gate again. " When we get back," I was saying to myself as I went, " I will lie in wait for her, and when she comes out like this I will carry her off to somewhere."

The wicket yielded and with long strides I was ascending the slope. I had no thought of what I was going to say or do. All my wish was to stand in her presence. Another moment and I was beside her. Then my heart dashed wildly against my ribs in terror, for one fleshless claw went up and dropped the covering from the face. Ayoh ! the face that looked out at me was a grinning skull, covered with

tight parchment, and holding two caverns wherein
burned and glowed two baleful fires for eyes.   My
lady of the peerless form was a grisly hag !  With a
choking gasp of dread I turned and fled again for
the ship.

I was but just in time ; the waves had lifted her
and every man was busy at his post.   Springing
aboard I fell down all my length in my place, as if
to catch my breath, for indeed between fear and
speed I was spent in good earnest.   Two men stood
holding the horses steady ; the eight rowers walked
with their backs bent above their long oars as we
swooped out upon the waters ; astern the steersman
knelt upon one knee as he plied his rudder oar, but
I saw only the shine of that ghastly jewel on the
slope of Castell Brynglas.

Then we turned southwest, parallel with the coast,
and I stood up.   The white line of the foam lay
along the strand like ropes of pearls under the light
of the moon.   The massed mountains lifted higher :
the eerie castle stood up taller ; the bare slim mast
above my head seemed tapering on up into heaven.
The veiled man beside me grew broader and bigger ;
only my own spirit seemed to be shrinking smaller
and smaller with every sweep of the oars as we left
the castle behind.

I felt that I was bewitched and that the sorceress
of the knoll had clutched my soul, so that my empty
body must come back to find it ; and then she
would have me, body and soul, to elf land for ever.
My ears followed the song of the rowers, wherein
the boding of the desolate sea moaned on through
time and chorus as they bent and lifted at the
sweeps.

My maid of the fire-flame eyes was a hideous hag, and I—I still loved her as the Lady of the Mound. I only wanted her to change herself again to what I had first seen her, and I would give all else for that. She dwelt in this haunted valley of Vortigern and it dragged at my breast as if it had been Eden I was leaving.

" Ochain, heart! my heart ! "—I sang dumbly with the rowers—" And alas for me that I looked in her eyes ! "

The great cape came sheer down upon our quarter. Far off and faint that jewel died out : the great cliff cut us off—but I knew that I should return again to the valley of Vortigern.

# CHAPTER VI.

WHEN I could no longer see the valley I sat down, quiet and dumb, for I had no desire to speak any more till I should see that castle again. I wished neither to know where we should land or when. I had only to set myself patiently to exist till I should return again.

Still the rowers kept the cadence of their song; still the captain stood motionless; still the cold breath of the sea seemed kin with the ceaseless voices of the wavelets breaking softly on the strand, a spear throw and no more on our lee. Then another cliff front stepped out a little from the land and our steersman held us straight for it.

The captain saw that and looked aft hastily, but the silent steersman only nodded. Another moment and we were under the looming bulk of it, the rowers shipped their sweeps, and we glided into a little cleft, shaped as closely to fit as if it had been chiselled by measurement to receive this shallop only. The men who held the horses now led them ashore, and, without waiting for any command, turned to the left and began to climb athwart the nearest face of the cliff, while the captain and myself followed.

When we had at length stumbled to the top we took

our horses and mounted, while the two men started
afoot forward as our guides.   Presently we came to a
track leading parallel to the coast, and midway between the mountains and the sea.   "That is your
way," said the speaker of the two, pointing along it,
and without more ado they both turned and disappeared in the direction of the shallop again.

When they were gone, and we had put our horses
into motion once more, the captain spoke.   But all he
said was, "There is a fair in Nevin here to-morrow,
and what I desire is that you let me do all the talking
that is needed in getting lodging and supper."

I answered him nothing.   I was thinking of what
I had left behind and he was talking of lodging and
supper.   So we went in quiet, our horses walking, for,
though the moon was bright above the hills on our
left, and the sea lay like a flood of quicksilver on our
right, yet the track was no freer of ruts and stones
than any other, and there was apparently no need to
lame our tired horses.

When at last we came to Nevin we found it a little
open town of a few score houses, with not even a
castle to defend it from raid or pillage.   Neither did
the church seem more fit for defence than what is
customary in better protected places.   But a square
pillar of solid masonry, rising in the highest part of
the town, indicated a reason for this apparent lack.
It would seem that the men of Nevin were themselves
pirates on occasion, and there is little profit in rob-
bing robbers.

For they had this advantage to tempt them ; they
could be pirates openly by way of reprisal for the
loss of imaginary ships which they had never owned.
At the most their punishment, if they went too far,

would be a fine on the corporaticn, or, in the
extreme, a forfeiture of their town charter, which
only their clerk could read.

To-night the place was thronged with stout merchantmen, mostly here by ships from Beaumaris, and
every house was full and open as we came to it.   The
ale and the wine were going ; the harp and the crwth
were helping the singers, and pipes and bagpipes were
reeling out the music to the feet of the dancers.   The
inns were hopeless for us, coming so late, and at
house after house the tale was the same, "not even
room for a stain on the wall."

"Well," said my companion at last, "the night is
fine and we have already supped at Brynglas : we
will lie out for this once.   Moreover, we shall be
saving an hour or two of to-morrow.   This way
then——" and with the word he started again in
the same direction as before, parallel to the coast,
but with the town of Nevin now behind instead of
before us.

Almost at once we found ourselves in a marsh.
Moonlight is little help in a quagmire, and we had
no guide, yet this man never erred by a hand's breadth
in the devious way as we crossed it.   But I no longer
cared for piecing out evidence concerning him ; all
my thoughts now were busy speculating as to how
soon we should get back to Nant Vortigern and the
lady of spells.   I even forgot the horse between my
knees, and it was no guiding hand of mine that
brought him safe through the marsh, but that I let
the rein swing slack upon his neck and so he could
follow hard upon the crupper of his fellow in front
under the captain.

I was thinking only that the nights were very short

after all, and that if the golden maid of sunset were also the witch of night and darkness, yet with the passing of the night she would become the glorious lady of the dawn too.   And those arms, which had been cream white as a narwhale's tooth, would shine anew all white as Mary's milk when day should send its first shaft to pierce and slay the night in her. And if to love her were to be turned into a demon at night myself, what mattered that if through the day I lived with her in her glory, I in my own proper form and being also ?

Aye, let us be done with this foolish errand of the lord of Brynglas and all this petty and unmeaning stuff of quarrels.   Let us get back to the shore of the valley again, that I might put my fate to the touch of the enchantress.   Yet I wondered that Brynglas himself should never have seen her : though perhaps she was only visible from certain places, or even to certain people.   Yea, let me get back again, for all the wide dome of the night seemed pressing in upon the emptiness of my breast, whence my heart had stayed behind in the valley of Voltigern.

Here, waking for a moment, I found that we had passed the marsh and that my horse still followed the captain as he turned toward the shore, where a long, narrow headland ran out into the sea.   Reaching this, he kept his way along it till, midway from the mainland, we pitched down into a narrow neck, where all beyond was fortified from us by a broad ditch and rampart, running from sea to sea on either hand.   In the middle, however, was an entrance gap, through which my companion pressed, I following him, and here inside he checked, saying : " This is Dinllaen.   Remember it; for you may have to

come here at night-time again on an errand for our
purpose."

I did not tell him that I no longer had any purpose as to Brynglas; or any other thing at all save
one; and so he went on speaking. "We will un-
saddle here and turn our horses loose to graze.
While we sleep here in the gate they cannot get out
and stray."

He lost no time in suiting the action to the word,
I listlessly copying him, and within a few minutes
we were both lying side by side in the gap, wrapped
in our cloaks to sleep. It did not move me to note
that he lay down on his right side; the bloody side
of the bandage. That stain then covered no wound;
the bandage was merely a disguise; a veil indeed—
only I cared no further about it.

Yet though the night was so soft and I was safe I
could not sleep at all. Last night I had couched in a
thicket like a roebuck and yet slept sound and sweet,
though I was hardly clear of those who had hunted
me from the Bala. But then I had a heart full of
quiet, while here I lay with an empty breast, turning
and tossing in strange disquiet for the heart that was
gone out of me. I was bewitched and the spell was
too heavy on me for sleep. Short as is a midsummer
night—and it had been already midnight when we
lay down—yet this was so long to me that before it
ended I sat up and leaned my back against the rampart and looked out over the sea.

The full moon still rode round and high, and in
the shimmer of its light upon the waters I thought I
could catch the blur of a ghostly ship standing to
and fro far off to the west. But my eyes were not
yet familiar enough with ocean and its burdens to be

certain, while my companion slept so sound that I did not like to wake him to ask questions of him. Instead I turned my eyes to the north, where the three peaks of the Eivl brooded across the sleeping coast and the glittering sea, and so at last by that way I came to the coasts of sleep myself before the first lark lifted to call the dawn.

The sun was an hour high when I awoke, and my first glance showed me the captain standing upon the upper ground beyond me, straining his eyes to westward. Turning to the north I saw no sign of the Eivl ; only a great white mist stopping up all sight that way, so that I wondered if that were more enchantment to shut me out from ever returning. And because of my disquiet I went over and joined the captain. "Are you looking for the horses ?" I asked, for want of something better to say after the greeting.

"Nay," answered he, "they would not stop up here on the dry uplands. They will be half way down the cliff, there on the north side, where the sweet grass is and the spring."

He knew this old fort then as he had known the marsh.

"But come," he continued ; "let me show you something," and with this he led me a bowshot farther along the high ridge to where a carn of fire-stained stones crowned the highest swell of it, immediately over the sea. As we went I saw that all the south side of the peninsula was set like iron with a dark fringe of cliff and reef, and all the blunt head of it was bald brown rock likewise.

At the carn the captain broke in upon me. "If anything should happen to me in the next day or

two, so that I should be prisoner in the power of
Brynglas while you should be free, then come here
and build a fire on this carn.  If it be night build a
bright one, and if it be day build a smoky one.  Now
come this way," and with the word he broke off
abruptly and led me across till we stood upon the
edge of the cliff on the north side : a cliff that swept
down like an arras of green velvet to the blue waters
of the curving bay that woke in the light beneath.

For this cliff was of earth, and all the moisture of
the land above sank down to the roots of the grass
that clothed its sides as close as a woven web, while
in one place near the foot was a little spring, where
now our horses revelled in the lush feast they found
about it.

" When you have fired the beacon," took up the captain again, "it will presently be answered by a tall
ship which will come here into this porth of Dinllaen.
If it be night kindle a little fire here in this curve
for a signal to the ship's people, and when they send
a boat ashore trust them and tell them everything
about me.  They will do all the rest, for they have
their orders—though had I known just what I was
going to do I would have given them a little differently.  And now we will catch our horses and
go."

When the horses had been brought up and saddled,
and we were once more mounted, it struck me that
this was a peculiar place for the men of Lleyn to
have fortified, and I said so to the captain.

" Nay," answered he, " this is a pirates' stronghold,
built in the old days when the black Northmen came
in fleets to ravage these coasts.  They used to draw
up their ships in the bay and then drive all the spoil

of the country into this fort, where they might sit
secure and feast till it was done. Then they would
sail away and devastate some other coast. That is
why every hill in Lleyn hath its top fortified so that
the people could be beforehand and take refuge there.
But in these days all Lleyn hath turned pirate itself,
so these fortresses are no more used—though the ship
I speak of may have need of this one perhaps."

With this he started back by the way we had come
in the night, and within a short while we were sitting
down to a breakfast in Nevin, where the fair was
already begun.

That fair was as lively and as throng a fair as a
man might wish to see. By kindreds the folk came
in from far and near, and the young men had gathered
into the churchyard to begin games from the moment of their arrival. It had ever been my wont
at a fair to try for the leaping, the running or wrestling, and especially the buckler play ; and many a
prize had I won in time past. To-day however I did
not even care to go and see how others shaped at it,
but instead walked listlessly at the elbow of the captain, as he went to and fro in the crowd, taking keen
note of every chieftain of a petty kindred as he
passed. Even the signs of hostility between kin and
kin no longer delighted me, though there was promise here of the fair ending with a general affray.

At last, when the sun showed yet a couple of
hours short of noon, I spoke. " How long is it still
before we begin to do something ? "

" An hour or two yet," said he. " But there is
one small business which we may as well despatch
now. This stall will do."

Here he stopped in front of a stall, the richest in

the fair ; and almost before I had time to wake up
and protest he had sold the old cloak off my shoulders and bought me a new blue one, goodly to see,
and laced with velvet broidered at the edges with
gold.  Moreover, my Monmouth cap must make way
for a Flaundrish beaver hat with a little feather, and
though my anger was choking me dumb I dared not
break openly with him in the midst of all that
fair.

But we were heading now for the inn yard again and
I went with a stride as long and as quick as his own.
In that yard I would tell him what I meant, thought I.
Behold, however, we were no sooner come out of
the crowd, and I opening my mouth to speak, than
he stopped it.  For in a flash he had drawn a broad
gold chain from some concealment in his clothes and
had thrown it about my neck ; a chain worth a hundred broad pieces if it were worth a penny.

In my impotence I laughed a little.  " What then !
we are to be mountebanks and you are bear-leader !
—is that it ?  In sooth I thought we had come to
use the steel !  But proceed ; what is the first trick
we are to practise ? "

" Keeping our temper," replied he, unmoved ;
" and next, keep out of all brawls for an hour's time.
Walk apart from the crowd—if to the shore all the
better—and then meet me at the foot of the watch
pillar.  Meanwhile there is a little something which
I can best attend to alone."

I stood irresolute.  To walk apart, to go to the
shore, was the very thing I desired ; but was I to obey
him as a good little urchin obeys, who fears the stick
or hopes for honey on his bread ?  I was a man, and
a man does not move at another's bidding for either

stick or honey, but only because he is satisfied that the end is worth while.

Pettishly I held out the hem of the new cloak. " This pest of cloak and hat ! this chain ! what are they for ?   I am tricked out like the fool of the fair, and yet am not told for what ! "

But he only waved his hand lightly towards me ; as who should say, " Patience ! good friend, ha' patience," and so turned him and was gone.   As to me, he had no sooner joined the crowd than I was already walking towards the shore.

At a field's breadth from the pillar I had reached the edge of the earth cliffs.   But for still more retirement I saw a little point run out to divide the two bays ; the Porth of Dinllaen from the Porth of Nevin.   Out then to the farthest sod of this point I went and there cast myself down full length on the grass with my face to the north again.

More than a hundred feet below me shimmered the little half-moon bay, round as my target and brighter than the bluest steel was ever burnished. The sheer front of the earth cliff that hemmed it in was green with the verdure of a thousand springs, soaking through from the marshes of the hinderland above.   Still blue bay ; soft emerald cliffs ; and the sickle of yellow sand that shone between—they made a scene to have fed full the eye of any man less distempered than I was then.   Yea, lifting the gaze to follow the bold curve of the coast beyond, the whole sweep made a picture such as would have beggared even 'AbGwilym's self to sing of.   Northward the hoary masses of the grey and naked Eivl shone softly through the shimmering haze like mountains of pearl, with the three peaks soaring so light above

that they seemed to float like their own eagles in the
tempered blue of the cloudless summer sky. The
long stride of the cliff that shut in the further side
of the valley of Vortigern made the other horn of a
great bay from this horn on which I was lying, and
all the sea between was ribboned with a hundred
tints that were neither blue, nor green, nor yet all
silver, but only pure loveliness, such as a maid
might dream of while she listened to the lark at
noon.

Still and calm and peaceful lay that vision, and
well I wist as I looked that it was some witchcraft,
since no mere earthly land could be so beautiful, but
only the land of faery. Had it been no glamour of
enchantment, but earth only and no spell, then would
men have come here to dwell instead of singing of
Paradise.

I could not lie still and look at it, for every minute
my longing to return to that thyme-draped mound
by the strand of Nant Vortigern grew into great
sighs that burst from me unawares. "I will go back
to the fair," said I ; and with that rose and went.

At the foot of the pillar I found the captain already
waiting, though the hour was not yet up.

" Come now, and keep close to me," said he quickly
—yet he did not seem to hold his sword any the
nearer to his hand as if there had been fighting to
come.

Neither did we hurry, but sauntered at a pace as
slow as that of any fair-loiterer there. In and out
amongst the booths we moved, till at last it dawned
upon me that we kept, turn for turn and step for
step, in wake of a lady who went closely veiled, and
of whom I could see no more than that she walked

5

with a grace which promised her a gentlewoman from top to toe. Now and again she turned her head, but all from crown to elbow was hidden by a caul-fashioned lombardine partelet of a purple gauze flecked with gold, that allowed nothing of her features or her hair to be seen.

" Have you a gold piece or two ? " whispered the captain in my ear : " if so then buy a gift of some sort : a silver harp-wrest or some such trinket."

Carelessly I obeyed, yet idly marvelling as to what this might portend. Only, with my hand upon my money I remembered that I had but one gold piece and some silver. " Have you the money ? " said I to him—" pay for me then," ended I.

For all his bandage I could see that he seemed a pleased man at paying, a thing not usual with men, so that I whispered next—" And what am I to do with this thing ? "

" What you will," answered he promptly. " It hath already served its purpose in being bought openly as we followed the lady. Come now," and he was starting again in wake of her as he spoke.

Like a breath from a kiln it came to me that I was being used to play the love-lorn gallant behind this lady, and all my expectation turned into disgust. " A woman I had never seen, and who might be as ugly as night ! " thought I on the sudden. I turned sharp to the captain. " Sir," said I, " I rode with you to help in a quarrel against Brynglas ; not to play the decoy to some lukewarm lover, or to feed the vanity of a silly woman. Stick to the quarrel and I am with you, but leave this or leave me."

" If you knew how closely you are sticking to the quarrel in doing this," he answered—and I caught a grim satisfaction in his voice—" you would laugh and enjoy it as much as I do.  I knew when I left Carnarvon that I should get satisfaction, but I never dreamed of so complete a satisfaction as this will give us in the end."

Then as I still stood fast, " Only believe for a little while," he went on, and you shall presently be glad that you did this now."

To have continued the debate was to have done it with hand on hilt, and the captain was a man to draw weapon upon only in a matter of life and death.   Bad as it was to have to ape the lovesick swain to this strange woman, it would be still more ridiculous to be slain over her in a fair.  I must wait till we could get out of this place and then avenge my dignity at the first fit chance.  " One thing," said I—" does this lead us back to Nant Vortigern ? "

" Are you afraid to return there ? " answered he, but without any trace of a sneer.

" The one desire I have on earth is to find myself in that castle there once more," replied I.

" Then be assured that only by doing this now can you ever get there again," said he, in a tone that I could not but help believe.

I threw my cloak across my face to hide the flush of shame as I started to keep pace with him again. I looked at the lady and I hated the grace with which she walked, and the poise of her cauled head as she turned this way and that in seeing what was to be seen.  She reminded me so of the one whose spell was upon me, and therein made my mock gallanting here so much the more bitter.  Twice in turning she almost brushed my arm at passing, but the lombardine hid even the light of her eyes from me.

At last I said angrily, "Is there much more of this ?"

"I wish there were," he answered, and I felt that he smiled over it. "I wish there were ; you do it so perfectly. I did this morning whisper it in the crowd that you were a young lord from Pembroke, who could not rest for hearing the harpers sing the beauty of the heiress of Castell March. It is known all over the fair that you are so desperate that I, your uncle, am here to counsel caution ; and all your open anger hath been taken for resentment that I still stick to patience. The new hat and cloak ! the gold chain ! Oh, you play the moody lover to perfection !"

Even in my anger I could scarcely forbear to laugh in answer to the merriment in his tone as he ended, and though my disgust stood firm, yet it was so much the less in that it was at least a famous beauty whose steps I followed.

Still suspicion would not down. " Why then does she go alone if she be both a beauty and an heiress ? Is there no gentleman of good kindred in all Lleyn to dispute the following with me ?"

" There might have been many," returned he, " but the man that overshadows this corner of the world hath daunted them all. So you may suck all the sweetness of knowing that you are the one man in Lleyn who dare cock his beaver at the lady of Castell March. And does not that please you ?"

I did not answer. Yesterday it would have pleased me beyond all things. Yesterday I would have ridden from one end of the land to the other to have done such a thing. But I could not tell him that now I was under a spell to love a night-hag and none other

in all the world.    I had no word to answer him and
so I walked in silence.

Then the lady turned once more, and, as if she challenged me, stood stock still for a moment in front of
me.    So plain was it that in mere courtesy I could
do no less than doff my beaver and bow to her ;
though as I rose I could have drawn upon the captain
for very heat at my discreditable part.    Straightway
then, and without the least sign of having seen that
I bowed to her, the lady turned and sauntered towards
her horse, which now I saw a well-armed fellow holding, close to one of the inns.

When she had mounted, there came six riders out
of the inn yard, all wearing the same badge as that
broidered on her glove and saddlecloth, and, as soon
as the seventh from holding her horse had mounted
his own, they set forth southwards, skirting the
eastern edge of the marsh.

Next moment we two were in the saddle also and
were following the lady and her party ; plain for all
the fair to see, while only the captain knew how deep
my anger was biting in behind the cloak that covered
my face.

But as soon as we were clear of the town I spoke.
" Sir, what next ?    Are we still to follow this lady,
as plain as she hath given me the scorn already ? "

Slowly he turned his face to me, and I felt that I
could almost have ripped the bandage off it to see
what lay behind.    " Follow her ! " repeated he, " aye
and more than follow her.    For you must carry her
off from her Castle of March."

# CHAPTER VII.

## TRACKING THE PREY.

THE words came out before I had time to think. "I'll not marry her! Quarrel or no quarrel I'll not marry any woman for the mere sake of killing Brynglas."

For the first time the captain laughed outright; "That thou wilt not," said he, "for then I should be balked indeed. I said carry her off."

"Where to?" demanded I.

"Nant Vortigern," answered he.

"But what hath she to do with our quarrel?" pursued I.

And for answer I got the old phrase again, "That you will see in good time."

I drew in a great breath. "Am I never to have any more answer than that?" protested I. "I am not a boy. I am expected to do a man's work; treat me like a man then. I can keep counsel."

"As you did at Carnarvon," railed he merrily; "when you boasted of having killed a judge; boasted to two strangers chance-met in a tavern in the town that is the seat of justice for all this part of the country. Yea, you can keep counsel."

"It was the wine," returned I sullenly; "I will take no more wine."

" But there are other things than wine, Rowland,"
he went on, " There is especially the torture. And
if it should be you who were the prisoner and I the
free man, then Brynglas would surely put you to
pitiless torture to make you tell all my plans. If
you knew them then out they must come and all
would be ruined ; certainly all hope of rescuing you
alive would be gone. So e'en trust me in this and
rest assured that within two days you shall be satisfied of everything."

He was right. After my braggart folly at Carnarvon what man would trust that I could keep counsel ?
But I said to myself that if once I got back to Nant
Vortigern, then the captain would need to explain to
the uttermost word of all his plans if ever he got me
to follow him out again.

To rouse my mind I straightened up and looked
ahead to count the chances of this thing in hand.
Seven lusty fellows, well armed, and mounted all
alike on black horses, rode comelily behind the
lady, while we were but two men. My melancholy
brightened a little at the promise of so brisk an action.
Nay, as matters stood I confess I did not quite see
how we were to accomplish the deed. Each man of
the seven had a steel cap to his head and an armolet
jacket to his body to defend him, while for use he
had bow and quiver, sword and target, and a long chasing spear held aslant across his saddle bow. Seldom
indeed might one see so pretty a train. Moreover
their horses moved fresh and free, while ours were
somewhat leg-weary. It seemed more like that the
seven should ride us down than we them. Without
doubt we should have to use some wile, for we could
not hope to succeed by force alone.

Yet the captain did no more than jog along in open sight, not a bowshot behind them, and at last, by the time we were come beneath the great hill of Carn Madryn, I began to fall into a fresh distaste for the business of following in wake of this lady. For every graceful motion of her body, as she sat her white palfrey so lightly and so firmly, reminded me again of the lady of the strand.

Here at this hill, too, the lady seemed to have fallen into a distaste of having us follow her. One of her men, by appearance the chief of them, turned and rode back to meet us, while the rest of them halted facing us.

Belike the fellow was puffed up by the goodness of his fortune in commanding so well appointed a company. Or it may be that he had bottomed over many cups at the fair ; for as he came near the sun picked out every ruddy bristle on his face, that sweated importance. Straightway he seized my rein to turn my horse about, with no other word than, " Take some other way, sirrah ! "

My smouldering anger at having to follow his mistress flashed into flame at his sauciness. My speech stuck in my throat and my glaive was the first to answer with a slash that had lopped his hand off at the wrist had he not jerked it away.

Instantly he reined about for room to run with his lance at me, while five of the other six were charging across the green at us in a level row of spears. But the captain turned my horse with his own and forced me into a path that threaded a little marsh, where their charge would have stuck fast had they not drawn rein in time.

They saw that they could only follow one at a

time, and so they came to parley; for no one of
them had stomach to face the captain singlehanded.

" Yield you prisoners !" cried their officer fellow.

" Come and take me !" I shouted savagely back,
shaking my glaive towards him in sullen defiance.

But instead—" Bows ! bows !" he cried to his
men, and they began to string each man his yew.

With that my companion put in, " Sirrah ! "—and
his voice was loud with deep impatience—" go not
so fast. Thy mistress will ill brook to have two
gentlemen shot at like wildfowl."

" I'll teach you——" began the fellow, when suddenly the seventh man of the company left his mistress and rode furiously towards us, shouting to his
fellows the while to hold their hands.

" Draw not ! draw not ! Our lady forbids ye to
do any hurt unless they be stubborn in following
her ! "

Their officer fellow liked it not, but he dared not
openly gainsay this command. Yet he tried another
way. " Will you pass your word to go back ? "

" Pish !" exclaimed the captain at my elbow.
" Wait and see whether we follow or not. Ride after
thy mistress now ! or thou wilt be left and lost,"—
for the lady had already begun to ride on as though
this affair no longer troubled her.

" Our lady says that you are to come back ! " urged
the messenger to the officer, and at that the fellow
looked first over his shoulder at his mistress and
next again at us. Then he mouthed out boastfully,
" Follow further if ye dare and you shall each have
a chasing stave through your carcases as the first fair
coursing spot you come to."

" Fellow," I answered savagely, " when next I

come near enough I will slit thy nose for thee and give thee something to use thy bull's voice in bellowing about."

He reined as if to ride at me with his lance, but the captain spurred broadside in front of me, crying over his shoulder, " After thy mistress, fool ! or thou wilt have half Pembroke landing some night to burn you all in your beds ! "

The voice was so confident, and rang so with seeming impatient disgust, that it took some effect, for three or four of the men drew off and galloped after their mistress.   Whereby I judged that there was no real authority amongst them, and that each man was liable to be rated in person by his mistress, instead of through their officer.   Women commonly meddle like that, to the ruin of all discipline.

Or it might be that they were but household servants armed for the day, with some butler fellow for an officer.   Certes he was little better in spirit, for at seeing the others draw off he began to move after them, only growling out great mouthfuls of threats as he went.

" Again ! we have done well again," quoth the captain cheerily as he watched them go.   " Of a truth, Rowland, if I had schooled thee to every word and action thou couldst not have done better."

" Better ? " echoed I bitterly ; " that is some new way of the word, doubtless.   And if to feel myself eaten up with contempt ; if to be parched with disgust ; to be a blind bear in chain and muzzle ; a dumb, ramping idiot ; is to have done well, then of a surety I could not have done better.   There is no man on earth could be so vile as I feel now and yet contain himself in the light of the sun.

"But now, good gentleman, continue; pile up this play; do as you will while you have me fast, it is but what I deserve for swearing faith with you with my eyes shut. Then when it is all done and ended I will burn these gaudy rags of cloak and hat, throw this chain to the first leper, and wash myself in every river of the land—a beggar with a beggar's staff and wallet—before I ever mix with wholesome gentlemen again."

He had not waited for me to finish all this speech, but had briskly led my horse out to the open ground again. "That is right, son," said he as I stopped; "I love to hear you relieve your mind thus. It is good for both of us."

Then, unabashed—"We will take this way now," he went on. "They will go by Llan Testyn and Nanhoron, but we will keep on this side the line of the Carns and come upon them as they near the other coast. They will not look for us there, since it is not every stranger who knows his way through this waste."

But I answered him nothing, for what more was there to say?

The ride was long and yet we made a good pace of it, since wherever the ground allowed of it we galloped, and even at the worst we crowded to a fast walk. Only this man must have a wondrous memory. "Did you say thirty years upon the Main?" I queried once, as we drew out from a piece of marsh, the worst yet.

He knew well what I meant, but all he answered was, "A man may forget what he learnt in manhood but not what grew up with him in boyhood."

Save for this we passed in silence under the long

line of the Carns that cross the land of Lleyn almost
from coast to coast.   Then between Carn Anneddol,
the last of them, and the Voel Vach we turned south
again and across a wide waste to the village of Mynytho.   Here the captain asked the way of a lad, the
only one to be seen ; though well I wot that he
needed to ask no road in Lleyn.   And the road he
asked was that to Castell March.

Then, as we were directed, we passed along a lane,
until at the head of it we drew rein to wait till we
should hear the coming of the lady and her train.
But when we caught the sound of their steel clank-
ing ; when I had begun to gather my courage ; to
fill my lungs ; to take my reins shorter and grip my
knees closer for the shock ; then the captain said,
coolly—"Now we will ride quietly along to meet and
pass them.   And do you doff your hat and bow to
the lady as we pass."

I had near drawn on him to fight it out then and
there.   "Diawl ! when is this thing to be done ? or
what is this lying in wait for ? " I cried.   " Let us do
or let us leave it, and not worry this poor lady like
a doe in chase.   Carry her off and be done with
it at once ! "

" Aye, be done with us at once, you mean," answered he.   " Carry her off now in open daylight,
from her own castle gate, through her own village,
and all the length of Lleyn behind us for our tired
horses to limp over !   Have done, and do as I ask ;
there is a reason for this, as you shall see within ten
minutes afterwards."

There was no time for argument.   Already he was
moving, trusting to my following, and he had asked
and not commanded—I had perforce to keep him

company.   There was enough of danger, too, to
sweeten the thing by making it less contemptible
than otherwise it might be.   If the lady should prove
irritable—but by this time we were abreast of her
and all her escort was scowling ferociously, as the
fellows came two and two behind her.

Nevertheless I did not doff my beaver, but instead
looked gently at her, for I was beginning to be sorry
for her.

When we had passed, as soon as we were out of
sight, the captain clapped spurs to his horse.
"Swiftly now," said he, and as I pressed after him
he headed by devious ways to the slopes of Llanbedrog Mountain, where it stands out into the sea.
For we were come to the eastern coast of the peninsula, looking upon the blue waters of St. Idwal's
Roads.

Gaining the mountain-side we came to a space all
rocks and bushes that hid us well from sight, where
we dismounted that we might the better look out.
"See yonder, that castled house," said the captain,
pointing : "that is Castell March.   Now watch it."

The low, wide square of battlemented buildings
showed plain and strong upon a long ridge beyond
and below us, looking over the sea, and while he
spoke the lady and her seven drew up at the gate of
it.   I marvelled that she did not at once light down,
but within three minutes out came a new seven men,
mounted upon grey horses.   These were followed
by yet another seven mounted on browns, and all
alike armed and accoutred as the first seven were,
save that the lances of each seven were painted the
colour of their horses.

Then the seven greys spread out like a bent bow,

with half a bowshot's distance between each man and his fellow. Next the seven browns followed, a bowshot behind and twelve lances' lengths from man to man, as they pricked at top speed after those in front. Lastly came the seven black all in a row together.

"St. Dervel!" I broke out impatiently; "what have we yonder? Something from the Dream of Rhonabwy or what? Are they set out to catch us! such a chase would not catch a lame cow. What fools a woman makes of a company of men!" I was as angry to see the lady thus squandering her defence as I was with myself for causing her to need it.

The captain answered nothing, only continued to follow the popinjays with his eyes as they went over the ridges until they disappeared. Then I broke in upon him. "Does this lady of Castell March live by the old romances then, and rule her household by every harper's tale? You said well that she is an heiress, and a rich one she must be to keep such state as that. One-and-twenty horses saddled in stall and one-and-twenty riders harnessed in hall to back them at a nod. She must think herself some princess of old story indeed."

"Doubtless," answered the captain this time. "It is the way of a maid to live wrapped round with dreams before she is wed."

"Shall we go down then and lift her now while all her fools are gone?" demanded I.

"Nay, for in good sooth she ordereth her castle by the old tales. She hath every one of the officers as the old codes lay them down for the Prince's palace, besides nine men that keep guard in the hall. No, we must wait till to-night."

Then as we sat, like a lull in a storm my anger broke down, and pity for this royal-minded maiden came over me. I felt well that every cunning town rogue in the land had learned of her weakness and was living on it; tongue in cheek, braving the day in costly harness; swilling her substance nightly till they snored down in the rushes; and fooling her from one end to the other to the top of her bent. If I could but come within reach of them to-night I would pay a few of the knaves for their impudence. And though I kept my tongue between my teeth yet my feeling showed itself in my face as I turned upon the captain.

He saw it and answered it quietly. " I see that you are still restive."

" Aye, restive and more. I am here to help you in this : but if anything comes of it that I like not for her, then be sure I will hold you to account for it. If I have been used to bring this lady to any dishonour——" I did not finish it in words ; the tone was enough.

Then for the first time he showed a kindly side. Laying his hand upon my shoulder he said, in the first soft tone I had heard from him, " Rowland, I tell thee this because thou art an honest lad. Although she does not know it, yet this lady of Castell March, that is so rich and lives so royally to-day, will to-morrow be a beggar unless thou carry her off to-night."

I held out my hand. " In faith ? " asked I.

And quiet and strong he smote his hand down into mine. " Aye, in faith and truth."

# CHAPTER VIII.

## THE SEIZING OF THE LADY OF CASTELL MARCH.

A SILENCE fell between us then, for his eyes had turned again to Castell March and all the wide sweep of sea and land spreading away from our feet. Something had stirred him. I had heard it in his voice and I read it now in his manner when he took two strides forward away from me, as if he did not wish me to see his face—showing that he had forgotten his mask of a bandage. His hands hung down by his sides, slack as those of a sick man, until, all of a sudden, he drew in a mighty breath and every line of him was rigid from top to toe. Well I wist some memory of past days was upon him.

Perhaps he feared I might read too much, for in the next breath he had recovered himself and was turning to me, saying in an unruffled voice, "Rowland, you slept but little last night; lie down and sleep now and I will wake you at sunset. The heather between those two rocks is soft and sweet. Afterwards I shall want you to watch while I sleep myself."

I was not sleepy but I was tired as a wolf and that did as well. Moreover much of my misgiving anent the lady I was to carry off was now done away with, and so I had hardly stretched myself in that cradle spot between the rocks before I was asleep.

80

At sunset he woke me and I found that he had divided into two uneven portions the food he had brought from Nevin. The greater portion was laid for me, and all he answered when my eye challenged him was, "Eat ; there is need of it."

Wine, too, he had set, tempered with water till I no longer feared it, and so we ate and drank in pleasant comfort. When the meal was ended he pointed southward. "Look ! " said he ; " yonder between St. Idwal's isles and the black bluff of Penrhyn Ddu—do you see that ship ? She is coming here. After dark watch the sea well, close in here under the mountain. When you see a light flashed three times then call me." And with no more ado he took his cloak about him and lay down to sleep.

Looking long at the ship I made it out to be some such a vessel as the one we had used last night, save that it seemed larger and that the sweeps had been shipped to let the southerly breeze bring it along by sail. Satisfied, I turned to watch the land. The white mists had begun to rise from every low-lying marsh and meadow. Faintly and slow the dusk began to fall ; and all to keep my mind from dwelling upon Nant Vortigern I fell to going over in my mind the tale of King March, who was king of this Cornish land of Lleyn in the days of Arthur.

I thought of the minstrel whom he slew because the pipe would play no other than "King Mark hath horse's ears," and yonder in that marsh the reed was plucked which brought death upon the poor minstrel by its truthfulness—a warning to all that live by royal favour. On that ridge yonder the foundations of his castle still showed, a bowshot from this later castle whose mistress we were lying in wait to carry

6

off. Southward beyond the little river was March Rhos, where he hunted at night when his court was asleep and his wife Esylt lying alone till Tristram played the consoler. In truth it were small wonder if the heiress of to-day copied the old state of the days of King Mark and the knights of Arthur's court.

But all this land of Lleyn was haunted, and as the dark fell I sat closer to the captain where he lay sleeping steadily. Presently I saw the lights begin to flicker redly out from the castle where one or two of the windows were left unshuttered—little they dreamed of harm who sat over the mead by the fire-light within. Then followed a quiet hour or two, and next off shore I caught the flash of a lantern run three times up to the masthead of the galley.

Touching the captain, "Sir," said I, "the light hath flashed."

"Come, then," said he, rising at once as if he had never been asleep : "we must go afoot, and lead our horses with us too, for we must leave them where they may be found by the castle people in the morning."

With this he began to lead the way down the mountain-side, for the moon was risen and the way was easy to him who knew it so well. Then as we came to where the bushes grew he tied his horse to a stem where it would be plainly seen in the morning ; bidding me tie mine near by. Next we began to ascend the hill upon which the castle stands, and looking back I saw the galley had followed and was pulling along the shore with sail furled and all its sweeps out.

Presently my companion stopped, while he uttered the long, mournful, liquid cry of a curlew disturbed at night, and straightway the call was repeated from

a point not four lances' lengths away.   Looking there
I saw something rise from the gorse bushes, and in
the moonlight I recognised our one-eyed guide from
Carnarvon.

At once I guessed that treachery was to be our
help in this, and in the first flash of the thought I
hated the fellow until I remembered that this thing
was for the lady's good, as the captain had sworn.
This rogue was a hanger-on of the huntsmen and
tended the hounds, therefore none of them would
give tongue to betray us—as the captain whispered
hurriedly in my ear.   And by that token I saw how
narrowly and with what nicety of detail this whole
enterprise had been planned.

" How many men are there in the castle ? " queried
the captain.

" Only the pot-bellied officers of the household
and the fat-eyed nine that guard the hall," answered
the guide ; and I caught the sneer of a full scorn in
his voice.   " The pretty one-and-twenty riders will
come back to-morrow, half drunk on the dregs of
Nevin fair, bringing some lusty lie with which to
befool their mistress as they commonly do."

" Is all ready ? " went on the captain.

" All ready," said the other, turning to lead the
way.

He went as boldly up to the gatehouse as if the
place had been our own ; for only your creepers and
stealthy steppers are suspected when seen.   The
porter was drunk or asleep, and the great door was
on the latch, as our guide had left it on coming out
after he, too, had caught sight of the light at the
galley's masthead.

Crossing the courtyard within, he led us to the hall

door which he had tied fast on the outside. Beckoning us to look through the window, "See them, like pigs, snoring side by side," whispered he. And sure enough in the moonshine we could see them lying as peacefully as though no long black galley were thrusting its beak into the sand of the shore, and as if we three had never met.

Then the guide led us along a lawn betwixt the length of the hall and the stables, and by a little side port gave us access to a room next to the end of the hall, whose inner door he had also previously fastened, so that the snorers within were mere prisoners in their own sleeping-place. Hitherto we had come as freely as sons in their father's house, but now we went stealthily as wild cats through chamber after chamber, till presently the guide caught each of us by an arm as we followed him, one at each elbow. Pressing us back for a moment he whispered; "Steady now; the next is the room."

I felt a catch in my throat as we started again, and none of us breathed in making the seven strides that brought us to where the guide threw open a door. "In there! quick!" he snapped under his breath.

One little push the captain gave me, and with a rush I was inside the lady's chamber. She was leaning out of her lattice, looking at the night, and as she turned at sound of me I saw that she was still dressed and had moreover wrapped her head and shoulders from the night air in a heavy shawl, so that even yet I could not tell what manner of woman she was.

Not till I seized her did she fully take the alarm, but then with a wild cry for help she roused the night so widely that I felt sure even those clodpates in the hall must break out and rescue her. Moreover as I

reached the door with her she got one hand loose
and with a swift snatch tried to draw my own dagger
upon me.

But I caught her arm again and held it.   How soft
and warm her supple form was in the gripe of my
clenched arms! how my armolet coat must have
bruised her rounded limbs as I crushed her in keeping her fast!   The guide was a stride in front of me
and the captain one behind, as with set teeth I
hurried on.   A clamour of shrill screams burst forth
ahead of us.   "Back!" cried the guide—"this way;
quick!" continued he as he turned aside through
another door just in time to save us.   Three strides
more and we should have landed in the midst of the
women and been stabbed to pieces before we could
have turned.

Now we were out into the courtyard and a wild
din of shouting came up from towards the beach
where the shipmen had landed and were running up
to help us.   Not for one moment did the maid in my
arms cease to struggle or to cry upon the cowardly
officers shut in the hall; nor I to run as fast as that
shapely burden would allow.

Fast I went, but the women issuing into the moonlight caught sight of us and like a cloud of half clad
witches poured after us.   At sight of that the maid
strove as if her heart would burst, until, with a last
wild, writhing endeavour, she tangled and tripped
me, and I fell headlong with her to the ground.

I had just time to twist myself that my body
might strike first and so save her the worst of the
shock.   But, alack for a round stone that lay half
buried in the grass!—her head struck against it and
she was senseless in my arms.

The women, with brandished knives, were almost upon us. Already the captain and the guide had drawn their weapons to try and overawe them, but they came shrieking on like demons. Then, just as it began to look as if we had failed, in through the arch of the gatehouse rushed the yelling seamen.

All in an instant the shrieks of anger turned to screams of mortal dread as the women fell back in a press of terror, for the leader of the newcomers was a man of no mortal height. Nay, I myself had almost loosed my hold of the maid but that suddenly I caught sight of a face below as well as a face above, and in a flash resolved it into two men—Foulk of the Feet mounted on the shoulders of a hairy giant who made no more of his burden than if it had been a feather.

The footless thief had an arrow nocked home and his bow half bent, but the sight of the weird double figure had been enough. The women fled; I picked up my insensible burden again, and with a run we were out and away to the shore, and presently wading out to the ship there waiting for us.

But, when we were all aboard, and the sixteen rowers were straining their broad backs as they stooped and tore at the long sweeps that lifted us through the sea, I knelt beside the shrouded figure of the maid where I had laid her, and doubt began to assail me. Turning to the captain I said bitterly, " Remember that you struck hands with me. By St. Dervel, but it were best you kept faith with me now ! "

And for all answer he laughed a free and open laugh; a laugh that perplexed me sorely, so that I even forgot to be angered by it.

# CHAPTER IX

### THE FACE BEHIND THE VEIL.

PRESENTLY the long-continued stillness of the lady began to trouble me. Had the fall slain her outright? "Wine!" I cried sharply. "Have ye no wine aboard, ye fools, to give the lady to bring her to again?"

The captain handed me a little silver-rimmed leather bottle containing strong waters, and I took hold of the shawl to uncover her face, so that I might revive her with a sip. But I found that she held the covering close, and in another moment I was aware that she was weeping as bitterly as silently beneath it.

My mind was all misery. "Lady," said I to her, vainly trying to take her hand, "I give you the oath of a man, that you shall be the better and not the worse for this."

But still she wept, not heeding my words, till my conscience pricked me to more protestations. "Fear nothing," I went on to her; "I that have done this, will, from this hour, be your truest servant. You shall command me to the end of the world—I swear it!"

Yet neither now would she make me any answer. I sat helpless in wretchedness till, to stop my mind, I gathered all the mantles that were loose in the ship and spread them for a couch to lay her upon. Then

I covered her with my cloak and, sitting down beside her, laid my glaive across my knees as if I had been her squire. For the moment I had clean forgotten the enchantress of Nant Vortigern; so full of doubt for this captured maid was I.

Thus we went surging over the breathing waters, while outboard the dip and the spray of the long blades made liquid silver under the moon as we passed between the lonely isles of St. Idwal and the black rim of Penrhyn Ddu.

Then across the mouth of Porth Ceiriad and round Pen Cilan, to where the sullen sheet of Porth Neigwl lay livid on our starboard, and the rowers as they swung to and fro on their sweeps chanted a time-old song to the dread spirit of that Hell's Mouth, as the steersman held us out and across the edge of it.

Past Talvárach under the shadow of its mountain; past many a brooding point and many a porth of demons haunted; past little isles that lay upon the midnight wave like seabirds sleeping; and then we drew through between the Braich and Ynys Enlli (of the English called Bardseye) and so turned and started northward, with the sweeps swinging easier and the hoisted sail bellying to the cool breeze that stirred along behind us.

Fresher grew the little breeze and faster we rode through the wide winged night. Porth on porth and point on point—we swept along the coast, just out of reach, till at last in the dawning light I saw upon our starboard bow the long thrust of Dinllaen, where we had spent the night before; yet long and long ago as it seemed now.

Then as the sun began to quicken the long comb of the high-ridged land I saw the white mists rolling

up the sides of the Eivl, till the three peaks tore
through the vapour and cast it adrift as an antlered
stag might toss loose from a hunter's mantle; and
with every length of the ship as we drew nearer so
did thoughts of the Lady of the Mound rise higher
in me.   Anon we passed the cape that had shut out
my eyes when we left, and once again I strained
my vision eagerly for the castle and the strand beneath it.

Whether it were in doubt or in hope I could not
tell, for the feel of the soft flesh of this living woman
beside me, as I remembered it when carrying her off,
seemed to thrill me through now with a strange
desire for the outer world and its free and open life,
as against the eerie dread that drew me to the enchantress of this valley of spells.

But the mound had no figure; the castle stirred
not so much as the opening of a shot-window, and all
the valley was asleep as we ground the shingle under
our stranding keel.

Passively the lady lay in my arms as I lifted her
ashore, all my blood tingling like fire to feel her in
my clasp again.   Silently and without complaint
she let me lead her by the hand up the path towards
the castle, only the captain following.

The slumbering porter at the gate let us drowsily
through, and the hall door had no warder save the
elfin boy sleeping across its threshold.

Up the hall we went until, as we stepped up on the
dais, the door beyond us opened and with eager hands
widespread to clutch out came the very hag I had
watched at sailing away.

Bale gleamed the wan jewel on her bony brow;
basilisk glowed the sunken eyes beneath, and fleshless

showed the talon hand which seized the hand of the maid from me.

Dragging her to the door, she checked there for a moment.   In that pause the maiden turned towards me and with a quick sweep of her free hand threw back the wrapping from her face.

"*Duw!*" I gasped in a flame of sudden wild torment.   For the face was the face I worshipped : the face of the Lady of the Mound !

Then, before I could stir a step, the door had closed and the captain and I were alone with the boy in the hall.

# CHAPTER X.

## THE MOCKING MASK OF FATE.

I WAS staring at the captain, trying to gather my wits, while he was saying quietly: "Now we had best get us to sleep for awhile."

With that at last I understood him and straightway broke out passionately: "Sleep. Pish! look you, Captain Meirion. I have helped you in your enterprise and now I want you to help me in mine."

"I will help you all the days of your life, Rowland, and cheerfully, as soon as we are done w-th Brynglas," answered he briskly.

"Brynglas! to the Pit with Brynglas! what care I about Brynglas!" I was trying to shout it, but he was smothering my mouth with a fling of his folded cloak, that no man might hear what I so recklessly shouted.

"I am for sleep," said he coolly, and at the word I took a stubborn and a wilful distaste to him and to all help of any man's. And yet I marvelled that I did not feel any resentment at that flick of the cloak, though I had never taken such handling from any man in life before. All my anger was that he should still stick to this miserable feud with Brynglas, when I wanted him to help me in a matter of such great

moment as the restoring of the lady of Castell
March.

But protest was mere waste; well I knew. "Sleep,"
he repeated and no more, as he still looked me in the
eyes, his hand upon my arm.

"Not in this accursed castle then," I said, shaking
his touch off, but otherwise passing as quick from
hot anger to still wrath as one stride is to follow
another. "Outside on the grass!—and remember"
(I could not help a grin of pleased wrath as I said it)
"now that we have done this thing for Brynglas, his
first work will be to have us murdered out of hand."

"No, not his first," replied the captain, still coolly.
"His first is to go to Nevin and hear the news of
the carrying off of the lady, so that he can offer a
reward to the man who finds out where she hath been
taken to. Thus all Lleyn will know that in this thing
at least Nant Vortigern had no part. And now do
you see why you were to dog the lady's footsteps in
the fair at Nevin and openly to follow her home
afterwards? All men saw you then, and now all men
are ready to clamour that it was you and no other
who carried her off. 'Brynglas is her injured kinsman only,' say men."

As I listened to this cool explanation of what had
so chafed and fretted me yesterday, I vow that at
first blush I could have run the captain through in
pure vexation at having been so made a tool of for
Brynglas. Then, as the picture came over me; that
I, of all men on earth, should have been so diligently
and so docilely engaged in carrying back that one
woman of all others to the last place and the last
fate in the world for me—that I, all distraught with
a rainbow dream, should have been busily risking my

life to shatter it for ever; my rage grew still with
concentration and I laughed in pure subtle tasting of
the situation. Aye, I could with pleasure have
throttled more than Brynglas just then; myself not
least, had that been possible.

Yet, too, while I laughed it dawned on me to
wonder savagely upon another point. "But why
should Brynglas have made all this pother of carrying
her off at all when she was here quietly in his power
yesterday?" demanded I.

"Because yesterday she was known to be here
openly on a visit, as his cousin, invited hither by her
aunt, his mother; the same lady who hath just
received her from your hands!——"

"What!" I broke in: "is that a human woman,
and did she ever bear a child, even such an one as
Brynglas? I thought she was a baleful witch: a
night-hag!"

"It would take many witches to outdo her in
evil," answered the captain in his hardest, coolest
voice. "And once she was so much a woman that
she thought herself a fit exchange for an old estate—
is that human enough for you?"

"Let be; never mind that; go on about the carrying off of this other," said I. "Why was she allowed
to go one day, only to be carried back the next?"

"Because," resumed the captain, "when she came
here four days ago, her aunt expected to fulfil a long
laid plan and secure control of the lands of Castell
March by making a match of it between the heiress
and Brynglas; her niece and her son—for she rules
her son yet for all that he is a grown man.

"But the heiress flatly refused. She hath a mind
of her own: and as she hath bought her own ward-

ship long ago her aunt could not override her. So Brynglas went to Carnarvon to find the proper man for this plan which his mother had made the moment her niece refused—she is never at a stand for long.

"He having found us, the heiress was next duly sent off with every honour and gallantly escorted to meet her own household people at Nevin—while you were down at the shore—there to be followed by the bold young lord of Pembroke; yourself. And now, while all Lleyn is putting to sea to search for the heiress, that heiress is here to be forced into marriage with Brynglas, will she, nill she; and after that, why, the whole business is done and there's an end on't, think they—save for the long laugh at the fools of Lleyn which Brynglas and his mother will have."

"And save for what I shall have to say in the matter," added I angrily. "But why should we, who came here on a quarrel with Brynglas, openly become his tools to help him to his heart's desire on this lady who hates him? You did this freely, though you profess yourself his deadly enemy. Moreover, how does this tally with your words when you told me that the maid would be a beggar if I refused to carry her off?"

"Ah, Rowland, to tell thee that were to tell thee all. Wait till we strike to-morrow night, and then thou shalt be satisfied."

"Nay," said I bluntly, "I will wait no more: I will trust no more. I will obey no more until you have first satisfied me. I have worked at your bidding and for your end till I have done myself a grievous harm. Now I will work to my own end, for I love this lady whom I have so evilly treated."

"Love! Aye? Aye?" said he slowly, looking steadfastly at me the while. "I hope not, and yet—thou art young. Aye, and why not?——"

He broke off and stood without movement, looking at me, who was waiting in moody savageness, eager to answer him roughly. "Aye, why not?" I put in at last. "I have done with you now, so you may out with it."

He lifted his head again. "Tush, lad," said he briskly. "Thou art in greater danger than I; that is why I wish to get an hour's sleep before the valley wakes. I shall be more wide awake in thy defence then." To cut all rejoinder short he let his cloak fall about him and prepared to lie down across the doorway, where the little lad had all this time been crouching.

But when I had first passed out I turned. "Trouble no more about me and my danger," said I, dogged and surly. "I can defend myself. Now I know that the Lady of the Mound is all of this Christian world and none of fairy or magic, I am well begun towards all I want."

"Aye, young men are a wilful folk," answered he, like one who comments on a gossip's tale. "I have no doubt I was once as stubborn. So, good sleep to thee, Rowland lad, and pleasant dreams. I will see thee after thou hast waked again."

I answered him nothing, but as I went I looked back into the open doorway and saw that he had wrapped the little lad in his cloak, while he himself was lying with closed eyes seeming already asleep.

As for me, a soul in torment could have easier slept on its gridiron than I on that soft grass in the cool, sweet glory of the June morning. Self-scorn;

dumb rebellion ; impotent black hunger for murder, and a restless gnawing anger at my own folly, made a hell that drove me to and fro, to and fro, like a chained beast, on the seaward slope of the bailey. How I loathed myself for having gone so blindly at the captain's bidding. I had gone like a hound in leash : he had carried me like a hawk on his fist ; jessed and hooded till the moment for flying me at his quarry—I that had fled from the Bala to Carnarvon feeding my pride fat with the belief that I was as goodly a tall man as any corner of the land could show. Whereas—whereas—and here my disgust choked all coherent thoughts and drove me restless on ; to and fro, to and fro, only with a longer stride.

Thus the time passed until I heard a stir on the other side of the castle. Going round I saw that the horses were being led through the gate for Brynglas and his party to mount for Nevin. Anon I saw them pass up the valley ; a dozen fellows only in the company which attended the lord of Brynglas ; and I marvelled that he went about this land with fewer men at his back than the pettiest chieftain of a four-generationed kindred would have thought safe or fitting. It would seem that the dread of his name was enough to hold most men in awe of him.

At that it came to me that it was time to have done with unprofitable self-revilings, and to set about retrieving the harm I had already accomplished. A few short moments I waited for the stir of this departure to settle and then I turned my steps to the hall.

## CHAPTER XI.

### THE ELFIN CHILD.

I HAD looked to find the captain within, but, as ever, the hall was empty save for the little lad, who now crouched over the hearth again where the first fire of the day was dying down to ashes.

" Where is Captain Meirion ? " I asked of him, but speaking gently, because his look was so hopeless. Moreover I remembered him wrapped in the captain's cloak.

" Gone to the Gwindy," answered he, as if he feared a blow, and grievous it was to see him shrink as he spoke.

So I continued softer yet, " Tell me then ; where is the lady whom I brought here this morning ? "

" I know not," he replied, this time with less fear. " My place is here in the hall ; they beat me if I go anywhere else save to the kitchen."

I stooped down and stroked his hair gently. " Wilt thou do this for me, little lad ? Find out for me where she is and I will give thee a penny for every blow they strike thee."

" I never had a penny," answered he, growing bolder ; " save one that Foulk of the Feet gave me, and then they took that from me and threatened to cut my feet off and salt them too, if I told him of it."

"If once you find where this lady is then I'll give you a silver shilling. Nay, more, I'll take you out of this valley to where you can spend it as you will," said I glibly then ; intent only upon moving him to undertake the errand.

"Will you take *her*, too, Madre Mia ? " asked he eagerly ; a new light making his face almost beautiful in its glowing anxiety.

"Be sure of that," returned I readily, thinking that he meant the lady of Castell March. Perhaps she had won him with some little kindness—for the "Madre Mia " was only child's talk to me.

"Then I will go," answered he at once and fervently. And without more ado he got up and went out through the door at the far end ; the one through which the hag had dragged the maid.

How long I leaned against the chimney cheek, and how long after that I fretted to and fro between the hearth and the door, I do not know. But all that time no one came in upon me ; only my own impatience echoed in the roof. So gloomy was the hall that the shadows seemed to grow quick and living as I looked into them, and presently the strange fact of its being always empty began to work upon my mind, reviving all my first eerie dread of such a place.

Old hag more hideous than any witch ; maiden more fair than any maid since Olwen cost Arthur half his knights and doubled his greatness ; and lean, ill-favoured lord, all were in and of this castle, yet all their servitor to uphold their worship in the hall was one poor boy, who looked more like a changeling than aught else. This Castle of Dread was a fit place for all art magic, and nothing was too strange to happen here.

Then, just as I had stopped and was standing looking at the door, meditating a push for it with glaive
in hand, the boy came limping back, tears shining in
his eyes and down his cheek ; pain and misery all
over him. I could not forbear but draw him to
my knee on the seat by the hearth, covering him
close to me with a corner of my cloak to comfort
him, as if he had been a babe indeed, so forlorn he
looked.

"Put this shilling in your pocket," said I. He
was so small a child, a ten year old at most, and a
shilling should have been a whole fortune to him and
salve for many griefs.

He stopped his sobs. "I have no pocket," said
he. Then a gleam of cunning, pitiful to see, came
into his wet face. "But I can hide it in my mouth,"
he went on : "then I can give it to *her* when I see
her again."

"Keep it for yourself," said I. "She hath already more than is good for her"—but I had no
sooner said this than his face fell and he stood away
from me, refusing the coin altogether.

I looked at him, standing so sullen now, who a
moment ago had been so open and eager, and I did
not understand. Neither in my own eagerness did
I care enough to try and discover what had altered
him. All my soul was in my business of releasing
the maid, and so all my point now was to soothe
him back again to openness. "Aye, you shall give
her the shilling, little one, and when I have seen her
I will add a crown piece more for you to give. Now
tell me where she is ? "

That offer of a crown was folly and only delayed
me by breeding new hopes in the boy. "Will you

give me a gold piece ?" he asked now, with sudden
miserliness as I thought.

"If she had a shilling and a crown for herself,"
he went on, "and a gold piece to promise with, then
she might get out afterwards if they should cut your
throat before you can get her out yourself ; " and he
smiled up at me now with winning openness of hope.
It would seem that it was not miserliness but merely
madness which moved him to bargain with me for
more money.

But again I only thought that time was precious
and that the boy was my one hope, and straightway
I promised. "Here is the crown now. The gold
you shall have when I have spoken to the lady."

He caught the crown eagerly, and this was more
folly in me, for it put him off the point and lost
more time again. Skipping to a part of the wall
where the gloom was thickest, he drew out a loose
stone that none would have suspected.

"See," said he, smiling happily ; "here is where
I always hide things till I can take them to her ; "
and he pulled out a piece of white bread in which he
had made a hole so that it should hold a piece of
broken honeycomb. A marrowbone was there stuffed
full of butter instead of marrow, and also a small
bird still whole upon the skewer used in roasting it.
"They beat me because they are sure that I steal,"
he said, looking at the food lovingly. "But I never
tell, and she likes these things."

Even then, in the face of all this, I still thought
that he meant the lady of Castell March, or that he
was a mad child. Yet his face showed plainly that
he never ate of these dainties. "Now hide them
again, quick !" said I, and sharp as he put the stone

back we hastened to the hearth again. "Now tell me where she is ?" asked I.

"They caught me as I came back and beat me," answered he. "But I had seen her then and they don't know that."

"Did you see her : did you speak to her ?" demanded I ; for I had need to be certain lest his madness should unwittingly land me in a trap.

"Yea," replied he ; "there is a little loophole in the door, latticed with iron, and she was looking out."

"The same lady that I brought here this morning ?" rejoined I.

"Yes ; and I told her that you were going to give me some pennies and take *her* away"—again that weight upon the "her."

But I was too eager for such a point. "What did she say then ?"

"That I should get no pennies, for you were a false and treacherous thief. But you are not, I know, for you have given me more than pennies and will give me more yet when you come back."

"You are right," answered I : glad that the lad should trust me in spite of her. "And now, how shall I get to speak to her—which way shall I go ?"

"You cannot go the straight way ; because at the second door stands one on guard. But if you say loudly now to me, 'Take me to the sleeping chamber,' then I will take you to that. When we get there I will show you how you can go through the secret door they use in killing those they put to sleep there. They do not know I have the key of that door. They thought they had lost it themselves and so they made another. Here it is," and, going to the nook between the chimney cheek and the wall, he knelt down in the shadow and dug in the earth with his fingers till he unearthed and handed to me the key he spoke of.

" But do they often murder men in that chamber ? " said I, aback at the unmoved way in which he spoke.

" No, because not many come here. There was one and then another, but the third got out. He tried to swim away but they saw him and followed him. They speared him from the boats. Now ask me to take you to the chamber ; loudly, so that they can hear you."

It was much like callling for one's shroud and murderers, but he was mad and I had no other hope. Therefore I called the words loudly, though it seemed that a very shout could hardly have reached to human ears through those walls.

" If you will follow me, sir ? " he answered in his high treble.

And so we started gravely for the door.

# CHAPTER XII.

## THE ESCAPE FROM CASTELL VORTIGERN.

Out of the hall he led me through three rooms, one after another, till by the form of each, a stone wall on one side and timber on the other three, I guessed that the castle was a shell of stone with all the rooms inside of timber, save the hall, which was of stone like the towers. Then up a narrow stair we went and on the landing the boy threw open the door in front of us and we entered a room lit by one broad window. This window had three iron bars to stop each half of it, for there was a thick stone jamb in the middle to divide it.

Those bars pricked my fears into fresh life. "How did the third man escape?" I asked the boy, under my breath for fear of eavesdroppers.

"Ah, they don't know yet, but I found out," whispered he, his face aglow with cunning. Closing the door, he beckoned me to follow him over to the window. "Look!" he whispered, and, taking hold of the middle bar of the farthest half of the window, he first lifted it up gently till the bottom end was free and then drew that end inwards and downwards till the whole iron was free in his hands in the room.

"Do you see that crack in the top stone?" whispered he, pointing. "All the wall above is cracked too, and so the bar will go up a good hand's-breadth. But they never noticed that; they swore I must have let him out and they would have beaten me to death if Foulk of the Feet had not threatened to shoot them all—Brynglas and all. Yet they had hurt me so much that I came up to find out, so that the next man should not get away. Only when Foulk did that then I would not tell them. I found it out myself and they don't know."

He was as pleased at showing me this knowledge out of the hiding-place of his mind, as he had been in the hall at showing me the food.

But I saw how dangerous such a boy could be to Brynglas and how valuable to me. Therefore I commended him greatly as I helped him to put the bar back. "And now this secret door?" I went on next.

"Ah, that is here," and he moved over to the opposite wall.

It was in truth a secret door. The wall was of roughly hewn oaken timber, and two rows of ordinary wooden pins went along it in a usual way from end to end; one row about hip high and the other at about the level of the shoulder. I saw nothing out of place in it to give me any clue, but the boy took hold of the lower peg nearest the corner and drew it out with ease. Putting then the key into this hole it found and fitted a lock beyond, and, behold, the five end boards had become a door which opened at his pull. Castle Murder indeed.

"When you pass through," whispered the boy, pointing to the door of the room beyond; "you step into a passage. Turn to your right and at the corner to the right again and you will find her door in front

of you. You may know it because it is set in stone
and not in timber, for the room is a tower one. Now
I am going back to the hall for fear they find me
out,"—and before I could make up my mind whether
to give him another crown or not he was gone. Patient as a worm ; secret as a mole ; he was more dangerous in this castle than a barrel of gunpowder at
the chimney cheek. And now to work.

First I fastened the regular door at the stairhead,
for I desired to be secure from all interruption, even
his, till I knew how the thing in hand stood. Then
with eager caution I passed out by the secret door,
locking it behind me, and with rapid stealth following the boy's directions found myself beside the door
of the room that held the Lady of the Mound.

Looking in through the iron-latticed loophole I
saw her standing beside the table, the picture of
smouldering rebellion. No longer was she shrouded
by any shawl or cauled partelet. Her hair fell in
burnished beauty behind her ; her rounded neck,
white as sea ivory, rose from her shapely shoulders to
carry her head with a poise as graceful as the poise
of a full antlered deer in a dew-wet August meadow at
sunrise, for no hind ever carried itself with so proud
a grace. Her arms were bare to the shoulder where
her slit sleeves fell away from their fastenings, and I
marvelled if there should be any damning purple
bruises to mark their matchless white beauty and ap-
peal against me with the record of last night's work.
Seeing her thus ; superb in beauty and yet prisoner
to another man through my surpassing folly ; smote
me to the quick till I almost cursed myself aloud.

But I would free her again. I would have her out
and in the open country once more where I could

make her understand the mistake and show her that
I had from the first planned to carry her off for myself from this castle, before she ever went to Nevin
fair. The sweat of my impatience broke out upon
me as heavily as if I had been wounded in cold blood.
And before I could catch my tongue, "Is this door
locked ?" I called to her through the lattice.

Yea, but her eyes flashed as she caught sight of me.
Her lips parted in fierce scorn and she looked indeed
a woman well worth the carrying off as she swept to
the door. "Aye," she cried, "you last of pitiful
curs ! And if I were only a man, for one five
minutes, you should be glad that it is locked as fast
as it is. Oh, to be so comely a figure of a man and
to be so vile in all that should redeem a man from
his native evil ! You are the worst thing that I could
have even dreamed of ; to steal me, not for yourself,
but for the next blackest villain that lives. Foulk of
the Feet and the worst of the poor crew that can do
no better than thieve with him are honest men compared with such as you.

"Yea, and to steal me for five gold pieces ; when
you were wearing a chain which would alone have
brought you a hundred ! Worse yet ; to pretend
that you were love-stricken and to dog me through
the fair and then home. Oh that was vilest of all ;
that you should ape an honest passion for a base five
pieces of metal !"—and here, God wot, she broke into
hot tears that amazed me with their passionate sud-
denness.

I tried to answer her, but I had got no farther than
—"Hear me, lady ! "—when she dashed back her hair
with one hand and her tears with the other. "Oh !
I could stab you to death with a bodkin !" she cried,

and for the next little while there was no word of scorn or contempt which a gentlewoman may use but she used it to me. And at last, for sheer exhaustion ending, "Hear you !" she repeated, "I did hear you when in the ship you made your lying protestations of devotion. 'I should be the better and not the worse,' said you, while all the time you had me in the very ship that was taking me back to the one man I most loathed on earth ! "

"It was no lie ! " I broke in. "I thought I was speaking true, for I was speaking as it had been sworn to me by a man whom I well believed in. Had I only known then what I was really doing : had I known it was you——"

"Had you known it was I," she burst in hotly. "Whom then did you think I was ? My grandmother or my granddaughter or what ?—you talk like a fool at a town fair ! "

"Not so loud," said I. "I am come to rescue you. Speak lower, or we shall be heard."

But nay, in truth she was a very woman and would rather lose escaping than leave her point. "Who then did you think I was ?" persisted she.

"I thought you were the lady of Castell March only. Not all the thieves in Lleyn should have carried you off if I had known that you were also the Lady of the Mound."

"The Lady of the Mound ?" answered she, hesitating in surprise.

"Aye," said I boldly. "When I saw you that evening, sitting on the mound here by the haunted shore of Nant Vortigern, all my heart went out of me in one great sigh to be with you for ever."

She left her fierceness for an instant and lifted her

face in quick unbelief. "Then how was it that you did not know me again in Nevin ? "

" Because you were so closely veiled, and because I was full heavily in the belief that I had left you behind me here at Brynglas, a hideous hag of the night."

" A hideous hag ! " she broke out and her lips parted red on her white teeth, till I knew not whether she would laugh or deafen me.

" Yea," I put in hastily. " When I saw you sitting at sunset you were so wondrous beautiful—just as you are now—that I could not think you were only a mortal woman, but deemed you at least one of the " Fair People."[1] And later, when we were in the ship about to sail, I saw in the moonlight a woman dressed as you had been dressed, jewel and all, and I thought none else but that it was you. I ran up, just once to stand in your presence again before I went, thinking that when I came back it would be for you. But the woman dropped the covering from her face and I fled, believing that you had been turned into that foul witch of darkness——"

" Pah ! " she flashed in upon me, all disgust. But I would not be put off.

" Nay, I did so think," I went on, resolute to be heard. " In very truth I did ; yet as I had sailed I could not take my heart with me again, and all that night till the dawn I could not sleep for thinking of you and longing to get back to you. For I thought that you were but foul in the darkness and would change again into the glory of the dawn when day came—this land of Lleyn is so thick with enchant-

----

[1] —Fairies.

ments and mystery that I dreamed no other of
you——"

She broke in again with a swift stamp of her foot
and a clench of the hands, eloquent of anger. But
for sore passion of love I heeded not, only shaking
my head once as I continued : " Aye, if I had only
known that it was you in Nevin ! But you were
shrouded so in that pall of a lombardine. Had
I seen so much as an eyelash ; the curve of your
cheek or a tress of your hair, then all would have
fallen out well for us both. Yet no, you would not
unveil, even so much as a corner ; not for a single
flash of your eye."

She drew up in quick disdain. " Was I then to
unveil in the midst of a fair ? with all the people all
eyes to see it ? I did stand once in front of you—
you looked so comely and so manly a man I could
have forgiven you then if by some pretty accident
you had brushed the veil from my face. I should
have been angry, but I should have forgiven you—
and what more shall a maiden do ? Is she to do the
wooing as well as the being won ? "

"You forget ; I was not wooing you," said I.
" Had it been so, then of a truth I might have more
than brushed your veil aside. But I was in love with
another woman already, as I thought, and so had
nothing but discontent for any other woman ; how
fair soever she might be."

" So you say," answered she contemptuously ; " but
no man in love with one woman would carry another
off."

" But I did not carry her off for myself," protested I.

" No ; you did worse. You carried her off—that

had never harmed you—for five poor pieces of gold!"

Sharply I spoke; "Brynglas may say that; it is but one lie the more with him. But it is another thing in you, since you know well that I did it for no such reason and that no gold would tempt me to it."

"How do I know?" returned she as sharply—she would not frankly confess that I spoke true. "You did the thing for Brynglas, and an hour ago he told me why; chuckling over it the while. What else are you, an outlaw, here in Nant Vortigern doing his bidding for? You are a redhand: a murderer!"

"I am no murderer," retorted I, pricked to resentment even through all the glamour of love. "My father slew a man in open quarrel and the judge hanged him. They did not give us our lawful right of compounding, though we of the kindred could have paid the blood-money out of hand, without asking for the legal time to pay in, or needing to go round the fringes of the kin collecting the spear-penny. No, the judge hanged him at once—what affair was it of his? The slain man was none of his kin. The dead man was a red reiver of Mawddy, and are there not enough of them under the Arans to avenge their own blood, or compound at the lawful price if they fear to take to the steel for it? That is the law."

"The law," echoed she. "Yea, the old law, but there is a new one now. The judge was sent from London to bring it into use."

"Then he had better have stayed and used it in the London where they made it," answered I doggedly. "If they want new laws in London let them have them. But here in Gwynedd the old laws are good enough for us as they were for our fathers. If I am killed I want no stranger judge to avenge me. Let the kindred avenge me, or let my name and death be for a shame and a by-word against them as long as they remain a kindred. I am no murderer : I have followed the old laws."

I knew that I had cleared myself; that I stood justified; and I looked for her to acknowledge it. But she would not. Instead of granting the point openly she left it and went back to the other.

"Your father and the judge had nothing to do with Nant Vortigern. Why are you here if what Brynglas said is not true ? "

"I am here to pursue my quarrel with Brynglas. He chuckles now, but I shall chuckle last ! "

"Oh! forsooth! here is a new way to pursue a quarrel. I thought that when men quarrelled they fought, but now it seemeth they fetch and carry for each other at spear point."

"Aye," returned I patiently; " it does seem that way to you who jump at half a tale. There is not time now to explain, but the thing is true nevertheless—I came to Nant Vortigern with Brynglas because I had quarrelled with him."

" And in your quarrel you cared nothing who else might suffer," retorted she. " You carried off a woman for him as if she had been a mere black heifer from a pasture. Her part did not come into your reckoning."

" It did,"—I grew more and more hopeful to hear her following the matter and arguing so closely though the tears shone like diamonds on her lashes the while—"I had it sworn to me that if I turned back from carrying you off, then I should be leaving you to a great misfortune, which only that could avoid."

"What misfortune?" demanded she with sharp new unbelief. "Had you given me the choice I should have told you that no misfortune on earth could equal this one you brought me to, you villain! What was it?"

"I will tell you when we are safely out of this."

"Did Brynglas tell you of it?" She asked it quickly, as one who suddenly sees light.

"Should I have believed Brynglas?" spoke I sharply, hot in my turn. "It was the captain. He saw that I had taken a sore pity for you, and as we lay in wait on the mountain he told it to me to comfort me. Nay, he struck hands on it."

"To comfort you?" echoed she in short scorn. Then, before I could repeat it, she went on—"And you believed it?"

"Yea, or of a truth I could not have gone on with the business when once I felt your sweet form struggling so pitifully in my gripe. If you but knew how I pitied you then."

"Aye, but your pity could not make you loose me and let me go," said she curtly. "I judge by deeds and not by words. Moreover that was at the end of the day. What moved you earlier when you so boldly followed me from Nevin?"

"Because only by carrying you off could I ever again get back to Nant Vortigern and the Maid of the Mound."

"Oh then; I was nothing! I was only the penny you were to pay for seeing your witch again. Truly you are a goodly sample of a gentleman!"

"It was you alone who were the cause of it,"

answered I stubbornly. "I am not to blame. I did not ask to love you when first I saw you on the shore. I had to love you whether I would or no. And if you were a witch, still I had no choice. Whether it were life or death, or between here and hereafter in the land of faery, I was still undone beyond any help of my own."

"But," she broke out, yet not so sharply, "you had but seen me once."

My answer came with a rush—"And seeing you once I saw you once for all. To look into your eyes is to be undone for ever. Can a man look elsewhere after looking at you? Olwen, Olwen! I shall never see light any more, save as you show me favour."

But she parried though she flushed. "And I shall never see freedom more, save as you loose me out of this prison and that soon," said she.

Yet I was not dashed. Her manner had less of scorn than her words—I had won something. She trusted now in me to help her to escape. Once I brought her free again to Castell March the rest would be easy, felt I. Aloud to her: "Wait," said I. "I am going to fetch something for breaking open this door with."

She eyed me doubtfully through the lattice as I turned, so that I lifted my hand. "I give you my word on it," said I.

"I want none of it. I will believe your deeds rather," answered she, moving away.

I turned and went, but as I went I looked behind and saw that she had come again to the door and was watching me with a strange soft look in her eyes.

At once I was back at the door. "Believe me;
3

Olwen; believe me. I am going only for tools. I will never desert you more. Never!"

"And I will never believe in you more; never!" cried she passionately at that. And while I wondered at such sudden new vehemence, she broke forth again into the storm of tears she had been holding back this while we had argued.

"I will not believe you," she cried again, turning away to the middle of the room. "You have betrayed me once as only a red thief would have done. No; I never will believe you more."

Then, as I stood and would have protested, she stopped me with: "Go, bring your tools and let me out. I never will believe you though."

Yea, what I would have said then, had there been time and had I been able to pass that door and take her hand and make her stop crying to listen to me! But the door was fast and so I went with savage strides to find a way of opening it.

I had this while been looking as well as arguing. The rough hewn door fitted against the doorposts instead of within them. It was fastened by one great lock, and I was now to find something that would force the staple. Reaching the sleeping chamber I stumbled over as goodly a maul as a man could wish for at a pinch; it was the heavy stool which was the only seat in the room. In form this was simply a piece, about a foot thick, sawn off an oak log some eighteen inches through, and its three short legs were stuck in almost straight. Here was a hammer; now for a wedge; and my next glance showed me the very thing.

A dozen spears stood on their racks against the wall; doubtless to lull a doomed occupant of this

chamber into security before he slept his last sleep.
They were not long horsemen's chasing staves, but
heavy stabbing spears with broad, wide-barbed heads
eighteen inches long, thickening back from the point
to the thickness of the shaft at the socket. I had but
to cut off the shaft half an inch from the socket and
I should have a wedge as strong as it would be silent
when struck. A coulter itself would not have done
so well.

Hastening back I found that she was looking out
over the sea. Yet I would not call her, for there was
no time to waste in argument. A single bold stroke
of the glaive would have cut off the spear head, but
also the sound of chopping it on the stool would have
echoed from top to bottom of the castle. Timber
walls and floors are like drums to one who wants
silence. Kneeling down I began with my knife to
nick the shaft round.

Whittling then, all my sinews in my knife edge
and all my eyes on the deepening scathe, I heard
her say suddenly, "I doubt this is some trick of
yours."

Now this was mere nagging, but I kept my temper
under and only answered: "Look you, Olwen!
Brynglas locked you fast in. If I am found trying to
loose you in his absence—for he is gone to Nevin—
then what do you suppose would come of me?"

"The death you deserve," said she shortly.

I would not answer more, for I saw that she was
set to revile me. But in my impatience I took out
my glaive and with one sharp sweep cut clean through
the shaft at the nick I had made. So keen and true
was the stroke, too, that there was scarce any noise
of the stool. "A woman's tongue may provoke some

good at times then," muttered I maliciously as I picked up the spear head and the stool.

But she disdained to answer, for now at last she seemed to take hold on the possibility of escape, as with strained lips she pressed her face close to the little opening to watch me. Her fingers were bloodless where she clutched the bars of the lattice in her sharp suspense.

Pressing my shoulder against the door I inserted the point of the wedge between it and the jamb, and a careful tap of the stool drove it in tight. With both hands then, and with a prayer to all the mercy of Christ, I followed with another blow as careful as the first, and saw that the door was straining back as I swung to strike again.

I had placed the wedge at the line of the keyhole, so that it would go into the staple, between the jamb and the bolt of the lock. Now, therefore, holding my breath in dread lest I should rouse the castle with a misblow, I began to swing and strike each blow heavier and more confident than the last.

Seven times I struck, and then with a little creak I heard the first movement of the iron staple giving way within. I heard a quick short sigh, too, but I dared not look at her for fear I missed the next blow and on the threshold of success should ruin all. Once; twice; thrice I smote again, and then the spear head was in up to the neck; the door stood wedged open by the thickness of two inches of steel. Drawing a mighty breath I flung my whole strength against the loosened door and with a swift clutch was just in time to catch the falling wedge as the staple clattered out on the bolt and let me in.

In the first great rush of my joy I would have

seized her hand and kissed it. But she drew austerely back. "Nay, I owe you no thanks yet. Put me back in Castell March and then I will think on't. We are not out of this castle yet."

Even here I kept my temper, saying only, "Come then," and so led the way back to the sleeping chamber. I wanted to get me another of the heavy spears for a weapon, for pure love of what I had already done with one of them.

"And now," said I, "do you know any way out of this valley besides that one at the head of it?"

"I do not know even that way," answered she. "I have been here but few times and then always by sea."

"Then we must e'en try the head of the valley," said I. "Here in the castle there is no one to stop us going out through the hall, but how to get out of the bailey without killing the porter and raising the cry I know not."

"That is easy," returned she eagerly. "There is the little postern double door below, and the wicket in the outer wall does not lock; it is barred only. I know the way; follow me."

Swiftly she led me back to the cross of the passage and there, turning to the left, found a little stair and took me down to where a door, on this face of the wall, opened to show us another door flush with the outer face. Only two oaken bars secured this last, and presently we were outside on the western face of the castle, with the easy wicket below to let us out.

But before we could move to descend to it the little lad stood before us, his white face flickering with excited hope and his lips parted to speak. I was beforehand with him, however. "Can you show us any way out of the valley besides that one at the head of it ? " asked I.

" No," answered he. " I have never been out of the valley."

" Come now with us then and I will take you out as I promised," said I, with a glow of fine feeling for his unhappy fate.

" But you promised to take *her*," protested he.

" And so I am doing. Is not this her ? " rejoined I.

" This ! " returned he, all his eagerness dying instantly at the stroke of the word. " This is the lady you brought here yourself. I mean *her ;* the one who was always here: Madre Mia."

" I thought that you meant this one," retorted I impatiently, itching to be gone.

" That one ! what does she know of this mark ? " he answered sullenly, slipping his left arm and shoulder out of his loose linen shirt. " What is that to her ? " and lifting his arm he showed me underneath it, in the armpit, a little scar in the shape of a cross not an inch in bigness.

I could wait no longer. The boy was of a surety mad. Drawing out a gold piece, " Here," said I, " take your key and the gold piece that I promised you."

But at a sweep of the hand he flung both from him and with a passionate gesture of hopeless grief turned sobbing away.

For a moment I watched him go, half-running and yet dragging his feet wearily. Much as I marvelled what it might be that he meant, yet there was no time to tarry. " Quick ! " said I to the maid.

And so we passed through the wicket.

# CHAPTER XIII.

## LOVE'S LABOUR MORE THAN LOST.

OUTSIDE, the bailey wall itself gave shelter from discovery by any casual eye at the castle windows; though here our chief security lay in the fact that the rooms most used were on the other side, looking up the valley, for fear of bombardment from the sea.

The carelessness of these outlaws did not end in merely keeping no watch here. All the space between the corner of this wall and the edge of the wood that belted the slope on the north side of the valley was strewn and patched with bushes instead of being kept clear. What with the rocky ribs that spined all the space, and these bushes that grew as they would, it was easy enough for us to climb up to the wood without discovery from a castle where no sentinel was posted. When the lord is away the underlings play is true enough anywhere.

Yet for all this screen, when we had safely reached the cover of the oaks I saw that the maid was white with dread of the chances, and as tense as a harp-string turned to the snapping point. And I was something pleased to see that she had the weakness of a woman as well as the uncalculating temper of one.

"Olwen," said I; "give me your hand now; this wood is difficult for the feet."

119

But nay, she had a woman's resentment too.  " My name is not Olwen, but Nerys," answered she, drawing herself away ;  " and I want no help of your hand.   It is red."

Though she stung me so sharply, still this resentment had its good use, for to quarrel with me took her mind from centring itself so fiercely upon the chances of escape.   Therefore I started again quickly, that I might keep her occupied with the slipperiness underfoot, where the roots of the close-grown trees laced and netted every handbreadth of space.

First we mounted through the wood far enough to escape being seen from the valley below, and then, turning to our right, began to make our way along it towards the head of the valley ; the only way out. But before we had gone very far we came to a place so steep that only by the help of the spear could I keep my footing in crossing it.   I knew she must have help, but I felt gentler towards her, and instead of proffering help in words, and so driving her to refuse, I simply held out my hand without looking at her, but only at the difficulties underfoot.

" Careful here," said I ; and then I felt her clasp in mine and the thrill of that first touch leaped through me like fire.

Yet I remembered wisdom, and with a great effort shut down on my tongue.   Only I took the roughest and the dimmest part of the wood for the space of a furlong or more, that I might still keep that sweet, soft hand in mine.   Dear heart ; death was but a petty pin-prick to risk for such a joy as that.

And, that I might continue this pleasure to its utmost, I in guileful mind began to lead her upward as well as forward, till, at a point half way along the

valley, we had reached also the upper edge of the
wood, where was only the broad belt of tangled
thorns between us and the cliff and wall that fenced
us in that way.  I might have cut a way through
the thorns.  I might even have devised some means
of scaling the walls in spite of their height ; but
it would only be to emerge upon the absolutely
naked back of the mountain and be seen at once by
the watchman on the peak.  Nevin, our only hope,
lay on the other side of the valley.  We must go on
and escape if at all by forcing the gate.

Here at the edge of the wood, though the light
was a little better, yet the way was very rough indeed.  Furthermore the jackdaws had built in a cliff
just in front and already they were beginning to wheel
and dash about our heads, scolding sharply.  Quickly
I turned and led further down again, lest the disturbed flight of the daws should waken suspicion in
some outlaw below or watchman above.  I only
prayed that they might settle at once and stop their
clamour.

Meanwhile the way was so bad that the maid panted sorely, but I was as cruel as any other lover and,
instead of making her sit down, I quietly took the
moment when she stumbled a little over a stone
and so slipped my arm about her to keep her from
falling.

Now at last I was in Eden, but no ; a lover thinks
he has nothing while there is yet anything to have.
A dozen times in the next dozen strides I lifted
my face as if I would turn and kiss her, for my
head was lighter than any bubble that a child blows.
Yet for fear of some angry exclamation betraying us
I kept that desire under with a strong grip ; the time

was not yet, I told myself.  Still I must nibble at temptation as if I had been a woman, and out of the corner of my eye I stole a glance at her face to see what she felt at having my arm about her.

That look undid me, for her face was full of all hope, and straightway I began to glance at her more and more openly, till anon she caught me at it.

Her face flushed hotly and she drew sharply out of my arm, but so confused that she could not decide what her first word of her anger should be.

I was becoming wise as the serpent and at once I put in before she could speak : " Sit you down now, Nerys, and rest you awhile; for you must have all your strength ready when we come to the head of the valley.   You will have to run then for Nevin while I stop and fight the guard to hinder them from following."

Such open guile was mere waste of words.  I wanted to stay her anger and to work upon her feelings with the picture of these brave and perilous things I must do for her, in thus securing her freedom at the cost of my own life perhaps.   But she took all the gold off it at once by her answer.   " Aye, it will teach you to carry any other woman away, when you find what peril it costs to right the wrong of this."

" Ah ! but it will be no more than a lost lesson if a foot of steel at the gate should put me beyond all care of any woman more in this world."   I had to stick to the picture or confess my guile.

" And will not my freedom be lost too ?—so you are in no worse case than I," retorted she.   There were to be no garlands on my shoulders from her just yet at least.

Then as I cast about for my next word, she spoke

again. "You well deserve it—to carry me off for
another man."

"Lady," said I in quick answer, "I verily believe
you had been well enough content had I carried you
off for myself."

"Content or no,"—and the calm way she spoke lay
heavier on my heart than any sharp words would
have done—"at least it had not so cut me to the
quick as to be carried off and given to another man,
with as little concern for my part in it as if I had
been a stolen heifer. I might in the end have forgiven you then, but now I never will forgive you—
though the rivers ran backward and the sun rose in
the west I would hate you still"—she looked to and
fro in the wood about me while she spoke, as though
I had been even less than a head of stolen cattle.

"Let us be going," said I shortly ; "unless you will
sit down."

"I want no sitting down till I sit safe at home
again," responded she, planting her foot to start
again.

Yet in spite of her hard words she took my hand
this time from the first, though I confess that the way
here was of the worst and that in the gloom we could
scarce see where to set our feet.   Presently however
we came to a place where, under a tall cliff, the trees
thinned in the upper part of the belt, so that I could
see well what manner of maid this was whom I was
helping.

And indeed she was no maid fairest at a distance,
for ever as I looked, I found her the more and more
beautiful while I noted, now the perfect moulding of
cheek and chin ; now the rare shapeliness of hand
and foot ; the poise of her head or the supple sway

of her form.  Small marvel then that in my heart
grew a dumbly stubborn determination to have her
for mine own, in spite of friend or foe ; of the captain or Brynglas ; aye in spite of her very self.  Her
lands and castle might go as they would, but she must
go with me.

A great sigh broke from me and all my thoughts
must have showed in my face, for perturbation came
into hers and I felt a triumph rise in me—I deemed
that I was beginning to prevail.  Once or twice she
opened her lips as if to rebuke me, and as often
checked herself, though she knew well that no sharp
words could turn me now from trying to free
her.

And each time as she closed her lips in silence I
thought I saw a faint flush stealing over her face,
whereat my tirumph took fresh courage.  Then here,
in the midst of my high hopes, came a rude shock.
Up from the very tree roots at our feet, broad and
high across the valley's head, shutting it in like a
world on end, the black front of Craig Ddu went
rearing up a thousand feet sheer into the blue of
heaven.  There was not foothold for a goat upon its
wet and glistening breast.

My breath came in a mighty sigh, and looking at
her I saw her face go white as the blossomed sloe for
dread as she turned to me for help now in this grievous outfall.  And—"Oh ! we are undone indeed at
last," said she with a dry sob.

I liked well to see her so.  Yea, I was glad of this
Craig Ddu in front of us that made her turn to me
for hope as well as help.

"Not yet," answered I with full voice ; "not
while I have steel at my hip and you have that glory

in your eyes.   Come now; we will go down to the
lower edge of the wood and see if we can cross the
valley at the foot of the rock, since over it we cannot go."

There was a world of woman's trust in the gentle
way she took my hand now, without a word of answer or debate, though she had flushed to wild rose
tint when I spoke of the glory of her eyes.   He
would have been an unlucky outlaw that had plumped
upon us at that moment : I could have cloven a man
then deeper than ever did Rhys Vawr at Bosworth.

It was difficult enough to descend, and I took many
and tender privileges of arm and hand as I helped
her down, the good spear steadying me at every step.
I was glad then that she had been prisoner in Brynglas, for so I had come to this rare delight of setting
her free again.

Neither were my spirits wholly dashed when from
the lower edge of the wood of oaks we saw that the
outlaws' town extended to within fifty yards of the
rock.   For all across the foot of the rock I saw also
that the fifty yards distance between it and the town
was oozy marsh, overgrown with alder and willow and
every other bush and sapling that lives best in the
wet lands.

We could but whisper now for fear of being heard
from the cabans, yet her eyes glistened as I said, under my breath, "This marsh hath saved us.   Keep
close to me now"—though I had never yet let go of
her hand since we began the descent.

Carefully we went until we were well into the
marsh, stepping from tussock to tussock, and then an
opening in the tangle ahead showed me a green round
spot where bubbled the spring from which the outlaws

drew their water. It was close under the foot of the rock, so that we should have to pass it, and, like the death of our whole enterprise, a little child, come to draw water, had set down her pitcher and was now straying joyously from point to point, gathering the wealth of meadow-sweet and the other flowers that grew there.

The maid drew closer to me when first we caught sight of the child. "Perhaps she will go away soon," whispered she unconsciously.

I saw small hope of that, for the little one was going from flower to flower as lightsome and as well content as a butterfly in a lush meadow. Yet while I looked a plan came into my mind—"I have it," whispered I. "We will go boldly on, and when we come to the child you shall take it up in your arms and kiss it, and so carry it with us up into the wood on the other side. We can set her down in the path that comes from the gate to the town. Then we shall be at the gate ourselves before she can prattle of us to her mother here below."

This plan I thought marvellous well in me, and I was all amazed that she drew her hand away, saying, in a voice that had something of cold scorn in it : "Deceive this child as you deceived the little lad in the castle ? I like not such deceits played on children."

"Yet you care nothing about the guard at the gate who must be killed if we win out," retorted I ; impatience firing me.

"That is different. Men only live to do injustice and to kill and plunder, while children have done no harm. But if your conscience is heavy at the thought of having to kill these men, then I will go

back.  It may prove better to be the lawful wife of
a lord of thieves than to put myself in the power of a
man who does thieves' work with so light a heart.
I have seen you how you have been looking at me as
we came through the wood.   All the way I have been
doubting whether it were not better to go back to
the fate I know of than forward with a man who has
used me so ill.   I doubt you would run thus into
danger for any honest purpose."

"Lady," said I a little grimly, "I may have done
you something of harm in carrying you off.   But I
think I have well paid for it all in having to listen
to your tongue since then.   Yet I am patient, therefore I tell you that I am doing this to set right the
mistake I made last night."

" Or is it not that now you want me for yourself instead of Brynglas ? " returned she.

"And if it is, am I not a man whom you yourself have called comely ?   I cannot help but want
you."

" But I have told you that I hate you," said she.

" What of that ?   You have the right to hate me
now.   But you will begin to think differently of me
when once I put you safe and sound in Castell March
again."

" Aye, but will you swear to take me back safe and
sound ?   Will you be a true knight now and do me
only honour till I come home again ? "

" Lady ! " said I, all my pride in arms ; " what
have I done that you should need me to swear it ? "

But she would not listen.   She shook her face with
a little gesture of impatience and then, suddenly, all
so sweet and all so maiden gentle, she stretched her
hands towards me pleadingly.   And—" Ah ! sir :

will you not swear it ? " begged she, in a voice like the ringing of a bell.

In my heart I could have kept silence for pure hope that she would continue pleading thus. To have this proud maid suppliant so : to see her leaning towards me with asking hands and parted lips, stirred me from head to foot with all the glory of life. Softly she repeated it, " Will you not swear it ? " and at the falling cadence of her voice again, sweet and low as it thrilled through me, I could keep the words no longer.

" Swear it ; aye, Nerys ; I will swear it.    Not for to-day ; not for an hour or any other part of time ; but for all the days that I shall live.    And I will be a true knight and have thee in worship and in honour as leal as ever a man did hold a maid since the world began.    Yea, and I will swear it, not by any relic, but by thy own golden self.    See ! "—and taking her hand I kissed it.

" Because," she went on ; all the tint of the wild rose stealing again into her face and neck as she spoke ; " because I am neither for you or Brynglas. I have been a plighted maid this two years past and sworn by every oath that can bind me to a brave, true gentleman."

The dew was in her eyes and the quiver in her lip as she spoke.    Soft and low the words came out, but I heard them every one to their last echo in my hollow heart, where all the life was gone out of me, so that my knees had no more strength in them and I sat suddenly down upon a fallen alder behind me.

" Sir ! sir ! " she said anxiously as I kept silence, only staring at her.    Then as I still sat dumb— " Remember that you swore it," she went on.

At that I roused myself a little and rose up.   Standing before her then : " Yea," I answered—and my voice was thin and stretched as if I had just fought through some great battle—" I swore it ; I will keep it."   And with that I struck hands with her in faith, for I had no thought of anything just then but to get away from that spot.

" Come ; let us go," I went on shakily, in this new stress forgetting the child.

But while we talked the child itself had wandered towards us, and a dozen strides brought me almost to treading upon it.   Nevertheless I felt no dread of discovery, or any other fear.   I was like a man that hath just taken a mortal wound in that I had lost all care of what should happen.   Still we were not yet undone, in spite of my numbness.   For, after the tender fashion of children, the little one lifted up her flowers with a shy smile towards my face and my heart-hunger went out to her, so that without a word or any other ado I stooped and lifted her gently in my arms.

I did not look back.   I knew by the rustle of her garments that the lady of Castell March followed me closely, and thus in this manner we passed the spring and came safely into the wood on the other side.

The little one smiled merrily at me as she held the sweet nosegay to my face, and I smiled back at her, though my heart was shivering in mortal sickness underneath.

**9**

# CHAPTER XIV.

WHEN we came to the foot of the slope on the other side, where the climb to the trail should begin, I set the little maid down. "Now you shall go and gather flowers again," said I.

But before she could go the lady of Castell March stooped down and kissed her; and straightway for that one tenderness the child pressed the nosegay upon her with both hands, in a shy pleasure that had no words. And from the bunch the lady took a spray of the meadow-sweet, together with a yellow flag and one of the tall red sprays that love the waterside. "I will take these for love of you," said she, and the little maid glowed with happiness as she was kissed again.

Then she went, and as soon as she disappeared in the thickets we turned to face the climb. I held my hand and she took it, without a word between us, and so in silence we worked our way up until we came to the track from the town to the gate. We struck it far up, indeed, but little short of the belt of thorns, and I waited till the maid should get her breath before I spoke.

Then I whispered, "We shall come to a belt of high thorns just above, and beyond that again is the
130

gate.   We must creep along the path through the
thorns till I get within distance of the guard.   When
I strike the first blow then you must rush out and
run as fast as you may towards Nevin, keeping what
cover you can as you go.   Never mind me; if I am
not hurt I shall overtake you, but if I am, then remember there is a watchman with a flag on the top
peak of the mountain here—keep out of his vision.
Now——" and with that I turned to lead the way
up again.

She had never seen the gate or its guard, and so
maybe thought the danger greater than it was, for I
saw the dread of it in her face as we started up the
trail.   But when we reached the belt of thorns I
looked again and she was white as ever living woman
was.   All her taunts were forgotten now, for she felt
this peril to come more than a man could well have
done.   Doubtless she thought that if we were once
past the gate all would be won; whereas I knew that
then would come the real heart of the work.

"It is nothing," whispered I to comfort her.   "A
cast and a slash and the thing is done."

She looked at me with hesitating eyes as if she
weighed my assurance, for I saw she did not believe
it blindly.   So I signed her to stoop low and come
carefully after me, while I went crouching up between
the bushes—if she were doing something she would
have less time to think in, and it is thinking of the
peril that plays havoc with the soul.

A few strides higher and then I touched her arm,
for through the twigs of the thorns we caught sight
of the three men of the guard, and I could feel her
shrink as she looked.

This time they were not playing chess, and because

the day was hot and they were but loose and idle
thieves, they had doffed their armour and leaned
their spears against the walls.   That one who was
supposed to be on watch had come down from the
rock and stood now with his back to us and his elbows
on the wall-top.   By his whole attitude I knew that
he was blinking lazily over into the heather beyond.
The other two were drowsing and grunting in the
hot sunshine : I could not have asked for better fortune, save that they should be wholly asleep.

The plan was plain.   A cast of the spear and a
rush with the glaive, and then the thing was done if
it were to be done at all.   Yet the sentry, at whom I
must level the spear, had his back to me, and in spite
of the need I liked not to strike him from behind.
The stroke would be more sure and certain, I knew.
Stricken at any point from the small of the back to
the nape of the neck he would be most surely slain,
but still I could not down my distaste for striking
him in the back.   And I reckoned that one more
item to the account of Brynglas whenever I should
come to a settlement with him.

We were not nine paces from the sentry but it was
uphill and so a tickle cast.   Stealthily I drew out my
glaive, holding it in my left hand ready for my right
to seize when I should have thrown the spear.   Then
I took and poised the heavy spear, javelin-wise, in
my right.   But as I planted my foot for the spring to
throw, she plucked at my elbow, and her eyes were
wide with dread as she whispered, " Oh, let me go
back !   This is terrible ! let Brynglas have me ! "

That whisper saved me the murder in front, for
instantly the sentry turned to look and the other two
pricked up to listen.

" Come," said I over my shoulder and no more, for
with all the might of my body I sprang up and sent
the spear at the sentry as he bent to peer towards us.
I saw the great blade drive up under his ribs, and swift
as he fell I was upon the others and had slashed the
nearest over the head, while the third, missing his
clutch for his weapon, fell back into the thorns below
before he could recover. The gate was won and
clear.

I had looked for her to follow me and was in the
passage befor I saw that she was still crouching where
I had left her. Springing down again I caught her
and half lifted, half dragged her up and out. There
was no time to speak, for the fellow in the thorns was
roaring out their gathering cry with a voice that woke
all the echoes of the valley, and up from below came
the clamour of a hundred throats bursting in answer.

It was no use to turn back to the fellow : the mischief was done and it only remained now to run.
From this height of a thousand feet all Lleyn lay before us, plain as a garden to be seen, and our one hope
was to get below some line of ridge and hide in bush
or brake till nightfall. "Now ; for your freedom ;
run ! " said I.

The flag was waving furiously on the peak behind
us as I took her hand and we broke straight for Nevin,
since on that side was the nearest help and also the
better chance of cover. The ground was brown and
even; all short springy heather. There was nothing
to catch her kirtle as she ran. Moreover after the
first furlong it was all downhill, and with my help
she was making good way ; but alack ; so soon she
began to pant that I felt hope dying almost in its
birth. Oh, for a horse ! I would have given all

Lleyn then for the sorriest nag in it, so long as it could have carried her while I ran beside it.

But, bearing a little to the right, I saw that where the mountain began to fall away to the sea there was a long width of alder marsh. If we could but reach that we might yet do well. We had covered a mile already : a quarter more and we should be in shelter, when suddenly I looked up and saw just ahead, another gwylva (watching place) with its sentinel waving his flag in answer to the one behind us. I looked back to see if there were time yet to turn and strike inland, but the first of the yelling outlaw pack showed on the rise hard after us. We must risk the arrows of this fellow in front, for none other hope had we but to reach that marsh.

And she was failing ; her lips were drawn tight and wide, and her breath began to come in gasps. But here the ground fell away so rapidly that she had but to keep her balance and the slope would do the rest. "Courage ! you have the rarest courage ever woman had," said I. Even in her distress for breath her eyes answered me gratefully.

I put myself upon the danger side of her, for the flag in the gwylva was down and I knew that the bow was bent to shoot at us as we passed. I kept a way as wide from him as I could : he should be a good archer if he hit us. Then the arrow whistled and my hat fell flapping off behind, for the shaft had cut the band and passed without scratching me. The next shaft shivered into splinters on the stones behind us, but a third from another direction came between our heads as we ran, and at the flash of it she flung up her arms so that only my hold saved her from falling.

That last shot came, not from the gwylva, but from the racing outlaws gaining on us behind. The thicket was not a score of yards in front. I thought of Foulk of the Feet as the long flight arrows clashed on the stones about us, and with a great lift I swung the maid up into my arms and the marsh was won.

Nor did good fortune end here, for almost in my next stride I plumped upon a roebuck, and he dashed away to the right towards the sea. " Thank God ! " I cried under my breath as I stopped, for I had startled him out of any path and he was crashing a way through the twigs for himself, so that I knew the outlaws would follow his line from the high ground without, shooting at the movement of the bushes as he went, believing it was our flight which made it.

When I stopped the maid opened her eyes. She could not speak, and her bosom heaved and fell as if it would burst while she tried to catch her breath. Yet as she heard the pursuit go thrashing through the furze and heather to the right of us she tried by signs to bid me leave her and save myself. For all answer I picked her up again and carried her seven or eight score paces further into shelter before I put her down.

By that time her breath was beginning to come easier. " Nay, but leave me now," she said. " I can go no further. You are free now ; save your own life at least."

" So I am endeavouring, for you are my life," replied I. " And as for prison, I am penned already in a prison stronger than any castle : my heart is fast held in the glamour of your eyes. If I go now to save this body then what use have I for it but to come back to Nant Vortigern and try to get you out again?"

She saw that words were but wasted on a stubborn man, and so, with a protesting shake of her head, she rose, saying, " Let us try further."

With that we started again, keeping to paths that the deer and goats had worn, so that we made good speed and at the same time stirred no bushes to betray our movements. Yet by the shouts we soon heard that the outlaws had learned their mistake and were now breaking into the marsh to scour the thicket for us. But what with alder and willow, thorn and holly, gorse and quagmire, they gained but little on us, and for a full half mile further we kept ahead of them, till of a sudden, as sharp as if a precipice had opened under our feet, we came to the end of the cover and found only a bare green swell in front of us.

Nevertheless we saw a waste of bush and bracken a few hundred yards away to the left : if we could only reach that unseen we might find hiding yet. There was no time to debate ; it was fight or fly and that at once. I could not fight a hundred men. We fled at top speed across the bare stretch between us and the brake.

Alack for that little sweep of bare land. Half way across it we ran full tilt into a party of horsemen coming over the rise : a dozen horsemen following a leader—Brynglas and his company returning from Nevin.

The twelve spears held me at bay with their crescent moon of points. Behind me the outlaws were leaping out of the marsh like hounds out of kennel. I looked at the maid beside me. "Aye," she said with a great dry sob; "we are ended. You must yield now or be slain."

"Which ?" demanded I, savage at my impotence.

"Not slain : let me not see you slain after so gallant doing for me," answered she, her hand upon my arm in quick dread and entreaty.

My glaive was bare in my hand. It was better to die out here in the sunlight on the open heather than to be carried back and turned loose in that grim valley to be baited to death for sport. But life was strong in me, and with that maid—and such a maid—pleading on my arm I could not believe in death. Life and hope are one and the same thing in a young man.

"Yield there !" cried Brynglas from behind his men.

Slowly I sheathed my glaive. "You hold the point against me : I can no other than yield," answered I.

Eight spears round me held me motionless and four men dismounted to find thongs to tie me fast. Not till that was done did Brynglas come to the front. "Now," began he, with a wild-cat snarl of joy. "You were running with good long leaps ; you shall have a leap the longest that man can take. It shall land you from here to hell. You shall go over Careg y llam."

At that word I flinched. So there was an execution rock : a Rock of the Leap, here in the Eivl as well as in Mowddy. "A short shrift and a long jump" was to be my end. I had yielded for nothing. "By St. Dervel ! Brynglas !" I shouted in passion. "had I known it before then I would have tried once to rid this land of Lleyn of the blackest coward in it."

And for answer he leaned down and smote me on the mouth with the shaft of his spear.

There was a cry at this ; not the maid's cry or mine, but the captain's ; for he had followed with outlaws from the valley and now stood by, seeing what was done.

" No more of that ! " he cried.    " The lad hath yielded.   Treat him honourably."

" Keep out from behind me and him," answered Brynglas darkly.    " I have used the fool for my purpose and now I will pay him for his insolence.   He shall go over Careg y llam : it is handy here as we go back."

" But he is my friend : you cannot kill him "—the captain seemed to be stirred out of his calculating moods.

" Why not ? " grinned Brynglas wickedly.    " And what is to stop me sending you after him ? "

" Your own faith to me.   You struck hands with me," replied the captain roundly.

The wisdom of years of danger flashed in that answer.   Had he blustered or threatened, then he, too, had been thrown from the rock with me.   To turn the danger's self, Brynglas, into his own security, was the stroke of a veteran.

The grin flickered indecisively in the face of Brynglas and I wondered how the dice would fall in his mind.   Then the cunning look came again.   " Aye : well.   But I did not strike grips with this red-handed fool.   He was on his way to Ireland when he turned aside to meddle with me.   Now Ireland is the nearest land west of the Careg ; there is only the sea between them.   He shall leap for it, and if he cannot jump as far as Ireland he will jump a good deal farther,

for he will land on the devil's threshold.   And that
is a little joke we have in Nant Vortigern to speed
the man who goes over."   He grinned like a chained
wolf over it.

The captain was dumb.   He looked round at the
outlaws to count the chances of a fight.   He looked
at me—and he drew down his hat over his eyes in
token of hopelessness.   Then, when I had thought
all was done but the dying, help came from the last
quarter in all that motley throng.

"Cousin," called the maid to Brynglas, and her
voice rang true as steel ; "you could have my lands by
killing me, I know, since you are the heir after me.
But I know you want to have me too.   Well, I had
never meant to say the word in church : I had meant
to die first at your hand.   But I will speak it freely
in the church to-morrow if you let him go free and
unharmed now.   And I will swear it here before your
men and him."

Brynglas looked at her craftily.   "Aye," said he ;
"and after he was free and gone you would repent
and refuse me when the time came to-morrow."

If scorn could have pierced him then would the
eyes of the maid have slain  him  outright as she answered him.   "I offered you my oath.   Hath any man
ever known me to break my bare word yet, let alone
my oath ?"

He wiped his mouth with the back of his hand,
for his shifty eyes could not look steadily into hers.
"You hate me so," he said at last.   "I fear you
would repent, or else I might do it."

"Will you do it if I swear to my word ?" persisted
she.

Long time he looked at her, blinking and shifting

in his seat, while she stood steadily looking back at
him. Then he said, "I will do this. He shall
come back to Nant Vortigern to-day and to-morrow
I will set him free after we are fast wedded."

"Ah, but I will not trust you," replied she readily.
"When did you ever keep oath or faith in your life,
Brynglas? But do this. Let him ride with us to
church to-morrow, and when we come to the porch
let him choose any horse he will of all your train—or
of all the valley before he starts if he likes. Let him
have his arms and his armour and then be free, and
when he is safely out of sight I will go in and wed
you."

And—so readily that I knew he was plotting deceit
—Brynglas answered, "Aye now : I will show you. I
will trust you." Then to the men he said, "Loose
his bonds but guard him closely. And give her a
horse."

I had stood dumb all this while, but when the
maid was mounted she rode close to me. "Sir," she
whispered, "I said a while since that an ill deed
done can never be set right again. But for the
noble effort you have made this day I do forgive you,
as freely as though I were safe in my own hall again.
And if I never can forget what you did last night ;
neither can I ever forget what you have done this
morning. The one was the deed of a redhand ; but the
other was all the deed of a true and noble knight."

I looked at her steadily as she spoke. From the
moment when the sob stuck in her throat at capture,
she had been as calm of courage as if she walked in
her own garden, instead of standing captive to the
man she hated. I remembered how she had nigh
swooned with dread only to see the fight at the gate.

And I remembered, too, how she had protested that she would never forgive me.  " Aye," said I to her quietly ;  " no river hath run backward, neither hath the sun risen in the west ; yet you have forgiven me."

She smiled sadly ;  " Ah, but what can that matter to you now, when I am to marry Brynglas to-morrow ? "

" To-morrow hath not dawned yet," said I doggedly.

" But I have promised :  I am promised," answered she, as she put her horse in motion, for we were starting back.

" Aye, and so you were promised before I ever saw you—but you are not wedded yet," said I to myself.

And so we took our way for Nant Vortigern again.

# CHAPTER XV.

## "MADRE MIA."

ALL the way back the captain kept at my elbow but said no word, good or bad. Nor did the maid look at me, or Brynglas speak ; neither any one of the outlaws. The only sound was the thresh of feet though bracken and heather, and the clank of weapon and harness. Once, however, as her horse stumbled, I saw how the jar of it shook down the tears that had been shining in the eyes of the maid. And little marvel was it that she should weep who had given up the man she loved to marry the man she hated, and all to save the life of the man who had brought her into this evil plight.

That thought was a shrewd blow to my jaunty confidence, and all the way as we went I brooded over it. Brynglas had pledged himself to set me free to-morrow, but I believed that it was but a wile in him to get the maid, and that he was certain to set some trap to have me taken again and done to death in the end. Yet in my heart I swore that if I did but get free, with a poor ten minutes' law allowed me, I would even the balance once and for all against him.

Thus we came to the gate again and I looked to see if the dead man were still there, though a new guard had been set. But only the blood lay blacken-

ing on the hot stones, and the noise of the women
wailing the corpse came clamorous up from below.
Yet Brynglas never so much as asked what man was
dead or how ; so little he cared for these his tools,
or else so full was he of triumph at having won the
maid for his own. And as we dipped down through
the thorns, the last light of the sun was the gleam
of it upon her head, making a glory of the chestnut
masses of her hair. Well might he feel triumphant.

When we came to the outlaws' town below, the
cost of our escape was laid out plain for Brynglas to
see. First, the fellow who had fallen into the bushes
was lying sprawling, half naked, and a woman was
plucking the thorns out of him while he cursed and
swore roundly at every fresh pull.

Beyond him lay the one slashed over the head, his
sconce now bound up with a great poultice, while
close to him his wife milked a cow and gave him the
hot milk to drink for the renewing of his blood. A
little further still and the body of the dead sentry
was lying stretched out on a great stone, and all about
it the women swayed and tossed their hair as they
wailed him. Aye, and they had laid bread and salt
upon his breast, though I wondered who would be
sin-eater to such an one as he.

Yet even here, with the wail in his ears and the
sight in his eyes, Brynglas did not so much as toss a
single word of contemptuous pity towards the corpse.
Only the maid shuddered and looked the other way.

The outlaws fell away from us ; some to the cabans ;
some to the drinking house ; some to the games ;
while we kept on for the castle. At the bend of the
valley, where through the trees it opens upon the sea,
Brynglas pointed with his spear to the great cliff

which cuts off the shore to the south. "That is
Careg y llam," said he to me curtly. "It is nearer
from the gate at the head of the valley than is the
Gorlech here, though the Gorlech is higher;" pointing
in turn to the twin cape that shut us in to the north.

But I answered him nothing, only pretending to
compare with a critic eye the heights of the two and
their suitability, until presently we came to the outer
gate of the castle, and in another five minutes I was
back in the sleeping chamber, a prisoner and alone.

The captain had whispered me in passing that he
must keep close to Brynglas for the next hour or
two, to study his mood and establish himself once
more in the fool's good graces—for by that word
did he betray his own opinion of the man who had
me prisoner, and who held the promise of the heiress
of Castell March to be his wife to-morrow. But I
took no notice of the captain now ; I had done with
him, said I to myself.

Here in the room then I leaned upon the window
ledge and looked out across yonder at the belt of oak
woods through which I had so lately guided the maid
I loved. Prisoner as I was, I yet felt now that the
attempt to escape was at least not all lost labour.
She had hated me before, while now her feeling for
me was full of forgiveness, even if it were no more.
She had said that she was sworn to another man, but
I would not cut myself too deep for that just yet. A
maid who is held ; half tied, half loose ; for two full
years, is held more by the habit of the bond than by its
own strength. A little resolution on my part and
she would snap it of herself.

Aye, though I knew well that Brynglas, in spite of
his promise, was stubbornly resolved to have me dead

by hook or by crook to-morrow, yet I would not have
given to-day, with my open danger, for yesterday
with my seeming security then.

The hour was not heavy while I leaned thus, dreaming of the maid and going over again the doings of
our flight ; indeed it was with some impatience that
I heard the door behind me open. Turning, I saw
that it was the elfin boy from the hall, bearing food
and drink, sent to me at the captain's desire.

The sight of the child, slack and sodden from exhausted grief as he was, brought up again the picture
of all his passion of disappointed hopes when he found
that I was going to leave behind me that mysterious
" her." Moreover, as I looked at him I saw that he
had done with me, and when he set down the trencher
there lay the token of his resolve, for the three coins
—the gold piece, the crown and the shilling—were
piled at the edge of the dish beside the loaf.

" Have back your money, sir," said he dully, turning to go.

I stood in front of him and stopped him. " What
nonsense is this ? " said I, pretending harshness.

But he did not shrink now as he had done in the
early morning. Instead he looked at me with a quiet
face. " I trusted you. No man before ever spoke
kindly to me, save only Foulk of the Feet once.
Foulk would not have promised unless he meant to
do : he keeps his word."

Yea, I had broken faith with him, and so I was
less than the worst thief in Lleyn to this child. He
was too small to understand my case and yet I felt a
shame of it as it came out of his mouth ; it sounded
as if I had in very truth done a dishonourable thing.
" Little lad, " said I ; " if I had well understood

10

what you expected of me I should not have promised, for I should have known I could not perform. But who is the 'her' you meant? Is it your mother?"

"No; I never had a mother. I was found in the boats, say they." By the look of him I saw that he was speaking truth as he knew it.

"Then who is she?" pursued I.

"I do not know," answered he. "She makes sounds : she does not speak like us, and she does not know what I say. Only she told me her name, Madre Mia, pointing to herself, and I saw that she was thin and sorrowful, and now I get things to give her. And always I say her name to her because she likes to hear it."

"How long have you been giving her things?" I went on.

"Ever since I first found out where she was ; a long long time now," answered he.

"Years?" queried I.

"Yes," said he.

"Then why have you not stolen the keys and set her free?"

"Because Catrin, mother of Brynglas, keeps all the keys of that part of the castle, and she never sleeps, or loses anything, or puts things down ; and if she caught me on that side she would flay me alive. Moreover, if I did get the keys and let her out, where should we go and what should we do? and how should we get out of the valley?"

"Wait a minute," said I. "If you cannot get the keys and dare not go near that side of the castle, then how do you give her these things?"

A faint light of his former smile of cunning stole into his face again. "Ah! I know!" said he.

"Aye, but I doubt if you be telling me the truth,"
I went on. "Take me to her once and then I will
see what can be done."

"No,"—and he spoke stubbornly. "You would
not take her this morning. You cannot set her free
now, and if I were to take you, then you would be
seen and they would shift her and I should never be
able to give her things any more."

And with that he went, for I heard a footstep
coming up the stair and I dared not speak more for
fear of being overheard.

The step was that of a fellow to bid the boy back
to the hall, and no sooner was the lad gone than the
door was locked on the outside ; the stair taken away ;
while through the crack I could discern a sentry
posted below where the stairfoot had been. Some
order was being taken to secure me then, thought I.

Yet I was the less troubled at that, in that I was
full of a guessing to know more about this mysterious
prisoner, who had none other comfort than the half-
starved elfin child. Nevertheless, since no better
might be, it were as well I sat to meat ; and the first
bite woke all my hunger, so that I remembered
sharply that I had eaten nothing before since the
rough, thumb-piece meal on Llanbedrog Mountain.

Also, when I had made an end of eating and had
drawn deep at the leathern jack of beer, I felt that I
had slept but little these last few nights, and presently
I had taken my cloak about me and was asleep.
There would be no treachery of that secret door now,
since Brynglas must set me free plain to the lady's
eyes before he could be wedded to-morrow.

When I awoke the sun was setting, as I could tell
by the glow on the mountain-side above the belt of

oak wood—for this chamber, as I should have said before, was on the north side of the castle and looked only that way.  The remnant of the meal brought by the boy did not tempt me, though a sudden desire to look about for a possible way of escape did move me. Wherefore I went to the window and drew out the loose bar to have a look round at the chances outside.

Thrusting out my head and shoulders I soon had the measure of what was there.  I could easily drop to the ground : a dozen feet was the full measure of the distance ; but what then ?  The guard at the head of the valley was doubled in number ; I had seen that as we returned, and it needed no prophet to tell me that it would be more than doubled in vigilance.  I could not escape by sea; the boats were chained as well as sentinelled and I could not swim the distance required to double Careg y llam.

Even could I have escaped that way, where should I get weapons and a horse for a rescue to-morrow, when all Lleyn was alive to earn the reward for capturing the man who had carried off the heiress of Castell March ?  The devilish cunning of Brynglas had stopped me there when he offered that reward for the "lord from Pembroke," who had followed the lady so close in Nevin fair.  I must wait then till to-morrow when he was bound to furnish me with freedom and horse and weapons himself, and after that—— !

Meanwhile my curious eye noted the fashion of the castle itself.  It was square, as I have said, but, being set with one corner facing the bailey gate, it appeared of a diamond shape to any one entering. There was a tower at each corner save opposite the gate, that corner having two, the better to defend the hall door which was between their feet. There were but two floors in the body of the castle, but each tower had three, besides a turret over all. The main windows of the towers looked along the castle wall, each into its neighbour opposite at the next corner, so that no shot could enter them except from a foe right beneath the castle leads, where it was supposed no foe could ever keep station long enough to shoot. Yet for greater security the lowest floors of the towers did not have windows at all, but only narrow arrow-slits, impossible of entrance by any attacking party.

In the tower to my right hand, the eastern tower, however, the arrow-slit had been blocked up by stones and the windows above had their shutters closed, making it look all deserted : whereas the tower on my left, the western tower, had its upper windows glazed and its arrow-slit closed only by the usual shutter from within.

My own window was in the middle of the castle wall, the only other openings in which were two narrow shot windows in other rooms, one on each side of me, midway from the towers. So much I saw and no more, so that for pure emptiness of purpose I began to watch the shadows creeping up the mountain-side opposite, where only the highest points could now catch the glow of the departing sun. Idly I watched the rose tint change to grey ; idly I saw the grass below lose the light, and then, without a movement of the eye even, I was aware of the little elfin lad, stealing along close under the castle wall.

He had come round the tower on the right, and immediately my interest was up like a hound to see what he would do.   I had not long to wait.   Sidling along, slinking like a prowling, homeless dog, he passed beneath me without looking up, till he came to the arrow-slit in the base of the tower on my left. Stealthily he tapped at the shutter; three gentle knocks.

Then, as if some one within had been waiting with hungry heart for that, the shutter flew open and two white, thin hands; not fleshless talons like those of the hag but the white hands of a gentlewoman in sickness; stretched out of the loop, one just above the other by reason of the narrowness, and, trembling and weakly eager, began feverishly to touch and fondle the face and head of the lad.

And ever, as if this were a thing of long and loving custom, he turned himself about, now this way and now that, so that the hungry hands might reach all parts of him from the shoulders up.   For, alack, he was too small to bring his chest high enough to be within reach.

And all the while, with endless differing cadences of tone, he repeated like a heart's own chant those two strange words, her name, " Madre Mia"; while out to him in answer came a crooning murmur, like all the thousand griefs of hopeless years of sorrow breaking in happy content.

Time and again he reached his own slim, bared left arm up into the loophole, as if in turn he fondled the face of the captive within; and time and again as he did so the restless fingers of the woman's hands would turn his arm round so far that I knew she was looking at the little scar of a cross on the under side of it.   Now wist I well all that he had meant when in the morning he asked me so resentfully—" What

is that mark to her ?" speaking of the lady of Castell
March,

At last, as if all the stolen time were up, he took
from within his jerkin the pitiful little hoard of food
which he had showed me in the hall, and one by one
he passed the pieces through to the one hand that
withdrew to receive them ; for even to take the food
the captive would not wholly leave touching him, but
kept one hand still fondling his hair.   Then, with
one last passionate pressure of his wan face, the
hungry hands went to his lips that he might kiss
them, one and the other, farewell, and so withdrew ;
though I felt that the shutter would not close till he
should disappear round the north-east tower.   And I
understood why he kept so close to the wall in going
—that she might see him longest.

Morevover, I knew well that the tears he shed as
he stole away were tears that he could no longer control in the desolation of his disappointment of this
morning at my hands ; though he had kept them
back from her lest she should see and share them.
And as I watched him go that little lad was holy to
me : the one white soul of faith and love in all this
den of evil.

Aye ; I marvelled no longer that he should have
refused to keep my money.   He would not offer the
gift of a faithless man to the one to whom he offered
his own righteous thefts.   "They beat me," he had
said, " but I never confess, and she likes these things."
I felt a shame that went deeper than any blow.

Of what tragedy was this a scene which I had
witnessed.   The boy, I knew, never would, even if he
could, tell me more ; for I had forfeited his trust once
for all.   And yet I was on fire to know.   If I could

but gain a sight of her, or a few minutes' speech, I might do good there yet. Then I bethought me of the coins ; the gold piece and the others, and straightway I decided that they should make my excuse. I would say that they belonged to the boy : anything to get speech of her.

The drop down to the ground was easy, but I must also provide some means of getting back again to the chamber, lest this loose bar be discovered by reason of some sentinel finding me wandering at large.

Buckling my belt therefore around the next bar of the window, I let the slack of it hang outside. Next, taking one of the broad-headed spears from the wall, I dropped the shaft down through the loop of the belt till the wide barbs caught and would go no farther ; for I did not know as yet why those barbs were splayed so outlandish wide. It did well, for it reached within a few feet of the grass, and in a trice I had passed my body through the window and was lowering myself to the ground.

Taking out the three coins I stole along to the loophole and there tapped thrice, gently, as I had seen the boy do. Open flew the shutter at once and the thin white hands were almost touching me when, with a little echo of distress as if a bell had broken, they were snatched sharply back and would have closed the shutter again but that I quickly thrust my coin-laden hand in to stop it. "Lady !" I whispered eagerly, "here is something of the boy's."

She would not take them, but moaned out words that I had no understanding of ; not Welsh at all or even English—for I had often heard English spoken. Only by the sound I knew that they were an agonised prayer beseeching me to leave her.

Like a harp wailing of sorrow she pleaded with me
in that unknown tongue, till from the mere pain of
hearing it I gave up hope and turned and went away ;
first dropping the coins within, not in the hope that
they would do her any good, but that she would tell
the boy of them and he could explain to her that I
was a friend. And not till I had climbed back by
the spear shaft to the chamber again did I remember
that neither the captive or the boy could understand
a word the other said.

# CHAPTER XVI.

## THE WITCH THAT WALKED IN DARKNESS.

GOING over the matter in my mind, the thing so moved me that I continued leaning on the window ledge, staring down at that shuttered loophole and pondering upon the sorrow of the one within. Dusk thickened to dark and still I tarried, looking out. Anon the dark changed into silver veiling as the moon climbed the peaks behind till she could look down into this black rift. Then suddenly I thought I heard a cry from the captive's place, and by the time I had snatched the spear and once more fixed it in the belt the cry had been repeated again and again.

Dropping out and running quickly to the loophole, another spear in my hand, I heard the sharp blows of a scourge, followed by the cries of the captive and the fierce, shrill curses of the scourger. Choking with swift wrath I lifted the spear and drove the butt end against the shutter with all my might, but it was too stoutly fastened to give way, though twice I repeated the blow. Yet it counted, for the scourger stopped to throw open the shutter wrathfully and see who dared hammer so. And in the moonlight as we peered at each other I saw again the hideous, livid visage of the hag, mother of Brynglas.

As she saw me she shrieked for very madness of anger, and at that sound forthwith all my loathing of her cruelty bit me sudden to the quick.  With a swift whirl I changed ends of the spear and, while in her rage she smote blindly at the loophole with her scourge, I with a dry gasp of wrath drove the spear in devilish joy straight at the gleam of the jewel on her forehead.

But, so quick that light itself is not quicker, she was already dashing the shutter to, and though the spear point banged it splintered back, yet the thrust was turned aside and only flashed past her temples instead of killing her.  Nevertheless the blow broke the fillet and I saw the jewel drop from her forehead as she drew back, though I knew she had escaped unhurt, for she rushed, shrieking wrathfully, out of the room.

I heard the opening and shutting of the door within and I felt that she was gone to have me seized and punished.  There was no time to stay.  Drawing back the weapon I ran and climbed again to my room.  Hastily I returned the spears to the wall; feverishly I replaced the bar, and I had no more than time to buckle my belt and lie down in my cloak before I heard the stair reared into place again.  There was a rush of quick feet: the door was thrown open— and I was found slumbering peacefully and only waking with a start as the first man strode over the threshold with resounding foot.

The captain was first; Brynglas at his shoulder and two or three spearmen pressing and peering close behind.  "As I thought," said the captain confidently.  "The lady was mistaken.  Our friend was here in his chamber fast asleep and dreaming."

Brynglas appeared relieved.   " I often tell her she
is mad," said he.   Then to me he muttered, striding
close, " If it had only been true then I wish you had
aimed lower so you would not have missed, and I
should now be a free man for the first time in life."
But I kept still and answered him nothing, for I
knew in truth that he was speaking to himself and not
to me.

So they turned them about and went, and I lay
still and wondered what should come next.   I felt
well that the hag was now my deadly, relentless
enemy, and I knew that she was one who would never
rest or turn aside from pursuing whomsoever she
hated, till she had the hated one under her foot.
Brynglas had held her off from me just for this first
moment, because his wedding to-morrow depended
upon me.   But though his sheer, selfish stubbornness might have baffled her open pursuit, I was none
the less certain that she had only been baulked in one
direction to try in some other.   Her blind fury would
think neither of the wedding nor of any other thing
but killing me, and that at once.

I did not fear the secret door to-night.   Brynglas
would keep the key of that secure for his own sake.
But the dread of this terrible hag, working, I knew
not how, somewhere in the darkness for my destruction, so grew upon me that I rose and took a spear
in my hand, as though I feared she would come in
person through the shadows of night to slay me.
Yea, anon I grew thankful to know that Brynglas kept
the doors fast upon me, and I blessed the sleeping
sentry at the stairfoot for his presence there, even
though he were little protection while he so slept.
He could at least wake and come to my shout if the

witch with her demon powers attacked me. For it was the fear of her demon powers here in this unholy castle that made me so shake with dread.

Then I looked at the bars of the window and was sorry that one of them was loose, for I had heard the whisper that the hag had sold herself to Satan for a hundred years' invulnerability. Now, too, as I remembered that, I saw well what had turned my spear aside when I thrust at her through the loop. Aye, and had notsome one said that the jewel she wore was Satan's token, which she must keep or perish ? But that was surely mere distempered folly, for did not the maid wear one too, only more beautiful ?

Nevertheless I would stand on my guard here at the window, lest she should shoot her magic at me unawares, and I be found to-morrow, dead, with only the purple print of five finger-points upon my breast to show that devils had taken the heart out from beneath. Or she might bring a cloud up from the sea to waft her through the bars and choke me. I took out a silver groat and made a cross upon the window ledge. I remembered also two slender javelins hanging on the wall, their shafts of the mountain ash, and in a trice I had broken one of them and tied it in a cross to the bars of the window. The other I held ready to cast if need be, praying that the charm of the wood should not fail against her witchcraft. Nay, I even gathered the bracken and heather of my pallet beneath the window, resolved that if I saw such cloud coming I would in the last extremity fire the pile. She could not cross through the flame without changing to her own shape, and better the risk of a Christian death by fire than the terror of a death under the claws of Satan.

Anon, about the hour of midnight ; I still standing at the window watching, all my hair began to crawl into icy life, for there, coming ghoulish round the captive's tower, I caught sight of the dreaded hag.   Body and soul, I stood in peril now indeed, and I could not remember even one poor prayer to help me in my need.

My eyes could look no other where but into her ghastly face, and when she turned in passing and swept a talon clutch towards the closed shutter, I moaned within my heart for the captive beyond.   Yet save for that flash of hate she had come eerily quiet and slow, and slow and suppressed she drew on now towards my window.   No green robe she wore, but crimson as the first blood from a wound, and I saw the broken fillet in her gripe, with the jewel smouldering in the ash grey shadow of the wall like the eye of a demon spirit.

Another moment and she was beneath me.   Then she lifted her face and I saw the glassy eyes lurid in the livid countenance and all my soul knocked at my ribs as she broke forth into a low, fierce, eldritch cry of hate and lust of murder ; as if some devil looked through heaven's gate and longed to murder those within.   Inarticulate, formless ; no words ; that cry pierced me to the marrow, for it struck me all and straight like an arrow ; not spreading to be heard of any other person, but concentrate to me.

The room was black behind me.   I had hoped she had not seen me yet, but now she shook the broken fillet towards me, till, as the wide sleeves fell back from her long skinny arms, I thought the talons grew up and up to drag me down, and a short sharp cry of dread burst from my slack lips.

At that sound all the wild fire of blinding hate flashed through her, while in her devilish ecstasy her glaring eyes seemed to smoke with intensity. Words failed ; sound failed, and her loose lips gibbered dumbly as she began to leap up at me. She seized the corners of her mantle with hands outstretched above her head : she was a vampire with wings : she would fly up ! Terror seized me : she was mounting nearer ! I laid the javelin across the ledge to cast at her, but my despairing soul believed her immortal: a demon !

She had come close to the face of the wall. See ! she was flying up now. I heard her talons scratching the stones as she clomb. She would have me now ! Silver, nor ash, nor cross would keep her out. She would tear me limb from limb, and with those tusky gums and loose lips would suck me dry of blood. I would have cast the javelin but that it would surely fly off from her unpierceable body, and I should be left defenceless before her. For I dared not turn to get another spear lest she should leap through upon my back.

Ah ! that was the hem of her crimson mantle touching the window ledge ! My flesh began to crawl ; my bones shook like the bones of a gibbeted skeleton. The cold sweat stood upon my frozen skin like icicles. A low despairing sound of mortal dread stole slowly from my dry mouth. My fingers loosed their hold upon the javelin ; my knees knocked. I was like to have given up the ghost for very terror, when suddenly she staggered back a pace or two from the wall as if to get a better spring—and then my staring eyes grew aware as well of the figure of the captain coming steadily along from the other direction.

I longed to warn him.  Quarrel and all I yet would
not have him die this dreadful death in the clutches
of a vampire, but my tongue was stuck fast with the
cold slime of fear  and I could not cry out.  He was
coming nearer, unwarned.  Another stride and she
had seen him.  One half-choked scream of rage and
she had seized the bandage with one claw and the
kerchief with the other, as if she would tear out the
flesh of the face behind with her teeth.  The kerchief
came off in one grip, the bandage dragged down
round his neck in the other, and all his face showed
openly within a hand's breadth of her own.

He did not move.  Stock still he stood, with iron
face ; but she : she flung both hands straight up above
her head : a wild, hoarse, long-drawn sound rattled
out of her stringy throat, and with a half turn away she
pitched full length and face down on the grass, while
the sound from my own lips stopped with a wail of
dread and I held my breath, waiting for the heavens
to crack forth the doom of this second castle too, and
for the earth to swallow it up.

## CHAPTER XVII.

IN my dread it had seemed as though my very soul stood out upon my lips, ready to fly, for terror of what should happen now that the witch had fallen. But no lightning struck : no Satan stood forth to claim his own. Nothing happened. Only the captain stood steadfastly regarding the still form on the grass while he might have counted a score. Then with a fierce gesture of hate he seized the haft of his dagger, and I cried out in quick fear lest he should stab her into life again.

At the sound he looked up. " Aye ? " said he, and then he wiped his face with his open hand and laughed ; a dry, unsteady laugh, that showed him as much shaken as I. And yet his features, now that I saw them, were all as high and bold as I had guessed them from the first. Comely, but with commanding comeliness. Stern ? aye ; but yet—what was it in his face that had stricken her ?

He was looking at her again, passion flashing through him and shaking him as the sheet of lightning shakes the dark of a summer night. Now the quick move of a hand ; now of a foot ; now of his head ; betrayed the pricking spur of a fierce desire to make sure of the witch with one wild, ferocious stab.

Once he muttered in his beard, but I caught no words, and next, not eagerly, but as one who did one thing while thinking another, he stooped and picked up the fillet from where it had dropped.

He looked down at it in his hands and started ; he looked up at me in the window and awhile stood still. Then he put the thing round his neck like a torques, his short ruff hiding it from sight.

" Nay ! nay !" I cried quickly. "It is hers : it is a token of Satan's to her. Do not touch it ! It is damned !"

" Aye ?" answered he steadily, settling his ruff again. " Aye, it is in truth a token that she is Satan's own—but you do not understand how."

My fear could not argue : I left that point and went on. " What shall we do next ?" said I.

" Kill her !" said he in an iron voice.

" Kill her ?" echoed I.

" Aye ; kill her ; strangle her ; cut her into little pieces !" cried he passionately. " If you knew how close we are to every torture that a woman's devilish malice can devise your bones would begin to crack in mere anticipation."

" Why ?" was all my shaking lips could reply.

" That is the bottom of all my reasons, as she is the bottom of all I am here to repay. I tell thee, if Brynglas knew what she knows now he would spend his last man to hold me fast. If she stirs hand or foot in returning life then she must die."

" Must ?"

" Must, or all is lost. But be not too quick : I shall not strike save at the last, the uttermost crack of hope. For to kill her here and thus would be to lose all but the bare item that she was dead : I should get only the naked satisfaction and none of the sweetness of revenge."

As he ended he bent above her, hiding all sight of her head or hands from me, so that only the garments and semblance of a woman showed. Like the spring of a loosed bow my mind went back to the fact that she was a woman, and first I held my breath in looking for the flash of his dagger and next I could no longer bear it.

"Nay; do not kill a woman!" cried I. "Let her come to if she will and let us die fighting like men. If we die fighting they cannot torture us— let us not murder a woman!"

"Die! thou fool!" he answered with cold weight. "I would kill a church full of such women as this she-devil first. Not kill? When thou hast lived longer and learnt more of women, then thou wilt judge them as they are and not as romances make them. They can be high as heaven, I know, but they can and do go lower than hell."

He was talking to himself as well as to me, but his eyes were fixed on the dishevelled form at his feet. Suddenly a great breath drew through the still frame : she was coming to. With set teeth I waited to see her rise and him strike.

He leaned a little in keen scrutiny as he clapped hand to sword, but the second breath came and she stirred not ; the third and still she lay motionless. Then her breath began to come and go regularly, but thick and heavy like the breathing of a sot in a sleep of drunken stupor. The captain loosed his hilt ; his rigid muscles relaxed and he drew a great sigh of relief as first he straightened up and then stooped again and turned her on her side, so that her face was in view, set in a snarl of fiendish passion. And at that sight he might have slain her if he would for all of me. She was the witch once more ; the hag ; the she-devil sold to Satan.

But he rose up and looked at me. "We are safe for awhile at least. I know by that breathing that she will not come to till she be let blood. Nevertheless we will wait awhile first and make sure"— and with that he took the kerchief from her clutch and tied it round his head as before. He picked up his hat and put it on and next lifted the bandage into place again ; though this time the bloodstain was in front, not on the side, and grim he looked with that black disc hiding his face. Then, still with his eyes on the face of the hag, he sat down so near that he could have touched her with his foot if he would, and I heard him muttering under his breath the while.

I said nothing, only continued to look out and to think of those two, while my pulse swung slower till at last it steadied again. The night was passing ; in another hour the white light of dawn would chill the silver of the moon, and I wondered what we should do then. But he spoke not, nor roused, and the sound of the heavy breathing of the witch was the only sound there until the first small bird rose to call the dawn.

"Now is the danger," spoke the captain at last. "Should any one see us in this posture then we should find ourselves in perilous state. But I have a plan ; I will tie and gag her and then carry her up and hide her in the woods."

He rose and stooped over her to lay her straight for tying, but at the first feel of her weight he stopped and laid hand on his knife. Even the long quiet of the cool hour before the dawn had not wholly served him to get the old iron grip upon his feelings again. I feared that if he were once alone in the wood with her he might yield to the temptation after all. " Nay," I said : " I have a better plan. Pass her up here and I will lay her against the wall and cover her over with the bracken and stuff of my pallet. My chamber is the last place in the world for her to be in ; they will never dream of looking here." ·

" But how can we get her through the bars ? " asked he.

" This way," and I drew out the bar.

" Oh ! So she spoke true. You did thrust at her with a spear—and then an hour later cried out upon me lest I killed her," ended he drily.

" Never mind that," returned I, suddenly seeing that I myself had tried before to do that which I now desired to prevent him doing. " The dark is drawing off ; there is no time to lose. Lift her up till I can reach her."

He slipped his hand down his beard as if he enjoyed some grim jest. But, " Pass me down a spear," was all he said.

Marvelling what he would do with it, I yet passed him that spear with which I had broken the witch's fillet. In a trice he had torn the broad hem from her mantle and with it bound her wrists fast to the neck of the weapon. " Stand by," said he, and then with a sweep he had lifted her, so that he held her, from the hips up, higher than his own head, while at the same time he kept the spear upright so that her hands were stretched full length above her own deathly head.

Clenching my teeth—for I would liever have touched an adder—I leaned out and down, holding fast to the next bar with one hand and stretching the other to its tips, till I gripped the wrists below and with a mighty heave brought the Thing up till its face glared at me level through the bars. So ghastly did that grisly visage grin at me and so close was it, with its arms stretched through into the room where I held them fast, that I had well-nigh let go my hold for the horror that crawled through my flesh. The locked, ferocious teeth ; the drawn lips, at one corner of which a little foam bubbled slowly ; the staring empty eyes ; the sunken cheeks ; the withered throat—so hideous was the whole sight that I shut my eyes ; thrust my head forward in desperation, and with a gasp of dread and resolution seized her round below the shoulders. One instant's effort, and then her limp body was following through into the room. If she woke now I should jump out, thought I, or else kill her in fear.

But she stirred not while I laid her close to the wall opposite and hastily covered her from sight beneath the bracken and the heather of my pallet, so that it should seem to a casual eye as if I had merely been saving a servant trouble. The thing was well done, even satisfying my peering eye as I rose and stood back to look at it ; for by this time day was so far spread that there was light enough in the room to see by.

Looking out, " It is well done," said I to the waiting captain.

" Good morrow then," answered he. " And now I must back to my bed before the others wake and discover it empty. But as we go to church ride close by me—I think I shall have that to tell thee then which it behoves thee to know ; " and with that he turned and hastened away, while I put the bar back and stood with spear in hand, watching the pile where the hag lay hidden.

The sun rose. Anon the sentry below roused up and stretched himself. A little while longer and the stair was replaced, that the same fellow might bring me a loaf and a pitcher and then withdraw without so much as a single glance round the room. He was half asleep yet.

Breakfast. I took it standing ; my back to the loose bar and my face still to the bedding that covered the witch, whose breathing I could catch by listening for it.

Then at last the fellow again. " Follow me now ; you are wanted in the hall," growled he.

## CHAPTER XVIII.

THIS time I looked to find that, for once at least, Brynglas should have a company sitting with him in the hall. But the eerie spirit of the place was not to be changed; it was empty as ever, and, as ever, only the elfin boy was there in his accustomed crouching place by the hearth. To my companion's questioning glance however he answered in words. "They are waiting outside," said he.

As we passed him a great desire swelled in me to fold my cloak about him and tell him all that I thought of his truth and loyal courage. But I was forced to go and say nothing, leaving him pale and hungry over the ashes, who should have stood in broadcloth and satin if deserving had any voice in such matters. And what he must think of me troubled me something, in spite of all that was before me.

Then we stepped outside and straightway I forgot him in the sight that was there. It was not the thirty picked men of the outlaws, mounted by nine and nine, each nine with its gentleman added to captain it ; neither was it Brynglas or the captain, cool and impenetrable as ever. It was the lady of Castell March, robed in green silk to defy the omens, and with a veil of French lace to hide her face.  The hag now hidden in the chamber must have counted securely on that wedding, for apparently she had provided store of all manner of gentlewoman's clothing ready, before she ever sounded the bride to it.

The maid was quietly sitting her horse, that pawed and fretted to be gone, champing his bit and tossing his mane for pride of the rich housings that tricked him so bravely, fore and quarter.  As goodly a steed he was as Brynglas could pick in the valley, and furnished with the costliest trappings that the castle could produce.

When through her veil she saw me, she was no sooner sure that it was I than she turned the other way ; as well she might, seeing all that I had brought her to.  As for me, so full was I of what should betide us twain in the next hour that I had nor eyes nor ears for anything else.

Thus it did not strike me to wonder that Brynglas should set forth like this to his wedding and no cry raised as to what had become of his hag mother.  Neither did it occur to me to be especially thankful when, dully and unconcernedly, my ear took in his dry explanation to the captain.  " We shall have to manage our wedding some fashion without the help of our lady mother.  It seemeth she took offence with me last night when I answered her that our redhand of Powys was in his chamber asleep and that she had been dreaming in hers.  So all to punish me she keeps her room this morning and will not answer the maids, knocking timorous on her locked door. 'Tis pity that our redhand should be leaving us ; we might have come by an occasional hour's peace if he had been tarrying here awhile to offend her at intervals."

"Aye," answered the captain, speaking with smooth gravity : "but you might be buying peace too dearly. Our friend is a hopeful youth and there is no telling what he would take into his head next.   Let him go, a-God's name, and be rid of him."

"For fear that where he failed with the wife he mighty try again with the mother ? eh," answered Brynglas with a dry grin.   "Sooth ! if I thought so I would keep him here awhile and try it "—he was in high feather this morning, Brynglas.

Then the word was given to mount and I found myself astride what was surely the sorriest pony in all Lleyn.   Bitterly I felt that ; for well I knew that it was done to make me ridiculous in the eyes of the bride.   A man afoot may be in rags and yet show manly to the eye ; but a man sorrily mounted is as sorry a spectacle as may be seen.

When we came by the cabans, all the outlaw folk were out ; women and children as well as men, gathered to see us pass.   With winks and nudges and with broad jests they greeted the bride and groom, as if this had been a wedding of true love instead of foul oppression and reft, and it burned in the bottom of my heart that the maid should have to hear and see these things, so merry to a willing bride and so bitter to such an one as she.   And, "Aye," thought I, as I looked at the crowd, "ye are thinking of the feast and the drinking ; the dancing and the merrymaking when the bride shall come back from the church.   But if one man can rouse a land then I will bring all Lleyn with torches to light the groom to bed at the end of it."

Then up the trail through the oak wood we climbed, all of us afoot for the sake of our horses save only the maid.   And when we came to the spot where I had cast the spear that slew the sentry she turned her face towards me for one brief instant as if to ask did I remember.   I would have given much then to have whispered to her in return that I would yet do greater deeds than that for her.

But I was too far off to whisper, and moreover Brynglas seemed to remember also, for he was looking at me, too, with a deceitful smile that ached in my very marrow.   Then through the gate we went and back for a piece by the way we had come from Clynog on the first day, until we came again under the high dark walls of the dead city, the City of the Javelin Men, that crowned the third peak of this Eivl.[1]   Here, however, instead of keeping between that peak and the main peak we turned to the right, by a green and ancient track which led down to a grey church standing in the bend of the pass between this mountain and the bare hills that lie round it.   And that church is the church of Aelhaiarn, in the pass of Llan'haiarn.

The trackway was just wide enough so that we went by two and two, thinly strung along from front

[1] Eivl is the mutated form of Geivl = Javelins—the Brythonic or Welsh equivalent of the Goidelic or Irish Laigin = spears or javelins also.   It is this " laigin " which as a tribe-name has left us " Le(g)inster " on the Irish side of the sea and Lleyn and Dinllaen on the Welsh side, to remind us that these two districts were once the country of a people whose weapon was a lance ; that weapon which we come upon time and again in the old chronicles as the "Irish dart," the "Scots spear" and the arm of the "Snowdon spearmen."

to rear.   For Brynglas had eyes only for the bride,
and the outlaws went all jocund, jesting each man
with his fellow, so that anon the captain made shift
to ride beside me.   There was room enough betwixt
us and those next in front and behind to make
whispering safe, and so presently he began to speak ;
but looking straight ahead the while.

"Do not ride for Carnarvon when he sets you
free," said he.   "Yesterday he sent a messenger to
Jevon Cutta and the Snowdon outlaws at Dolbadarn
—there is old friendship between them—and to-day
every thief in Arvon is come down to help to catch
you.   They are stretched, seven score or more of
them, in a line from sea to sea : from Dinas Dinlle
on the shore of the west to Criccieth on the shore of
the east, and they are to sweep southward this way
to net you as they would net a partridge.

"There is a hundred gold pieces to the man that
catches you, and a feast for them all at the bridal
spread afterwards.   Brynglas hath set his heart upon
putting your head between the blankets to greet
the bride when she goes to bed to-night—he is his
mother's son in that and will pay any price in money
to revenge your handling of him.

"So now, when you are free turn and ride for
Dinllaen, but skirt Nevin wide, for Nevin is ready
to catch you too.   Fire the beacon on Dinllaen and
when the ship comes in then let some of the crew
beset the head of Nant Vortigern while the ship
itself attacks from the sea.   And when the fight
begins let the ship send a landing party at once for
me to command—but all this storm must not break
till the dark begins to fall to-night, for I would have
an eye for an eye in this "—ended he.

Yet it was not alone the closing up of those behind us that made him break off.  I think he was as full of his near purpose of revenge as Brynglas was of his near bridal.

This then was what mine enemy intended.  I had expected some treachery, as I have before said, but not quite so cunning and complete a plan as this.  He had well caught the spirit of his mother in the womanish vindictiveness of this plot.  Nothing was too great or too small to be bent to my destruction, and then he would repay the bride's scorn of himself by putting my reeking head to greet her as she went to the bridal bed.  It was a pretty notion, in sooth, and would have sounded marvellous well in a song, or a tale to be told in hall over the drinking horns.  I looked at Brynglas and I looked at the horses ; as many as my eye could reach and weigh, and a plan came into my head which I doubted little would save it from greeting the bride in any blankets, except it were fast and lithe upon my own shoulders.

Thus presently we came to the church porch, and here as we drew rein Brynglas smiled wickedly on me.   "Well ; redhand of Powys, I promised that you should be set free to-day, with all your arms and armour and the pick of the horses beside——"

"Aye ; and you have broken faith," said I, "for you have mounted the bride on the best you had, so that I could not ask that one.  And afterwards you took the showiest horse for yourself ; thinking that I would surely choose the one you rode.  You call me a redhand of Powys, but if you knew anything of Powys you would know that we breed good horses there and can tell a horse from a cow without looking for the horns.  The horse you ride is as worthless as

yourself "—thinking of the net stretched to catch me
made me speak hotly, and moreover I knew that he
dared not harm me yet. "He does not limp on the
near hind, neither does he flinch on it more than one
stride in ten, but as soon as he gets well stretched to
go he will come down crest and quarters together.
Aye, you picked him for me, well I wot ; but I will
pick a better one, the roan here that this gentleman
rides ; "—pointing to the leader of the nine that had
ridden farthest in front.

The officer did not wait for the curse that broke
from Brynglas, nor stop to argue. "By the Dream
of Rhonabwy, thou art a good judge of horses !"
cried he, dismounting at once. "Aye, I'll give him
to thee gladly for thy skill. Never a horse in Lleyn
can catch him. I had to go in the dark myself when
I wanted to catch him—though that, it is true, was
from my own brother's stable."

Little did Brynglas relish the joke, though he
durst not chide the maker of it, for all the company
laughed as at a privileged and known wit as well
as a tall man of his hands.

As for my armour, I had but an armolet jacket and
that had never been taken away from me, but when
I was mounted and they brought me my glaive again
I shook it to feel if it had been loosened in the hilt,
and also I looked narrowly to edge and point to see if
they had been tampered with by any deceitful hammer stroke. My dagger, too, I examined, and then,
when I had put them up again, satisfied : when I had
taken good grip of the horse with my knees and felt
his mouth with a light lift of the rein, I turned and
looked at the maid to see how she took it all.

For a full minute she could not open her lips to

say farewell to me, and I could see that she was all
a-quiver with the tension of her feelings.   But she
kept all tears under bravely, though she was of a
white piteous to see and her hand trembled as she
gave it to me.   Then as I kissed it she said, out loud,
"Nay, sir; you have lost nothing by this.   If it had
not been Brynglas it would have been another: it
could still never have been you."

"But the other would have been a man of your own
choosing," answered I.

"Still not you," insisted she, and I saw her lip
twitch as if she was on the edge of a laughter that
would burst in tears.   And lest she should break
down I answered her never a word more but lifted
the rein and turned to ride away; keeping my teeth
upon my tongue the tighter for seeing the livid grin
of triumph on the face of Brynglas.

The track from this church to the church of Clynog went down the pass towards the sea, between
the peak of the dead city on the left and a bald
stony mountain on the right, and this pass I followed,
as if I had been bent to return to Carnarvon.   I
saw a meaning grin go round the company of outlaws, and I had my own secret smile that I dared
not show too plainly, lest I should have broken into
taunts and betrayed my hidden hope of triumph.   I
went but slowly, for I knew that till I disappeared
from their sight where they stood at the porch the
wedding could not proceed, and my plan had need
of my horse being fresh if it were to be carried out.

The captain's plan was well enough as he looked
at it; but he wanted only revenge, and that according to some long conceived and fantastic plan, whereas I wanted first and foremost to save the maid from

any touch of Brynglas.   I could not bear to think of all those long hours of torture for her between the wedding here in the church and the attack by the shipmen after dark to-night.   Her heart would be broken in dread  meanwhile looking forward to the future.   The captain had said that it would be an ill day for the man that took Brynglas out of his hand ; but the maid was more to me than the captain or any other man on earth.   To save her I must end Brynglas : the wedding itself I could not prevent, but I could try and cure it before harm fell of it.

Coming to where the track dipped steeper down towards the shore I turned to see if the flagman were still on the highest peak of the Eivl mountain.   I found, however, that he had come down from that and was standing upon the great carn of the dead City of the Javelin Men, looking directly down on me.   Yet my idea required that he should miss me some way ; for I intended to ride back to the church and do or die to rescue the maiden.

Planning then, I saw that if I went some fifty yards further down I should be lost to his sight, for the road from there forward was hidden for half a mile at least by a tangle of trees.   What I must do was to enter that hidden stretch ; dismount, and there abide for a little while until the flagman should be expecting me to emerge into sight at the other end.   Then, while his eyes were strained on that end, I from this would ride quietly out and back again towards the church once more, trusting to escape his observation till it should be too late to matter overmuch.   Slender as such a hope was, it was yet the only one possible and so I fain followed it.

Being so simple a chance it naturally succeeded,

and I regained a point on my backward journey from whence I could plainly see the church while the flagman must still apparently have been looking the other way. Here before me I saw exactly what I had already suspected. No sooner had the bride and the rest gone into the church than the last nine men with their captain had stealthily remounted to ride after me and either cut me off for themselves or drive me headlong into the clutches of Jevon Cutta's men.

They had not followed the road : they knew the country too well. Straight in front of them a bald waste of strong, boggy mountains seemed to bar all short cuts to head me off, but they had taken up a slack slope of it, and presently, while I watched them, disappeared behind the barren swells. Save for the flagman on my right the whole scene was clear for me to ride in.

Moving then I pushed back at an ambling pace towards the church again. I looked neither to the right nor to the left ; I sought neither bush or rock to hide me as I went, for nothing could help me now save a bold stroke and the fortune of adventure. There was no turning back : if the flagman on the peak should be still straining his eyes to where he expected me to emerge into sight again, half a mile the other way from where I disappeared, then well and good. But if not ; if he should look this way and see me now, I could still only push on. There was no other for it.

And see me he did, his flag going furiously to warn the ten would-be pursuers, whom now I saw high up on the mountain to my left. Would they notice him ? If so it would still make no difference to my going forward, I could no other than go. But so fast they pricked to overtake me, as they thought, that they

12

never looked behind : never saw either me or the futile flagman.

And now my danger lay with those in the church. If they should have left a man to stand guard over their horses outside and he should see the flag, then I should ride right into the swarm of them as those inside hurried out to meet me.   I looked ahead : only the horses and the yew-trees and the green smooth sward appeared in my sight.   I never thought of a prayer, but my lips were parching and my tongue be-gan to stick a little as I thought of winning the maid, and the chances of losing her should I mistake and be slain.

Yet when I reached the churchyard, the soft turf drowning all sounds of hoof-strokes, there was no man on guard and at a glance I saw that the careless crew had not even opened the shutters of the windows, closed aforetime to keep out birds and bats.   The wedding, then, must be going on inside with only the light of the glazed high window above the altar for them to see each other by : the fools !

With that the sight of their horses, tethered here in loose lines and clusters, bred a new lift for my plan. I would turn them loose ; all save the horse of the bride which I should need.   Every moment of con-tinued good-fortune made me bolder : and boldness was all that my plan had to speak for it.   To have weighed it would have been to damn it : it would not bear thinking on.   Hastily I rode from horse to horse till all were loose, and then softly and feverishly I started them away towards the north, all save the horse of the bride—that one I made fast to my own saddle bow.   Now if any one of the loose horses should begin to neigh and scamper off I was undone.

My heart swelled tight under my ribs ; my breath
began to come in quick catches and great sighs that
startled my straining ears with fear lest those inside
should hear me.  Reining close to the door of the
timber porch, but just out of sight, I bent eagerly to
listen for the clatter of feet which should tell me that
the wedding was ended or that I had been discovered.
There was none yet, however, so while I hearkened
there I also cast an eye to the country over which I
must escape if fortune should be with me.  A green
track led away to the southward, the way that I wished
to go, and a glance over my shoulder showed me that
the flag upon the walls of the dead city was still
waving.  More, far up on the grey waste towards the
Carnau, I saw that the nine riders and their captain
had seen the flag and were turning back in obedience
to its summons.  A dry grin cracked my lips as
I settled myself deeper into the saddle.  In a few
minutes those riders would be here : in a few minutes
then I must have won or be past caring more.  It all
depended now how long it would be before they ended
the ceremony inside.

Then the drone of the parson within ceased.  I
caught the loutish step of the groom and the light,
sad foot of the bride ; but not till they were half way
down the aisle did I hear the first stride of the others
following.  That was well.

My heart was cold granite in my breast : the fire
of excitement dried all my mouth to dust : I tried to
spit on my hands for the grip, and found my parched
lips had no moisture in them.  But I swept the sweat
from my temples with my open hand, and the wet of
that glued my palm to the hilt of the good glaive as
I drew it.

Brynglas was at the church door. His foot was on the step. He was in the porch. Two strides more I heard—Brynglas was here. I lifted my quivering horse with the bit while I flung him forward with the spur, and at the lift of the horse I lifted the glaive. One hoarse cry from the man as the hoofs brushed his breast and then I brought the blade down in a sweep that should have cloven him to the breastbone.

I felt steel hard under my own steel, yet he went down like a stricken ox, while I leaned over and clutched the bride. I was a giant : my lungs were brass and my arms were steel and I lifted her to the saddle before me as light as a thistledown. One stroke of the spurs and we were gone, while a mighty voice behind us was roaring out—"Shoot ! Shoot ! a hundred pounds of gold to the man that brings him down."

That voice was the voice of the captain.

# CHAPTER XIX.

### RENUNCIATION.

THE first stretch of the green track leading southward was smooth and level beneath the roaring hoofs
as I bent above the burden in my arms, urging the
good steed that was straining till his heart was like
to burst between my knees. Swiftly the outlaws
bent their bows behind us, but we had covered ten
score yards before the first shaft flew, overshooting
us, and the second was a twelve score shot that yet
fell short, so swiftly we went. The wind in my ears
drowned all other noise—God be thanked that he
made horses to carry men at need.

Upon our right the flag had summoned the rest of
the outlaws from the valley of Vortigern and the first
of them were crowding over the ridge by the Rocks
of the Giantess. But that was a long mile away and
more, and little I cared for them. Behind us the first
of the church party were catching and mounting their
horses, helped by the ten riders who had tried to cut
me off; but I had scorn for a chase a mile astern.
In front of me rose the perfect shapeliness of Bron y
Wyryv, the Virgin's Breast, with its nipple of red rock,
and as I looked at it my heart swelled up in triumph
against the burden in my arms. Shapely as that hill
was so shapely I wist was she—well might I be stub-

181

born now.    Furlong by furlong we swept along, heading always a little to the left and always the bride's horse keeping stride for stride alongside as if he asked for his share of the burden, till we came to a waste of gorse and bracken, marsh and boulder, stretching away to the south.

Pulling up, "Sweetheart," said I, "I am loth to let you out of my arms, but here is your own horse : we have many miles yet to go."    And with that I put her into her own saddle and away we went again ; this time at easier speed.

Never another word we spoke as we covered the miles till at last I thought we were well beyond pursuit.    Then as we drew down to a walk, partly by reason that the horses were beginning to be spent, and partly that we ourselves needed a little ease, I could wait no longer.    Now while the iron was hot was the time to strike ; now, while she would be full of thankfulness to me for saving her from the clutches of Brynglas, was the time to plead mine own cause, when gratitude in her might well aid the passion in me to win her.    Yet whether this were the fittest time or not mattered nothing in the end : the words came out of themselves.    "We are safe now," began I.    Then, "Nerys," I went on—and sweet the name was to speak at that moment—"Nerys, yesterday you told me that an ill deed once done can never be balanced again.    But I have balanced this one, as I think, and more, for yesterday you were but the heiress of Castell March, while to-day I have added Nant Vortigern to your portion.    Brynglas made you his wife and I made you his widow, all between dismounting and mounting again.    And what say you to that, sweetheart ? "

"That ye have done all that a man may do," answered she, and not a word more to it.

She was pale still and trembling from the terror she had just gone through, yet it was not want of breath alone that made her speak so few words in reply.

But my hunger was sharp and I went on—"Aye? but a man can win your love perhaps—have I done that?—Lady of spells! Olwen! have I done that?" —all my heart was suddenly in my voice as I pleaded.

She turned her face the other way as she answered. "I told you when I parted with you at the church that I was pledged to another man. I am still pledged to him."

Fire rose in me—"Then where is this other man?" demanded I. "Where was he to let me carry you off from Castell March so easily? and where is he now that he never showed steel in Nant Vortigern to rescue you again? How is it that he left it to me to save you? A leaden lover must he be, good lack!"

She turned her face to me again and its pallor warmed into the light that shone in it yesterday when she promised to marry Brynglas to buy my life from him. "Ah, sir," she said, "if I did but know where he is, then the rest would be easy; nay, I could almost do it myself. But I know not where he is except that he is in some prison oversea, treacherously betrayed and sold to the Spaniard upon whom he made war so long."

Then in a passionate voice she flung all to the winds. "Oh, sir! if you only knew the foul treachery that betrayed him! If you only knew his wrongs: his cruel wrongs. Oh, so foully dealt by! it crieth in my ears day and night so that I have no peace in anything save in hoping and planning release for him. If I could only tell you all ; but the story is too long ; too black ; to tell it here.

"All these years I have lived in hope ; waiting and praying to find some noble gentleman to do this thing for me ; to go on quest and find the prisoner and bring him home to me.  Sir, you are of the old type of Arthur's knights ; daring all and fearing nothing so you may right any wrong.  You have done so much ; will you not now do this other and I will shrine you in my memory as the one true perfect knight—will you not take this quest and find him now for me ?  He hath been so dealt by !—what does it matter, to marry me or not, if only you be noble and right the wrong that he hath suffered so long ! To marry me is no more than if you plucked a dog-rose as you rode ; what does it matter whom I marry if you are but doing a great thing and a noble !——"

Sharply I broke in.   "It matters all the world to me.   You have mistaken me.   I am no knight but a redhand of Powys, as Brynglas said.   There is nothing noble about me.   To me you are no dog-rose to be plucked or not as I ride.   You are the end of the world for me ; its two sides and its four corners.   You are all there is in the sky above or the place beneath. You are the woman I want and the woman I will have, in spite—aye, in spite of yourself."

She stopped her horse at once.   "You swore faith to me yesterday that you would do me no dishonour, but set me safe at home.   I trust you," said she, shaking yet from past fear in the flight, and whitening with fresh dread.

"I do not mean that," retorted I.   "Of a truth I will bring you safe to your castle again.  I mean after that ; for I will watch, and wait, and work, and do, till I wear you down to loving me."

" But what good is that if I am sworn to this other man ? " persisted she. " Bethink you : it cannot be altered. I have sworn faith to him."

" Aye, but I will do as I have said. I always keep my word," returned I stubbornly.

" Do you so, sir ? " said she, all so quick and all so sweetly : " then indeed I have found my knight in you at last. Do you remember how in the ship you swore to me that you would be my servant to serve me to the ends of the earth ? And this is only to the coast of Spain I wish you to go. Sweet sir, tell me your name that I may speak it once and then wrap it in my heart for ever sacred."

This was woful fortune on me. If only I had never sworn so foolishly in the ship, or, failing that, if I had not boasted now that I always kept my word ! In sooth it is ever a man's tongue that runs his neck into the noose. Well I knew as I looked at her that my own words had undone me. Her lip still quivered a little ; doubtless the danger had so shaken her heart that she could not steady its palpitating all in a minute ; but there was a pretty triumph in her face the while as she looked so eagerly at me. One might almost have sworn she was but merrily jesting with me. And yet deep in her eyes I saw that she laid all her hopes upon this pretty play.

But—that I should go and release another man that he might take her from me ! " You know that in the ship I spoke only to comfort you," answered I sullenly.

" What is your name ? " said she first.

" Rowland." I gave it bitterly.

" Rowland, then—how pretty a name it is—Rowland, will you deny that you meant it from the bottom of your heart when you swore it in the ship ? "

The lie was in my throat, but as I listened and looked at her it died behind my teeth. Never did a woman's voice so wander over the tides of music as hers did then in pleading. " This pestilent fellow with his misfortunes ! " I broke out. " I know you : it is only his ill fate that makes him so lucky. If he had been a free man : if he did not suffer wretchedness and cold and hunger and fever, you would never have cared a wisp of straw for him. But fate hath given him all the advantages, and so what chance shall a free and lusty man have against him with you ? "

I stopped. I was full of a savage hesitation and she saw it, for she looked me between the unwilling eyes and began to plead with me. Never was she so fair ; never was she so sweet as then, till for very fear of yielding I broke her short. " Nay ; let us get on to Castell March. I will hear you all then when we are safe."

" Oh no : not wait. Promise me now," urged she.

I did not answer ; silence was safest when she looked so.

She thought I was yielding. " You will not promise then—Rowland ? " Lingeringly she spoke the name.

Short and sharp I answered. " No."

Tears welled into her eyes. " Oh, I have failed ! " she cried. " You have failed me. I care not now to go to Castell March or any other where. All the world hath turned upon me, for there is no other man to grant what you refuse."

I tried to put her from the point, making pretence

that we were being chased, but she refused to press her horse to speed. " I care not now," she answered me. " What does it matter what becomes of me now ? And I thought so truly that you would have served me. All the way as you followed me from Nevin fair, I thought at last the knight had come who was to take this quest for me ; the more when you so gallantly defied my men. Even yesterday when we tried to escape it was that you would sail my ship for me that I was glad."

Savagely I broke out, " How cometh it, madam, that this point is so stubborn with you to-day ? Yesterday, when you promised to marry Brynglas, you seemed only to trouble because you hated him. You made no such ado about this other man then——"

The look she gave me had no anger in it, but it smote me like a steel gauntlet in the face. Straightway I saw what I had said, and with a bound I put my horse closer to hers. " Nay, Nerys ! " I cried ; " but you shall forgive me. I am the very vilest of men to have said that, when well I know that you promised Brynglas because there was no other way to save my life, though it was I who had brought you into that jeopardy. But you shall forgive me : I will not be denied. Nerys ; Nerys ; forgive me."

Slowly she lifted her face again, but she could not open her lips at first for the hurt I had given her. Then I began to say to myself that perhaps if I took this quest it might turn out well, for maybe I should find this other man dead. Yet no ; to look at her cut me to the quick ; I could not abide to see her quivering thus—" Yea ; I will be your servant ! " I cried eagerly. " I will go and bring this other man home to you—and then I will find some waste place where

no eye of man shall ever see me more.  Olwen !
Olwen !  I am ruined for ever by the loving of you."

I held out my hand to swear faith to her, but for a
moment she held back.  "Do you speak wholly and
freely now, or do you grudge and keep back something
in your mind—Rowland ?"

Her lips remained a little parted as she finished
speaking, and her eyes that held mine fast seemed to
grow wide and wider as she looked the question into
my very soul.  Then she leaned a little towards me,
and her eyes suddenly swallowed me up as her voice
came low and pleadingly again.  "Rowland ?"

At that word all my stubbornness fled and all my
heart went out as I answered.  "Wholly and freely
and without grudge I give you my word ; and freely
as ever the tide went out to sea will I go on this quest ;
all for the dear love of you."  And there as we struck
hands upon my faith I leaned over and kissed her for
the first time in life.  The other man surely could not
grudge me that.

And so we put our horses to speed, and all the way
as we went I was thinking of what I had just done,
when out of my own mouth I had bound myself to
seek out a stranger, and from my own hands to give
into his all the glory of the world.  For what is this
world but heaviness to a man unless he first have
the woman he loves ?

A hundred times I looked ahead and called myself
Fool ! Fool ! wondering at the madness that had made
me throw away the world at the woman's asking.  A
hundred times again I looked at her and saw there
that I had no other thing on earth but to do her bidding for ever.  Though it were sorrow to work for
giving her to another man, yet it were a thing not to

be thought of to fail of my faith that I had pledged.
If I could not have her love for my own I must at
least have her trust and good esteem, for I could not
longer abide to live if she should think of me as unworthy.

I could not bear to pass out of her life entirely, and
if she were happy with this other man, at least she
would owe that happiness to me and would think of
me tenderly for that ; if for that only. Heigho !
With what crumbs will a lover feed his hungry heart
if he may not dine full at the table. It is hard for a
man to love a woman, and he shall think it harder
before he be done with his lesson.

So we rode in silence till we came again to Castell
March. Only, as we drew near to the castle gate she
turned and said, " Rowland ; at last I may walk by
day with a happy mind and at night sleep sweet once
more. Now that I have you for my knight my heart
swells lighter of its load with every hour. For in keeping your promise you are taking a shame from me,
since, till I marry this man, I am profiting by the guilt
that betrayed him."

But I troubled nothing as to what this last sentence
might mean. I only noted how passing fair she was
and thought what I would give to be this other man,
suffering in prison somewhere over sea.

## CHAPTER XX.

As we had come through the village of Mynytho, just behind, I had noticed that it was all deserted, and by that token I guessed that the tenants had been summoned to guard the castle now, after the mischief had been done. Some one of her rosy-nosed officers had done that, thought I. Yet I was greatly indebted to him for it, none the less, since I had been full dubious of making good the castle should I find there no better fighters than the cozening rogues who were her own household men and guard.

When we reached the gate a pompous fellow challenged us from within, though there was a loophole there through which to see us had he been less a-shake with fear.

The lady herself answered him. "It is I, thy mistress. Let me in, good chamberlain."

"Ah ! but let me see first if it be you or treachery," quoth the fellow.

And certes he would have waited to look, but that a jeering voice inside cried out, "You lob ! do you not know her voice ? Open ! Here ; I will !" and forthwith the cross beam was shot back and the gate flew open for us to enter, while a great shout went up to welcome the lady back.

190

The first glance showed the place swarming with the tenants ; all with their families and goods crowded about them, and in the midst the paunchy chamberlain, red in the face from rating the squint-eyed, red-headed boy who had first jeered him and then thrown open the gate to us.

"See you, mistress," protested the chamberlain, holding out his wand of office to her impotently, "they will not obey me at all. They mind me no more than if I were the wind howling. Ever since you went they have driven me well-nigh crazy with their contempt of all authority."

This was my opening. Turning to his mistress, "Make me now captain of the castle," said I as I lifted her down from the saddle.

"An if I do not then you will but make yourself captain," answered she. "Take it, but remember that my people are not used to have a man in authority over them."

"No, or they might have been of some use," muttered I to myself.

Yet I knew that it would be but lost labour to try and open her eyes just then to the true worthlessness of those deceitful rogues, who had so well gotten on the blind side of her. Neither would it have profited any to warn her of the danger of trusting to such painted reeds. It is ever a thankless task to teach a satisfied mistress that the trusted servants are but knaves who cheat and deceive her. Even if you prove the point you are not soon forgiven. All I could do here was to take sharp order with them at the first possible moment, while keeping her in ignorance till the danger should be past.

Therefore I waited but to return her to the eager

arms of her clamouring women and then I set about taking hold of my authority.  Seizing the wand of office from the flabby fingers of the purple-visaged chamberlain, I stopped his apoplectic protestings by driving him out of my presence with it.  Then I offered it to the nearest of the three grey-haired chiefs of tenant-kin, bidding him take the office with it.

He put it back, however, saying, "I am come here with my kin to defend the place, not to be chamberlain."

"Then appoint me a man to bear the wand !" said I.  But no man would speak ; they were too proud to take an office which its holder had brought into contempt.

Breaking the wand across my knee I flung the pieces out through a window.  "So much for officials : now for captains and men," said I.  "This is no time of romance, but of hard everyday living and doing, for we have three battles of men coming against the castle.  There is Jevon Cutta and all the Dolbadarn thieves, seven score and more of them ; Foulk of the Feet and all Nant Vortigern men that are five score at least ; and Captain Meirion with his shipmen from the Ooronoka—and if I could be well rid of the same captain and his men I should have good hope of defying the others.  As it is we must fight every gasp that is in us if we would come well out of it.  How many be we here ?"

"I have six and twenty men that wear weapons," said the first chief of a kin, a tall man whose beard was brown and full yet, though his head was grey under his cap.

"And I have one and twenty men fit to fight,"

added the second : hard his muscles showed as he dropped his frieze cloak from his shoulders.

"I have seventeen only," spoke the third : "so many of my kin went out in the ship that never came back."

"Ah, then that makes three score and four," answered I. "And there are the thirty rogues in armolet jackets and steel caps. They are no great stay for fighting, but they have good weapons and their defensive armour, which I perceive your own men sadly lack. Now where be these gallant thirty that we may strip them ? "

"They are all crowded together in the upper chambers of the gatehouse that they may parley for their own safety if it come to any danger of attack from without," shrilled the red-headed lad. "They have been there from the first."

The chief of the boy's kin chided him for his forwardness before he confirmed his words, adding, "And now the chamberlain hath gone up to them to tell of what befel him at your hands just now— they will assuredly betray the place at the first push unless we take some order with them."

"Go then," answered I, "and summon them to come down. And you "—to another chief—"stand ready with your men to take the weapons from the fools as they come, and strip them of their armour."

But when we reached the stairfoot the thirty refused to yield, for every man stood upon his office or his terms of service to obey only his mistress. "Faggots ! " cried I at once to the tenants : "pile up the faggots and we will burn them out ! "

With loud cries of satisfaction, which told of contempt and derision long held under, the tenants ran

13

to the fuel heap and flung the faggots together about the door at the stairfoot. The fellows above had only one window looking this way and so they dared not draw shaft upon us to stop us, for fear of being shot as full of arrows in return as their bodies would hold. Yet still they thought to parley, and one of them cried out—"This is the man who followed us from Nevin. It is he stole our mistress."

"A torch!" cried I at that foolish waste of speech, and out from the hall came the red-headed lad, bearing a lighted brand and dancing in glee at the prospect of roasting the thirty. It may be that the pompous knave of a butler had denied him anything stronger than whey in time past.

Then I advanced with the torch to lay fire to the pile, and at sight of that the courage of the thirty sank away. They knew well that I could burn the gatehouse and still leave the rest of the castle untouched and fit for defence. "Mercy, sir! We yield!" they cried, all that could crowd about the window clamouring at once. "We yield!"

"Come down then, quickly, before the outlaws are here!" answered I, still holding the torch in menacing closeness to the pile.

Sullenly they obeyed and little they liked the scornful jeering of the young men as they stood to be stripped; thirty of them, who had been good men perhaps had they not been so long without a master. The household officers, too, were peeled and plundered by the young men before they had time to protest, but I bade the chiefs to restore all save the weapons.

Then I divided the thirty by ten and ten and sent them, ten back to the loft of the gatehouse again,

ten to the barns on this north side the castle square,
and ten to the west or hinder side ; leaving to each
man his bow and quiver only. " And hark you," said
I at parting, " I shall send men to pile fuel below,
under all of you, and if the outlaws once win inside
the castle then that fuel shall be fired and ye left to
perish in the flame. See then that ye shoot well
and closely, for I have a grudge against you and
will burn you like rats if you let them come too
close."

And they had great dread of me and only asked
for more arrows, " Since," said they, " if we be short
of shafts then we shall be burnt for no fault."

The household officers went not with the others,
however, for I was minded to teach them also their
own proper lesson. Therefore I divided them in
proportion to the chiefs of kin, to be servants and to
fetch and carry to the kindreds as they were ordered.
Also they were to be soundly beaten if they ran not
quickly at the word. When all this was ended I
felt that I had done well, for it was all the fault of
those varlets which had in the first place delivered
their mistress into the hands of Brynglas through
me.

Thereafter I bade the chiefs divide the arms and
armour amongst their men, and so we were ready by
the time the first outlaw came spurring up on to the
ridge—to get an arrow whistled into his thigh and to
spur back out of range, faster than he came, amidst
the jeers of us all.

While the laugh was yet upon our lips, however,
there came the whole thirty of those who had ridden
to church with us ; all save the one whose horse I had
taken. The thirty knaves in the lofts, however, with

their bows, shot all so closely together, having the fear of the fire in their hearts, that the outlaws turned and pricked back pell-mell in a cursing medley; while the tenant-kin cried out in derision, "Ho! they thought there were none here to keep the gates than the fools we have just newly disarmed!"

Whereby I gathered that the men of the Lady Nerys were the laughing-stock of Lleyn and that it was her own kinship with Brynglas that had been her best protection in time past. Yet I marked that they had shot wondrous well now, and I began to be sorry for them.

This first onset being beaten back, I felt that we should be no more troubled till the main body of Nant Vortigern men could arrive, and also the Dolbadarn thieves under Jevon Cutta. Whether they would then attack at once or not I could not tell, for it might be that the captain would bid them wait till he could sail round with his shipmen and attack us from the shore with the ship's cannon.

It was when I thus thought upon the cannon that my mind misgave me, for this castle was too weak to stand against cannon, while our numbers were far too few to make a sally and cut our way out. Moreover, to what point should we cut our way, with the sea on three sides of this land of Lleyn, and to the north only Snowdon and all the other mountains of Eryri, full of thieves?

If we had but had a ship of our own, thought I, then we might in this interval have escaped. Short of a ship, only the winning of a stand-up fight could save us, and as I thought of that a bitter hatred of the captain rose in my heart. For I might have looked to beat the loose bands of thieves by themselves ; it was the presence of the captain with his pitiless purpose of revenge, and his cannon to effect it, which made our case seem so hopeless.

"I need not have troubled so long about giving my word to Nerys this morning," said I between my teeth to myself. "If I had only looked ahead a little to this moment then I should have hurried her to let ns take the quest at once and get on board the ship and begone with all speed. I greatly doubt that the prisoner oversea will get much good of the oath that seemed so great a thing to the lady and to me out yonder in the waste an hour ago."

With a savage heart I set about arranging the defence of the castle to the best advantage, apportioning to each chief of kin, according to his numbers, his part of the castle, for which I would hold him responsible ; and his share of the thirty stripped men whom he must keep to their work. That done, I felt a little better till, on my way back to the hall as I finished, I thought I heard the voice of the chamberlain complaining to his mistress, and, turning to look—this being the woman's part of the castle—I saw it was indeed he, pouring out a whining tale so fast that the words overtrod each other as they came. I saw, too, that the face of the Lady Nerys was darkening as she listened.

Promptly I went to check the fellow and drive him back to his work ; but in that instant the lady stood between us. "How now ?" she broke out in wrath. "What is this that you do? that you strip my able household men to arm the silly tenants, and beat my officers and make them servants. And you would burn my men too ! Sir, I'll see sharply to this !"

I saw that only firmness could prevent mischief,

and straightway I menaced the fellow with the spear in my hand. "Fellow! back to thy duties or I will have thee hanged over the gate for thy meddling, thou whining whelp!"

He tried to get behind her skirts while she made to catch my spear, but with a quick leap I came round and thrust him an inch deep wound behind that would keep him from sitting down awhile. "Begone!" I shouted in a great voice, thrusting again at the same place; and with a howl of dread he rushed out, while his mistress, for lack of words in her indignation, tried to hold him back by clutching at his collar. But so fearful was he that he tore away from her, leaving the piece in her hands; and yet if he had not been wondrous nimble for a fat man she would have caught and kept him by the scruff, so angry was she.

She faced me in a towering rage but I did not wait for her words. "I am captain of this castle for you," said I. "I am responsible for you, and I must do what I think best."

"And I am mistress of it," flashed she, "and you are responsible to me. There shall be no more of this; beating my men and with a spear driving them from my presence. But I'll alter it all!" ended she, starting for the door to follow the man.

At once I stood in the way and closed the door, "Back, madame," said I firmly. "If you had waited till I explained the matter to you then you would have understood. But you have listened to a fat servant's whining and condemned me unheard."

"Unheard! what needed I to hear more? Could I not see when in my very presence you wounded my trusted servant?"

"Aye, trusted indeed," retorted I, savage that this new trouble about nothing should be added to our dangers. "If you had trusted them less they would not have been able to hoodwink you so, till your name is a byword in Lleyn for one deceived." The beginning of rebellious despair had made me forget the beginnings of courtesy.

She looked at me, white now with hurt and wrath, "You—redhand!" she said at last. "Well did Brynglas say truth when he told me that you were but a redhanded outlaw."

"Redhand; aye, I am. I slew a judge upon the bench—and now are you content?" demanded I, wilful to seem as though I cared nothing for her opinion.

"And I thought you an honest gentleman all this while," she went on.

"And now you find that I am neither honest nor a gentleman," retorted I, taking a vile and unmanly pleasure in pricking her romantic notions of me.

"I will have no more of you," answered she. "Give back the wand to the chamberlain or I will call the tenants to bind you."

"Will they obey you?" replied I, too sullen to be other than unmanly still. "And your own men are in trap."

I knew that speech had hurt her. I saw it in her face, where all the anger died out to white calmness and her breath came in a long catch that I could plainly hear. But I paid for it when she said quietly, "A little while ago I thought that at last peace was mine, for that you had promised to take the quest for me. But now, I would rather the—other man—

should die in prison than you should attempt to free him."

And without waiting for sign or word from me she turned into her own room and closed the door in my face.

# CHAPTER XXI.

### THE CAPTAIN CAPTURED.

"THAT is well : now there will be no more meddling till the fighting is done," said I to myself, though every fibre of my heart knew that it was not well.

Then I began to make excuses for myself, but there was little comfort in that, for through it all the fear was tearing at my soul that she had cast me out from her life, and that she would no more look to me for hope or help, or to take that adventure for her which she had so long prayed and waited on. An hour ago I had been hesitating and denying her when she pleaded with me to be her knight and do her desire, while now I would give the Crown of Arthur, if I had it, to have her accept me again to be her man and serve her in that quest.

She had pleaded with me ; now I would plead with her. Would, nay, must : must was the word, for I was beginning to shiver with a mortal dread that I had undone myself for ever with her. Yea, she should listen while I explained the desperate peril we stood in, and the according need for stripping her men. She must bear with me till the fighting was done and then the future should show how well I would repair the seeming discourtesy of to-day.

But to my knocking she returned no answer at
201

all, neither to my voice calling her to open and listen
to me.  I tried the door, meaning to go in unbidden,
but she had barred it fast, and in that minute I believed her anger mortal ; though this, again, bred in
me, not grief but impatient anger.  Then I could
stay no longer, for by the clamour of shouting from
the men at their places I knew that the outlaws were
stirring without.

Yet for all my anger I went heavily, and lament-
ing at every step that now I should not be allowed to
sail oversea to rescue the prisoner.  All this, moreover, though I knew well what scant hope there was
of my ever seeing the morrow, since there was no way
of our winning through this present danger save by
sheer close fighting ; plain hard handplay ; in which,
as captain, I must be foremost.

When I reached the loopholes on the north side I
found that all the rim of the ridge that way was
fringed with the outlaw steel, for Jevon Cutta had
come, and with him the Eivl men as I guessed, since
I saw the footless Foulk of the Feet riding round and
compassing the castle, keeping just out of range of
the bowmen in the lofts.  On the broad ridge itself
we were shut in by a half-moon of spears, and doubtless the lowland between us and the shore in front
was laid with men also, though there was no sign yet
of the ship which I dreaded because of its cannon
and its captain.

Then, while I looked, a horn was sounded and presently I saw, coming across the tableland, none other
than the captain himself, advancing to parley.  Going to the gatehouse I waited at the middle window
above the gate till he came near, and there demanded
his errand.

"Ah, good friend," answered he, as if he met me unexpectedly. "I thought you would be at Dinllaen."

"Doubtless," returned I bitingly : "especially as the last thing that I heard of you was your roaring offer of a hundred pounds of gold to the bowman who should bring me down."

"Well, of a truth that was something to be accounted with in casting up the reckoning," said he coolly. "Still that was all a little over-haste on my part, when I thought you had taken our friend Brynglas out of my hand. But now he has sent me to recover his wife for him. I am therefore here to command his tenants——"

"Stop !" I cried ; "do you tell me that he is still alive ? "

"Why not, seeing that he hath not lost a single drop of blood. That was a shrewd blow," he went on with grim appreciation— "and doubtless had you known what was in his hat it would have gone through to his chin. But his new wedding beaver was lined with double steel, padded with leather. Your edge went through the steel and then the leather saved him the rest, except that you drove his neck so far down into his body that he is an inch or so less of stature."

"Tell him then," I answered savagely, "that the next time I will see that the blow finds him where no steel is."

"Aye, aye, but meanwhile you will doubtless restore his wife to him."

"For why ? " replied I, beginning to jest too. "It were a cruel thing to cause a gentlewoman such weariness. She hath already ridden from the Eivl

here, and why should she now ride back merely to
put a poultice on a broken head which I shall so
shortly put beyond all need of poultices ? ”

" Do you refuse then ?　Remember that every outlaw from Comot Maen to Arllechwedd is gathered here
to beset you ? ”

" You speak like a herald in a child's tale," retorted
I.　" Could I give up the castle ? even if you had
every thief from Ardudwy to boot behind your summons ?　But these walls are high and I trust yet to
make them good, since naked outlaws cannot stand
up to good shooting.”

" Still, you are not master here yet, good Rowland.　Methinks the lady of Castell March will hardly
like to be kept from the arms of her lawful wedded
husband.　Tell her therefore that her husband is well
and waiting.”

" Doubtless ! ” jeered I.　" And then she shall
yield the castle to you and leave me naked to the
same husband of hers, who is well and waiting for
me too.”

" It is truth you speak there," returned he coolly
as ever.　" He intendeth that you shall be tied with
nine feet of rope to a stout stake and then baited by
the young boys with their little bows and spears.
When I left the boys were all wild with delight, clamouring and pushing to get to sharpen their arrows
on the dead man's stone.　Come ; it were churlish
to baulk the children.”

I laid my spear's neck on the window ledge ready
to cast at him.　" Have you done ? " said I.

" Not yet,"—he spoke as gracious as if he had been
some chief granting me some petition—" I have to
warn all these poor men, the defenders of the place,

what fate there is in store for them if they refuse to give you up.    They are to be fastened in the hall and then burned alive, as Reinallt of the Tower burnt the men of Chester."

" Then lift thy voice to call out but one word of it to them and down thou goest," answered I, my voice swelling out slow in cold wrath as I slid the spear a hand-breath up and down to give it aim and force.

"Nay," said he ; and though he had a target on his wrist he never lifted it or moved to shield himself.    " You will not throw."

" Why ?——" I paused.

"Because I am your one friend in Lleyn and you mine."

" A rare friend, i' faith !" returned I scornfully.

" Aye, that is truth ; a rare friend I am, for even now I wish to save you "—his calmness angered me beyond all bearing.    "If you would only trust me once for twenty-four hours on end.    But no ; each time you have broken loose if you were but five minutes out of my sight ; spoiling my plans as often as I lay them.    You even refuse to join this one, though it is the last one and the best."

" You are shooting at the wrong mark," retorted I bitterly.    " It is not my life that I want to save, but the happiness of the lady of this Castle.    You take no count of her and think it nothing that a woman's life should be ruined so you be revenged in some fantastic way."

" Woman's happiness ! woman's nonsense ! a mere romantic wench ; what should she know of what is best for her," returned he, for the first time speaking impatiently.

My passion of revolt blazed up. My eyes were beginning to burn dry in my head. "Have done and go !" I cried, drawing the spear back to throw.

Without a word or menace he turned on his heel and sauntered off, cool again, till he came to the corner ; too close in to the wall for me to cast at him from the window. Then, all as calm as ever, he turned the corner to go and speak to those in the barn and buildings on the north side, as if I no longer existed.

He had defied me in that, even as he had used me as a puppet and a boy all through. But now he had broken through the limitation of a herald, and I was free of all friendship to him. He might call himself my friend, but he was here to try and make my men turn traitors and deliver us into the hands of Brynglas. I would show him that I was a man to be reckoned with.

Darting down the stair—"After me !" I shouted to men at the gate, as I slipped the bar of the wicket door and rushed out.

Turning the corner headlong, I was upon him before I knew it, and my glaive came down involuntarily in a half-hearted blow at his head.

Alack, his buckler struck it aside, seemingly as if it moved of itself, and his cloak was round my head blinding and smothering me before I could lift to strike again. But I heard the sound of a quick scuffle and by the time I had rid myself of the folds I found the captain lying upon his back under three lusty men of the tenants, while the spear of a fourth was at his throat.

"Hold !" I yelled. "Harm him not ; he is my friend," and I rushed to stop the spearman's hand.

For now that it came to the point I could not see him done to death. " No : keep him prisoner ; that is all. And now let him up."

As the captain stood to his feet he spoke. " I said that we were friends, did I not ? and yet you would not believe it till you found that you could not let me be killed." He was laughing a little by his voice as he said it. Then looking round, " Quick ! " he cried, as one alarmed ; " inside, before they charge us ! " and he began to hasten round for the gate with a dread so lively that we followed in a manner as if he had been our captain and we his men.

We were inside and the wicket barred fast again by the time I had wit enough to see that this might be but a wile to get within and work upon the garrison to surrender their mistress and myself. Before I could open my mouth, however, my eyes held me dumb, for the grey chief of kin, whose post this gate-house was, stepped in front of the captain as if he would begin a speech ; while before he could utter the first word the captain had commanded him to silence. Aye ; for though the word he spoke was not Welsh, yet there was no more mistaking its meaning than its effect. The chief stood back with every sign of respect to let him pass.

I was in a whirl to know what this might mean, but before I could do or say aught I saw the Lady Nerys herself approaching. Again the captain was the readiest man there, for in a trice his hat was off and he was making a lusty low leg before her, and saying—" Madame, I am come here upon embassy to you from your husband."

She did not flinch at hearing thus that Brynglas was still alive. She had been pale with anger and

determination as she came and now she went whiter
still as she stood for a moment receiving him. Neither
did she deign so much as a glance my way for help in
her answer. Rather her manner showed a set contempt for me. I even thought I caught a certain
triumph in her eye at the news ; whereat my anger
puffed up my pride so high that I spoke never a
word of dissent as she replied : " This way then, sir : "
and so led him away through the hall to her own
apartments.

All the way as they went I noted the buzz that ran
before the captain amongst the tenants, and marked
the deference in the attitudes of the older men as
they watched him pass, with all the eager looks of the
younger men as they whispered to each other at his
coming. It smacked of an understanding betwixt
them and him ; some such an understanding as that
which had caused the one-eyed guide to betray his
mistress to us in the first place.

" Aye," said I to myself. " Doubtless they have
already sold themselves to him, and us to Brynglas.
All my efforts are naught. I am undone now ; I am
like water poured out upon the ground : spent and
no more heard of."

Then the two passed through the farther door of
the hall and I stopped, for I would not follow further
after having been so plainly ignored before the men
and so pointedly set at nought. Instead I went
moodily to the turret in one corner, climbing the
stair as if I desired to look again at the enemy without,
though the truth was that I cared no longer about
those outside, believing that they would do nothing
without the captain's command. Why should they
attack now, when the chief leader of them was here

in the very heart of the citadel, and all the garrison sworn to him already ?

I was right, for no outlaw moved or made any sign. Then I fell a-thinking and in a while my misery so stirred in me that I made up my mind to go desperately and beard the captain to the lady's face, and tell him that I knew he had agreed with this garrison to have me prisoner to Nant Vortigern. So said, so done. Going down then, I reached the last step and stood in the hall at this end just as the captain came in at the other, leading the Lady Nerys by the hand. And I saw she had on her habit for riding, as on the day at Nevin.

At that sight all my gloomy and distempered wretchedness dropped off me with the cloak that I let slip from my shoulders to the ground. I could at least try the matter out with the sword, and I felt a man again at the thought. With long strides I gained the hither door and straightway locked it.

Taking the key with me I met them midway, answering the lady never a word as she put in so quickly—" My husband hath sent for me."

That was her revenge, well I wist, only I cared no more about it but turned my face from her without listening further, and flung down the key at the captain's feet. " You shall win it before you use it," said I.

Then, drawing my glaive and continuing—" Aye ; well I wot that I am bought and sold like an ox in the stall when the butcher is buying. But you shall fight : you shall not have me cheaply to run tied to your stirrup. Come, now ! "

As I stood there, glaive in hand, all my heaviness had lifted from my breast, as a cloud lifts from a

mountain top and lets the sun shine warmly in. I
was come to my last stand, thought I, and nothing
mattered now, save the sharpness of one good honest
fight and so a manly end of life and all its shames ;
all its mistakes ; all regrets. A smile was on my face
I know, and if that face were more white than ruddy,
yet the passion which shook it was one which shone
out of my eyes with good unflinching challenge. All
my blood was like a sparkling wine within me, and I
felt as light as a bird from head to foot. I was drunk
with an ecstasy of eagerness to show my contempt of
life and death alike by daring all odds of skill or
numbers and dying defiantly, face up and sword in
hand. What are women ? what is wealth ? what
are a few poor builded stones with a patch of the
miry fields of this clogged earth about them ? to
the wild temper of such a sudden frenzy ? What
mattered courtesy even ? I leaned forward toward
the captain and would have smitten him on the
mouth with my gloved hand but that he put up
his buckler.

He had stood quiet from the first of this and now,
instead of showing anger, he said quietly, "Thou
hast taken it to heart too sorely and taken it wrong.
Yea, I almost repent me now that I did not do differently." Then turning to the lady, "Madame," he
went on, "I think there is a better way yet of doing
this thing. I have a plan that will suit all of us as
well as one."

She stamped her foot with impatience. "But I
have not. I am going."

"Aye, aye," said he quickly and smoothly. "That
is not what I mean ; what I mean is that it were best
you should go openly and with a fitting company

equal to this of your husband. Not as if you were haled back a prisoner."

"And where shall I get an equal company ? You do but stuff me with words to put me off because of what this man hath said. But I am mistress here."

"Of a truth, yea," answered he ; "but still, trust me, I can bring you for convoy as goodly a company as ever was seen in Lleyn. Meanwhile, do you but rest awhile till I come again "—and with the word he was trying to lead her back.

"I will not," cried she. "Am I to be commanded in my own house by every man that comes into it and chooses to take authority to himself ? "

"Yea, madame," answered the captain with a fine smoothness : "woman must always yield when the steel is out and danger to the fore. Then when it is over she hath her revenge, for that she commands the victor and punisheth him with double authority." This captain was as full of fine phrases to befog her understanding and put her off her purpose as any knight of court.

"But—I will not," said she firmly, planting herself to keep her ground.

At once the captain changed and was all reverence. "Madame," said he in a low voice, "do but wait here till I return and then——" the rest I could not catch, for it was no better than whispered in her ear and I would not have it thought that I cared enough to strain my ears in listening.

I saw her lips part a little and her eyes open wide, but whether it were more in dread or in surprise I could not tell. She made no further attempt to resist, however, as he took her by the hand and led her away to her own rooms again.

Then a minute more and he had returned. Stooping, he picked up the key. "Come," said he, thrusting his arm though mine.

I went as unresistingly as the lady had gone. What did it matter! I was out of it all. But at the gate as he passed out he said : "Rowland, I think I shall come back a welcome man to thee. I see what has happened, but she will speak to a different tale when I return. See that thou look at things in the largest light then and keep thine eye fixed upon the worthiest part. For thou hast the makings of a man in thee, Rowland, when experience shall have brushed the cobwebs out of thy head. I was proud of thee yonder in the church porch when I bade the bowmen bring thee down ; I was proud of thee now in the hall, defying me and all else together. I shall be prouder yet if thou dealest rightly by this maid."

But I was not to be entreated. "Aye ; cobwebs," I answered. "What else! I am but a fool who, it seemeth, may not even die manly when he hath made living too bitter in the mouth for further tasting."

"Ah !"—he had changed all in a breath—"thou wilt have forgotten all that by the time I get back. A few strokes of the steel will put all the salt back into life for thee—and strokes promise to be plenty with Foulk of the Feet so near."

# CHAPTER XXII.

## THE UTTER DEATH OF HOPE.

THE captain went away from the gate and across the plateau with a cool and easy swing that did but make me the more hard as I watched him. Not that I trusted or distrusted him : I simply cared no longer what happened. I had a sword, and beyond that, nothing. I could only fight when the moment should come, whenever that might befall, whether it were against those open thieves without or these uncertain friends within. I did not even wish that it might come quickly, for I felt no suspense, but rather a distempered pleasure, in waiting and watching how it should fall in the end.

I saw the leaders of the outlaws crowd to meet the captain as he reached their lines. Foulk of the Feet I knew, and the short fellow with the great black beard who rode beside him was pointed out to me as Jevon Cutta of Dolbadarn, the scourge of all Arvon. These questioned eagerly with the captain and there was much talk and crowding amongst them, but I did not wait to see what they would do. Neither did I give any more orders to the chiefs of kin or any other man, but went back to the hall and up to the top of the turret again, from whence I could see all the country. Yet even this was not from any desire to watch for the first move of the enemy, but only that

I might be as much alone in the body as I conceived myself to be in heart amidst the people of this castle.

The day dragged on. With idle eye I watched the sea below, now shining white and placid beneath the glistening sun and now deepening from blue almost to black where some sudden little breeze whirled along it. No ship came, nor did I peer to see if one were coming : the mere lazy beauty of the water was enough. All the land shimmered in the heat, and by the way the spears shone motionless in the glare I guessed that the outlaws were sleeping and waiting for night to cover their attack, if attack it were to be. Though if this garrison were bought and sold then there was no need for more than one man with a single well-aimed shaft to bring me down.

Not till evening came, bringing the memory of that evening of the day before yesterday, spent yonder on the dark slope of Llanbedrog mountain, did I rouse from that strange folly of reckless quiescence. Then as my mind called up again how we had lain in wait there to carry off the lady of this castle, and as from that I followed on through all that had happened since, from carrying her off to bringing her back again, I rose and shook myself, and heard my scab-barded *'sgian ddu*—my dark brown slicer—clank against the target upon my hip. And at that sound I swore that I was a fool in every way and in everything that I had done, from the moment I had ridden in through the east gate of Carnarvon till now.

And being a fool, and having come from folly t' folly, each a step worse than the one before, till now my next folly must be my last; why, I would make the most of what time remained. A dinner of good meat ; a draught of good ale ; an hour's rest, and then throw off the shirt ; tighten the belt ; spit on the hand and make the brown slicer whistle as one stepped out to challenge, first the garrison of the castle to know if they were true men or not, and then, if true, to sally out and beat up the outlaws : to fall upon them just when they were gathering in the earliest dark to assault the gate.

After that, well, at least a good fight and a brave straightforward end, with no tangle of any man's fantastic plots or cobwebs of any woman's romantic follies. That would be in any case a free and wholesome finish to make by way of offset for my distempered follies of the last three days. So I went down.

In the hall things were much as was to be expected. The young men were practising with the better weapons taken from the stripped thirty. The older men were talking earnestly together upon some subject which they stopped as soon as they were aware of me standing there ; and the women were busy making each her place comfortable for the children and the men when sleeping time should come. The dispossessed butler was standing dejected in the midst, and him I commanded to lead the way to some more private room and bring me food.

Night is seldom more than dusk in June, and this night the moon would be up in little more than an hour, so that it was in that one hour that we should be attacked if at all. If I went round the defences now I should learn if the garrison feared any attack ; in which case they would be holding themselves ready. And if they did not prepare for any such attack then I should know that they were in league with the outlaws.

After I had done eating then I went the rounds,

beginning first with the disgraced household men in the lofts, and them I found full of all preparations and making ready. There was a great sharpening of arrow tips ; a brushing of feathers, and a testing of strings. They at least expected no other than a fight, and indeed looked eagerly for it as a consolation in their present dejection.

Down below, in hall and barns and gatehouse alike, I found things of a quieter cast. True, each post had its defender and the rest of the men were near by and ready ; but there were no shining eyes and eager talk amongst the boys ; no jests amongst the young men ; no grave alertness amongst the older men.

" Are they not to attack, then ? " said I at last, curtly, to the chief of those in the gatehouse.

" That is more than I can say," returned he cautiously.

" But if they do attack then what time will they choose ? " pursued I impatiently.

" That is more than I can say," repeated he again. " If it were only Foulk of the Feet, he would wait till the moon was up, so that he could see to shoot, because he is proud of his shooting. But Jevon Cutta—he loves the dark so that he may creep up, and then, in the rush and the hurly, while all men are busy fighting, he flings the torch into whatever will burn. He knows that the flame and the smoke will drive men at last out of any buildings and then he hath the best of them as they stagger out, gasping. It is for Foulk and him to decide when they will attack."

" And what of the captain ? Hath he no voice ? Doth he allow them to decide for him ? "

" I think you will find that he does his deciding for himself,"—the old man's voice seemed to rouse and unfurl itself.

" Then what time does he choose ? " demanded I as of one who knew.

" His own time," responded the chieftain ; a new ring in his slow voice.

" And when will that be ? "

" It is more than I can say. You will learn in time," answered he.

Here was that same old phrase of the captain's again to plague me, and in my sharp impatience I could have quarrelled with the chieftain for his using it. And indeed it stung me to an answer of childish weakness. " Who is this captain then ? " demanded I, again as of one who knew.

" How should you ask that of me ? " rejoined he, unmoved and without any pretence of surprise—he did not even think me worth deceiving. " Did you not tell us we were not to harm him because he was your friend ? "

He had put by the question but I thrust again. " Is that why you took orders from him the moment he set foot within the gate ? Is that why you let him, when he left, set your duty for you while he should be gone ? "

" He set my duty ? " Again the ring roused a little in his voice, this time with somewhat of scorn in it. " My duty was my duty before ever I was born. My duty is to help defend this castle with my kin, as it has been the duty of my kin from generation to generation. That duty was before either of you were born and will be when you are both dead."

I saw that it was no use. Not only he did not

intend to answer me, but he was a chief of kin and had begun to dispute of tribal rights and duties. He would run me through presently to demonstrate some privilege of his particular kin, and then bury me with all pomp to illustrate his duties.

One last test remained by which to learn how I stood in the castle. I would give an order. "You say that Jevon Cutta loves to attack in the dark. Set then some of your young men to tying up faggots of gorse and straw, heather and the like. Have them ready when the dark falls and then light one and fling it as far out as you may from the top of the walls. As fast as one burns out, follow it with another—they will give light enough to betray any creepers in time to shoot. Do that here for the gatehouse and I will go and see to the other sides doing the same."

I watched him narrowly as I spoke, but from the first word he seemed to listen and to weigh the project all the way through to the last. "Yea," said he then. "Jevon Cutta will be puzzled at that. It is a good plan indeed. Here! Badi, Owain, Howel,"—and forthwith he set the young men by name to work at making the faggots.

But I had learnt nothing from his answer, for he had considered it before he spoke it.

As to the other two chiefs of kin, the test with them was no test, for they had been looking on from their posts, and had seen the young men running from the gatehouse to do the work. They made no demur to my order therefore, and so I was none the wiser for my attempt to discover how I stood with them all. The making of the faggots was something and nothing, for it might have been done merely to befool me. Moreover I had not in truth given an

order at all, but merely proposed a plan of defence,
giving the arguments for it as I unfolded it, so as to
move them to accept it. By that token, then, my mind
had of itself shrunk from any real test. Unaware I
had shown to myself that I was at bottom afraid of
finding the tenants against me ; though I had boasted
myself so valiantly up in the turret. After that I
could only wait.

Anon dark fell, and I saw them light the faggots,
one on each wall, and then, with a swing and a
whirl from a spear point, fling them far out into the
gloom. Jevon Cutta must sit still at that, thought I.
Through the dusk until the moon rose the faggots
blazed and flickered, and never a shire or a shaft of
outlaw did we see that while. Neither did they stir
as the moon rose, though when the silver disc stood
all so white up from the dark sweep of Llanbedrog
Point, her soft light flashed back in a flickering rosary
from the serried circle of steel that fringed us in.
For now I caught the glint of spears in the lowland
betwixt us and the sea.

What is there in the round white moon to a young
man that it should loosen all his resolution ! I had
no more than cast my eyes once over the lustrous
scene than I was dreaming again of Nant Vortigern
and the Lady of the Strand. Nor could I shake it
off. I went down from the turret and paced moodily
from post to post within the walls. Yet it was all no
use ; the longer I thought of her, the fairer and
more gracious rose her image before me. Sweeter
she seemed in every picture as they followed in soft
succession before my mind's eye ; and viler and more
unmanly seemed what I had done and said to her.
Higher and higher rose the warm blood in me with

every pace I took : emptier ached my breast ; hungrier did my soul cry out ; stronger and more imperiously did her door seem to draw me towards it, till at last I stood before it, pausing to gather my thoughts and order my words before going through. For it was come to this ; that I was ready to say or swear anything to gain her favour again.

To my knock I found the door ajar and, pushing it open, I found the room within all empty ; lit by one candle only.  Fear seized me lest she might have stolen away to the outlaws—a thing which would have explained their quiet—but stepping further in I saw another door on the other side, standing half open, with a brighter light shining through into this room. Softly then I strode across, not with any desire of surprising her ; conscious only of being almost in her presence, and so the picture that I came upon within that second room smote me the more like a death stroke.

She was still habited as if for riding, just as I had seen her in the hall, but it was not herself so much as the room that was so notable.  For the room—a small one—was in everything furnished after the fashion of a man's room and in nowise such as a woman fits for her own use.  Weapons and implements of sport hung round the walls.  A high harp stood in one corner, and at the table, close under the window, a chair was ready as if waiting for some accustomed user's return.  A lute was on the table leaning against a pile of learned books in divers languages ; a sheet of music half covering both.  Still more—where in answer to her mute gesture I stepped up to look—there, side by side, lay two other books flat open ; the one a printed book of Hebrew, the

other a written book of Welsh.   Aye, and the written
book stopped half way down a page ; half way through
a line ; half way through a word; nay, half way
through a very letter.   It was a translation of the
Old Testament and it stopped at that passage—" And
cause them to return to this city ; and they shall fight
against it, take it, and burn it with fire."

Neither was that all there was to read.   Underneath
the half-finished passage was a dark stain that was
yet not ink ; a stain that was of kin to the long, deep-
grooved, double-edged, hollow-ricassoed blade, half
drawn from its scabbard, and whose silver hilt lay on
the upper half of the open page.   I asked no question ; I did not look at her, but I guessed at once
that here the prisoner now oversea had been betrayed,
and that that dark spot was the first drop of the
blood from the wound by which his enemies disabled
him in the moment of surprising him.

I stood upright again, looking straight at the
candle nearest to me on the table ; but looking without seeing, for I was keeping myself still till the
pain should finish eating itself in through every vein
and muscle of me : the pain of that despair which
follows the utter death of hope.

Now I knew that in very truth I could never have
won this woman to my wife.   Now I knew the full
weight of what she had been saying awhile ago when
she called me by that one word, "redhand !"   When
she said that, she had in mind all the contrast between such an one as I, a rude mere fighter, armed
only with common glaive and target, and this other
one, a scholar by this book ; a courtier by this rapier
and this lute ; a commander and a travelled man by
all these costly weapons and rich armour.   Yea, I

read now many signs aright which before I had taken to
my flattered heart in foolish satisfaction.    Especially
I understood what she had meant when at the church
she said, " If it were not Brynglas it still could not
be you." How could it indeed be I, when all the
while she was thinking of this courtly vanished one.

And if at first my heart rose up in heat to say that
she had played me fair and false, in that she had not
told me what manner of man this was whom she
loved, and how well fit and furnished he was to take
and keep a woman's heart without even conscious
effort ; I yet had presently to admit that she had
pleaded with all the fire of honesty and love when,
out on the waste this morning, she had begged me to
be her knight.    Only, I loved her and she knew it ;
it had been more merciful in her to have asked some
other man—but when had a woman in love any
thought for any other man, save the one she loved ?

And yet, even there she was justified, for had she
not offered to give up all hope of this prisoner, and
instead of him to marry his opposite, Brynglas, only
to save my life who had put her in such peril ?  She
had some show of right then in asking even the
greatest sacrifice of me after that.

All this passed through me as I stood, and whether
the time were long or short I do not know, for I was
trying to get a grip upon myself again ; to quite understand what the death of all my abeyant hopes
should mean to me ; to forge some resolution which
like an iron belt about my breast should keep my
heart from bursting and hold me together for the
future.    At last I turned and looked at her.

In her face however was neither defiant taunt nor
fear ; hope or despair ; or any other feeling so much

as indecision and half puzzled expectancy.    But I
did not stop to probe her mind.    I had but one idea
and that was to say my one speech and be gone.
" Lady ! I see now : I understand better about this
prisoner oversea.    It is not worth your while to keep
your quarrel with me.    When this matter of the outlaws is over I will go upon your errand as soon as
you like, unless you have some other man whom you
would rather send.    Moreover you need not trouble
about the afterwards.    Afterwards I am for the Ooronoka.    Good-night."

It is true that I had hoped that she would use some
grace in answering me, even if it were but to bid me
a good-night in return.    It is true also that the resentment in her tone hurt me when she spoke, yet
that was a small thing compared with what she said—
" You need not trouble yourself further in the matter.
There will be no fighting to-night, and the prisoner
is no longer oversea.    Before to-morrow he will once
more stand in this room ; sit in that chair again, and
finish that half-written word.    The captain is now
gone to fetch him home at last."

A little while I stood, steadfastly upright, quite
still, keeping from flinching, till at length I could
take breath without showing any quiver of the face.
Then—" Ah ! if that be so—good-night," I answered.
And I bowed and went.

# CHAPTER XXIII.

### DARKER AND DARKER.

NOT till I was beyond the door did it occur to me to wonder what would happen now that the prisoner was come home, while she found herself wife to another man through me. Neither at that moment could I guess what would be the upturn of it all—save only sorrow for me. Aye, sorrow was the word I rolled and tasted between my teeth so bitterly; for as my love had been so high when I went in, so now was my melancholy as deep when I came out. All my bones had melted then of grief but that a shock of sharp help came to rouse me at that moment when I needed it most.

She had said that there was to be no attack. Whether that was something which the captain had told her, or whether her woman's mind had jumped to that conclusion, prompted by the desire to say something which would wound me, I did not know. Neither had I any need to decide; for here in sharp time the words were proved mistaken. Stepping across the courtyard from the hall to the gatehouse, I was some half way over when suddenly a long streak seemed to cut the moonlight above the wall, and in the same instant an arrow splintered on the hard-packed gravel close by.

224

Stooping, I found the fragments of a long flight-shaft, hanging together by a set of strings which had been tied from barb to butt of it. This was so strange a thing as caused me to fear at once that it was some settled signal between the outlaws and the garrison. Drawing my glaive then I took the shaft in my left hand, meaning to charge the chiefs boldly with treachery, and to abide by whatever might befall of it.

I found the first of them sitting in the gateway where I had left him ; a young man holding a torch beside him to give him light, over a horn of bragot which he was drinking. Stretching the string-hung splinters towards him, I had got out the first words only, " What do you think of this ?" when he rose up with a quick cry.

" Foulk of the Feet ! his challenge ! Ware at your posts all ! Send it along the wall, ' Foulk of the Feet hath bent his bow !' Now be men if you would ever see to-morrow."

He caught the wonder in my eyes. " Do you not understand, sir ?"—and I was glad of the " sir," for it showed that he looked for aid from me now in the danger. " Count those strings : five strings, black, brown, red, yellow, and flaxen white. It is the sign that Foulk of the Feet hath sworn to attack—and win. Aye, I see you have not heard his story, there is not time now to tell it, but fight, sir, now—if ever you fought in life, fight now ; " and with that he took his spear and began to go from post to post to stiffen his men.

There was need, for as I turned to look back across the courtyard I heard the clash of a hail of arrows, shattering on wall and pavement, with the cry of the first of the wounded among the defenders. Then

15

from the four quarters without came a wild shout
of "Eivlogion! Eivlogion!" mingled with the
shrill clamour of the Snowdon outlaws crying
the name of their fortress, "Dolbadarn! Dolbadarn!"

Two steps at a time I rushed up to the middle
chamber, the one above the gate; for that gate as I
thought was the weak point of the castle. Elsewhere
the great wall of stone, six feet through, would
laugh at the torches of Jevon Cutta; but here,
though we might beat back the first rush, yet in the
hurly-burly their swiftest runners might come close
enough to fling faggots of dry stuff against the
wooden gate. After that, it was but to shoot fire-
arrows into the pile, and though the stout oak timbers
might have defied sledge hammers, yet fire would
find a way to let the next rush in. It was this danger
which had prompted me to give the gatehouse to the
keeping of the strongest of the kindreds and which
kept me here now till the first rush should be beaten
back.

Just as I had reckoned, so it happened. I was
standing in the chamber, telling the archers to hold
their shafts till they were sure of their shots, when
with a new and greater shout a wild cluster of the
outlaws came charging for the walls. Then was the
moon our enemy, shining squarely against this front
wall, for it showed the windows in it so plainly that
the best bowmen of the foe kept up a stream of
arrows, aiming always for them, so that no man
of us durst stand at any gap to shoot but straightway
he should be pinned and skewered with more shafts
than a fowl for the spit. We could but stand side-
ways against the wall, waiting till their spearmen

should come below, the only place where we might get a shot in return.

The archers who shot so hotly at us were the men of Foulk of the Feet, but the spearmen who rushed to the attack were the men of Jevor Cutta, famous for the endless wiles that made his name a terror. Cunning as ever, each man came running, bent and crouching, and holding before him on the point of his spear a close bound faggot of brushwood, long and broad enough to cover him like a shield, and thick enough to stop a shaft from the stoutest bow. Neither did they come close under the walls, but from a distance with a mighty heave they tossed the faggots towards the gate, and though most of them fell wide or short, yet there were enough landed against the timbers to burn it through when light should be set to them.

Lastly came three, the swiftest of them all, who must trust only to their speed, for they carried their faggots loose and blazing.

Here was the moment that should test us. " Shoot ! shoot !" I cried, and every man knew what depended on it.

Then with a proud word on his lips one youth sprang forward to shoot and save us, but his half-drawn bow twanged the shaft idly out, for he fell dead, with three shafts through him, before he had well stiffened to shoot. Another and another stood to the fatal loophole, only to fall like him, and then a grey old archer, with his breath full drawn and his bow bent till the barb nigh rested on his knuckles, threw his foot over the first corpse and looked out.

The pitiless hail of arrows struck him to death, but, slain though he was, he did not waver as he

stood, a dead man, holding back his soul from flight
between his locked teeth till he should see and shoot.
His bow twanged ; the first of the three torchbearers
fell ; a smile came over the old archer's set face ; and
in that smile his ghost went out into the night and
there was another corpse in the room with us.

He had not altogether saved us, but he had heart-
ened us, and straightway as he fell his own son stood
across his body and with a fierce cast of his javelin
slew a second of the flame-bringers, so that his fire,
too, sputtered idly out of reach of the faggots, while
the lad who had dropped him stood back, unharmed
and whole.   The third however, light as the roe and
headlong as an eagle, had reached the gate ; dashed
his blazing burden down in the midst of the pile,
turned, and was gone, before another spear could be
cast.   Neither was any shaft drawn upon him as he
went swiftly back.   He did well.

Just then the chief of kin came up to see why the
blood dripped through the boards upon him as he
went to and fro below.   He looked inside at the dead
and he looked outside at the fire just catching in
front of the door—" Aye," said he, " I fear we be
but dead man in this gate."

" Are we ? " returned I, a new thought flashing
through me.   " I am a forfeit man already.   I may
do this then at least."   The arrows had ceased now
that the fire was burning, and in a twinkling I had
squeezed through the narrow middle window and
dropped to the ground outside.   I worked like a
madman tearing the piled faggots aside ; kicking
them, casting them, dragging them—even a spear's
length away was far enough—so that they should not
set the door to burning.

I heard a wild clamour of shouting from the outlaws when they realized what I was doing, but the
smoke of the blazing faggots rose thick and curling
betwixt me and them; too thick for them to see me
plainly or to take good aim. That was well, but in
a gasp or two I felt different; better be slain by
arrows than die of the smoke like this. I had begun
to stagger, my eyes were burning in my head and my
groping hands were reaching blindly towards the
flame, when at that moment the wicket in the great
gate opened behind me.

"Here!" shouted a voice, and as I spun round the
old chieftain dashed out, seized me, dragged me in,
and the wicket was banged and barred again, all in
the taking of a breath. I had escaped with no more
than singed hose and an arrow through the fleshy
part of the thigh, though my armolet coat was stuck
so full of shafts that I feared some bard would see
and name me "the hedgehog" for evermore.

"Sir," said the old chief as he cut off the barb
and drew the shaft out of my thigh, "that was a deed
to tell of. You have saved us."

"Have I? Then remember it to me if ever
you see me without a friend in time to come," answered I.

"Shall we forget it; my kin or I?" demanded he
with rising warmth. "We are all gathered here in
this gatehouse, men, women, and children; youngest
and oldest we are all here. A young man, as thou art,
might have escaped in the hurly of the fight, but not
we, having our families with us. Nay, we shall never
see thee lacking a friend, for thou art a kinsman to us
and upon the privilege of kin from this day forth as
long as the kin endures."

"Aye, but that will hardly do to stand by, for except to you I am a redhand," answered I.

"What of that? Foulk of the Feet would have had us cheap but for thee," persisted he. "If thou art a redhand then our hands too shall be red before any avenger take thee. Yea!" he went on, stretching his hand towards me : "I am the chief of my kin, but thou shalt swear me by what token thou wilt that we will keep this compact with thee."

"Nay," said I, though he had touched me to the quick : "you cannot swear that, for you be men of this Castell March, and to-day the Lady Nerys married Brynglas. He is your lord now and you cannot admit me to the privilege of kin without his consent."

"Aye?" responded he warmly : "but I say that even if he were our lord now, as you think he is, I would still count kin where I will, without the leave of him or any other. A lord is a lord, and his rights and his dues and privileges are known in the laws, but I am a chief of a kin, and the lord may not go below me and meddle with the kin——"

He would have said more, and proudly too, but I was eager to follow one point. "I have told you that the Lady Nerys was married to Brynglas this morning—how then do you say that he is not lord of this castle?"

"Because the lady herself was not lord of this castle when she married him," replied he stubbornly.

"Then who is?" demanded I at once.

"The man who was born to it ; and a man indeed he was," answered the old man. "Aye," he went on, warming as the words came ; "if only he had not cared so much for the sea! But the first thing he did

was to build a tall ship—it was the lands of gold and
the tall ships that carry the treasure to the king of
Spain that fired him.    And that is why the kindreds
of Castell March are so few men to-day : he ever took
as many of his own people as he could.   And so it
went on till at last, twelve years ago or so, he was
wrecked and drowned in the Western Indies "—here
he stopped a moment and shook his head.

" Aye ?" said I to move him to continue.   " And
what then ?"

" What then ?   Then his cousin, son to his father's
brother, came here in his stead.   That cousin was
father to this present Brynglas, but he had an elder
brother, who suddenly sailed home from being long
lost, and the elder ousted the younger and was lord
here in place of the drowned.   He died here two years
ago, having no son but only one daughter, the Lady
Nerys, whom he had brought back with him when he
came home.   She succeeded him.   And that is why
Brynglas wanted her to wife, that he might have the
estate his father had been put out of.   His mother
ruled him to do it though."

" But," said I :  " if the born lord of the castle be
drowned, then how do you say that the Lady Nerys is
not lady of it now by inheritance ?"

" Because the drowned lord was not drowned, and
because before the day breaks he will be here to take
up his lordship again," rejoined the old chieftain
triumphantly.

" Did you learn this from the captain ?" demanded
I quickly.   " Is this what made you so ready to his
nod to-day ?"

" It was the captain who brought the news," answered he simply.

" But did he show you proof ; are you sure that
there is no mistake and that the lost lord is alive and
well ? "

He smiled a little at that. " Wait but this one
night," he said, " and you will be sure also, for you
yourself shall see him in the flesh, with your own
eyes."

I was thrown back into a tangle again. This
chieftain told me that the rightful lord was coming
back to-night ; the captain had promised to bring him,
though he had been so long believed to be drowned
off the Spanish Main. The Lady Nerys, however,
also expected the captain to bring back with him a
man who had been betrayed from a room in this very
house. Further, she had never seen the lost lord of
the place, for she had only come here as a child from
the dim outer world when her father sailed home to
oust his younger brother.

There must be two men returning then. One, the
oversea prisoner whom she loved, and whom she had
desired to marry that he might have the lands of
Castell March in recompense for his betrayal—perhaps
at her father's hands—and another, the rightful lord,
who by resuming his rights would strip her of all
and leave her therefore unable to recompense the
other man, even when Brynglas should be slain out
of the way.

Yet, stay ; the two men who were coming home
might in some strange way have become friends, and
that might be the captain's real reason for desiring
that the lady should marry Brynglas. For after
Brynglas was killed, then his wife would be owner
of Castle Vortigern and all its lands, she being his
cousin as well as then his widow. Thus she could

still recompense that lover. Aye ; clearly there must
be two of them returning. Yet whether there were
two or one or none I saw that my dream of the Lady
'Nerys was dust and ashes now. The Ooronoka was
my only hope henceforth.

And that brought me back to the captain himself.
Who was he and what was his quarrel with Brynglas ?
I could not guess. All I could do was to resolve to
work with him readily in future and make his quarrel
mine. Then we would rescue that captive lady, and
the little elfin boy.

And after that—the Ooronoka.

## CHAPTER XXIV.

### CRY DOOM TO NANT VORTIGERN!

I HAD fallen silent while trying to straighten out the tangle, until presently it struck me to ask the old chieftain who the captain was, and whether he was foster kin to the lord of Castell March, or any other kin which would explain his interest in it. My chance was gone however, for the first word of the question had hardly left my lips when a new and greater shout went up about us. "They come! They come!"

Instantly the old chief went springing up the stair again, I after him, for the prick in my thigh was still warm, so that I did not limp at all yet. In the loft the smoke of the scattered faggots was rolling in through the open windows so thick that I was forced to stop and stoop to gasp for breath. Not so the old chief, he stood upright, looking at the men crouching with their faces to the floor for air. "For shame!" he shouted; "I have seen a worse smoke than this in the hall at Christmas and you sat and laughed over the ale then. Up! do you not hear? they come!"

Sheepishly they stood to their feet again—they had but wanted rousing—and some put the shutters to the windows, for the new attack was not in front;

234

the fire prevented that.  But as we rushed to the loopholes in the north end of the chamber we saw that the breeze was drifting the smoke across the plateau, and the outlaws had seen their chance in it at once.

On they rushed, only their spear points, fantastically tall, flashing in the moonlight above the rolling smoke to show their coming.  Not till they were within javelin cast of the wall did their bodies leap into view, and then at last I saw well why the blades of their spears were so long and the barbs splayed out so wide.  For as each man came to the wall he lifted his twelve foot spear full length above his head and set one barb like a hook on the top of the wall. Then with a high, quick spring he swarmed up the shaft to the top and was ready to leap within.

One man alone of them was mounted, Foulk of the Feet himself, but an arrow from one of the men at my elbow shot the horse dead in his stride, and the shock of the fall stunned the terrible rider, stretching him out like a corpse himself.

As if that had been a signal, straightway all the chamber and the loft above was alive with the whipping twang of the bows, as from every loop and window hole the archers plied their shafts.  We knew by the din and the shouts that every side was beset, but on this front was the real onset, as we saw ; the rest were not meant just yet.

" Keep the archers to it ; I am for the yard ! " I shouted in the old man's ear, and then, with drawn glaive and buckler in front, I dashed down the stair to head the press of those who fought in the yard against the stark thieves dropping from the wall.

But to win so far had turned the outlaws into mad-

236 THE LADY OF CASTELL MARCH.

men, drunk with half-victory. Starkly I drave a way to the front of the fight. Yet that grey shadow of the high walls seemed to vomit new demons in clusters, while they seemed also to rain down from above so quick that for a moment my throat stuck fast with a sudden dread that they would win after all.

Then however came help—help that was the better worth because it was so strange. For the women, who had been boiling great pots of porridge for their men, to keep them better awake for the watching, now suddenly snatched up their pots and with their ladles flung the boiling stuff into the faces of the swarming thieves. Front and rear flew the scalding mess, and the fellow behind or in the midst got as much as one in front. Their eyes were blistered out of their heads and in their agony they flung their weapons down, stooping and running blindly to and fro, shrieking in pain. And there we slew them as they ran, for we had no time to hang them as prisoners.

Yet it was strange, thought I, that no more of their number followed over the wall to help them, even though the archers in the lofts shot so closely, and stranger still that such a sudden quiet should fall on all. There was a stairway next the barn to give access to the wall top, and I darted up to see what was happening outside.

The reason was plain at once. No need for peering or craning of the neck. Broad from the west, the moonlight dancing on their steel coats and caps as on the rippling surface of a wanton river, marched with steady step a stark battalia of as goodly men as ever shook weapon in the field of war. Nine score at least they were, their sixteen foot pikes level in front of them as they advanced across the plateau—

small wonder that the first glint of their line should paralyse the outlaw, shout on lip, hand on weapon, foot lifted in charging ; and little marvel if, at the next breath, Eivl and Dolbadarn men alike should break into shouts of dismay and fly like startled deer away to the north and the nearest mountain.

Barefoot and half naked, the redhands were swifter in the broken land than any mounted men that could have followed, so they went unpursued, while all my own attention was absorbed in watching our unexpected allies, as they marched after the captain towards our gates.

A sharp shout from the gatehouse chamber startled me, and, turning swiftly to look that way, my eye in its passage caught the reason. Foulk of the Feet, rousing from where his fallen horse had thrown him, had risen on his haunches and with his short bow bent in front of his chest was drawing a heavy shaft up to the barb against me. Instantly I stooped, holding my target in front to ward the shaft, but even so the shock of its striking staggered me a step backward.

That step found only space ; I had forgotten that this was only a narrow wall and not broad earth. I remember the myriad stars that flashed as I struck the ground in falling, and then I remember no more for awhile. I was senseless.

When I came to myself again I was lying quietly in the gatehouse, made comfortable on some heather and blankets, while by the light of the torches I recognized the face of the old chieftain as he sat on the ground beside me. Two or three wounded men were lying at the other end of the room, and a cow had been led in that her milk might be given to them fresh and warm for the renewing of their blood. All their wounds, too, were fully bandaged; everything in fact went to show that I must have lain a long time, perhaps an hour, unconscious.

Next I saw the captain enter, with soft foot and anxious face; at which my brain stirred itself a little, for the bandage was gone and the face of the man was open to be seen. Coming to where I lay he knelt beside me, first looking closely at me and then saying something across to the chieftain on the other side. But he spoke in a language not Welsh; a strange language, which yet I had heard before; heard, as I presently remembered, from the poor captive in the castle of Brynglas. Straightway my confused mind flashed the thought into speech— "Why, that is the same language as Madre Mia's."

For an instant the words startled both of them. Then a glad smile, half a laugh indeed, broke over the captain's bold, high features. Taking my hand in his, "Ah! Rowland," he cried, "thy wits are wandering yet. 'Madre Mia'—what knowest thou of such a word? Thou wert born of a good Welsh mother I'll warrant, while madre mia is Spanish, and means, 'mother mine.'"

"Oh," answered I, "then that is why the captive gentlewoman taught the little lad to call her Madre Mia. I thought it was her name and so does the boy. And that is why she could not understand what I said to her. She speaks only Spanish; poor prisoner!"

The smile froze in the captain's face as I watched it. His eyes were gleaming like burnished steel into mine and his voice was fierce with eagerness as he said hoarsely, "What prisoner? What little lad?"

"The little elfin lad that crouches by the hearth in the hall of Castle Vortigern. And the lady hath been a captive in the witch's tower for years. He steals food for her and she taught him to call her Madre Mia."

I broke off, not for lack of words, but because the captain's grasp was suddenly crushing my hand out of shape. "Go on!" he half shouted. But I was fain to seize his grip with my other hand—"You are mangling my fingers," cried I.

"Ah!" he looked down as if to see whether his hand had hold of anything. "Aye!" he said, opening his grasp and holding my crushed hand now as if it were a little wounded bird. Nay, in the tumult of his mind a sudden weakness seemed to sap his nature and for a flash I thought he would have kissed the hand, as a mother kisses that of her little child to make it better of a baby hurt.

Snatching it away I spoke on. "The little lad was taking some food to her that night—last night was it not?—when I was a prisoner in the chamber at Brynglas. I saw him give it to her, and I saw that she delighted more in him than in the food. So after he was gone I got down through the window to give her some money, but she was frightened and closed the shutter against me. Then I heard a great cry as if she were being tortured and I hammered on the shutter, and when it was opened and I saw the hideous face of that damnable hag, mother to Brynglas, I drove the spear at her and cut the fillet from her head : the fillet that you fastened round your neck."

"Aye! aye!"—he clutched the jewel under his collar where it lay, but he bent his face still nearer into mine, and the agony of hope in his voice struck me to the heart as he went on. " Aye ! aye ! but why did she teach the little lad to call her mother ? Did he say she was his mother ?  Why did she ?——"

" He said that she was not his mother for he had none," answered I.  " But I think what moved her to it was a mark that is under his left arm, the scar of a cross, for she turned him about till she could see it, and while she patted and petted it she made him repeat the words every time she touched it."

The captain did not answer to me, but he tore the fillet from about his neck and held it across me towards the old chieftain.  " Is it her ? " he gasped, his eyes blazing and his voice choking.  " I gave her this jewel myself ; but the mark ! the mark ! under the left armpit ; the mark of the cross !——"

" Yea ; it was the cross," I put in.  And—" I think it is she," answered the old chief steadily.

Like an eagle the captain turned to me again. " Let me be sure ! " he cried, " O God, let me be sure !  Tell me what she is like.  Is she as beautiful as midnight under the stars ?  Does she move as stately as a white-winged ship across a summer sea ? Hath she all that woman ever had to draw men's hearts out after her ?——"

" You do forget," broke I in pity.  " She hath been captive year upon year to the cruel she-devil of Nant Vortigern.  White she is and wasted to the bone, yet still she showeth a gentlewoman to see."

He stood straight up to his feet, his hands clenched out before him, his face white to the iron lips.  Up to full stretch he swelled, spreading his chest above us till he seemed broad as a door.  Then smiting his breast he broke forth into words, "Dolores! Dolores! wife, my wife! O God!"

With that, suddenly, as if all hell were tearing him, his voice came in a roar of rage. "After me! after me! We will burn Nant Vortigern with fire; we will pour the sea into it and wash it down to the bare rock: we will overturn the mountains into it and fill it up!"—he choked; he mumbled; wagging his head like a palsied man; all his joints loose and moving; his frenzy shaking him from head to foot as if a devil shook him with red-hot pincers.

Then he stopped, all in a breath standing as still as stone. Next he turned and his voice came husky as an old man's. "After me!" he choked out thickly, and with his bloodshot eyes sweeping the room over his shoulder he strode out, shaking aloft in his hand, not the sword his mind imagined, but the broken fillet with its jewel gleaming in the smoky light.

And out in the courtyard we heard him hungrily repeat, "After me! after me!"

16

# CHAPTER XXV.

WITHOUT another thought I rose to follow the captain, so much moved that I was up and standing shakily on my feet before I remembered that I was supposed to be hurt. With that I took a step or two to try my bones, and right glad I was to find that I had escaped with no worse than some very sore bruises on my body and a great swelling on the back of my head which caused me to stagger somewhat giddily as I walked. Beyond this the arrow hole in my thigh was beginning to be a little stiff and sore, but I minded that the less in that I should in any case have had to ride, and not march, to this attack on Nant Vortigern.

Then I saw again how long a time I must have lain unconscious, for when I emerged into the courtyard I found that all the bodies of the slain had been removed, and all the men of the defenders had looked their fill on the captain and were well in hand again. Here now at his shout they were ranging themselves in proper order to march with him, mounted, however, not on their own wiry little nags, but upon the goodly steeds which theretofore had served the household men of the Lady Nerys. Seeing me standing there, one of them led forward my own roan that had

242

carried me from the church, and immediately I mounted, for luckily it was my right thigh that was pricked and not my left.

My head was still singing ; it felt half the size and all the weight of a tower, and the sudden lift in mounting caused me to wander a little in my mind again. The old chief, however, saw that and, being now mounted himself, his kindly arm steadied me in the saddle for a minute or two while the rest filed out of the gate after the captain. By this time my mind came again and we set forward also, but at the gate I drew rein, for I saw that the company which the captain had led to our rescue was now marching away after him with the rest.

" Who, then, is going to keep this castle and protect the Lady Nerys while we are gone ? " demanded I.

" We shall protect her," returned the chieftain : " we shall do it in the surest way—by attacking the enemy at home. Are not our own wives and little ones left here, too ? Besides, the lady hath her own household men left to her. They have their bows, and it is truth that they shot well this night—better than most of us looked for," ended he heartily.

" Aye, but in that case I want to speak with her a moment before I go," said I. " And you had better ride fast after the captain, for he is marching yonder without his head. I will overtake you presently."

The chieftain smiled, yet he went readily enough while I turned and rode back again across the court-yard to the hall. The door stood wide open ; the light of many torches shone within, and without thinking further of what I would do I pressed my horse through and rode hazily on up the hall ; for my first dazzled glance had shown me a picture that

drew me forward as surely as a rope might have
done.

In the midst of the room, a pace back from the
edge of the dais, stood the Lady Nerys, where my
entrance had caused her to halt on her way as she
was coming. Her ruddy officers, now pale but glad,
held up their torches about her head, making a halo
of her shining hair, while behind her crowded the
thirty archers whom I had degraded.

Resentment was in all the faces of the men and
many a murmur broke from them until their mistress
with a lift of her white hand commanded them to
silence. But I troubled nothing about them, I had
eyes only for that rare vision which she made, standing there in the light of the torches. The chief's
words came up in my mind hazily—"She never was
lord of this castle, the rightful lord will be here before the dawn."

Looking at her there, dazed as I was, I wondered if
she knew yet that she was now no longer the lady of
the castle. Then more of my memory came to me
and I remembered how she had told me that the
prisoner from oversea was to have returned also before the day broke. A great desire came over me to
know if he were here and, if so, why he had so soon
allowed her to escape from his company? And my
blurred mind had no other thought than to put the
question bluntly to her. "Hath the prisoner returned?" said I, my clouded brain not dreaming of
discourtesy.

She had been ivory white before, she went milk-
white now, and had my senses been clearer my eye
must have understood that she winced under the
words. But blurred and all I yet could see the dis-

dain that was in every line of her as she drew herself
up before answering : " You have before boasted
that you were a redhand.  I have not questioned your
word ; there is no need therefore for you to prove
yourself a cowardly lout as well."

"A cowardly lout ! "  Some futile anger clouded
my dizzy senses still thicker as I tried to decide what
the speech meant.  Moreover the effort to think
caused me to lurch a little, so that I leaned forward
and steadied myself by resting my arms on the saddle
bow.  " How ?—yes, I am a redhand," said I thickly,
my mind falling back to that as one clear point.

Then, as she remained silent, only looking at me
with cold scorn, I roused a little.  " I forgot.  I came
to tell you that the captain and all the men of the
kindreds have started for Nant Vortigern ; so I turned
back to tell your household men that they were to
defend you and the women and children in the castle
till we came back."

"Aye, to defend us," returned she with cutting
disdain.  "After you have stripped and disarmed
them you leave them to defend me and tell them to
guard the castle."

"What ! there is no danger," retorted I with hazy
stubbornness ; " they have their bows and they shot
well to-night.  They will do.  If I thought there was
danger I would send back a company of the captain's
men or one of the kindreds."

A sudden gust of anger moved her.  " Why did
not the captain, as you call him, come to me himself
instead of sending you ?  Go and tell him to guard
his castle with his own men, I'll none of it——"

" He did not send me ; I came of myself," interrupted I, not clearly noting the latter part of her

words. "The captain hath gone to rescue his wife ; could you expect him, then, to remember anything else in the moment when he first found that his wife was still alive, a captive through long years ?"

My face had fallen forward so that I was not watching her as I spoke, but I heard her repeat under her breath : "His wife !"

"Yea," I went on, looking up. "He is like a madman at finding that she is still alive ; he hath loved and mourned her these many years as I guess. But I must go if I am to catch them in time. Good-night," and so I turned round and rode out of the hall, and I have wondered often since that no man of them put an arrow through me as I went.

At the gate I found a lusty man of the tenant kin ; well mounted—the old chieftain had sent him back to guide me and bring me safe up with the captain, and verily the man proved a great help to me, for in my numbskull state at starting I must of a surety have gone wandering aimlessly across all Lleyn, perhaps to perish miserably in some marsh.

The cool air of the hour before the dawn helped me, however, so that what with that and a wet cloth upon my head, which cloth we dipped afresh at every stream, my mind was clear again by the time we came up with the rest.

Afoot and heavily armed as they were, the shipmen could march but slowly, and the state of the captain's mind was shown by his being so far in front. He would have ridden on alone with his own sword but that the seamen would obey no other than himself.

When I reached the side of the old chieftain again, recollection of his words in the gatehouse flashed

upon me.  " You said the lord of Castell March was
to come home before the dawn.   Did he come ? "

" You should know.   Yonder he is," answered the
chieftain, pointing ahead in the moonlight to the
captain.

" The captain ! " was all I could answer.

Then my mind went back and I remembered that
the sword which the captain was wearing when he
knelt beside me in the gatehouse was not the one ho
had aforetime worn.   Yet it was one I had seen before ; it was that long and costly blade which had
been lying half-drawn, with its hilt upon the open
book of the translation.   It was the sword which
waited the return of its former master, the prisoner
oversea.   A light struggled into my mind—" And is
he the oversea prisoner, too ? " I asked the chieftain.

" Did you know then that he was a prisoner in
Spain ? " demanded he, turning in his saddle to look
squarely at me.

" We did not know," he went on, while I held
dumb.   " We thought him always dead till you
brought him in a prisoner yesterday.   How did you
·come to know the one and yet not the other also ; that
he was the lord of Castell March as well as oversea
prisoner ? "

" I did not know the other either," answered I and
then again fell silent for awhile.   For I remembered
now how the Lady Nerys had bidden me go back and
tell the captain to guard his castle with his own men.

She knew all, then : knew that the prisoner from
oversea was lord also of this castle which she had
thought her own and which she had looked forward
to bestowing upon him with her hand in marriage.
Yea, I was silent now, for I was seeing again in my

mind that picture of her in the torchlit hall ; disin-
herited and disillusioned ; all her dreams shattered
at her feet, standing with her disarmed and disgraced
retainers, to listen to me thickly telling her that the
captain could not be expected to remember her at
the moment when he was mad to rescue his long-lost
wife.

Well might she think me a cowardly lout, though
I, in truth, spoke innocently, by reason of the blow
upon my head.

# CHAPTER XXVI.

PRESENTLY, however, my thoughts came to a check. If the captain had disappeared by supposed drowning in the Spanish Seas, before Nerys ever came here, then how had she fallen in love with him —a man she never saw ?

Again, he had disappeared at sea : the man she loved had been betrayed from a room of Castell March. Above all, if the man she loved had been the captain, she would have recognised him from the first : love can see through thicker things than linen bandages.

No, there were still two men, and of the two only one had come home. The prisoner oversea was still a prisoner, and the sea was still between him and the woman who loved him. The explanation must be that the captain and she had misunderstood each other, whereby she had been misled into expecting that the prisoner whom she loved was to have returned with him, whereas he spoke of himself only. The incident of the sword must have been a mistake.

Yet she was still in pitiful case, for now she could not endow the prisoner with Castell March even if he did return. Also she had no means left of seeking him out, or of keeping her archers, unless indeed

Nant Vortigern should prove, after we had slain Brynglas, to be more than a mere den of thieves.

All the while as I rode I could not take my mind from dwelling upon her, till anon I could hold no longer, but asked the chieftain to give me a man to carry a message back to Castell March from me.

He chose again the same one who had guided me, whereby I perceived that the man had the reputation of being discreet. This pleased me greatly; so much indeed that I amended my intention. I had purposed to pluck a spring of the heather, with a sprig of the gorse and a tuft of the white cotton grass, to send them to her for a token with my message. But now I would do more.

Daylight was stealing wide about us like a wan, ghostly tide as I took the man aside till the rest had gone on. Plucking then the sprays I fastened them in front of my armolet jacket. " Seest thou these three ? " said I. " Go now back to Castell March and the Lady Nerys. Greet her from me and tell her that I have just for the first time learnt that the captain is that lord of the place who was supposed to be drowned. Tell her that I now understand what it was I said and did in the hall, and that I pray her to pardon it. And because it still remains to rescue the prisoner oversea, say that I am ready and eager—aye, eager—to fulfil the quest I promised to her yesterday as we rode through the waste from the church of Aelhaiarn.

" And for a token to myself I have plucked these three plants that grow in the waste where my promise was made. Before they have time to wither I shall have returned to her, ready to start on my voyage. And for a token to her—here," I went on, taking

the hair above my forehead and parting one goodly
lock in front from the rest ; " cut this lock and give
it to her ; so shall I be her servant till I have done
the thing I promised."

Taking my proffered knife he cut the hair close to
my head ; leaving a bare spot there whereby all men
might know me for a man shorn and sworn. Then
he wrapped the tress around the haft of the knife and
so bore both away in his hand southward to do that
errand.

I would liever have been my own ambassador, but
I could not turn back from this ride against Nant
Vortigern. Moreover, my heart was lighter of a
heavy load now that I had sent back so patient a
protestation of renewed faith to her.

Daylight was full and broad by the time that this
was ended, and as I lifted my rein to overtake the
men again I saw that it was time to rouse the captain from his befogging madness of murderous desire,
and make him show us somewhat of his captaining.
His shipmen had marched from the Dinllaen on the
west coast across to Castell March on the east, and
now without food had marched almost an equal distance back again, while from the direction taken it
seemed as though the captain intended them to continue on to the Eivl itself.

This would have been double folly. To begin
with, men clad in steel from the knees up would no
more be fit to fight than to fly by the time they had
struggled through the heather of the Eivl. While,
even supposing we did win the head of the valley,
then the outlaws had merely to take to their shallops
and so escape clean out of our hands by sea, carrying
their prisoner with them. Moreover to leave the

ship itself out of the attack was to waste the power of
her great ordnance, and I had a keen recollection of
how much I had dreaded those same guns yesterday,
when I took in hand the defence of the castle behind
us while thinking that the captain was my enemy.
The walls of Castle Vortigern had been built to stand
any siege and all but the largest cannon.  A ship's
great guns might open us a way into it ; nothing less
would.

Putting my horse to speed I passed the labouring
seamen, and presently overtook the captain just as
his horse hesitated at a marshy strip, doubtless wondering why its rider took no heed of its thus being
brought to a stand.

I was at his right elbow before he noticed me, and
as he turned his face my way all the glory of the
dawn, shining full into it, could not soften the fierce
hunger for battle and murder that made it grim to
see.   That which in other dangers and former adventures had been quiet firmness, cool steadfastness,
was now pitiless ferocity which would have spared
no single thing alive betwixt him and his present
purpose.   His bloodshot eyes blinked impatiently at
me as he questioned me with sharp peevishness—
" Aye ; aye ? "

But I had no set speech, and the change in him
took me so much aback that I could only blurt out ;
" Your shipmen, sir, are beginning to tire.   They
have marched all night, afoot and in heavy armour ;
they should rest now and take breakfast if they are
to be fit to fight at all."

" Rest ! " he  broke out impatiently ; " and food !
What is this march across Lleyn in the cool of the
night to them !—to the men who marched over

mountains and through forests; swimming rivers and wading neck deep across tropic marshes, following me to the sack of Nombre Dios ? [1]   And if they stop now then all these rogues of the damned crew of Nant Vortigern will have gotten back to their fastness and be ready to beat us off.   A beaten foe must be followed and his stronghold captured before he can take heart and rally again."

I saw how much his rage must have upset his brain when he could talk so of following these nimble outlaws.  "Nay, sir, consider.  We are not yet more than half way there, while you know well that the slowest of the outlaws is not only safe at home by this time, but hath before now bandaged his hurts with linen and comforted his heart with a good breakfast.

"Moreover, unless we attack both ends of the Nant at the same time, you with the ship from the sea and I with the kindreds from the highland, we shall do only harm.  If we all fall on at the head of the valley then they will escape to sea, carrying your wife and child with them."

"By sea they could not escape," burst he.  "The sea to its farthest edge is no more to me than the palm of my hand.  I know it from rim to rim.  It hath no thick forests or savage rocks ; no high mountains or deep valleys for them to hide in.  They could not pass out of my hand."

"But they could kill your wife and your son before your eyes if you brought them to a stand," retorted I

[1] It was another Welsh buccaneer—Sir Henry Morgan, to wit—who made the final sack of that famous stronghold, under circumstances which showed the race of buccaneers at their best and worst in one.—ED.

boldly. "Consider," I urged : "consider what you do. Are you set forth now only for vengeance on an enemy, or to rescue your wife and son ? "

He caught his breath with a snap and let it go with an oath of savage rage. Twice he opened his lips to begin a fierce reply and twice he shut them, dumb again with passionate wrath. The words were in his breast to damn and defy my promptings of good, but they did not come ; they stuck in his throat instead, while his red eyes for a full minute looked burning into mine. The question had struck home to his vitals and all the fume and spume of his anger could not down his recovering reason. At last, in a thick, hoarse voice, he snapped out, "Thou art my friend ; my true friend indeed in that question. But—I could with joy put thee to the torture for it."

He turned his face from me northward to the Eivl again, and rebellious grief, passionate love, and surging hate stirred him to the bottom of his soul as he burst out again. "Wife ; my wife ! in the power of that hell-hag all these years. Dolores ! Dolores ! had they foreknowledge of what should be when they christened thee Dolores ! Dolour indeed hath been thine—but I will end it now and soon ! "

In his torment of torrent feelings he kept his face away from me, still to the north, for a long, long five minutes, fighting the battle with himself for mastery over his hungering rage. I had put up my hand for a warning to those behind and the old chieftain had halted his men from the first. I kept my breath ; I sat my horse as still as if we were but painted man and horse. I hardly dared to blink lest I should dis-turb that good fight within his breast.

And at last I had my reward, for he let the breath

out of his rigid body in a great sigh that told of
victory won.   Rage was in him still to do vengeance
upon those who had so foully dealt by his wife, but
love for her and fear for her safety were now over all.
He would be the cool, compelling captain again presently, and we should win.

In his weakening mood the habit of his prison soli-
tude came back upon him and he began to murmur
his thoughts aloud to himself, but still so low that
with his deep voice I could not catch the words.
Yet by the cadence I knew that love and grief were
in his mouth and I was glad, for next he would pass
to plotting out the manner of rescuing her he loved.
True enough he presently fell to silence and, picking
up his rein, began to press his horse to cross the
marshy breadth in front of which I had found him
halted.

The horse, however, mistrustful of the footing,
went no more than his own length before he planted
his hoofs stubbornly on the edge of a strip of clear
brown water, scarcely a half leap across had it been
good ground beyond.   Pressed again, he snorted and
looked about this way and that for some other place
of crossing, thus showing that the other side was a
quagmire.   And I was glad to note that the captain,
though he would not believe till he had looked for
himself, yet refrained from spurring or in any other
way punishing the nag for his refusal.   It showed
that his mind was clearing again, though at the
same time his looking so steadfastly in front and not
glancing hawklike to right and left for a better spot
betrayed him still pensive.

In no hurry, he measured the yonder side with his
eye and then looked down at this side, where the wet

was rising round the fore hoofs of his horse as he stood waiting and anxious to scramble away. Yet the rider still lingered, looking down as if probing the water with his eye for some sign of firm bottom. Then he started a little and began to pull his beard about, now this way and now that, watching the effect on his reflection in the water below.

With that he began again to speak his thoughts aloud, this time clear enough to catch. "Aye; a beard. It maketh a marvellous difference in the aspect of a man. And I was twice as old as she then, yet looked much younger than I was. Now I look old enough to frighten her. And she told me often and often that she liked not a beard on a man, save the upper lip. I must get to the ship and shave myself and put on some better apparel, or she will not know me, neither trust me for being in truth the man she loved."

With that he sat up straight in the saddle again and turned his horse about to the firm ground. Then, not dreaming that I had heard his words, he looked me in the face with all the frankness in the world. "Aye, Rowland, I am thy debtor for stopping me," said he. "We will divide; the kindreds to go with thee to the mountains and my mariners with me to Dinllaen and the ship again. But we must march together till we come to Morva Nevin, for we all need breakfast, one as well as another. Nant Vortigern will not be won on empty stomachs." He was become the old cool commander again: he was going to his ship—but he had not said openly that it was to shave himself and change his apparel.

A single sweep of his eagle eye to right and left and then he turned his horse for a passage further

west.   Gladly I picked up my rein to keep alongside
him ; a glance over my shoulder showing me that the
men behind were in motion again to follow.   We
should do well now.

17

# CHAPTER XXVII.

## THE LORD OF CASTELL MARCH.

CROSSING at the new place we rode on at a foot-pace in silence till presently the captain turned suddenly to me. " The little lad, sayest thou ? Was that the little one that sat in the hall ? Is he my son ? "

" Yea," answered I ; " the one you wrapped in your own cloak to sleep with you on the threshold, that morning when we took the Lady Nerys prisoner to Brynglas."

A smile pitiful to see lit all his dark face at the words, and his mouth was soft as a woman's as he broke out. " Aye, he did sleep in my cloak ; did he not ? And he smiled too as he slept. I wonder if he knew : I wonder if he felt anything. I had his head on my arm ; he looked so pretty a little lad. He is a pretty boy, is he not ? the prettiest I ever saw."

I was brought to a stand. To think of him ; his father's new found feelings cheating him into fond memories of that unconscious moment—so pitiful it was I knew not what to say. Already he was crowding his horse to a faster pace and his eye began to burn again. " Aye, he is a pretty boy," I burst out desperately : " but he is more. He is the bravest boy that ever a mother dreamed on. Sir, when I think
258

of him, helping me because he thought I was going to release his mother, I feel like a branded man. And he showed me the food he had hidden for her. Sir, sir !——"

I picked at my rein fumblingly : I dared not go on to speak of all the lad's starving of himself that he might feed that prisoner who knew herself his mother, though he knew her only for a prisoner, whom he loved because she had none other friend on earth save him.

And I thought of her, she knowing him for her child ; her little son ; feeding her hungry heart on him ; watching and waiting for his visits ; spending her love in words he could not understand ; teaching him to call her "mother," and yet knowing while she listened that he knew not what he said—I thought of all this and I dared not look at the captain as I ended—"Thank God, we will soon have them free."

I was staring straight ahead, but at once I felt his hand upon my arm, while his voice came fierce and husky, "Rowland, thy cheek is wet——?"

I shot one glance at him. His lip was quivering under his beard and the tears stood in his burning eyes. "Tell me ! tell me all, Rowland. Remember it is my wife and my little son. I will be thy debtor for ever if thou tell me now." And if his entreaty had not moved me to speak, I saw by his face that he would soon have taken other means. Never a wolf's fangs gleamed hungrier than did the white teeth between his parted lips.

Hurriedly I went over the story, furtively watching him from the corner of my eye as I spoke on, and wishing that he would draw out some flask or other and wet his mouth with that, instead of licking

his parched lips with a dry tongue and wiping them
with the iron gauntlet that covered his sword hand.
And when I was done, to the last word, he broke the
fever of his silence with a string of incoherent words,
not blasphemy, neither any oaths, but a long rolling
moan of desire that could finish no phrase or sentence
of the wild thoughts that burned in his soul like hot
irons.

At last—"Thank God, your spear only broke the
fillet and did not kill that hell-hag before her time.
Oh ! to think that I stood there with only a wall between me and the wife I would give my soul to free
if no better could be !  And my little son, whom I
had never seen in life ; I had him sleeping on my
arm and in my cloak and did not know it !"

A little while we rode in another silence, and then
he turned in his saddle to look me in the face as
he broke out again.  "What devils women can be !
Think of this one, mother to Brynglas.  When I was
a lad of twenty, newly come into Castell March in
the room of my father, this woman was the beauty of
this part of the world.  She set her heart on Castell
March—though she said it was on me—but I was
eager to get to sea and seek for El Dorado.  And
when I showed my impatience of her love-making
she drew a dagger upon me—the scar is on my face
yet ; I did not ward the blow entirely.  Yet I only
laughed at that, neither did I heed when she swore
she would be revenged on me.  "You only want to
have Castell March for your own," I told her.

" ' I wanted you,' she snapped, 'but now I'll have
Castell March instead ! '

" Three years after that I came home and found
her married to my cousin, and twitted her for hav-

ing married the younger of two sons, but she said she
had taken the younger because the elder was dead
somewhere at sea.   She had a son of her own then ;
this present Brynglas.

  " But my cousin, her husband—he was lord of the
Eivl and Nant Vortigern—had always been a good
friend of mine, so I troubled nothing for his wife's
spite, but fitted my ship afresh for the Spanish Main ;
and in that manner I came and went till I had been
a sea rover for nigh upon twenty years.

  " Then in a great storm I was washed overboard
in trying to save one of the men.   Some wreckage
kept me afloat, but I was picked up next day by a
great Spanish warship and carried in to Cartagena, a
prisoner.

  " Other prisoners were there already, waiting the
coming of a certain Cardinal from Spain to open an
Inquisition.   So many were there that the Governor
vowed he had no more room, and requested Don
Alonzo Penalva, the captain, to keep me ironed in
the ship till the Inquisition could take me in hand.
But by the grace of God that Cardinal never arrived ;
a Plymouth ship laid him aboard and he went the
same way as his vessel's crew.   Therefore when in
due time Don Alonzo had to sail from Cartagena, he
transferred me to the keeping of the Alcalde of the
town.

  " That Alcalde had a daughter, and that daughter
had a duenna who could deny her nothing—and so
it comes that that duenna was strangled in front of
the Cathedral of Cartagena and that daughter is a
prisoner in the Castle of Vortigern."

  He broke off for a little while and we rode in steady
silence till he picked it up again.   " Aye, the Span-

iard is not so cruel as his priest and my captivity was not so strict but what the daughter of the house got sight of me two or three times. And from that she allowed me in turn to get sight of her two days in succession, so that my thoughts were arrested. And after that—why after that what else but that we two had only one desire in the world.

" At last, one day, she came into the room where I was confined, and I thought her duenna walked a little differently ; as well might be, seeing that the duenna's dress covered a shaven priest. What story she had told him to move him to consent I do not know, and I cared less, but answered according as her eyes bade me, so that for my reward presently I was being married to the woman that I worshipped. Aye ; married ; a prisoner and all—but it was done for her own protection, for we could contain ourselves separate from each other no longer.

" Then—that was heaven on earth till it was discovered and I was thrown into the foulest dungeon in all the castle. I had been there a month or two when a message was conveyed to me in secret to say that my wife had escaped from her father's house ; had hired the rascal captain of a ramshackle ship to put to sea, and so sailed for Castell March to rouse my people to come and rescue me from prison.

" When she started she knew nothing of Welsh but my name and the name of Castell March. She thought Wales was but one eyrie for the breeding of sea eagles, and that all sea eagles speak some Spanish, since that is the language of those they prey upon. If she had thought it of Lleyn or Arvon she would have been nearly right."

Again he broke off, and though my lips were parched

with eager excitement to hear what happened next,
yet I dared not break in upon him, for it was
plain as plain might be that he was telling this story
over to himself much more than to me.    Then a
stumble of his horse roused him to speech again.

"I was not long in escaping after that ; the priest
who had married us helped me out; perhaps he
feared his share in the matter might be discovered.
I hurried home, coming to Carnarvon as bare as a
beggar man and full of a project of giving my beautiful one a joyful surprise.    The first man I met, the
first man I spoke to, was my cousin of Nant Vortigern ;
in the same room of the same inn ; aye, at the same
table "—he suddenly turned to me—" the same table
where I met his son the other day when first we three
came together.

" The first word that I heard was the bitterest that
man could hear, for while we were yet shaking hands
he swore false to me telling me not only that my wife
had not arrived, but that her ship had been found
stripped and sacked and set on fire by Lundy pirates.
Every soul aboard her had been murdered, and only
the ship's name, when I spoke it to him, served to
connect it at all with any place in the world.    It was
a vessel of his own which had found the half-burnt
derelict after the fire had gone out.

" Then all my blood was up to go and sweep Lundy
and Lundy men out of the sea ; but he went on to
tell me that the Spanish Ambassador in London had
procured a special decree of outlawry against me, and
that an officer was at that moment in Carnarvon to
enforce it.    I cared nothing for the outlawry, however, save that it made it hard for me to get a ship
and men for the harrying of Lundy.    All that I

wanted was vengeance, and he swore to help me up to the very hilt of it. So I trusted him and allowed him to smuggle me home to my own house of Castell March in the dead of night, and to hide me away in the rooms behind the hall. Even my own people were replaced by his, lest word of me should go abroad through careless talk. There I was to lie hidden till he could prepare an expedition.

" Meanwhile to keep my temper in hand I proceeded with my translation of the Bible ; which I had been working upon in the spare moments of the last seven years at sea.[1] I was sitting at that one midnight when the door opened behind me, and, before I could draw my sword from its scabbard on the table, I was struck on the head from behind and knocked senseless upon the book I was writing in. When I came to myself I was fast ironed in the lazaretto of a French ship, which my kinsman had hired to carry me to Spain, where I was to be handed over to the Inquisition.

" We did not get to Cadiz. Within two days of that port a Barbary rover took us prize, and I was a slave to the Moor for eight years before I made shift to escape to sea in an open boat.

" Picked up by an expedition which was sailing to

[1] Another Welsh (virtual) corsair, Captain William Myddelton—brother to Sir Hugh of New River fame—made a metrical translation of the Psalms into his native tongue, during his spare hours at sea while engaged in the godly work of harrying the Don. He it was who hung upon the flanks of the great Spanish fleet—sent to trap Howard off the Azores—for three days and then slipped away with full information to warn the admiral, who took the wind in time ; leaving Grenville, however, to immortalize himself in death.—ED.

waylay the Lima galleon, I have worked day and
night ever since, with head and hand and heart and
soul, till at last I made myself captain of a ship and
filled it with a crew strong enough to come home here
and take vengeance ; a vengeance that should be told
for a hundred years to come.   But when I had laid
all ready and landed at Carnarvon I met there an
ancient friend of mine in time past, a lawyer, and
heard from him that I had never been an outlaw and
that the whole tale of the outlawry was a lie of my
cousin's from end to end.

" When I was washed overboard my ship had returned to Carnarvon, reporting me crowned, and my
cousin at once claimed Castell March as my heir.
After that he must, by capturing my wife, have
learned that I was alive, and so made up the tale of
outlawry and the plan of kidnapping me, ready for
instant use if ever I should return.   He felt sure
that in shipping me to Spain and the Inquisition he
had done with me for ever.

" He had ; for though I am here yet he is dead.
His wife Catrin, the hag, is alive, however : his wife
that prompted all the harm against me ; his wife who
keeps my wife prisoner and in whose power my little
son is.   And by that token there must have been
some confusion when the outlaws captured my wife's
ship, as it drew in to the coast, and in the medley the
babe was not suspected of being her child.   Had
Catrin Brynglas dreamed for a moment that the boy
was heir to Castell March, then she would have done
him to death at once.

" That was why I wanted to wait till Brynglas
should have married the Lady Nerys before I struck.
By holding my hand till Catrin thought she had ful-

filled her long cherished intent of securing Castell March—through her son, since she ruleth that fool—I should that way give double edge to the blow."

He fell silent. He had come to the end of his story. I knew now that he was the prisoner from oversea. But still that strange betrothal of the Lady Nerys remained. "Sir," said I, "the Lady Nerys is betrothed to some prisoner in Spain. Who is that prisoner ?"

The fierceness that had been in his face turned to a gentle smile ; yea, a loving smile, as of one who watches his children playing in the sun. "I am that prisoner, Rowland," said he.

"How then was she betrothed to you ?" asked I quickly.

"It was her warm woman's heart, Rowland. The tale is in truth a tale for harpers to carry far and wide, for all maidens to hear and dream upon. When my cousin had kidnapped me, he liked little to have his own elder brother turn up and oust him. And if he liked it little, his wife Catrin was eaten up with fury to lose what she had at last won, as she reckoned. But though she was baulked she was not beaten ; she only set herself to wait for another chance. Before he died the elder brother knew that I had been kidnapped, and as he lay muttering on his deathbed his daughter heard just so much of it as made her think her father had done it. When therefore Catrin made a new start by proposing a marriage between her son and Nerys, the maid spoke up and told her that Castell March was not hers at all and that she intended to find me and restore me to my own.

" Then Catrin used the old lie again and added another, telling her that even if I were yet alive it made no difference, since I had been outlawed and my forfeit estate bought by my own uncle, father to my cousins, and grandfather to her, Nerys. She found the maid as stubborn as herself, however, for forthwith Nerys swore that she would first save enough to buy my pardon from the Council and then fit out a ship to find me. When I was found she would give me back my lands by marrying me, and after that would tend me all the days of my life with love and pity in recompense for what I had suffered by her father.

" Aye, only a young maid would dream a dream so fond and foolish as that ; so noble and so beautiful as that. Rowland "—he turned full face to me and his eyes were shining—" I heard somewhat yesterday, and more in the night, of thy promise to aid her in finding me. God bless ye both in your innocence ! for ye would have forgotten all else in the wide world but your two selves before you had been a week at sea. It is when two such children get hand in hand on some such quest of wondrous unwisdom that beauty and sweet glory are born into the world, like a rainbow against the clouds."

" Children ! " The turn of his speech as he ended put me off my feet for a moment, so that to cover my confusion I could only repeat, " Children ! "

" Aye, why not ? " replied he. " We do not live by the almanac. Children ! yea, for only a child would have answered with a denial of childhood. And she, too ; she would have gone to church and married me ; but as for the rest, for being in sooth a wife, she would have turned to thee in wonder ;

pouting that I wanted what was not in the game : "—
he broke off in a musing smile.

Plainly he thought her a child, and that her quarrel
with me was a child's quarrel, to vanish in merry
eagerness over the next feather that whirled past in
the wind.   But well I knew that she was a grown
woman, with all a grown woman's resentment.

Before I could fashion to speak, however, he broke
out again.   " But here we are at Nevin—now for
my wife and son !   Now for vengeance ! "   And all in
the speaking of that last word his face set hard as
iron again and he gripped the hilt of his sword to
loosen it in its sheath.

He was happy now, if such a thing might be for a
man in his position.   He had left the Ooronoka behind him and before him was his wife and child and
vengeance.   But I was at the other edge of the sea ;
I had left love behind me when I so mortally offended
Nerys, and before me now was only dreary fighting
and the weary Ooronoka.

" Yea, here we are at Nevin," said I also, for I had
no other word to say.

# CHAPTER XXVIII.

## TRAPPED.

WE had in truth come to Morva Nevin by this time, and at the first suck of his horse's hoofs in the quagmire the captain dropped his hold of the hilt while he measured all the immediate world, as it seemed, with one keen sweep of his eye.

" Nevin is not yet astir," said he, as quietly as if in that long explanation just ended he had talked all his passions out. " That is well for us, since I believe that there is more than one of Nevin men in the pay of Nant Vortigern. Take the kindreds then, and stretch a line of men to the north of the town—that will daunt the townsmen so that they will keep quiet while you take breakfast. Then mount and ride again till you come to the Eivl and there beset the head of Nant Vortigern so closely that not a field-mouse even can slip through your line.

" Keep a lookout, and when you see my ship put out from Dinllaen to reach up the coast, then fall on with all the noise and threatening that you may, but not coming to hand grips because you are too few. What I desire is that the outlaws be busy with you at the head of the valley while I land suddenly at the mouth of it and sweep their castle clean before they can come to the rescue of it. For I dare not use the ship's great guns lest I harm also my wife and little son."

He gripped my hand ; " I was lucky when I found thee for my friend," said he.   And so we parted, he to lead his seamen across the marsh to Dinllaen and the ship, and I to take the men of the kindreds and come between Nevin and the Eivl.

Crossing the little brook I caused the men to dismount beyond the church.   " We are now to breakfast," said I to the old chieftain.   " Have ye any food with you ? "

" Nay," answered he ; " Nevin shall furnish us with a meal.   What else is a town for save to be a market where men may buy and sell ? "

" Have you, then, money ? " asked I, knowing that I had none.

" I have better than that.   I have the name of Gwilym 'apJohn, lord of Castell March.   I have but to say that he is come home again and then the man who will not give for love of us shall give for fear. It is but to wait for the next fair day and then to raise a bickering.   The house of any certain man is easily sacked and burned while all the fair is busy at the blades.   Aye, it will be a small thing to get breakfast here, now that we have a leader again."   He looked ten years younger as he rode away into the town.

It was not breakfast alone that he brought with him when he returned, for with him came a dozen of lusty townsmen, some for far kinship with one or other of the kindreds of Castell March, and some for long nursed feud with Brynglas.   Yet from their speech I gathered that they reckoned little of Brynglas himself, holding him for the mere tool of his hated mother. Now that my eyes were opened I saw well that this land of Lleyn had beer hag-ridden by her.

We spent little time over the meal, and all the way after we started again I had to check the eagerness of the men, lest we should reach the Eivl too soon. For the captain's seamen would need good rest after their night of marching, and we must not begin our attack too early, lest the outlaws should discover it for a feigned one and so send back their main body to defend the castle.

Passing the Pistyll we came presently to the high ground by the Cnydd. Here we saw the watchman in the Gwylva first signal our coming to his fellow on the high peak of the Eivl beyond and then incontinently fly before us as we drew nearer. Some of the young men, in the pride of being mounted on such unaccustomedly good horses, would have chased him. "But why," said I, "seeing that we purpose to destroy them all, root and branch together? —let him join his fellows in peace then."

Thus we came at last to the high sweep of brown heather at the head of the Nant, and I wondered that the outlaws should let us draw thus near without even so much as a flight shaft shot at us. The more so since they had all Jevon Cutta's men to increase their numbers. Not one of them, however, stepped a foot out this side the gate to meet us; not a single blink of steel showed in the dark waste, only the flagman on the Clogwyn—the rocky boss by the gate—flapped signals to those in the castle far down in the valley below.

Seeing this I mistrusted some wile; some trap for our destruction, for they were enough to have swallowed us up quick had they come out to meet us ; save indeed that we were mounted and so could move the quicker on that level sweep. Yet I must do something and that quickly, for already the ship had left Dinllaen and was speeding like a white-winged bird of ocean over the short space between.

Choosing, then, ten of the lightest men on the swiftest horses I drew them out in front. "Now," said I, "it is needful that we discover with what strength they hold the rampart here by the gate. Therefore I will ride swiftly across their front, keeping a distance of some three score paces from their wall. Their bowmen then will let fly at me as I sweep past, but as soon as I am well started I desire that you should follow me, one at a time, two or three lances' length after each other, the first man close under the wall, the next a spear throw out in the open and so on, some near and some far.

"For this purpose, each man as he rides must note the number of shafts shot at the one before him, as he shall see the archers rise to shoot over the wall ; for this wall hath no loopholes but only a parapet. And because they will not see us in time, as we follow one another, therefore they will shoot hurriedly and we shall run in little danger of being hit ; while we, when we come back here, can decide upon their number, whether they be few or many that hold the wall."

When they had heard and perceived my plan, the three chiefs of kin that sat by approved my skilful captaining greatly. "Verily," said one to another, "his wisdom is grey though his hair be not." By which I knew that I could trust them to obey, and that cheerfully, whatever I might order.

As I had planned, so we followed it; I myself going first and that so swiftly that every man who shot at me from the wall top shot late and hurriedly. Not one struck even my horse, let alone my own body. And because they were all looking after me and marvelling what I was doing, so they were not aware of the second man till he was abreast, each archer in turn then drawing upon him and shooting late and hurriedly again as before. So with the third man and all the rest to the tenth, and of them all only two were hit in the flesh and one horse slain; so cheaply did we learn the strength of the defenders.

I was more disturbed now than before, for by the observation both of those who rode and those who sat still at the starting point, there were not more than a score or so on all the wall. I had the greater doubt then that some trap was set, and yet could not guess what it might be.

Trap or no trap however we must fight, and that at once, cost what it might, if we were to help the captain at all. We were three score and five men, counting the men of Nevin. With so many men we ought to do much, even against secret cunning, if we but fought all that was in us.

Calling then for five-and-twenty of the best archers to dismount, I sowed them thinly through the waste in front of the line of the wall, bidding them vex all the defenders of it, so that no outlaw should dare rise up to shoot over at those who should charge. That settled, I took the other two score to assault the gate; yet, because my thigh was sore and stiff from last night's arrow, I could not go afoot, but must keep my horse and lead them from the saddle.

Then at a sign from me the archers ran forward a

18

score of paces or so from where they had stood, till
they came within range of the wall.  Halting, like
one man they drew and shot, sending their shafts
well up into the air that they should come down like
the rain behind the rampart on those that kept the
passage.  That was enough, and while the bows were
bent next to keep the wall top clear, I with a great
shout led the spearmen to the attack.

But I was mounted, and because my horse was
champing and raging to go, and because also my own
blood roused like a strange, cold, cloudy madness in
me, I forgot that the others were afoot.  Head down,
a broad spear stretched eager in my hand, I drove
the spurs home with a chill delight, bursting with
eagerness as the good horse leaped away like an arrow
for speed.

I forgot those who were behind ; I looked neither
right nor left ; I saw only the narrow gap in the
rampart and the two spearmen who suddenly stood
into it and set their points against me for the shock.
An arrow struck my steel cap with a force that made
me wink, but I kept on, my flesh all cold and crawling
as I looked at those waiting spears.

My own point was stooping to strike : my knees
were gripping close as any vice, when suddenly a
shaft from behind me flashed past and slew the near
hand one of the two.  His spear fell, my own just
parried the other, and all in one wild leap the good
roan lifted me through and beyond, into the midst
of a clustered score of outlaws and a sheaf of gathered
spears that defended the gap.

All that place was steel, and gleaming eyes, and
panting blows, and a snorting horse that maddened
more and more between my knees ; for the ground

dropped straight down from beneath his hoofs to the tops of the trees below, while behind him and on both flanks were furious men, and over all the mighty shout that deafened even the blows.

Time was not; all things did themselves in the same second like a pictured scene, and then an arrow struck into the near shoulder of my horse. With one wild scream that checked every hand for an instant, the frenzied steed rose on his haunches; rose and turned to the right and leaped; leaped so high that I could see over the wall to those without again—and then we were going on and going down, for he had jumped over the edge of this corner of Craig Ddu and we were hurtling down through space into the depths of Nant Vortigern.

And yet as we went it was not the picture of the death beneath that flashed upon my mind, but of the trap which had been set above to catch us. For as my horse first leaped I had looked over the wall and had seen, broad and swift over the ridge behind my scattered archers, the torrent front of the Redhands of Dolbadarn, sweeping down to engulf my men.

All the kindreds of Castell March were caught between them and the wall : there seemed no way of escape.

# CHAPTER XXIX.

## THE ELFIN BOY'S REVENGE.

THAT one picture—of the outlaws and the fighting in the morning light above—flashed into my mind indeed, but only to be swallowed in the same instant by another flash; a flash of blackness; of black crag at my elbow; of black tree tops and black depths that seemed to shoot up lightning swift to meet me from below. A mighty wind roared in my ears; a crashing sound filled all the world, and then—then I found myself below patiently trying to stand upright by the help of an oak sapling, while before me, a lance's length downhill, the mangled body of my poor horse was quivering against the stem of a great tree. The bushy tree tops which had broken our fall had killed him while saving me.

Well was it for me that the jump had been from so near the corner of the craig, where the depth was so much less than what it would have been a few strides beyond.

My armolet coat had defended my body from being pierced by any splintered bough, but I was bleeding from the ears, my head felt as if it would burst in pieces, and every bone in my body seemed to ache separately. Yet because I was so sore in every sinew and so stiff in every muscle, I did not notice so much the pain of my wounded thigh till I had staggered and scrambled some little way from where I had alighted. Then, as by degrees my brain cleared again and I began to separate my sensations, I first remembered that other things had happened before I landed in this wood, and next, so sharply that for a moment I forgot all bodily hurts soever, recollection of the fate of my men above stirred me to the bottom of the soul.

Lame and sore and useless as I was, I yet could not bear the thought of what was happening now over my head, and I began to struggle towards the path which ran up from the outlaws' cabans to the gate. Limping and scrambling I made but slow way, though I was burning with a fire of dull impatience. In my mind I saw each separate man of the kindreds die in a dozen different ways while I struggled pain-fully along. But when at length the path was gained. all things changed in a flash, for I almost stumbled over the little elfin boy from the castle ; the captain's son ; panting and out of breath as he climbed.

"Ah, laddie ! come with me now and you shall be safe at last ! " I was so joyful that I clean forgot the danger I myself was in and the scant prospect of making my own escape, let alone of freeing him also.

But he was only startled instead of comforted. "Nay ! " answered he, jumping out of my reach and beginning to climb again, "you spoke false to me before, I want no more of you."

I stretched my hands, imploring him to wait a minute. "Stop ! stop ! " I cried. "Come down again. Foulk of the Feet and all the outlaws are up there——"

I was going on to tell him that they would kill

him; that he could not escape that way, and so forth, but he cut me short. "Yes, I am come for him to help defend the castle. A great ship hath come——"

"Aye," I broke in. "That ship is the captain's. He is coming to rescue Madre Mia and you. He is your father and she your mother—come back before Foulk sees you."

"Ah! but you broke faith before," he called back, still climbing. "I have no father or mother, and this ship is going to batter down the castle and burn it. That is why I have come for Foulk, so that he can save it, or else Madre Mia will be killed in the tower."

He had almost disappeared through the trees above. Loudly I called, "Come back! Come back!" but he only went the faster. I tried to overtake him, but in my lame state he went two yards for my one. Still I struggled on. "Wait! wait!" I cried, but I cried in vain, for he would not trust me.

How I cursed my impotence and his folly as the distance between us lengthened. "Oh, if I were only sound again for five minutes," muttered I.

Then, as he reached the upper edge of the wood, the thought of all that he was doing to baulk his father and to harm his mother and himself drove me to despair. "You fool! you little fool!" I groaned, halting for breath.

"Ah!" cried he, turning upon me in triumph. "Now you show what you think. I know. But hide you in the trees now or else Foulk will see you as we come down. I don't want you killed!"—then he sped on into the belt of thorns.

Nevertheless I followed on. Even though it were

climbing into the arms of Foulk of the Feet I could
do no other.   I could not go back into the world if I
as captain had led my men into a trap where all were
killed.   If I should find them all dead under the
walls then the sooner I were slain too the better.   So
I toiled on.

But from the thorn belt I saw only a corpse or two
at the gate, and when I reached the gap itself I saw
well why.   For three score men and more are not
slain offhand as one might wring a fowl's head off.
Apparently the men of the kindreds had got wit of
Jevon Cutta's men in time to turn and make a running fight of it as they retreated.   Nay, they had
given ground, it is true, but only in order to take a
better position behind them.   For as I stepped out
over the dead spearman in the gate I saw that they
had taken ground on the high ridge to the right,
overlooking this rampart, and there, back to back
and facing every way in a ring, they were now
bearing up the battle against three times their
number.

Many a man had been slain on both sides as they
retreated ; the brown heather was sown thick with
stark corpses and with writhing men, but the great
slaughter was to be on that high hill, where already
the shafts were flying close as a storm of winter's
snow.   And I saw well that if the fight lasted there
much longer then Castell March should be all widows
and orphans, for now Foulk of the Feet was picking
a band of special men to follow him in a charge.

Many a riderless horse stood in that brown waste,
and in a moment I was mounted again.   My first
thought was to ride after the boy and bear him off
to a distance before I returned to the fight.   But as

I looked I saw him stop beside the footless Foulk, holding to the outlaw's empty stirrup, and speaking up to him as he stooped from the saddle to listen. It was a grievous thing to me, to see him appealing to his enemy for help against his friends.

Aye well, there was nothing left therefore but to charge in and carry off the boy if possible, for there seemed no longer any hope for the kindreds ; they must be all slain.   A spear was in my hand and now I shortened the rein, ready to ride at speed into the press ; but I had pricked scarce a dozen lengths across the heather when I was suddenly aware of a new company of men, coming over the rise as if they came from Nevin.

No well housel'd or gallant men they looked, it is true, for they were mounted but upon country ponies. Neither had they any armour but motley of cloth, and indeed the one good thing about their array was the line of their points, for every man carried a broad, barbed, long-bladed spear, like these men of the Eivl.

I looked again, and then I understood.   At their head rode a woman—they were the despised household men of the Lady Nerys, following their mistress in the field ; bent to give back my scorn of them by proving themselves in battle.

Whether she were here to fight for us, or whether she were here to revenge her shattered dreams by fighting against us for her unloved husband, I could not guess ; but at once I pressed towards her to put it to the touch.

Checking in front of her—" Lend me your men that I may save the kindreds," cried I.

" Ah, you are glad enough now of those you de-

spised aforetime," she answered in scorn, though yet
she paled in looking at me.

" Aye, but I have been learning since then," replied
I, turning to the men.

" Now !" cried I to them. " Follow me and I will
be squire and groom to every man of you hereafter if
you bring off these men !"

Little they loved me, but a white smile lighted all
their faces as they took their reins shorter and stooped
their faces and their points to charge in after me.
The land lay level betwixt us and the ring of Eivl men.
A hundred yards of a trot that crowded faster with
every stride, and I flung my spear arm up and
—" Charge !" I shouted.

I had thought I should outstrip them far, but their
ponies raged behind me like wild beasts, and wilder
than wild beasts their riders spurred them on like men
demented. No shout they gave, but a long low
moan of desire broke from their lips, and as we struck
the startled ranks of the foe the great spears stabbed
like lightning for speed and deadly doing. Aye,
these disgraced men, these stripped and flouted men,
fought with a fury that might have daunted fiends
fresh from the Pit. Back we bore the redhand ranks,
sweeping them before us, driving them apart till we
met the first of the kindreds, now springing down
the slope to help their own deliverance with their
own steel.

St. Dervel ! but that was a goodly fight and not a
man of us all but felt compunction for the stripping
of these succours yesterday. Yet when the press
broke and the outlaws began to give ground, then I
remembered the boy again and lifted to look for him.
Yonder he was, carrying a spear that he was not big

enough to wield, and though his face was white with
dread of death, yet he was bravely copying Foulk of
the Feet and crying to the outlaws to turn and face
us again.

How I wished his father could see him now ; I
could have kissed the child for his high courage, in
spite of the mistake of it.  But I could not come
near enough to capture him, for Foulk of the Feet
was raging like a mad bull between us.  With oaths
and curses, with threats and blows, he was working
like a demon to rally the redhands.  His bow was
broken in his hand and he was using it as a whip to
sting his men to turn and bear up the fight against
us.

The running fight had reached abreast of the gap
in the ramparts again.  Now if only they would
divide, the Snowdon thieves to the north and the
Evil men to their valley again, we might get the boy
in the end, thought I.  True enough, Jevon Cutta
and his men had indeed had all they could carry of
Lleyn and of fighting in another man's quarrel.  This
country was too open for them ; home to the crags
and forests of Snowdon was their word, and in a
loose mass they began to draw off over the heathery
sweep, by the way we had gone aforetime to the
wedding.  But the Eivl men went too, mingling
with the northland thieves ; not daring to break away
for the gate of their own valley, lest we should bend
all upon them and so cut their few selves off to the
last man.

Then I roused the men to another effort, for I feared
that despair and Foulk of the Feet together might
bring them to make a stand while yet they had the
upper ground of us.  Already they began to draw

close together ; to set their points more evenly against
us and to go with stubborner step.   But, stabbing,
hacking, spurring, we pressed them sterner still, and
presently, though they were locked now in a fast ring
bristling with points on every side, yet the dangerous
ground was past ; we were on the comb of the ridge
and the outlaws had begun to drop down across the
sweep of lower waste on the other side, towards the
Rocks of the Giantess.

With that I grew more hopeful ; the boy must now
fall to us soon or late.   In the long retreat from
here to Dolbadarn there must come some moment
when a quick charge, pushed resolutely home, would
of a surety succeed in seizing and carrying off the
boy.   So well for us did things look now that I chose
seven men of the kindreds ; men of grave beards and
scarred faces, and sent them, well-mounted, to be
for convoy and protection to the Lady Nerys, who had
perforce remained alone upon the ridge whence I had
first led her men away in the charge.

This was hardly done, however, before my hopes
received a rude rub.   For, instead of heading down
into the valley past Llanhaiarn, the outlaws kept the
high ground, drawing by the green trackway straight
for the dead city whose frowning walls, black and
forbidding, encircled the bald head of the eastward
summit of the Eivl.

Of giant height and thickness, those grim walls
struck a doubt into my exultation.   If once they
reached the shelter of that fortress then only hunger
could reduce the outlaws.   I raged ; I strove, yet I
could not stop or turn them.   Foulk of the Feet
was not more fierce in fight than cool and ready to
take every advantage now that his remnant of men

were well in hand again. And while he kept his rear rank steadily locked against us as he retreated, Jevon Cutta was getting his own Dolbadarn men into form and order beyond, where he led them towards the gate of Tre Ceiri, the dead town.

Within a short while indeed, in spite of every shift and effort we could make, the thing was accomplished; the outlaws were safe within the walls, and neither could we effect a lodgment by pressing in so close as to enter with them. Jevon Cutta had posted the foremost of his thieves to man the wall of an outwork, under which the road to the gate climbed up; and with great stones they beat us off, tossing down boulders that crushed man, horse, and armour into one bloody mass.

And the one to shake a spear and taunt me from the town wall beside the gate was, not Foulk of the Feet nor any outlaw, but the little boy whose father was blindly raging now round the castle of Vortigern; fiercer than any tiger to recover his wife and this young son, who stood here triumphing in the defeat of his father's men.

He was repaying me for my breach of faith. Alack! that breach of faith.

# CHAPTER XXX.

## FOULK OF THE FEET.

FOR the moment I was baffled. Of a truth we had
not wholly failed; nay, in some aspects we had
gained, since now the outlaws were cooped up within
the walls of a city set upon a naked high hill. They
could not get away secretly, and in the end, if we
should fail to carry the place by assault, they would
doubtless be only too glad to give the boy up, whole
and sound, in exchange for safe conduct back to
Snowdon. Only, it would take time.

First, then, to restore my men to order and get
news of how the captain fared against the castle; for
we had heard great guns discharging this long time
past. I marvelled, too, what guns they might be,
since the captain had said he could not use his own
for fear of destroying his wife in the ruins of her
prison. Therefore I sent three men up the mountain
to the watch place on the highest peak, from whence,
after ousting the flagman, they would be able to see
well all that was happening between ship and castle.
After that, one was to come down and ride to tell
the captain what things had passed with us.

Other men I sent back to where the chief fight had
been, round the gate of the valley. These were to
gather such arrows as they might find unsplintered

on the field—all our quivers were empty, like those of the outlaws—and to catch any riderless horses there. Also, if they came across any of our men wounded they were to bind up their hurts.

When they got back to the field, however, they found themselves forestalled in this last, for even the seven men whom I had first sent to guard the Lady Nerys had found her kneeling by a wounded man, where the great stand had been made , and where the bodies of dead and wounded were thickest. But she had bound up outlaw and honest man alike, at which the seven demurred, as not only taking up time which were better bestowed on her own party, but as also needlessly causing subsequent work ; the work of hanging those outlaw men, to wit.

But to that she had answered that they were not to be hanged. " When they are well they shall become new men ; honest men ; my men. They are like me and have no one to turn to ; it is fit therefore that we be friends, they and I, who are alike wounded and forlorn of hope ; " thus she had ended, a little defiantly.

This was told to me by the chief of the seven, when he presently came back with her, riding to where we kept the leaguer against the ancient city. Having finished binding up those who were hurt, she came now to see what should next befall.

Yet she did not come near where I was, and when I started towards her she put her horse into motion again and moved away, which put me in great doubt as to what she had thought of my message sent back to her this morning. Nor could I ask of my messenger, for though he had come back with her, and was one of the thirty who charged with me, yet he was not here with the survivors of us : he must be lying dead or wounded at the head of the valley.

Pondering the words she had spoken when tending the outlaw just now, I could not keep my eyes off her. The more I pondered and the longer I looked at her, the more did my own heart move me to play the man towards her, and to go manly over to her and say all that was in my mind to say. And indeed I had done it there and then, but that a white flag rose on the dark wall of the city and all the men behind me cried out, " A parley ! a parley ! " at which I had to turn again and to business.

I had no white thing about me wherewith to answer the sign, and when I asked the men for some white cloth one of them put spurs to his horse and dashed out to the Lady Nerys. Glad was she at that, for she thought that now this killing should cease, and so she hastened her horse and came to me, offering the shawl of white silk from about her shoulders. But I was looking rather at the white hand that gave it and the white face that would not look into mine. It was all that I could do to keep my lips from breaking forth into all that I wanted to say. " Thank you," aloud, sounded so like a fool's bells jingling beside what I was repeating in my heart.

It was Foulk of the Feet himself who came with the flag and it had significance that his first word to me was not of greeting but of threatening. " See ! " said he, turning in his saddle and pointing to the top of the wall of Tre Ceiri. " We have the boy fast : the captain's son, as now we know at last. If you play any trick with me then he will be killed there before your eyes."

I looked.  He spoke true, for on the wall stood two outlaws, each with a bare dagger in one hand and each grasping the collar of the little lad with the other.  " Make but a single treacherous move and they cut his throat from ear to ear."

Anger rose up in me, both at the lad's danger and at this fellow's callous cruelty.  " Aye ? " answered I.  " And if any harm do happen to that little one, I swear to you, by the spear and shield of St. Dervel, that they shall hear of my vengeance through the four quarters of Britain.  You fool !  do you not see that you are fast, whether you kill him or keep him alive ?  You cannot break out now, for we are all mounted and can reach and ride you down from whichever side you sortie.  If you do harm him then I will visit it upon you all, every man of you, with a terribleness that shall make even outlaws shudder. "

A devilish sneer came over his fierce face.  " Will it be more terrible than that vengeance which gave me my name and made it feared as far as it is heard ? " demanded he.

" What vengeance was that ? " replied I.

" Aye !  I knew well you had never heard or you would not have bragged so like a fool of vengeance to me," returned he.  " I am Foulk of the Feet ; the feet I have not got, because of what I did years ago. Listen to the tale of it.

" I was a lusty young man ; the merriest thief that ever rode away with a merchant's packhorses while he was dining inside the inn.  I was no red-hand then, but on a day I sat with a red-haired serving wench in the guest house at Llanvair, drinking and making love while I waited for the coming of some merchantmen who were to pass that way.  And she put a drug in my drink, and when I woke all five of the merchants were sitting round the table drinking, with me lying on the board between them, tied and trussed like a sheep for the spit.

" ' Ye ha' been captured oft, good Foulk,' said one of them, dropping a splash of beer on my mouth. ' And often, too, ye ha' gotten away again. But this time you go into Carnarvon and hang over the east gate of the town like any other thief not half so slippery. This time is the end of you, good Foulk,' laughed that one with the beer in his hand.

" They had been sitting a long while over the ale ; another half hour would see them drunk, and they must have been nearly that when they tied me up, for a single knot on my breast was the king of all my bonds. If that were loosed only for a second then I was free. Said I then—' You have but to leave that knot as it is and I'll slip you yet betwixt here and Carnarvon.'

" ' Will ye ? ' said he, and he reached for it to tie it with a fresh turn. He had no sooner caught hold of the ends than a jerk of my body set me free and with a leap and a laugh I was beyond them all and running for the door. Then the wench again ; she did it this time too, for she tripped me with her foot as I passed her on the threshold. I was caught once more.

" They laid me on the table fast bound this time. ' Aye ? ' quoth him of the beer, Black John Skinner. ' So you were at your old tricks again.'

" Then they all laughed at that, and in my anger, ' I am not yet in Carnarvon,' said I, ' and I'll wager that the five of you will never take me there in life, for all these bonds.'

19

" With that they swore one upon another that they would make sure. ' And what will you wager to us, Foulk ap Madoc ? ' said Will Rhuddyn.

" ' All that I have, against the best you have—my life against yours,' said I. And—' Done ! ', answered he, smacking his open hand down on my tied one.

" Then one whispered to another till the last of them spoke up loud, ' Ye'll give us the slip, will you, my merry gentleman ? But not if ye have no feet to run upon withal. Wench ! bring us the chopper and the block ! ' And I saw that they had drink enough in them to do it and laugh over it.

" For that one time in my life my blood forsook me ; the sweat broke out from head to foot of me and I begged for mercy.

" Well, they did it : they chopped them off "—here, God wot, I, Rowland, saw the terriblest smile that ever made the face of man awful to see, as Foulk stopped for a moment and wiped his lips with the back of his hand.

" There was a great pot of porridge boiling over the fire and into that they dipped my stumps to sear them and stop the bleeding. Then they put me back upon the table—' Will you escape us now ? ' quoth Black John Skinner.

" But I could only lie and let the tears run down for sheer pity of myself, that had never drawn blood of any man save in open quarrel, and now was but-chered like a hog for merchantmen's sport. They saw me in tears and they sobered, because for the first time in life I had no word to answer with.

" Then they began all together to make excuse, and because I still answered them nothing they

added promises of recompense and of the livelihood
they would secure for me in some town.   At last I
spoke—' Ye have promised what ye will do ; now
give me each a hair of your head for witness.'   And
they gave me the five hairs, one red, one black ; a
grey, a yellow, and a flaxen white ; and so next day
they parted.

"But at parting I said, ' You must all come and
dine with me this day three months.   I shall be well
then and you shall see me fit and moving again.'
They promised that, too.

" A month from then I was learning to get about
on hands and knees.   Two months from then I had a
short bow made and began to learn to shoot kneeling
instead of standing.   Three months and then I took
from a firkin behind my bed something which I had
kept secret in the brine and, putting it in the pot,
began to cook the mess that the five were to dine
off.

" They all came, every man with a smile on his
face to cover the dread in his heart ; and every man
with a wondrous tale of what he was going to do for
me.   Then I had them all sit down and I made the
wench sit with us, though she was white with a mortal
dread, because I had never reproached her yet for
betraying me.

" And I bowled out the mess, to each man a
savoury portion of flesh and bone and pottage, and
the steam was in their nostrils, and they smacked
their lips and flourished their spoons, and swore by
the spit and pot that I was a savoury cook.   And I
laughed and pressed them to it—and I ate none
myself.

" Then when they had licked up clean and had

begun to comfort their hearts of their fear, I spoke up—' Yea, but I forgot to put the garnish to the dish. Yet better late than not at all. See, here is the garnishing.'

" And there, while they looked, quaking in dread to see, I laid out the ten toe nails round the dish. ' Ye have eaten the feet,' said I, ' now scrape your beards with the nails.'

" Then while they stared at me, sick and shivering to the marrow, I threw an arrow on the board— ' And pick your teeth with that when ye are done,' I ended.

" Every man of them looked at it and each man saw a hair of his head wrapped round the shaft ; black or red, or brown, or yellow, or flaxen white. And while they stared and shivered I shuffled out and on to a horse that I had tied by the door. Then I looked back through the open window and gave them my parting word.

" ' You laid a wager with me before, your five lives against mine, that you would take me prisoner into Carnarvon town. Ye have lost that wager, gentles, and I claim it ; to take the forfeit when I will. Ye may live long or ye may live short, according as I choose. Only if any man of you try to escape by leaving the country then I will strike at once.'

" With that I rode away, and one by one thereafter I took their forfeit lives, just when I would. This one I slew at the altar upon his wedding day ; that one as he came out of the gate of Carnarvon where he had threatened I should hang ; and always each and every one of them when he felt himself most secure. Last I went to the woman, but she had been wandering mad from the day she ate of the feet, and now at sight of me she dropped down jibbering and died. And I am a redhand from that day.

" And will your vengeance be more terrible than that ?" ended the speaker, his grin devilish to see.

# CHAPTER XXXI.

## THE DEED OF THE DISINHERITED.

ALL the while he was speaking, the outlaw's face had been like hell's smelting pot to watch, with the light upon it changing, now lurid, now dark, now flashing vividly fierce. All the more grim it was in that it never bubbled into rage; never overflowed; but was kept under, smooth, smooth, though a hundred lights of demon passion played over it.

It was an old tale to him, he had even told it many a time I wot; but still it was a raven's beak tearing at his heart, piking and pulling; and the pain of it and the rage swelled in him every time as now, till the veins in his neck and temples stood out like bowstrings. I was the only man there who had never heard the story before, yet I wist well, though I could not turn my eyes away to look, that every man felt himself the colder at his heart for hearing it from the doer's own lips.

I dared not show such a feeling myself. I was captain and I must keep a front to this man, if he were Satan's self. "Doubtless," answered I—but I almost feared he would hear my tongue parting stickily from the clammy roof of my mouth— "doubtless any threat of vengeance I may make will seem little to you. But with your men yonder it is another matter. You are more reckless than they and grimmer, or you would not be their leader now. They will be afraid then and will keep the boy safe."

I had pricked him there and forthwith his rage at last boiled over. He forgot all need of cunning or hiding his purpose. "You have clapped in the clout," he burst out with a furious oath. "Aye, if Jevon Cutta and all his skulking calves of men had as much pluck amongst them as my little finger has, then I would have seen you in the Pit before I would have even pretended to offer terms, I would cut the lad to pieces before your eyes. After that you might win if ye could, but the tale of the fight should be told for a hundred years to come."

He stopped, more to catch breath and wipe the foam of his rage from his lips than anything else, and I put in with a word.

" What want you then ? "

" Nothing ! " snarled he. " I want nothing save what I have and what I can take. When Foulk of the Feet wants anything then he seizes it. But these Dolbadarn squealers—hares to run and rabbits to hide they are ; foxes to snap up poultry and never a fang of a wolf amongst them to pull down a high deer—they talked of terms. They had the captain's son, said they. They would bargain for safety, the boy's life for theirs. That was why I came out ; I came myself so as to keep you and them from bargaining against us of Nant Vortigern."

" What are the terms you speak of then ? " demanded I.

" Terms that you cannot grant," he broke out again with a passionate sneer. " Terms that only your captain, Gwilym 'apJohn, lord of Castell March, can agree to. Bring him here to meet me, then, and while you are gone I will ride back and tell the Dolbadarn men that you have refused all grace but a withy to hang such as ye do not kill in battle. That will put some pluck into their sheep's hearts, if it be only of despair."

" Dost thou not fear to speak thus ? " demanded I. " What if we keep thee now ; thy life for the boy's ? "

" There are not enough of you all to do that ! "— boastfully he spoke as he took us in from flank to flank with one scornful sweep of the eye. " Moreover I thought of that before I came out and I left order that if you made a single move to take me it would mean that you had broken truce, intending to kill and hang us all without mercy. I picked the two men I put on the wall with the boy : they are two who never repented of murder yet. They would as lieve kill the lad as not, and I told them to do it the instant they saw treachery in you."

Look at him as I would I was forced to believe that he spoke truth ; grim truth. I could only try to gain time. " These terms then ; what are they ? " said I.

" Take them from me to the captain," answered he with wolfish glee. " Tell him he must come and strike hands with me on them. He is to draw off his men now, and then for ever leave Nant Vortigern alone and unmolested ; all its defences standing as he found them. When he has sworn to that he shall have his son back."

" Aye ; but his wife also : his wife that is prisoner in the castle ? " responded I. " You agree to give her up as well as the son ? "

"I have nothing to do with his wife. Catrin of Brynglas has her"—a dark smile was on his face as he said it.

"But will you answer for it that the hag gives up the wife?" pressed I.

He laughed ghoulishly. "I am Foulk of the Feet," he said; "but Satan's self would not answer for Catrin Brynglas. The son I have; the son I offer. Go, bring the captain then to bargain with me for my half of what he wants."

I wist well that talk of such terms was foolishness. But if I could keep the outlaw haggling here awhile, then the captain might meantime win the castle and rescue his wife, after which the boy might be saved on the conditions just laid down, which would no longer be foolish. "Stay here then till I send for the captain," said I.

"Not I," retorted Foulk. "I am going back. When the captain comes, tell him what I have said. Then let him ride out, with a white flag, under the wall where I shall be standing with the boy. If he can see and hear his son then he will be the quicker to strike faith with me."

A thought struck me. "You call him the captain's son. What proof have you, that I may send it to the captain? He never saw this boy till three days ago."

"You need no proof," retorted he. "You proved your own belief by what you told the boy when you tried to catch him in the wood. He has just told me the whole tale of all that ever passed between you and him from the first. He trusts me while you broke faith with him." And here the footless thief stopped to laugh in my face.

While I tried to swallow my choler the fellow went on. " But I knew long ago. When the Spanish wife sailed from the Main to come to Castell March, her captain steered for the Eivl here—it being the boldest mark in Lleyn—and my boat was the first aboard him. It was I who took her prisoner because of her beauty, and it was I who took the babe from the breast of its dead nurse where she had been slain by an arrow meant for some man.

" I thought the babe belonged to the dead woman, and it was not till Catrin Brynglas, who knows some Spanish, shut up the prisoner the moment I landed her, that I began to guess. Within two years I found out who the prisoner was, and that the boy I had given to the kitchen wenches was hers ; though she thought him dead, for she supposed she had seen him slain with the same arrow that killed his nurse. But I knew I was right, for she had cut a little cross under his arm, just after he was born, because she was bringing him to a heretic land. I kept my secret to myself though, for if the she-wolf Catrin had known of the boy she would have torn him limb from limb. She kept the mother alive for the pure joy of torturing her ; the child she would have done to death at once."

" Why did you keep the secret, Foulk ? "—I asked it gently, hoping to hear that the bloody soul had been moved to sweet pity once in life ; even if it were only for a poor helpless babe that a wild beast might leave unharmed.

But no—" I kept the secret for use against just such a day as this," quoth he with savage triumph.

" Kept him to save thy skin with then ! " retorted I in quick scorn.

"Are you sure of that?" rejoined he with a devilish grin—"or did I keep him that I might some day cut his throat before his father's eyes?"

"Thou devil!"—I shouted the words—"what hath his father ever done to thee to provoke such a devilish deed as that?"

Straightway his rage broke into foam again. "What need of his father having done me hurt at all? What do I need of any reason? Had I done anything to those who mutilated me? Is it not enough that I am footless; tied; shackled by the want of ten toes? I was to have been hunted and harried by every man alive but that I made them fear me. I will do as I list in scorn of you all and that is reason enough for me!"

"Aye," he ended, over his shoulder as he turned to ride back: "ye shall see. Now bring Gwilym 'apJohn : I will give you an hour to go and come, and then, if he does not appear, I will kill the boy on the wall yonder and you may do as ye will. I am Foulk of the Feet who once in life asked mercy and will never ask it again."

Hot I was, and a dozen times it plucked at my heart to ride him down as he went. But each time as I poised the spear in my hand I remembered that the first stride of my horse meant death to the boy. I thought of the light in the captain's face when he had cried, "Is he not a pretty boy?" and at that my spear trailed again. If the lad were to be doomed then his father must doom him. No other man would dare do it.

Until he reached the gate of the dinas again I sat and watched him, trying to decide the chances. Would his lust of cruelty prevail, so that he would

murder the boy and thus force the rest of the outlaws to die with him; their backs to the wall and
curses on their lips ?   Or would the love of life prevail and move him to keep the terms he had just laid
down.

I could not tell.   It lay as much with the Dolbadarn men as with Foulk.   They had only come down
here from Snowdon in the first place to earn money
cheaply by capturing a fugitive, and now that they
found themselves, not only out of all prospect of
money, but in near jeopardy of being put out of life
itself, their one desire was to get away on what terms
they could make.   Not so Foulk.   His demon hatred
of all men raged in him to join battle again that he
might kill and kill.   Nay, his remorseless courage
perhaps even looked for victory, since the outlaws
shut with him in the dinas were at least as many as
we who held them there.   Moreover had there been
but two more like himself with him now, I also should
have reckoned his chances worth while.   I was torn
in two with doubt.

I looked round at the men clustered behind me,
but never a word said they till a Nevin man on the
flank spoke up.   "I fear the babe is but dead, kins-
men," said he.

Then I turned to my other elbow and found the
Lady Nerys, looking me through and through with
eyes of agonised eagerness.   "Charge the city.   Why
do you not charge at once ?" she cried.

"And have that butcher kill the child before our
eyes ?" asked I gently.

"But we have archers," panted she.   "They are
good marksmen all.   Can they not shoot the two
who hold the boy upon the wall and then keep all

others from him while you are taking the gates? Oh, see him yonder ; surely you will save him ! "

"Our archers cannot shoot so far," answered I, "and if they attempt to advance within range then we break the truce and the boy is dead."

"What will you do then ?" demanded she desperately.

"I know not yet. We have an hour to do it in whatever it is," replied I. "The captain must decide. I will divide the men, half yonder upon the high ground opposite the gate, and half in the valley on the other foot of the hill. The outlaws cannot escape then, and if we do not save the boy we can at least take full vengeance for him."

"Vengeance !" she cried in tearful scorn ; "what is vengeance if the child be dead ? Can his mother dress up vengeance and set it in her lap and kiss it and call it pretty names ? Vengeance !" She broke off for a breath and then—"Oh, if Foulk of the Feet were only on our side, he would save the child, I know," burst out she.

I answered her nothing to that but divided the men ; sending one party to beset the side towards Llanhaiarn, while I led the other up to the high ground, opposite the gate of the city. The lady moved no way, but stayed her horse where it was. . And since there was no danger there I left her alone, till she should come to see the hopelessness of any attempt to save the lad except by strategy.

When we were halted in our new position I set another chieftain to take charge of the men while I should be gone to bring the captain. Yet as I went I could not help looking back at the city crowning the peak, and on its wall the child in jeopardy. But in the first glance I saw more : I saw that the Lady Nerys had left her place and was riding fast to join the men opposite the gate.

At once it struck me that she would try to get them to assault the gate in a mad attempt at rescue, and though I did not turn immediately, yet I rode with my chin upon my shoulder, watching her every move. And in truth I found my fear correct, for as soon as she reached them she began to call upon the men, pointing the while to the little one, where he stood against the skyline between his captors.

Straightway I turned to ride back, for I saw another figure appear upon the wall, a figure that went upon hands and knees ; Foulk of the Feet himself ; and I knew that if the men but so much as fidgeted overmuch in their saddles, then the lad was sped.

I pressed my horse to speed, and whether that drove the lady to mad action, or whether it was the sight and the fear of Foulk of the Feet, I knew not ; but a great groan broke from me as I saw her lift her rein and urge her horse at breakneck speed across the slope towards the wall where the tragedy seemed impending.

I was in time with a shout to stop the men and to snatch the bow and arrow which one of them was drawing uselessly against so far a mark. If one of us should move now then both the woman and child were gone, yet in that heat I forgot all sense. "Back, you !" I shouted with a black oath to the men, while at the same time I plunged the rowels in and drove my horse at whirlwind speed after the woman I worshipped.

Well for us then that Foulk had only eyes for

the lady spurring below.  Her good horse kept his
footing with all the sureness of headlong speed,
through whin and heather as she went, holding a
level line across the slope that would bring her right
to the foot of the wall at the spot where all things
centred.

I heard the voice of Foulk from above.  " What
want ye, woman ? " and I saw the lad and his captors
craning likewise to see.  Wide stretched the lady's
arms as she looked up from where her horse had
stopped.  "Jump! oh jump down!" she cried in
agony, and forthwith, like an eaglet answering the
call, the gallant boy obeyed.

He missed the lady's arms—well for them both
was that—and, lighting in a great boll of whin and
moss and heather, rolled down the slope a lance's
length and more.  Quickly she put her horse about
to get below him and take him up into the saddle,
and had she been a second later she would never have
moved more in this world ; for Foulk of the Feet,
snatching the sword in fury from the man beside him,
had leaped down after the boy, striking at her as he
came.

But I looked no more at him, for without feet to
light upon he must be driven senseless, or even killed
outright, in striking the ground.  All the mad rage
that drove him to the act could not bear up such a
shock.  What I feared was another figure that rose on
the wall behind him ; the short, squat figure of Jevon
Cutta poising a spear to throw.  The bow that I had
seized was still in my hand, the shaft nocked home
and ready.  I had not time to aim, but with a cry to
God I let fly, and headlong backward from the wall
fell Jevon Cutta, the shaft in his body, up under the

short skirt of his brigandine as he bent back to cast his javelin.

A glance over my shoulder showed me Nerys trying to lift the boy to her saddle. Forthwith I whirled about. "Go!" I shouted to her as I seized the boy and swung him up before me. But I saw that she did not move. "Come!" then I shouted, starting myself to fly; anything to get her out of that danger; for I saw that she was standing upon some point of stubbornness.

When she saw me start she started also and not before. "Ah!" gnashed I to myself: "Foulk of the Feet here in my hand to be slain with a single stroke perhaps, and yet I must leave him, all for a woman's stubbornness." But even while I spoke I saw her face lose all its light and I put my horse alongside hers just in time to keep her in the saddle. For she had fainted—thank God we were now safe out of range of the walls.

# CHAPTER XXXII.

NOT so much as a single shaft had been sent after us and a glance ahead explained why. The old chieftain whom I had left in command had no sooner seen me ride after the lady, than he led a headlong charge at the gate of the town, to draw off the attention of the outlaws from us.

He had hardly hoped to win, but just as he came to the shock a mighty clamour rose from those within—"Foulk of the Feet is dead headlong!" shouted some; "Cutta is slain!" shouted others, and at once the outlaws broke and fled, scaling the walls where they were lowest on the inside. Only a handful of the Eivl men stood stubbornly up to the steel, dying amid the ruined houses rather than follow the Dolbadarn men to Eryri.

But those who fled did not all escape, for the party I had sent down into the valley crashed into them and scattered them like chaff; and it was stealthily and by one and one that the remnant reached their mountains again in the end.

All this time, however, I had a dearer task in keeping the two horses moving at their gentlest walk only, so that while my bridle arm was round the boy as he sat in front of me, my other arm was round the waist of her whose unconscious head was on my shoulder. In this posture I was heading for a spot of smooth greensward in front of me, where I should be able to dismount and bring the lady round again. And in this posture, too, I was when a headlong horseman suddenly drew rein beside me and with a cry of fierce heart hunger snatched the boy from me and folded him close to his iron breast. It was the captain, battered and bloody and all disordered, hot as he had spurred up out of the valley on the horse of the man first sent to tell him that his son was prisoner to Foulk of the Feet, in the dead town of Tre Ceiri.

He spoke no other word to the boy, but "Son! my little son!" over and over again, repeating it in a voice so hoarse and cracked that I looked quickly away lest he should break into tears and I see it.

I had another feeling, too, for the waist within my arm and the head upon my shoulder showed signs of returning life. I looked at her, and I had no sooner looked than in the same movement I kissed her quickly. I had no sooner kissed her than she opened her eyes and in the same moment drew off indignantly and pressed her horse away. I looked at the captain, wishing him away that I might have this matter out with her once for all, but he looked only at me—"I saw Foulk of the Feet come down from the wall. Is he dead?" demanded he.

"I do not know if he be even hurt," answered I. "But he must be yonder yet, for there was no horse for him this time and he cannot go far without one."

"Cousin!" said the captain now to the lady— "Cousin, will you keep my son here for a minute or two. These men shall be your guard," pointing to

the two coming down from the high peak of the flagman behind.

She bowed ; " Give him to me," said she, holding
her arms out.

But the little lad would none of that. " I will
stand here," said he, slipping down ; his manhood
ruffled at being proffered to a woman as if he had
been a babe.

His father laughed as merry as a youth at that.
" Aye, son, thou art a man already," said he ; his
eye lingering on the lad, more loth than a miser's eye
parting from gold. Then he picked up his rein,
" Come ! " said he to me, starting towards where
Foulk had fallen.

As we went I saw some of those who had taken
the town now coming out through the gate again,
and I motioned to them to follow after us. We rode
openly, for I had no thought but that we should find
our man with broken limbs at least. Therefore I
drew rein in amaze to see the flash of an arrow that
stuck fair in the pommel of the captain's saddle.
Three fingers higher and it had done for him.
That arrow had five threads of colors wound about
it ; it was the grim shaft of Foulk of the Feet himself. I remembered that I had dropped the bow
after shooting Jevon Cutta ; the arrow must have
been one Foulk carried for a token, since he had
no quiver when he leaped down. " His last shot in
this world then," said I as we pricked our horses to
speed.

No need to peer, and seek, and crane the neck,
however. When he saw that his shaft had gone low,
the redhand rose up on his knees above the bracken,
shouting defiances as we came.

The captain's sword was in his hand as we drew rein, but he sat still for a moment and looked at the face before him. Then—"Seize him!" ordered he to the men, who were already dismounting.

They ringed the outlaw round with spears, pressing in upon him with all their points at once. "Foulk of the Feet is sped," said I in a whisper to myself.

But he was not done yet. From hands and knees, as if he were indeed a wolf, he sprang forward upon the spears. One pricked him in the breast, others in other places, but with a mad yelp he seized one of them by the neck and with a giant's strength plucked its holder forward, face downward on the ground.

One other leap, one short sharp shout of exultation, and he had driven his dagger to the hilt in through the man's neck and slain him.

Next instant he was fast, all his bones cracking in the wrenching hands that seemed rather to be ready to tear him bone from bone than merely to be holding him. Only the captain sat still and looked awhile again before he spoke.

"Aye, now I remember thee. It was thou, crawling noiselessly into my room, who struck me down from behind that night when they kidnapped me from my own house of Castell March. Aye, thou wert the thief."

"Yea," snapped Foulk, "and, if thy cousin had not been such a stubborn fool, I would have stricken thee down so heavily thou shouldst never have risen again, save in men's hands as they carried thee out to hide thee in some secret grave. But the fool wished to have thee tortured in due and formal manner by the Inquisition. He feared the news of thy

escape from Cartagena would come and upset the
tale of thy being drowned, by which tale he had
succeeded to Castell March.  He thought if thou
shouldst once come to a well-established end by rack
and pincers of the priests then he could not be disturbed in his position !  The fool !  it is a pity he is
not alive now, to receive the reward of his folly, instead of his son."

The captain listened with an iron patience till the
last word, and then, as if nothing had been said, went
on.   "This arrow in my saddle ; look at it : is that
thine too ?"

" Aye," snarled the thief, straining in the gripe of
those that held him.   " And if I had had my own
good bow, instead of the lathy boy's plaything of a
stick that this fellow dropped, then it would not have
stuck in thy saddle ; it would have carried higher
and thou wouldst never have come a stride nigher or
been croaking over me here."

" Tie his hands behind him," went on the captain
quietly.   And, when that was done—" Now hold him
properly, ye, and thou "—turning to one who stood
by—" take thy sword and cut off his head."

The doomed man was already kneeling, having no
feet.  One man behind him gripped his arms and
held him firmly back.   One man in front seized him
by the hair and dragged his head forward, bending it
down.   The one with the naked sword stepped up to
do as he had been commanded.

But he was a Nevin man, and a dread of Foulk of
the Feet had been bred in his bones.  So faintly he
struck that at the first blow the outlaw broke into
ribald curses, and at the second blow he wrenched
his face round and with a mighty oath, "If I had

thy neck under my sword I would make it take better edge," snarled he.

While he yet spoke, all in one movement the captain had leaped down and seized the blade from the loose fingers of the Nevin man. One step he took forward ; one dry gasp of rage he gave as he whirled the steel and smote, and then the man holding the head had all its weight in his hands.

He would have tossed it down into the valley but the captain checked him. "Nay," said he ; "take it and set it up on the high place of stones at the north end of the city. It shall be there for a token that no redhand shall ever again ride by day or night in Lleyn."

So died Foulk of the Feet.

# CHAPTER XXXIII.

## THE COMING AGAIN OF THE HAG.

THE men had been gathering back to us from the chase of the flying outlaws, and, as if striking that one stroke of the sword had roused him, the captain was all quick to be gone again. "My wife!—we will tear that castle stone from stone but what we have her out," cried he to me, starting his horse before he was well into the saddle in mounting.

We reached the place where we had left the Lady Nerys and the little lad, and the captain drew sharply in that he might take her hand for an instant. "At another time I will prove to you my thanks for what you did when you saved my son—how should I have comforted his mother if I had only freed her to find him dead?"

He had kissed her hand and dropped it before she was ready to speak, and her intended words turned into a sad smile as she saw that he had snatched a cloak from one of the men and was folding it on his saddle bow to make a pad for the little lad to bestride.

"Come up, little son," said he, leaning down. "I want thee to tell me which way the rooms and passages lie in yon castle where Madre Mia, thy mother, is." With that he swung the boy up and set him astride before him.

311

In the interval I had already portioned the trusty seven again to stay behind with the lady for her guard, and now with the rest I followed hard after the captain, spurring across the slack for the valley of Vortigern once more again. At breakneck speed we went, and the captain could hardly bring himself to dismount in descending the steep pitch through the wood. To possess his son seemed only to burn him up with a fiercer eagerness to clasp his wife also.

For myself I was forced to keep to the saddle all the way, both by reason of my wound and because every joint in my body seemed to be groaning loose ; in this lull in the fighting all my flesh reminded me of my fall. My mind, however, was tugging busily at me, for it went back beyond that to the night before last ; the night I had spent in this castle we were now to attack. Keenly I wondered what had happened to the hell-hag whose unconscious form, breathing stertorously, I had left hidden in the dry bracken of my pallet. Once again I pictured her and how heavily she had fallen, when, snatching the bandage from his face, she recognised the features of the man she had first so loved and then so hated.

The captain had said that she would not come to consciousness again till she had been bled ; but who was to find her in that chamber ?—the last place in the world to look. Brynglas had been only too glad, before he rode away to his wedding, to think that she had taken umbrage and secluded herself, and if he so thought of her at that moment, who then should trouble about her subsequently. For while half a dozen men had borne Brynglas home, helpless and barely conscious, after the blow wherewith I had felled him at the church door, every other man from

the valley had followed the chase to the attack on
Castell March.   These had only got back an hour or
two ago, and meanwhile there had been no one to
direct things in the castle or to concern himself over
closely for the hag whom all feared and most of them
hated to boot.

Vaguely I hoped then that she was lying there still,
comatose or dead, for if she had by ill-fortune recovered, then it was certain that she would murder
her prisoner the moment we should effect an entrance to the castle when anon we assaulted it.   Yea,
fervently I hoped that she were dead, or too far gone
to remember the poor captive whom we were ready
to spend so many lives in rescuing.

Presently we were in the bottom again, and as the
captain mounted he told me jerkily what had happened in his assault on the castle.

" We dared not use our own ship's guns, but they
have a battery of four on the roof of the castle, where
they had been hidden.   Our ship was forced to lie
out of range while we landed in boats.   They sank
one of our boats and beat off my attack as I led the
rest of the crews to the assault.   I dare not fire the
castle because I should burn my wife.   Give me
then some counsel, good Rowland," ended he : "for
my wife's danger palsies all my thoughts."

I looked down the valley towards the castle to see
how the battle stood.   The musketeers of the seamen
were lying, hidden by bush and stone, too far away
from the castle to do any good and yet blazing away
their ammunition foolishly against the towers.   They
dared not creep near enough to be of use for fear of
the archers of the defenders.   " I see no way of doing," said I,   " but that you spend men resolutely to

capture the bailey gate here from this side.    Then a forlorn of men shall carry fire and powder to blow in the hall door.    It will be costly, but I see no other way for it."

"Take thou the command," begged he eagerly. "I will be a volunteer under thee.    Certes I am not fit to be captain.    All the years of my slavery to the Moor I thought my wife was dead.    To find her living ; to see only the thickness of a castle wall between her and me, makes me no captain but a mere murderer of the men I should lead.    God help me ! I would take them to the unpierced wall and curse them if they did not stand and be shot down like sheep while they could do no better."

I saw that he spoke truly, for there were dead bodies of his mariners where no corpses should be, had they been properly led.    "Then gather two score of your stubbornest men," said I, well knowing that when once he found himself leading the actual assault he would be himself again.

Choosing next a dozen of the best archers of my own men I sent the rest into the outlaw cabans at the head of the valley to get a score or so of blankets. For each blanket then we cut two hazel rods, tying the tops of the rods to the top corners of the blanket.

"Now," said I to the captain and his men, who stood by wondering, "learn a trick that Prince Madoc brought back from America, three hundred years before Columbus ever sailed.    Take each a blanket by the two rods and hoist it in front of you thus."

Here I lifted one up, and the two rods, bending a little, held the blanket before me like a screen, not quite touching the ground below, and at the top rising a foot and more higher than my head. " As you run to the attack," I went on, " stoop a little, yet keeping the blankets upright before you at arm's length. But do not run behind the middle of the blanket ; keep to the one side or other. Then, when they shoot, their shafts will all be guided to the middle of the stuff and will slither harmlessly down because the blanket will but baffle and not resist the shock."

The captain left his son astride his saddle while he jumped down and took the first blanket from my hand. " Said I not that thou wert fittest to be captain ? " laughed he, pleased as a boy might have been with some new way of winning an old game. Then sharply to his men : " Quick ! get you the blankets ready."

A score of them hastened to obey, and they were as full of jokes and laughs as if they had never been anything else but boys, though indeed that is commonly the way of mariners. When they were ready I set my archers to ride well within range of the bailey gate, there to commence shooting at once, while the blanketeers should charge. The second score of mariners I kept to follow the first when those should have reached the gate. " Now then ! " shouted I. " Forward ! "

I had looked to see some bloody work before that bailey gate was taken. And indeed at the moment when the archers rode out to shoot there was all promise of hard handplay presently. But no sooner did the blanketeers advance their screens than all the archers from the castle walls bent their bows against them ; deeming them the head and front of all the business. And it struck fear to their hearts and palsied their arms to see those flapping blankets still advance in spite of all the shower shafts that sang against them.

Then they thought of spells, nor could they divine aught better, for the only two men slain of the attackers fell backwards so that their blankets covered their corpses and betrayed nothing. " Witchcraft ! witchcraft ! it is the black art ! " shouted the defenders of the gate, and forthwith in terror they turned and fled over the causewayed path to try and gain the shelter of the castle. The barbican was won without a stroke of the sword.

I had followed on with my reserve of men, thinking that we should still have first to blow in the gate to give us entrance ; but I found that the seamen needed no doors. They had swarmed up the portcullis, climbing from the top of that through the missile way, and all the bolts and bars were in their hands to draw. Some had lifted the portcullis ; some now threw open the gate, and in went the rest of us, the captain leading.

In my excitement forgetting all pain, I had dismounted and now went afoot with the rest, active as any there. The blankets had been thrown down by the men. We were all like eager hounds ; leaping to pull down the quarry, for the outlaws who had fled from the gate were running round and round the bailey ; beating upon the hall door, stretching their hands up to the windows ; crying pitifully upon those within to open and give them shelter.

In chase of these went the men ; a wolf-like business at best, and I followed after the captain to bring him back and take means for blowing in the hall door. I found him indeed, but all semblance of coolness was clean gone ; all other thoughts burnt up in one. He was standing at the loophole of his wife's prison, hammering madly at the shutter, and through all the din of howls and shouts, of groans and clashes, he was calling upon her name, with a hundred endearing words of Spanish to aid him in his wild appealing.

I seized him by the arm. " Let us beat in the hall door," I shouted in his ear.

Drunk with passion he looked at me with an instant's dull stare and then, not as if he heard my words but as if the sight of me reminded him of something, he snatched up a spear and with a spring attempted to fix it on the ledge of the sleeping chamber above. At the second attempt he succeeded and I thought the place was won.

" An escalade ! an escalade !" I shouted, calling upon those nearest to follow where I prepared to mount after our leader. I looked at him as he reached the ledge and caught the bars : I watched him shake them fiercely and heard his furious cries as he tried to open a way, but no way showed there. Quickly seizing another spear I mounted up beside him, thinking only that his eagerness was at fault. Alack, the bar was no longer loose ; the heavy firing of the battery of great guns above had shaken the castle to its foundations ; the headstone of the window and the wide crack in the wall above had settled tight together again ; the bar was fast and firm.

He looked at me with a gnashing curse upon the immovable iron, and I in turn broke out with only, " Yonder in the heather and bracken is where I hid the hag in her swoon !"—pointing within to the pile at the foot of the opposite wall. For from the non-answer to his hammering at the loophole I thought none other than that the hag was risen and had murdered his wife.

" Aye ? " he yelled, more like a wild beast than a man.   He was kneeling on the ledge, holding by the grip of his hand on the upper part of the bars. " Aye ! " and instantly he had seized his spear from the sill at his knee and hurled it with all his might through at the pile of bracken.

Then, as we knelt, I trying to shake him into coming down to burst the hall door in, and he madly jibbering and cursing through the bars, a horrible stir of life shook all the bedding, and the spear fell down from where it had been stuck through the pile into the wall.

And—" Ah ! oh ! " came long drawn out from my shaking lips, for the pile parted and up from the midst of it rose the livid visage and the ghastly figure of her I had hidden there in the dawn of yesterday.

" The hag ! the hag ! " I whispered in terror, all my bones loose to see her rise up thus who should have been dead, lying there so long unfound.   Ghastly ; awful to see she was, with that parchment face drawn tight on the bones beneath and one gaunt, skinny arm stretched out, dripping blood from the spear wound whose running had brought her to life again.

# CHAPTER XXXIV.

## THE LAST OF CASTELL VORTIGERN.

I CAUGHT my breath in dread to see her stand thus, staring vacantly at the blood ; and all the din of the fighting below us was but a far-off, futile monotone in my ears as I strained to catch what speech should pass between these two. The captain was first and his fury burst like a gunshot in the one word that pierced through all her dazedness, stinging her to recognition of him and of what was happening.

A weak, high, quavering cry : a cry that by its terrible yearning should have been the cry of a mother clasping a long-lost son, but which by its undertone was the cry of a choking, maniacal hate ; broke from her as she came towards us. I wished to drop down and get away to some other place, for I felt in all my bones that she was not mortal. But the captain—a sudden ferocious cunning had glozed his rage into a tigerish stillness. A hungry smile was frozen, horrible, upon his face, and his eyes burnt like live coals newly uncovered as he waited her approach.

Then a sheer whimper of murderous desire broke from his lips and both his arms shot through the bars to clutch and tear her asunder. But his fury was too soon ; by a hair's breadth his reach was short, and as

319

she drew back one quick step such a blast of impreca-
tion belched from him that even she was daunted
for a moment. Yet only a moment ; the next instant
she looked at him with a smile that froze my blood.
" I'll kill her now while you watch ! " she shouted.
" Go listen at the loop and you shall hear her screams
in dying ! " and with that she turned and left the
room with tottering strides.

" Come ! " gasped the captain, dropping to the
ground and darting to the loophole in the tower.
He had drawn his dagger to hammer again upon the
shutter, but to his furious knocking came no answer. "Oh Christ ! is she dead already ? " exclaimed
he.

Then ; then a little hand touched him from behind and a brave little voice said quietly, " That is
not the way ; she does not know that. This is the
knock she knows ; " and here, up on to the stone he
had set stepped the little boy ; come through all the
hurly to tell Madre Mia that help was here at last.
He knocked the same soft knock that I had heard
before, and straightway the shutter, that had been
fast to all the horrid din, flew open, and the two white
hands came hesitatingly out to touch him.

A wild cry of joy broke from the captain and he
had seized those hands and was kissing them madly.
Then a long, long golden note from within answered
him—and I moved away to gather a party of the
nearest men to help me to break in the door of the
hall ; for we must either win an entrance at once or
see the captive murdered at the moment of rescue.

The men in hand, I turned to call the captain and
found him stabbing fiercely at the wall, trying to
crowbar out the stones to let him through. But the

spear broke in his hands and with a savage curse he flung the splinters down. " Oh ! and she will be murdered ! " he shouted like one demented.

A sudden idea seized him. Snatching his dagger out he passed it through the loop into the captive's hands, bidding her take it. Then in the next breath he had torn a wheel-lock pistol from the hands of one of the men and passed that through also. Another second of time and he had picked up the boy in his arms and was running back to reach the hall door, stooping as he ran that he might shelter the lad's body with his own against any missile from above.

Following him, I found that our archers had occupied all the bailey gate, and from its shelter their close shooting had got the upper hand of the bowmen in the castle towers facing them. They had cleared every loop that should have defended the door and so there was none to hinder us as we lifted the battering ram, a heavy log of oak which a party of the seamen had brought from the edge of the wood near by.

Once and again with all our might we drove the heavy log against the door, and once and again the thick ribbed timbers did but rattle sullenly in answer ; for the great beam of seasoned oak drawn across behind it might have been iron in its strength.

" Powder ! powder ! " shouted the captain hoarsely. " Put down the log, so ; "—guiding us till we had laid it down with its massive end butted close against the door in the corner of the threshold.

'Into the close space between the butt and door and doorway wall, the musketeers emptied their powder horns and the one who carried a reserve for them set his keg, hole downward, on the pile, filling

21

up all the space.   A match was laid, a great stone
piled on top of all, and then we drew back for shelter.
The match was lit ; there was one moment's suspense,
and then with a roar that deafened all the valley the
powder caught.   The very ground seemed to shake,
grey chips of stone and long white splinters of oak
flew through the air, and next, while yet the smoke
was eddying too thick to see through, the captain had
charged into it, bending almost double.

In after him went his seamen, and I had to drag
back the boy or he would have gone too.   By the
time I had made shift to enter I found the hall half-
won, for Brynglas was bedfast yet somewhere within,
and there was no indisputable man, like Foulk of the
Feet, to take command in his place.   Yet did the
trapped outlaws fight hardily and even put us to it
to hold our own.   And while for a moment they bore
up against the press there came one to help them
worth many men ; aye, and many leaders.

For while the captain raged in front, the door beyond us opened and out stepped the hell-hag potent
for dire hurt upon many there.   In her right hand,
poised on the palm of it, above her head, she held a
wooden bowl full of a quick oil : in her left she
clutched a lighted brand.   At sight of her all the fight
stood still for a moment and through the pause her
voice came stridently as she cried out, " Welcome !
love Gwilym ; here is warm liquor to welcome thee ! "
—And with the word she lifted the torch and
dropped it into the bowl above her head.

Forthwith the flame leaped hissing up, shaking
the shadows from the blackest corners of the roof.
" Love  Gwilym ! " she  screamed  again ;  " Love
Gwilym ! " and with both hands flung the fiery bowl

at him.  Wide rained the crackling flame splashes on friend and foe alike, but the main flood of it came blazing straight for him.  A shout was on my lips— a shout of horror at his fate ; but quicker than the shout, quicker than the flame, the captain had seized the woollen mantled outlaw in front of him and swung him up for a shelter to shield his own head.

It was all done in the catching of a breath ; the throwing of the bowl ; the lifting and the dropping down of the man, and then the hall was one appalling hell of shrieks and flames, and a mass of burning men who jammed themselves and fell together in a writhing heap, choking the door through which they were trying to escape.

That sight by that door I saw in one single glance behind me, and then in front another glance showed me the captain rushing forward through the other doorway in chase of the terrible woman who had done this devilish deed.  I could not get out by the door behind, and already the unburnt men within and the fresh men without were busy aiding the burning ones.  There was but one thing to do : I followed the captain.

I knew which way he went, by the doors left open and the smell of burning which hung in his wake where he had beaten out the small flame spots from his clothing as he ran.  Yet her knowledge had baffled him, for presently I met him turning back ; gasping, and drawn-lipped ; he had lost her.  " Which way ? " he yelled at me.

" Leave her ! leave her ! let us save your wife from the fire," I answered.

At the words " wife " and " fire " he winced. " Aye, let us save her first," gasped he, yet still looking fiercely over his shoulder for some trace of the other.

I had put my hand out to seize him by the shoulder and drag him away, when a door at my elbow opened softly and a half-dressed man stood on the threshold, a sword in his hesitating hand. With quick impatience I whipped out my dagger and drove it through him, lest the captain should stop and waste time questioning him as to the hag's passing, before killing him. Every second was so precious. Not till the captain snapped out—"Who is that?" —did it occur to me what I had done and whom I had slain. "Only Brynglas," answered I.

"Brynglas?" repeated he, turning the body with his foot to look at it. "That trumpery fool!" said he next and said no more. That was Brynglas and that was his epitaph. "Come!" said I, starting back.

My work was to seek whatever corridor might lead to the door of the captive's cell, and well I wist how short the time was till the flame should lick up the whole castle, and how little hope there was of our finding that door in time. At every step as we searched we stood in peril of coming upon armed defenders—"Ah! if the little lad were only here now to guide us," said I out loud.

As we went we found that the smoke had begun to belly through the passages, and that in striking back to choose another way we went into it thicker at every stride. "We must be going back to the hall then," said I; and the words were yet on my lips when through the reek in front I heard a little gasping voice cry out, "Oh Madre Mia! I am choking!"

"The boy!" exclaimed I. And—"Son! my son!" cried the captain, rushing forward and snatching the little one from the floor where he was kneeling, overcome.

It was not the smoke here, however, which had distressed him. It had been in passing through the fiery hall, for in spite of my command he had followed me in, and had but stopped to dig up his buried keys before rushing through to find the place where his mother was shut up. Straightway his courage rose again as the captain picked him up. "Through the door on the right," said he : "the big key opens it."

Through the smoke we found the door, but it was wide open already. And so indeed we found all the doors unlocked as we went, until we came to a door at sight of which the lad cried—"That is it! I knocked at it last night and she answered, though she could not open it then."

He slipped from his father's arms and knocked his knock at the door. I had begun to fumble at the keys to try them in the lock while the captain snatched up a stool to break it in. But there was no need of either, for, instant to the knock, the door flew open and out stood the pale, dishevelled captive. With one swift snatch she had the little one close to her breast and then with a heart's cry of "Gwilym! Gwilym!" she flung her right arm out to clasp the husband, whose voice was ringing through the place with a wild cry of "Dolores! Dolores!" as he strained both in the grip of his long arms.

They had forgotten all else in the world, but had I also lost the keen remembrance of our danger, the smoke which had followed us and was now beginning to thicken even here, would have speedily roused me. "Sir!" said I, breaking in upon them. "We must out or be burnt in the fire!"

The captain started at once. "Which is the way out, little son?" asked he gently.

"This," said the boy, turning to go. And within two minutes more he led us out by way of that postern entrance through which I had aforetime escaped with Lady Nerys.

We were but just in time. From the first step the captain had carried his wife in his arms, and not alone because she had fainted from excess of joy, while I had held the little lad by the hand to help him, for the smoke was hot now, as well as thick, and wellnigh overpowered us all. Had we lost the way; had we but had to go another score of steps farther or found the door fastened, then all our bloody doings of this day had been done in vain. But we found the door wide open as the escaping defenders had left it in flying from the fire; and I was glad, between my gasps for breath, to see that they had for the more part been taken prisoners only, instead of being slaughtered.

Ready hands bore us up from falling, the while they led us back to the shelter of the bailey; and all the way my eyes were closed up tight to ease the smart of smoke and fire. Even when I had been led into the guard-room, I had to call for water to bathe them, whereas when I opened them I found that the captain's bloodshot eyes still gazed hungrily at the face of his wife, where he had laid her down while he tried to revive her.

The roar and the crackle of the flames without grew louder and louder. Then a shout rose over the

din : "The hag !   See the hag !" and at once a score
of voices echoed the cry :  "The hag! the hag !"
adding a long drawn "Ah !" which roused me to
know what caused it.

Stepping outside, the heat of the fire struck my
already scorched face like a blow, so that instinctively
I threw up my bent arm to shield my cheek.   Under
my arm I could see that the fire was belching out
of the broken hall door as well from the windows
and loopholes on each side of the castle.   Then I
looked up and saw a sight that shook my very heart-
strings as I stood.

Like a roaring furnace shut within some giant kiln,
so blazed and leaped and swirled the fire in the tim-
bered bowels of the castle, shut within the rocky
thickness of its stone shell.   Every loophole spouted
its hissing flame ; every window shot out its sheaf of
crackling fire.   Great swaths and sheets of flame
tore loose and flashed up to dash themselves against
the under side of the pall of black smoke above, as if
trying to drive it higher and give them more room
for play.   Only the tops of the towers, roofed as they
were with massive beams of squared oak, laid close
together, still battened down the flames that were
making the walls red beneath them.

And on that tower which was the hall front, facing
us there at the bailey gate, with the grey green smoke
rising like a waving curtain between her face and
ours, stood the hell-hag herself, stretching her arms
and chanting some mad song whose words were
drowned in the steady roar of the conflagration.

I turned to call the captain, but he too had heard
the shout and now was stepping out to look.   In that
same instant as he cast up his eyes to her so she

looked down and saw him. "Ah! Love Gwilym!"
she screamed with a shrill power that pierced through
all the din—"Ah ha! do you hear? your black
foreign wife is burning; is burning down below. Go
listen at her shot-window, Gwilym: go hear her
scream!"

The fierce look came into the captain's face again,
where for a moment pity had been struggling. With
long strides he dashed within the gate chamber and
then came out, supporting his recovered wife. He
looked up at that weird figure on the tower. "Here
is my wife!" he shouted in a trumpet voice and with
remorseless triumph kissed her lovingly, plain for the
other to see.

I looked at that and I looked aloft to know what
after it would happen, I was just in time. With a
wild, heartshaking scream of demoniacal fury the
tortured hag snatched the kerchief from her head;
tore at her grey locks; beat on her bosom; the
bubbling foam hanging at the corners of her lips, and
then, while the horrid scream was yet freezing our
blood, the roof dropped down from under her feet,
and up, up to the lurid pall in the lift above, leaped
a red awful blast of fire, that seemed to sweal the
heavens themselves with the wash of its sheeting
flames.

"She hath gone home by no postern but by the
front gate," quoth a Nevin man, blinking with the
heat where he stood. And no man added any more
to it. She died as she had lived, alone in her own
breast and cut off from even the least word, that
kindly sorrow hath. Unless, indeed, that were in
truth sorrow which I did not speak aloud—"God
help her!"

# CHAPTER XXXV.

THE falling in of the roof of the tower forced the flames of the hall out through the door in a level spout of red fire that drove us pell mell back into the bailey gate-house, lest we should be licked up. For myself I cared no longer to stay there, looking at the leaping, snaking streamers of the element which was purging this dark valley of its foulest spot. The ravening excitement of the struggle just ended began to ebb away ; and my hurts, my weariness, and my utter exhaustion came upon me like a sickness ; so that I staggered for pure weakness as I passed through the gateway to the outer air, beyond the heat. The pain of my thigh which had been so great, and which in the attack upon the castle I had so completely forgotten, was not so potent to prevent me walking as this sickness of the stomach was.

My horse still stood where I had left him in dismounting, and I caught hold of the saddle, meaning to mount him that he might carry me across the bowshot's distance to the woods ; for all my flesh was longing to lie down in the green shelter of the trees and sleep. I had taken the rein in my left hand, my fingers locked in the mane, and with my right was holding to the cantle for very weakness, when I was

329

aware of the Lady Nerys, drawing rein on the off side of my horse.

I looked up at her and never a word had I to say, she looked so high and defiantly at me. Then as I kept silence, "Well?" she said; "I hope you are satisfied at last. Ye have slain my people and burnt my castle : ye have carried it high, I trow—I hope you are well pleased now at the counting of the game."

"Slain your people? burnt your castle?" repeated I dully.

"Aye, my people and castle," retorted she. "I was no more Lady of Castell March since the lord of it came home; but I was and am the Lady of Nant Vortigern, which you have swept with fire and sword from one end to the other."

Now this was not all true, for the cabans of the outlaws were still standing untouched, and though the women and children had fled and scattered, some to the woods and some to seek their dead on the mountain-side, yet well I knew they had not been scathed. Weary I was ; soaked through and through with utter tiredness ; my bones aching for the soft greensward under the long arms of the leafy oaks, and my scorched face parching to press itself against the cool earth of the grass roots. All my soul was sick to lie down and rest, if only for one little minute.

Thus then to hear her speak so unjustly—though yet she had good cause of grief herself—brought a quick answer up, but sickness shut my teeth upon it for a moment. Still to avoid too great discourtesy I filled the pause by mounting, though it needed all my stubbornness to get me up into the saddle. And as

soon as he felt my weight in the stirrup the horse
began to walk away, so that by the time I checked him
he was two lengths or more distant from her.

Looking over my shoulder, while I pulled the nag
round again, I found she had taken it in dudgeon,
thinking maybe that I had done it out of contempt,
and so had turned her own horse away and with her
back to me was dismounting. "Well," said I to myself wearily; "what does it matter? And I am
deathly sick: I want to lie down." I had turned
for the woods again before I had finished muttering.

I looked back no more, being full of the work of
holding myself in the saddle; and as soon as I came
under the first tree I lurched off, plumping heavily
down full length, my face upon my arm. Seeing me
thus the horse stooped his muzzle to smell at me,
whereat I looked up at him. "Good horse," muttered I wearily; "there is none of the jade about
thee. Eat now then"—and with that I reached up
and loosed the throat-lash and slipped his bridle off.
With a quiet snort and a swish of the tail he stepped
away and in his second stride was already grazing,
while I stretched up my other arm and, pillowing my
face on both, gave myself up in quiet to the sickness
that possessed me. The hissing and the crackling of
the fire sounded soothingly a little while in my ears.
"Aye; I am for the Ooronoka now," said I, and so
must have fallen asleep.

When I awoke, all the land was dark, as I thought,
but my hand proved the darkness to be but a cloak,
thrown over me to keep out the chill of the evening
breeze from the sea. Throwing it back I rose to my
elbow and found the old chieftain, sitting with his

back to the tree and his face showing ghostly grey in
the last light of the far-off afterglow, which was lying
like a primrose pennon to the west betwixt the sea
and sky. He saw me stir; "How art thou, son?"
enquired he soberly.

"Stiff," answered I; "and aching in every inch
of me. Hungry too, and my mouth thick for want
of a draught of something; anything; wine, ale, or
mead, I care not."

"Yea," answered he soothingly. "I looked for no
other and so I have wine here. Drink then and
presently there will be a bite of rock venison and
barley bread for thee—it is being prepared now."

I took the flask—"That is not from the gwindy :
that is from the ship," he went on, as I let the
mellow liquid warm its way down to my chilled
heart.

"It is good," said I—"wherever it came from, it
is good."

"Yea," answered he, "the sun shines hot where
that came from."

"Did it come from the Ooronoka?" I asked him
quickly. "You have been to the Ooronoka, have
you not?"

"There and thereaway," answered he pleasantly.
"The wine did not come from there though—but
here is the supper," he broke off, as a lad appeared
with food in a wooden trencher.

While I was eating I felt that my wound had been
attended to—"Ah; did you dress that arrow hole
then while I was sleeping?" demanded I.

"And put fresh hose on you," laughed he out of
the dusk. "You were so dead beaten, son, that
you could only have slept face down. And being

face down nothing less than another wound would have waked you till you had slept your fill."

"Well," said I, thinking of the unforgiving anger of the Lady Nerys towards me. "When I am in the way to do a good turn to any one in time to come, I will look to it that it be done to a man and not to a woman. A man rendereth measure for measure afterwards, as he conceiveth."

"Aye," answered he gravely from the shadow where I knew he was smiling. "Therein a woman hath the upper ground of a man, for she rendereth, not measure for measure, but all that she hath in return for the mere little that another hath given her."

"Doubtless," returned I, unpleased, "but she returneth not in kind. If you give her toil and worship and all that the heart hath of goodly endeavour, then she repayeth you more than full measure—but it is of scorn."

"Aye?" came his voice, railing softly upon me. "Aye? but that is because you take the scorn instead of brushing it aside and seizing the heart underneath. But one moment, son; hast thou been paying some of this toil and worship into the exchequer of any woman's heart lately?"

I answered not. He knew well what I had done for the Lady Nerys. He was but railing on me in lovingkindness, but he did not understand that these things hurt a young man to sit under. His beard was grey; how should he understand that his words were like a harrow going over my soul;

And because I kept silence—for the sigh that broke from me escaped all unawares—he went on further. "I ask thee, son, by reason that, if so, then it were

well thou kept her name from the Lady Nerys.    Thou
hast played such tricks with her these few days past,
dealing so high-handedly with her dearest and most
womanly weaknesses and running her into such perils
and mischances, that thy feet are shackled somewhat
at least of their stride.    And what of so affronting
her in her household men that she could not rest till
she had brought them into the field, there to shame
thy treatment of them by proving their bravery
plain for us all to see—art thou altogether free after
that ?

" Why, son, I tell thee, thou hast carried things
so with her that she may well be held excused if she
take her only possible revenge by recounting the tale
of it all to this other woman, if she shall find her out.
And then thou art undone, for that woman will at
once swear kin with the Lady Nerys and have no
more to do with thee till thou hast made amends and
won pardon for thy past ill-doings."

" Hath the Lady Nerys been speaking all this in
your ear, father ?" said I.

" Nay, son, not so.    All she said, when I had been
seeking and enquiring for thee of every man in the
valley and had found that no one of them all knew
what had become of thee—all she said then was, ' I
think you will find him yonder under the trees.    The
fighting being all done—and fighting being that he
careth about—he had no else to do but rest.' "

" That is wrong," interrupted I.    " See how wil-
fully she misjudgeth me ever.    I care less about
fighting than most men.    I like to enjoy my life, not
put it in jeopardy.    But she would deny me any
Christian virtue at all, though a bench of bishops
should testify of me."

"Aye; maybe, maybe;" went on he. "But though she might deny the bishops she could not well deny what the words of thine own mouth presently proved. For, when she brought me a piece of her own robe for a bandage for thee, and I stirred thee to bind thy wound, she could not help but hear the words that came so thickly from thee in thy sleep— 'I am for the Ooronoka.' That and no more was all the word thou hadst when she asked thee if the pain were very great."

"But I was asleep," said I impatiently. And because I saw well that he did not understand how stubbornly things stood between the lady and myself, but rather let his wishes colour his hopes and words, I desired therefore to change the subject. "Give me some meat, father," said I, leaning and stretching my barley-cake platterwise.

"I have given thee a bone to pick," answered he, reaching forward and laying the piece upon the cake. But I wist well what he meant, for what he laid upon the bread was all meat and no bone.

I thanked him for it, however, and so kept quiet till my meal was done. Then, as we sat in the dark, I tried to open his lips upon the Ooronoka. But he put it by pleasantly by dwelling upon the wrong end of it, for all his words were of the happiness of home-coming; of the wives and sweethearts; and never a word would he say of the joy of setting sail, with a bright sword eating its way into the soul from its scabbard on the hip. "But then his beard is grey," said I to myself.

At last, when I saw that he would still stick to one thing—"Where is the captain?" I asked him.

"At the gwindy," replied he. "His men have

fitted it up with stuffs from the ship for this night. His wife was not yet fit travel to Castell March."

My horse was grazing near at hand. "Let us go to the gwindy," said I : "I wish to speak with the captain."

I did not tell the old chieftain, but all the way I was ordering the words in my mind wherewith to claim fulfilment of the captain's promise—made as we rode south from Carnarvon—that I should be put in the way of sailing to the Ooronoka. And as I rode I rolled the word like a muffled drum in my mind to stifle another name that ached in the bottom of my heart.

The door of the gwindy was open ; a lamp shone golden on the wall beyond and under the lamp a couch was set, covered with the rich stuffs from the ship ; while on the couch, wrapped all in softness, lay the rescued captive, white and weak, but sighing with pure happiness as she looked from the son that leaned against her breast to the husband that sat beside her and held her hand.

My heart swelled out in a mighty sigh to see that sight. The Lady Nerys was not there. She had no men ; no ship full of rich stuffs to make a lodging for her. No roof had she ; her castle was burned ; her lands harried, and she would have none of the help I ached to give her. I could not bear to look longer—"I had best ride about a bit first ; not break in upon that," said I to the old chieftain. And before I was aware I had spoken on—"Till I see you again then "—and so left him with the farewell as if I had been going on a journey.

My heart guided my hand as I reined the horse along the valley towards where the sea lay like dull silver below.  As I went the moon lifted and sent her rays reaching down into the depths, and the burnt out castle on its hill at my elbow showed all its empty shell, like the desolate castle of some legend or fairy tale.  At sight of those now roofless walls, with the moonlight streaming through loop-hole and window-gap to mingle with the ruddy glow from the bed of still smouldering embers inside, my thoughts crowded in on me to suffocation.  I could not take my eyes from the place, with its thin wisps of attenuating smoke drifting and vanishing athwart the sky, but rode with my face upon my shoulder, turning my body next, and all to look back at that fitting scene of my ruined dreams.  Alack !  the castle was not more empty now of all that it had held than my heart was of the hope it had so cherished.  Not till I found that my horse had stopped at the edge of the sea did I rouse again.

One look I sent across the sea and then turned to ride along the shore.  One length I went in the new direction and then I drew my rein, for I was come again to that little mound where I had first seen the Lady of Spells.

And I was lighting down from the saddle.  I was shutting my teeth to kill the pain in my body as I walked, slow and straight, three paces before me.  I was holding out my hands and crying like a forsaken man, "Nerys !  oh Nerys !"

For there on the mound, looking up the desolate valley, the moonlight from the east shining upon her face and flashing from the jewel on her brow ; fairer now with the tears in her eyes and the loneliness in her heart than ever she was in the plenitude of fortune, sat the Lady of the Mound.

22

And she rose : softly and queenly in her sorrow she rose up, and her white arms stretched yearningly towards me as she cried her own heart's answer to the cry of mine,—

" Rowland ! oh Rowland ! "

www.ingramcontent.com/pod-product-compliance
Lightning Source LLC
Chambersburg PA
CBHW022207010726
47493CB00002B/446